New York, 1899, and the police department's best ally is the secret Ghost Precinct, where spirits and psychics help solve the city's most perplexing crimes . . .

There's more than one way to catch a killer—though the methods employed by the NYPD's Ghost Precinct, an all-female team of psychics and spiritualists led by gifted young medium Eve Whitby, are unconventional to say the least. Eve is concerned by the backlash that threatens the department—and by the discovery of an otherworldly realm, the Ghost Sanctuary, where the dead can provide answers. But is there a price to be paid for Eve and her colleagues venturing beyond the land of the living?

Searching for clues about a mortician's disappearance, Eve encounters a charismatic magician and mesmerist whose abilities are unlike any she's seen. Is he a link to mysterious deaths around the city, or to the Ghost Sanctuary? Torn between the bonds of her team and her growing relationship with the dashing Detective Horowitz, Eve must discern truth from illusion and friend from foe, before another soul vanishes into the ether . . .

Visit us at www.kensingtonbooks.com

Books by Leanna Renee Hieber

A Sanctuary of Spirits

Leanna Renee Hieber

REBEL BASE
Kensington Book Corp.
www.kensingtonbooks.com

First Electronic Edition: November 2019
eISBN-13: 978-1-63573-059-3
eISBN-10: 1-6357-3059-7

First Print Edition: November 2019
ISBN-13: 978-1-63573-062-3
ISBN-10: 1-6357-3062-7

Printed in the United States of America

Prologue

Manhattan, 1899

Monsieur Dupont, career undertaker and director of a Manhattan viewing parlor for the dead, considered a postmortem body the most beautiful treasure. For him, the tired cliché of an undertaker being obsessed with death was transcended; he rejoiced that the dead made him feel so alive.

The dead were the key to the kingdom of heaven.

His craft had started innocently enough. Locks of hair. The obsession progressed. Other tokens and trinkets were next, taken and procured with exquisite care. Subtle trophies.

No one would know or see. No one could. Grief was such a strange, ever-changing beast, but one constant remained: no one ever noticed *all* the details of a corpse. No one would notice if some small thing wasn't exactly as it had been, as death had already made the familiar strange.

Memory rewrote itself. He'd seen the proof of it time and again. The dead were transformed and made perfect by their loved ones. In that perfection it was just so lovely, so sacred, so beautiful to take a small scrap of that elevated, exalted existence…

So, he began. Tokens of his little saints made into sacred objects. Tiny souvenirs from the world's most innocent: children. Taking something from a child was the most sacred of all transactions. Procured and placed into sacred vessels. Surely no one would mind. Their bodies were photographed for posterity, and a souvenir was taken in private just before the body was taken to the grave.

No one but the ghosts, that is. Spirits of children noticed what was gone but didn't understand.

Then there was Ingrid. *His* Ingrid. The child that by all rights should have been his if fate hadn't been so cruel. Heinrich Schwerin, thinking the girl was actually his, had interfered and ruined everything. He took the little girl's body, presenting her dressed and anointed as a saint and giving it as a gift to an orphanage when worship of her should have been done in private. A promising apprentice gone mad. None of it had gone to the grand design. As a divine architect, Dupont had lost control of the lamb that wandered from the flock and had to be fed to the wolves, never knowing the child he'd gone mad over wasn't even his.

He stared out the third-floor window of his viewing parlor and watched as boisterous theatre folk tumbled from their boarding house. There was such life in this city, and to juxtapose it with constant death was high art. He took on the sorrows of those who did not wish to, or could not, greet death in their own homes. He took it on for them, an extension of his undertaker role. Wakes were usually done in the home, in the downstairs parlor, but for those who couldn't bear it or didn't have a suitable place to host an entourage for days, his viewing parlor stood in for home. Families could consider calling their parlor instead a "living room" because he was displacing death for them, banishing it from their doorstep.

Thankfully, the spirits had been banished from his.

The best thing about meeting his business partner Montmartre at a lecture about the mapping of the human mind three years prior was that the man had devised a way to keep out the ghosts. The children floating outside the window, pointing at what had been left behind in Dupont's cabinet of treasures, simply didn't understand. He'd tried to explain it to them, but if children had a hard time grasping divine mystery in life, it was even more hopeless after death. He wished he, like most people, didn't see ghosts. He supposed his ability was an unfortunate symptom of a profession in death.

Montmartre had devised the ghost barricade, but out of the corner of Dupont's eye, he could see them marching around the exterior of the building like striking workers on the line. He couldn't allow their constant parade to distract him, so he stared at a fresh child laid out on the slab and dabbed rouge on cold blue cheeks.

He feared his careful enterprise would be revealed after all the nonsense with Ingrid. Part of him relished the edge of danger. Part of him wrestled to regain a simpler life he'd left behind once his mind had been opened to the grander possibilities of his artistic rituals. What was it his friends would say? *Arte Uber Alles.* Art above everything.

Turning to another work in progress, a waxen sculpture standing against the wall, he affixed a hint of color to the lips of the new seraph that adorned a pedestal of the stage set. So very realistic. He stared at his work and swelled in pride. No amount of danger could dull this rush.

He stared at the lovely little faces. He would make saints of them all.

There was a knock at the door. He scowled, put down his tools, and went to answer it. His stomach twisted with dread when he saw the tired face he'd once found sweet, years ago, when she'd worked as his maid. But now she was a troublesome card he had to strategize how to play.

"What did you do to my daughter?" the mousy-haired woman demanded, barging past him into the entrance foyer, her wide eyes full of rage. "And *why*?" She shrieked. Whatever beauty she'd once had was now sunken by grief and pierced by the sharp knife of poverty.

"Shhh, my Greta, my love," he murmured. "You've come back to me. Now we can grieve, together…"

He clutched her passionately, forced her to acknowledge him. Their past. Their little Ingrid. Their illicit child. He held Greta as she cried and tried to soothe the wildness of her sorrow with sweet nothings.

The thought occurred to him that they could try again. She could be his Eve and he could build something new, with all of his prizes collected in an Eden of his design. Perhaps, finally, he could feast with all the saints…

Montmartre wouldn't like it. But that man had his own agenda, and Dupont planned on leaving him to it.

Dupont seized Greta roughly. "Come with me, and we'll make hell a heaven."

Chapter One

Union Square
Manhattan, 1899

"Maggie." Eve Whitby waved at the distracted ghost who floated before her, a transparent, greyscale and luminous form. "Answer me. How could you, of all spirits, simply disappear? And what brought you back?"

"I *am* dead; we do that sometimes, you know. Vanish," Maggie said with a laugh. She turned and began floating north, in the direction of the train depot where they were headed. The wraith was a visual echo of the lovely young lady she'd been in life, dressed in a fine gown of the early eighties.

"Don't you be flippant, my dear," Eve chided, lifting her skirts and hurrying after the specter, running directly into the cold chill of her wake. "We've been distraught for weeks," she continued with a shiver. "We knew you'd never leave without telling us! We couldn't even catch a *trace* of you during our séances!"

The dark-haired man taking long strides to keep up beside Eve cleared his throat.

The generally drawn pallor of Eve's cheek colored. "I'm sorry, Detective." She turned to him without breaking her pace. "I forget you can't completely hear or see our subject here."

Tall and lithe, with a neatly trimmed mop of dark brown curls that bounced in the breeze, dressed in a simple black suit with a white cravat, Detective Horowitz, in his midtwenties, was as sharp in wit and mind as he was in features. The angles of his face curved and softened as he smiled. His ability to shift from serious to amused was as swift as it was attractive.

"I'm catching pieces here and there," he replied, "but to be honest, I'm more enjoying the looks you're getting from passersby, averting wary, disdainful eyes behind hat brims and parasols."

"Oh." Eve batted an ungloved hand, caring not a whit for the fine details of sartorial propriety, as gloves often got in her way of tactile experience important to her work. "Mad folk walk New York streets daily and no one stops them; it's one of the glories of the city—minding one's own business!"

Horowitz laughed and kept pace.

The three angled along bustling Broadway as it slanted up ahead of them, the ghost at the fore, dodging passersby with parasols and weaving past horse-carts, careful to mind their droppings. Eve grumbled as the stray foot of a businessman's cigar was lifted by the wind onto her shoulder, and she brushed off the embers before they caught the thin wool on fire. She wore an adaptation of a police matron's uniform: a simple dress with buttons down the front, but in black, having donned constant mourning in honor of those she worked with and for, the spirits of New York.

The detective didn't seem to hold Maggie's interruption against her, despite the fact that he'd been leaning toward Eve in a near-kiss when the spirit's incorporeal form had appeared between them. That the detective even *entertained* the idea of a ghost was a blessing. That he could slightly see and barely hear fragments from Maggie was incredible progress. Just weeks before he'd been a confirmed skeptic. Perhaps Eve's Sensitivities were rubbing off on the practical, level-headed detective. The idea that she might be able to draw this man further into her world was an equally thrilling and cautionary prospect. Eve reeled in more directions than one.

Maggie Hathorn had been Eve's dearest friend since childhood, the most trusted spectral asset in her Ghost Precinct since its recent inception, and the spirit didn't seem to be taking her own disappearance seriously. Yes, ghosts often came and went as they pleased. But they were generally creatures of habit with particular patterns of haunt. Eve's Ghost Precinct of four mediums relied on the constancy of their stable of specters, Maggie at the core. Until she'd vanished with no word.

"If the Summerland draws you and you wish to go, Maggie," Eve said earnestly, reaching out to the floating figure and touching chilled air, "just tell us. I love and need you, but I know I mustn't keep my dear friend from her well-earned peace."

"Oh, my dearest friend." Maggie turned and reached out. A transparent, icy hand brushed across Eve's cheek. "None of this was about wanting to go but wanting to *stay*, to help. But come, there are details I can't trust myself to remember. I'll take you to where the Sanctuary left me. You can't go in, but you of all people should know where I came out." She turned and resumed her float. Eve and the detective tried again to keep up.

The spirits that pledged themselves to Eve's Ghost Precinct promised they wouldn't go on to the Sweet Summerland, as the Spiritualists called their idea of a heavenly plane, without telling their coworkers. It was a way of ensuring that the delicate channel between the precinct Mediums and the spirits did not tear itself into injurious pieces. An open, psychic channel to the spirit world hurt if torn away and not properly shut. A wounded third eye could never properly heal. It had injured Eve when Maggie had been ripped away. It seemed the spirit hadn't thought of that. Eve swallowed back a reprimand that would seem ungrateful considering how glad she was to see her dead friend.

"Eve, who *is* this gentleman trailing you?" Maggie waved an incorporeal hand toward the detective. "Have you started hiring men since I've been gone?"

Eve shook her head. "Detective Horowitz and I have been consulting on strange cases that have unexpected, intersecting patterns. He's been a critical liaison for the department and a valuable friend."

"To be clear," the detective added, looking vaguely in Maggie's direction as they continued uptown, his gaze focusing and losing focus as if he faintly caught sight of her spectral person then lost her again. "I do support Miss Whitby and her precinct, even if I don't always understand it."

The public at large didn't know about the existence of the small Ghost Precinct, technically part of the New York Police Department. The few lieutenants and sergeants who did know thought the whole thing preposterous. "Full of hogwash," Eve had overheard one day in Mulberry Headquarters. The fact that the Ghost Precinct was made up of women didn't help the force's estimation, and it had been Eve's hope that Horowitz championing them would help win over some colleagues. The ones who didn't similarly judge him for being Jewish, that is.

The unlikely trio made the last fifteen blocks to Grand Central quicker by jogging over an avenue to catch an uptown trolley line, hopping on the next car that clanged its bell at the stop.

Maggie looked around with fierce interest in every sensory detail as the trolley dinged along, her luminous eyes taking in every storefront and theatre. The venues grew grander as the blocks ticked up their numbers. The ghost seemed to study every horse and cart, carriage or hack; every passerby, be they elegant or ragged, watching the shifting sea of hats along the sidewalk, from silk top to tattered caps, feathered millinery to threadbare scarves, forms dodging and darting like fish in a narrow stream.

Eve saw it all pass around and through the ghost, her transparent image superimposed over the tumult of midday Manhattan.

"I've missed you," the specter murmured to the metropolis. Eve didn't hear New York reply, but she felt it in her heart. When one genuinely loved the city, the soul of New York took note.

Watching Maggie watch New York was a study in eternal eagerness. Love kept the good spirits tethered to the tactile world. Moments like this were Eve's lesson about life taught by the dead: drink it all in, the chaos, the tumult, the bustle of existence and its myriad details as much as possible, as one's relationship to it all could change at any moment.

Once inside Grand Central Depot, a noisy, dark, crowded place filled with glass and trestles, soot and steam, a building dearly overdue for an upgrade to a full station, Maggie gestured toward a particular platform.

"Transit is with us, and if we're quick, you can be back within the two hours I quoted," the ghost exclaimed, wafting up train-car steps on the northern line. With a screeching rumble and a billowing burst of steam, they were off. Eve and the detective took a small bench at the rear of a car before pausing to consider whether it was wise to trust the demands of an excitable ghost.

Greenwich Village, Manhattan

Three mediums of the Ghost Precinct waited for their manager to return, sitting primly at their séance table on a crisp late autumn day. Hands clasped together, they were ready to begin. The lancet windows of their rear office had been cranked wide open to hear the clamor of New York City meld with the rustle of falling leaves and the constant whispers of the dead.

Cora Dupris, Antonia Morelli, and Jenny Friel had been left alone at the Ghost Precinct offices after having given their leader, Eve, a bit of a hard time about leaving again on a whim with the detective to whom she seemed to have a growing attraction. They knew that to wait for her to begin their séance would waste a precious opportunity for new information regarding the many loose ends of their cases. The three young mediums came from vastly different backgrounds and circumstance but were brought together by their gifts and calmly began their ritual of communing with the dead.

Cora, Eve's second-in-command, a year behind her at age eighteen, struck the match.

"Good spirits, come and speak with us, in the respect of your life and your cares in this world. Is there a spirit who would like our attention?

We still seek our friend Maggie. We still seek answers for that which remains unsolved."

Two ghosts appeared, their transparent, greyscale forms fully manifest on either side of the table. The two girls, little Zofia and the elder Olga, were immigrants from Poland and the Ukraine who had died in the same garment district fire years prior. Their spirits, most keen on keeping other young people from similar fates or myriad abuses in the vast, churning, industrial behemoth city, quietly stood watch over the proceedings as devoted spectral assets to the Ghost Precinct. Zofia chose to remain a consistent haunt; Olga chose to manifest only during séances. Both girls were silvery, luminous, with dark charcoal hair pulled back from their sharp-featured faces. The darkened, singed hem of their simple dresses was the only reminder of how they'd died.

The appearance of these precinct assets—ghostly, serene faces staring at their living friends—heralded the opening of the spirit realm to mortal ears.

There was a rushing sound through the room, in an ethereal echo, as if a great door had been opened.

"There's a host of children," Zofia said, uneasy. "And they've been wronged somehow."

"We are listening," Cora responded, speaking loudly to the spirit world as a whole but nodding at Zofia to make sure the girl knew she was heard and understood. So often spirits spoke, trying to help the living, and were ignored.

A thousand whispers crested around the mediums like a tidal wave, a jumble of woe, impossible to make out one word over the next. Little Jenny clapped her hands over her ears. Antonia, her tall, wide-shouldered body sitting starkly still and bolt straight, winced. Cora released a held breath carefully, slowly, as if she were lowering a great weight onto her delicate shoulders, untucking a handkerchief from her lace cuff to dab at the moisture that had sprung up on her light brown brow.

There was another sound, a scuttling behind them, though they could see nothing. They felt presences they could not see. Ghosts were unpredictable in the ways in which they manifested. The scurrying sound, accompanied by the same wash of urgent whispers, swept over to the locked file cabinets against their rear wall.

The young women turned their heads very slowly.

Just because one worked with the dead didn't mean they couldn't be frightening. Spirits were often creatures of startle and shock.

The precinct file cabinets flew open.

All of the women jumped.

"But we don't even have all the keys," Cora said, wondering how the ghosts could possibly have unlocked the dusty old wooden cabinets filled with incomplete and shoddily taken case notes from earlier decades of corruption and disarray.

Below one of the four desks scattered about the long room, the center drawer creaked open of its own accord. Then another desk's drawer. Then a third. Papers rustled, and a few flew out. Then a few more.

Jenny edged over to the seventeen-year-old Antonia, who held her long arm out for the little girl who had become a surrogate sister, and the child tucked in against her. Antonia kept herself calm and collected, for Jenny's sake if nothing else. The little girl didn't need to sign, or write a note to be understood, her small form shook, making Antonia hold her all the tighter. The child didn't need to have any further traumas added to her condition of selective mutism.

"Spirits, what do you wish to tell us?" Cora demanded, finding her voice.

"And why this display? You've never been the sort to give us poltergeists!" Antonia exclaimed.

"Find us..." came a murmur that consolidated from the voices, the words racing around the room in a freezing chill, though no spirits could be seen to have made the declaration. It came from the fabric of the air itself, repeating again, in aching earnest. "Come find what we've lost!"

Chapter Two

As the train rumbled away from the depot, heading north, Eve felt driven by something beyond her control. The spirit world was like that, a runaway train, but so too was flirtation, and she was driven by another excuse for she and the detective to be together. Alone. Without a chaperone. For an extended period of time.

For a moment back at the park she and the detective had leaned in, so close, intimate. She wasn't sure how she felt about their near kiss, but she wanted more time to sort it out. The detective wore a pensive, faraway look, his elegant angles turned toward patches of dappled sun blinking through trees as the train gained ground level again. Perhaps he was as dazed as she felt about what was happening.

She and the detective had agreed to "court" on the pretense of averting their parents' mutual pressures about finding someone to marry. A convenient ruse. Whether the courtship was a mere act anymore wasn't something Eve dared ask.

"You know, there's so much…" Maggie began, taking on a thoughtful gaze as the city rolled away, opening to patches of green and less dense buildings.

"So much what, dear?" Eve asked, accustomed to reminding a ghost to make its point. Sometimes spirits were just as distracted as a young person trying very hard not to fall in love.

"How much there is in the city to block us out," Maggie said. "So much noise. It's a wonder you and the girls can ever hear us. We're going somewhere quieter."

"Can you hear her now?" Eve asked the detective. "Maggie?"

He turned away from the window, looking at Eve and then off just behind her, near to where Maggie floated but not exactly. "Bits and pieces."

"Take his hand, Eve; if you want him to hear, you know that will strengthen the channel," Maggie said. Eve tried to cool her blush, but it bloomed on her cheeks regardless. "And it seems to me you *want* to hold his hand, so…" Maggie murmured, a draft against Eve's ear.

"I do not—" Eve said to Maggie through clenched teeth.

"What? What's wrong?" the detective asked. His brown eyes ringed with striking blue pierced her, searching.

"Nothing," both Eve and Maggie said quickly.

Eve did not take his hand, and they returned to their pensiveness as the Hudson Valley came into full and glorious view. The scenes of bridges, sweeping vistas, grand mansions and dramatic tree lines in full autumnal glory along a glittering, wending river rendered them reverently quiet.

It occurred to Eve after taking in the picturesque scenery that she didn't know what had happened to Maggie in the first place. "Maggie, tell me what happened the night you disappeared. Before you show me what saved you, what threatened you? Where were you?"

"The Prenze mansion."

Eve shot a wide-eyed look at the detective.

He cocked his head to the side. "Did I just hear the name Prenze?"

"You did," Eve said in an undertone, careful to check her surroundings. Other passengers, in a mixture of simple business wear or more elegant finery, seemed preoccupied with the view, newspapers, or books. Caution was wise, as the Prenze clan was prominent and powerful. The patriarchs were twins, one alive and one presumed dead, and they cherished their younger sister. None had children that Eve knew of. The Prenze family had made their fortune off dubiously healthful tonics, and the family name kept circling in Eve's precinct for reasons she hadn't yet determined. Because of their prominence, she didn't want any gossip to escape via eavesdroppers. She didn't need more detractors.

"What about them?" Eve whispered.

"There's something wrong in that house, with that family," Maggie stated, caring not a whit for the passengers who could neither see nor hear her, save perhaps for one wide-eyed child in a pinafore and straw hat staring all the way across the train car, but that couldn't be helped. "I was drawn into the mansion by a child," Maggie continued, "who wanted me to launch something off the mantel. Turns out the box was full of postmortem photographs. Caused quite the scene."

In a murmur, Eve repeated what Maggie had said, realized a parallel to another case, and explained it to Horowitz.

"Vera, another of my valuable spirit operatives, was drawn in by a similar instance and asked to do a similar thing," Eve explained. "But in the *Dupont* house. The complaint filed against my department for interference regarding the *Prenze* family must have come from Maggie's experience, right before she disappeared."

"Odd that there's a connection with the postmortem photographs," Horowitz mused. "That seems too specific to be coincidence."

"Agreed," Eve replied before gesturing that her floating colleague continue.

"The man of the house ushered everyone out of the room," Maggie explained, "after I'd launched the box of photographs. Cruel, he turned to me and raised the dial of the electric lights to a blinding, painful level. I blinked out as if there were a spectral knife in those lights. I was cast into a nothingness, thrown into utter darkness. Aware, and yet lost. It was hell."

"How, then, did you escape?" Eve asked in a breathless murmur.

"Why, I begged for sanctuary, and I was granted it," the ghost replied as if that were the only sensible answer. "Bless an express line, we're nearly here!"

The train squealed to a stop at Tarrytown.

"The Sanctuary is in Sleepy Hollow? Really?" Eve asked, cocking an eyebrow.

Maggie just laughed and wafted through the train wall. Horowitz stepped into the aisle and gestured for Eve to go ahead.

On the train platform, Eve took a moment to get her bearings. A change of light sometimes meant spirits' incorporeal forms were hard for her sensitive eyes to see. Donning her dark glasses was a help, as too bright a light was painful. Maggie floated at the less crowded end of the platform, leading away from the crowd, gesturing to them.

"This way," Eve said quietly to the detective.

"Lead on, ladies," he said amiably.

Descending onto a gravel path, Maggie turned away from what would have led to the village's main thoroughfare and headed instead toward a copse of trees that were darker and denser than one would expect. They walked along a shaded, gravel lane.

"Washington Irving knew there was something odd and important about this whole area; he just didn't know *just* how spiritually charged it all is," Maggie stated.

The gravel gave way simply to a footpath through close pines, and they followed that for countless yards, into a pine barren where the path gave way to a spongy floor of brown needles.

"Are we…trespassing?" Eve asked the ghost hesitantly.

"No, this is public land, an extension of a park along the riverside; it's just that this specific parcel of land hasn't been cleared."

They mounted a small incline and came to a place where pines and beech trees, intermixed in a strange assortment of dark and luminous barks, growing in patterns that weren't usually so intermingled, opened to a little circle. A pile of stones sported tendrils of ivy across its cairn, and from this pyramid rose one stone-hewn side of a Gothic arch the size of an average person.

It didn't appear ancient or worn but was instead modern masonry, the ghost of a window whose chapel had never been finished beyond these initial stones.

"What's this?" Eve asked, gesturing to the unfinished monument.

"It's one of the living world's few anchors to Sanctuary," Maggie explained. "I was told a devout young Episcopalian woman wanted to build a chapel here for travelers' rest and meditation. She had the support of local deacons but was foiled by her family after these first stones were set. Nothing else was done.

"The church owned this part of the land and asked that it be added as a quiet addendum to the park," the spirit continued, "to honor the young woman's idea. It's said the trees grew immediately thicker and denser, as if to hide this sliver of sacred stones. The spirits say that woman's heart created a doorway even she couldn't have known would open and that the unnamed woman lives still, perhaps never knowing the seed her heart planted. It's the thinnest part of the veil between mortal and spirit world. It's here where I tumbled out when I came through, when I asked the Sanctuary to return."

Eve turned and shared with the detective the things he hadn't picked up on his own.

"But you didn't enter Sanctuary here," Horowitz clarified. "You were ejected here?"

"Correct." Maggie nodded. "After the lights blinded me in the Prenze mansion, when I regained a sense of myself in the darkness, I could hear a few other whimpering souls but nothing else. I was there what may have been hours, but it felt like days."

"It was nearly a month," Eve reminded her.

The spirit wafted between pine branches that rustled in an autumn breeze as she related her trauma and in turn Eve shared with the detective; while it was clear from the turn of his head and the focus of his eyes he was picking up a few words, it wasn't a connected narrative for him as it was for Eve.

"I prayed and prayed, so very hard!" Maggie pressed her luminous hands together. "I tried reaching out to you, Eve, to the strong bond all our séances have built. I felt you close to me a few times, as I thought you and the girls might be reaching out for me too—"

"We were, please believe us, Maggie," Eve assured. "We tried everything to reach you. I think I did, once, in that darkness—a painful automatic writing session. But it wasn't enough to break you out of that limbo. I even went into the depths of the Corridors for you—"

"I know, dear friend." Maggie floated close to pass a cold hand over Eve's warm cheek. "You went too deeply toward death for your health, but I managed to shove you out toward life again, and *that's* thanks to what I learned in the Sanctuary."

Eve circled the stone arch as Maggie explained the place. "Sanctuary is connected to the Corridors between life and death, but it maintains separate autonomy. It's quite complicated. Sanctuary isn't a space *between* life and death like the Corridors are; Sanctuary is a space permanently of and for death. It was made for the dead by the dead, as a refuge for those not ready to go on to eternal rest but needing a place to 'live' and to belong—a place of respite for spirits who have pending work with the living but need a place to recuperate. The ways of the spirit world are complex and mysterious, even for you who deal with us daily. Our realms are not like those of the living, and Sanctuary is an even different place still."

"Do we, then, have permission to enter?" Eve asked warily.

Maggie shook her head firmly. "No, you do not. There are places the living aren't welcome. But you need to see this place, in case anyone else goes missing or if something strange from the spirit world can't be reconciled. You might be able to come and ask for help from here, from the outside. One of the Sisters who maintain the Sanctuary might come and answer. They do listen. Especially here."

"The Sisters?" Eve raised an eyebrow. Maggie gestured to the half-finished arch before them.

"It's like an abbey, the Sanctuary," Maggie explained, and Eve repeated her words quietly for the detective's sake. "It's maintained by Sisters, but its votaries and attendants come from all varieties of cloth and belief, all of them spirits. It was founded centuries ago when like-minded ghosts needed a cloistered, safe place to recover from trauma."

"By whom? Who founded it?"

"None of us know, exactly. Her Holiness is hundreds of years old. It's said she built the Sanctuary with her own spiritual gifts and since then it tethers to places like this…a place that a noble, innocent heart begged to be made a sacred place of peace."

Maggie reached out to touch the stone arch, this uncanny portal. A tiny piece of sandstone tumbled down the arch's slope and onto the leaves below, moved by the phantom caress. Eve wondered how many stones were worn smooth not by time but by the gentle brush of spirits.

"Some have guesses as to Her Holiness's identity," Maggie continued, "such as an early saint or reformer, but no one is certain. She carries music with her like magical spells, old, eerie—the stuff of divine mystery. She spoke to me through light. I did not see her; no one can see past her Living Light, as it is known. But I explained what our Ghost Precinct does, and I was granted leave and permission to tell you this. I was also asked to give you a warning."

"A warning?" Eve touched the cool stone as Maggie had done. It was as ice-cold as a spirit, but it seemed to vibrate, full of life and magic.

"Our modern practice of Spiritualism, of holding séances to contact the dead, is a boon for all it has done to bring comfort to the grieving and to affirm the existence of spirits. However, the Corridors that connect life and death are being polluted by clumsy living souls rummaging around and leaving their anger and fear behind."

Maggie had been pacing before the stone, but when Eve gasped at the word "polluted" the ghost stopped and turned to her, wavering before the arch, her eyes wide and shining.

"That must be why the Corridors between life and death were so dark and murky," Eve exclaimed. Gathering her skirts, she sat upon a small rock to the side of the arch, looking up at the wavering specter.

"The Corridors changed when I went in to find you, Maggie. It wasn't just the long, warm, worn hallway between life and the beyond I'm accustomed to in a séance or a trance; it was pitch black, and I could gain nothing from that space. It used to be full of life, energy, and visual moments from which I could glean insights and predictions, but now it's as if there's a dark smog inside, damp and devoid."

"Yes," Maggie said sadly. The trees rattled dried leaves in a passing breeze as if in agreement. "And in time, that cumulative pollution of mortal woe will make the living sick in ways we can't understand. All the Sanctuary was buzzing with this talk, and fellow spirits agreed I had to bring this to you so that you might begin to strategize how to help the Sanctuary stay sane and keep mortal troubles out."

"I'm very glad to know about this place," Eve said, rising excitedly to her feet, "this force of nature that rescued you! I want to see it protected and unpolluted. I certainly don't want Spiritualism's mortal séances to have a negative effect. All I want to do is be a help to those here, there, and in between."

"Of course, dear. I hope Sanctuary will learn to trust you, even if it can't trust the tradition of Spiritualism in general," Maggie said gently. "But before I left Sanctuary's light and beauty, it looked like a storm was coming. The Sisters began to shutter the abbey against it. Whether that's metaphoric or literal, time will tell."

Eve glanced at the detective. His expression was far away, his brow furrowed. Matters of one's spirit were so difficult to speak about when they were often the most intimate things a person could feel or think. She didn't press him, especially since his traditions were different from hers and she wanted to be respectful in every way.

"It's getting darker," he said quietly. While Eve knew he was indicating the day, it felt like he was commenting on Maggie's experience.

"Yes, indeed," Eve agreed. "Now, Maggie, it's too late for me to return to the offices, but I need you to stay with me. There's someone else who needs to see you, and you know it."

The ghost sighed wearily.

If Maggie was Eve's dearest dead friend, her closest corporeal friend, the woman to whom Eve owed *everything* was her namesake and grandmother, Evelyn Northe-Stewart. Fondly known as Gran.

Maggie was Gran's niece, and while Gran hadn't made a big fuss over Maggie's spectral disappearance, Eve knew it was breaking her heart, as their relationship had been complicated and strained during life, a fact that had haunted Gran deeply since Maggie's untimely death two decades prior.

"Yes, I suppose you're right," Maggie said finally. "Lead on, to Fifth Avenue."

The detective gestured ahead of him, leading the way back out of the wood, glancing once back behind him at the archway, brow still furrowed, lost in thought.

A spattering of poetry played through Eve's mind, regarding woods, paths, and hearts.

But Maggie's revelation of storm clouds encompassing beauty was something out of Poe's imagination, and it was a new concern for the dawning of a new century.

Detective Horowitz kindly took his leave at Grand Central depot, giving his colleague and the ghost an overwhelmed smile. "I don't really know what to say, so... Until next time?"

"Until next time, Detective," Eve replied, adding sincerely, "Thank you for your company."

"And you for yours. Ladies." He bowed his head to Eve, then in the direction he likely thought, due to the distinct chill, must be Maggie. He was almost on target, and Maggie waved even if he couldn't see it.

"Pleasure, Detective. It's lovely having you on our adventure! Do call again soon!" the ghost said with genuine warmth, ever the welcoming socialite even in her spectral state.

After watching him go, Eve turned to stare a warning at Maggie, a look she hoped was sufficient to instruct that not a word be said until the gentleman was well out of sight. Eve held her head high and gestured uptown.

"We'll walk," Eve declared. Maggie bobbed along for a bit as they exited the noisy depot filled with steam and the squeals of steel, but the ghost broke into a little giggle once they headed north along the avenue.

"Well, well, well," Maggie said.

"Not you too," Eve muttered.

"Me too what?" the ghost responded coyly.

"You're at me about the detective too?" she murmured. New York didn't seem to mind someone who appeared to be talking quietly to themselves; seemingly discreet madness was fine. The city just didn't appreciate it when it was an interruption to everyone else's busy day.

"Well, why wouldn't I be?" Maggie exclaimed. "He's handsome, smart, and kind! Haven't we spent several years now, gossiping about beautiful people together?"

"Because I don't want a suitor, Maggie, not—"

The ghost folded her arms and floated directly in front of Eve, forcing her to step right through Maggie, a frozen blast across her face.

"We have agreed upon a courtship as a *ruse*," Eve clarified, "to placate our respective parents. Goodness, isn't it an obvious ploy and nothing more?"

The ghost grinned. "Ah. A ploy. Of course. Yes. Clearly. A ploy and nothing more. Quoth the raven," the ghost said, tittering a laugh.

Eve set her jaw and charged forward. "You have to explain everything to Gran, you know."

"Yes, yes, Auntie will be cross with me I'm sure, for charging into the Prenze mansion without securing your Preventative Protocol," Maggie declared. "You and your blasted precinct paperwork! But Auntie will see the worth. *She* taught me to judge a higher calling. It's why I felt confident in giving my life to a worthy cause and why I make a good fighter between realms."

Eve nodded in appreciation. "That you do, my friend. You should be considered a decorated hero. I have missed you, you know."

"Of course you have," the ghost said with jovial haughtiness.

"The girls will be so excited to see you, none so much as Zofia. She was inconsolable when you left."

Zofia, a regular Ghost Precinct haunt who died in a garment district fire and now spent her spectral life looking out for other vulnerable souls in danger, had taken to Maggie like a sister.

Maggie put a transparent hand over her mouth. "My girls," she exclaimed, tears glittering at the corners of her bright silver eyes. "For those of us who can never be physical mothers, the power of our found family rises above all. My bond to all of you is what kept me from being entirely torn apart."

Eve put a hand to her heart. The sentiment was overwhelming. There would be time to regroup and recover, all of them, as Eve's side of the "Fort Denbury" townhouses had become a refuge for the living and the dead.

The Ghost Precinct mediums lived in Eve's townhouse communally and their best ghostly assets pleasantly haunted their halls. The reunion would be quite an event, but there was a hierarchy to attend to first and Eve wanted to make that point quite clear.

"We'll all be home soon to celebrate you, my friend. But for right now, we must attend to the woman to whom we owe everything," Eve said, leading Maggie up the walk to Gran's door and crossing the threshold of the grand matriarch's home.

Evelyn Northe-Stewart's Fifth Avenue townhouse was an elegant bastion of splendor firmly planted in the styles of Art Nouveau and the Tiffany Studios, Gran having been a fan of the designer long before he'd become the talk of the town in luminous stained-glass interior design with its spectacular effects of pattern and iridescence.

Eve let herself into the foyer and unpinned her small felt hat, leaving it on a peg by the entrance hall mirror and taking a moment to note her reflection in the mirror. Windblown black hair and flushed cheeks made her sickly, pale complexion far less bleak. All the blushing she'd been doing since working with the detective was doing her pallor some good. It helped sell the ploy, she reminded herself. The ghost floating behind her in the mirror, transparent and still holding back a grin, seemed to say otherwise—that she wasn't fooling anyone.

"Gareth, is that you back from the museum already?" Gran asked from the parlor.

"No, Gran, it's me, not Grandpa," Eve said, stepping up to the parted pocket doors.

"Ah, hello, dear, come in. Your mother's here."

Eve and Maggie stared at one another a moment.

"Should I go?" Maggie whispered. "I doubt your mother wants to see me."

"She'll want to know your spirit is well," Eve replied. "We were *all* worried."

It was no secret that Natalie, Eve's mother, had long wanted the paranormal aspects of her youth left behind. The fact that Eve had inherited the spectral world as her own was a constant source of family tension.

"What's that?" Gran called. "Do you need something? Ring for one of the girls if you do. I've got my arms full of unwieldy wildflowers doing battle with a vase."

"Gran, Mother, I've brought someone by," Eve stated, stepping inside the well-lit parlor decked in lace curtains, gilt trimmings, colored glass, and brocade upholstery. Maggie wafted in behind Eve.

"Hello Auntie Evelyn," Maggie called. "I've missed you!"

The ever-elegant Gran lost a few wildflowers that tumbled to the fine Persian carpet as she whirled around to face the ghost calling her name, her peridot silk day dress edged in emerald beads whooshing and clicking as she turned. Maggie floated closer to both women, who stared at the presence before them.

"And hello, my dear Natalie, I've missed you too, if you don't mind my saying so," the ghost added, addressing the pretty, auburn-haired woman in a simple linen dress of a rich plum color with lace trim. Natalie's eyes were less focused; she couldn't see spirits as well as Gran, but she felt the presence.

"Hello...old friend..." Eve's mother said haltingly, shifting toward the center of the room where Maggie floated. "I'm...*so* relieved you're safe," she said earnestly, tears glittering in her green eyes. "All I've *ever* wanted is for your peace—"

"Oh, you darling! Your dear daughter brings me all the peace I need, thank you," Maggie said brightly, wafting over and placing cool drafts of a kiss on each of her friend's cheeks. Natalie tucked an errant auburn lock the ghost had unsettled back into a loosely braided coiffure.

Maggie's shimmering greyscale form then floated toward Gran, whose hand was on her mouth, tears glittering on her cheeks. Eve wasn't sure the guilt Gran felt about her niece's death would ever be fully healed, and the spirit's disappearance had only heightened old wounds.

"I know, Auntie," the ghost cooed. "I love you too."

Statuesque and compelling even when taken aback, Gran sputtered a chuckle amidst tears.

"Would you all…like to talk business?" Natalie asked awkwardly. "I'll go."

"No, stay," Maggie stated. "Three generations should hear what I have to say, as it's for the good of us all. There's no stopping Eve from being involved." She wafted forward a step and added, with gentle sternness, "You might try not to fight it for once, Natalie."

Eve was glad the ghost said it, not her. Natalie opened her mouth as if to retaliate but, after a moment, clenched her fists and sat in a high-backed chair near the window.

Gran picked up the wildflowers from the floor and set the ones that hadn't managed to fit in the vase on a side table beside her stepdaughter's chair before taking a seat next to Eve, patting her granddaughter's hand as she looked up at her ghostly niece.

Maggie explained Sanctuary and its benefits as well as the potential danger Spiritualism posed if the pollution of mortal energy left behind was not more carefully controlled. Gran was rapt, Natalie wary.

"How did you get out?" Natalie asked.

"Sanctuary is hesitant to allow a spirit to return to the living unless they've mission and focus." Maggie floated along the farthest wall, the flocked brocade wallpaper creating undulating patterns behind her transparent skin. "I fit that bill, and Sanctuary wanted to relay the message about mortal pollution. It was Eve's deep dive into the Corridors that drew me out. When she went after little Ingrid from her case, searching for me too, her efforts reconnected my spirit to the mortal world—almost at a perilous cost to Eve."

Eve remembered that moment when Ingrid Schwerin's spirit was being ushered toward the light and the child gave Eve a message for her mother, Greta. Enraptured by the light, Eve had wanted to follow that beauty no matter where it led. But Maggie's spirit had shoved her back with a loving scold, and Eve had fallen away into two days of unconsciousness.

"Pushing Eve away from death's door," Maggie continued, "propelled *me* toward the living, and I finally tumbled out in Sleepy Hollow at that archway."

"Where… Where did you say that unfinished monument was?" Gran asked quietly.

Eve shared the exact location and Maggie told the story about the unnamed young woman who had wanted to build a meditative abbey there and how her commitment to peace had tethered access to the Sanctuary there.

Gran sat back in her chair, and the tears rolled down her cheeks once more.

"What…" Eve reached out for Gran's soft, veined hand. "Did you know that woman?"

"I… I *was* that woman. That was me!" A shaking hand went to her hair, the crest of her silver coiffure adorned with a peridot hairpin that had come loose during her reaction. She adjusted the shimmering green stones as if realigning a crown. "I never knew what had sprung up in my long-lost hope's place!"

The room sat, and floated, all stunned by this powerful revelation.

Gran had lived a long life filled with adventures, battles, stories, and glories untold, and Eve knew only a fraction of them. There were so many ongoing, unfolding mysteries of Evelyn Northe-Stewart that Eve wondered if she'd ever know all of them.

"It was…you?" Maggie finally murmured in awestruck reverence. Spectral tears glistened on the ghost's luminous cheek. "The spirits said the door to the Sanctuary had been set by the heart of an unusually powerful living spirit. Oh, I'm so proud!" She clapped her hands, the sound to mortal ears merely an echo of applause.

"The spirit world gives me too much credit," Gran said, waving a hand. "No wonder the Sanctuary rescued you; it must have known you were family," Gran said quietly. "I never knew what happened. After my parents foiled my attempt at a woodland chapel meant for the weary traveler and halted construction, that arch was the only evidence of the dream I abandoned. There were…other complications at that time in my life. Infinite cruelties I don't want to talk about. I have all of you darlings now, my recompense." She looked at the generations of women who considered her a mother figure. "I have no complaints," she said, glancing upward as if making sure the heavens knew she was a grateful soul.

"The veil between life and death is thin there, by Sanctuary," Maggie said, wafting close to Gran and placing a luminescent hand on her silver head, "because of your love and faith, imbued into that solitary arch. You have always connected our worlds."

Gran nodded. There was so much Eve wanted to ask, about her past, about all the things she didn't know and perhaps had been too self-absorbed to ask. One never fully knows their loved ones, not truly, especially not those who had lived as fully and as bravely as Gran. But Eve remembered there were pressing reasons why she had come and current cases that depended on Gran's help and insight.

"Now, there's business to discuss," Eve said and shifted the tone. "Beyond what happened with Maggie at the Prenze mansion, which confirms our suspicions that something is rotten in that house, there's a new development with the family. Just before Maggie returned to us, the detective and I were closely discussing..." She felt the words fall away as she thought of their near kiss in Union Square Park. She stammered to recover. "We were...talking, and he showed me a paper related to the dead Dr. Font whose body was found in the Dakota—"

Eve's mother rose. "Here's where I draw the line. While I'm glad the Sanctuary can be a refuge for spirits in need, when it comes to case details and dead bodies, that's your world, Eve, not mine. Just see to it that you're safe. No more kidnapping of either of you, or I'm going to take this family far away, never to speak the word *ghost* again. Thank you for the tea, Evelyn." Doling out a kiss on the cheek to her stepmother and to her daughter, Natalie paused at Maggie's floating form. "It *is* good to see you, dear. Don't disappear on us without warning again. I don't think our fragile hearts can take it."

"Why, you sentimental *darling*!" Maggie cooed as Natalie walked away.

"Don't press your luck," Natalie said from the parlor door and continued out into the balmy dusk to return home. Her unceremonious rebuttal got a chuckle out of Eve. For all that her mother didn't like what she did, Eve had learned her stubbornness, fortitude, and occasional cutting wit from her.

Gran clapped her hands, ready to get back to business and all the loose ends that surrounded them. "What's this about the Prenze family, then?"

Maggie again described what had gone on: that she'd been drawn into the mansion by the ghost of a child, saw the child's face in a slew of postmortem photographs she sent flying across the parlor during a dinner party, and then was driven out by blinding light before being cast into utter darkness, only to be saved by Sanctuary.

Eve jumped in to explain the latest Prenze mystery. "Detective Horowitz was investigating the odd death of a Dr. Font, who happened to be the presiding physician listed on the Prenze twin's death certificate. Dr. Font was found dead recently in the Dakota, in a room with no furniture. He didn't live there; he was just *there*. A relative says he was 'scared to death' but wouldn't say what about. The detective had a bottle of tonic examined that was in Font's effects, what with poison a possible cause of death. A label was recovered from within the empty bottle. One side read Prenze, as it was a Prenze company tonic. Two words were scrawled on the other side: *Isn't dead.*

There was silence as Gran pieced the label and the note together. "Prenze isn't dead?"

"That's what the clue indicated, that the twin might not have died after all."

"Do you think that's who could be behind the threats to the Ghost Precinct?"

"I honestly don't know," Eve replied. "I wish I did."

"Well *one* of the twins tried to snuff out my spirit," Maggie said. "That's for certain. Blind me into nonexistence. It's bad enough to be killed once. But twice—"

"Horrific," Gran exclaimed. "My poor girl. *How* have I failed you so?"

"Auntie, you'll miss the truth of things if you keep clinging to the past," The ghost replied with a sudden vehemence and passion. "Half the time, mortals can't hear what the divine asks of them because their ears are stuffed full of the voices of their own insecurities. They can't see the divine path ahead because they're blinded by guilt, jealousy, or any mortal failing that gets in the way. Auntie, please, let go of a past we cannot change, or I cannot help you in the future."

Gran blinked back tears. "My *wise* girl."

"How can we find out more about the Prenze family? Safely?" Eve asked. "They're powerful. I don't know how to do this without bringing more trouble down on my head."

"I've an idea," Gran assured. "I think I can gain access. I met Alfred, the living twin, at his family soiree, and it's he who maintains an outward social life. If the other twin is alive, he's in hiding. I'll reach out to see if Alfred Prenze would like to sponsor a charity function. Under the guise of society chatter, I'll see if I can get more out of him. We'll convene again soon. Let me get to work."

Gran kissed Eve on the head and reached out to pass her hand through Maggie's outstretched palm, looking at her with a complicated expression before exiting toward her library. Eve could read everything about her elder, her mentor, and best friend: heavyhearted but her powerful mind whirling, spirit churning, plans being set in motion.

* * * *

Eve stepped up to the door of her home, a townhouse adjoining her parents' townhouse, catching the reflection of her weary eyes in the oval glass etched with phantom flowers. Turning a beautiful silver scrollwork key in the ornate plate of her lock, she leaned her full weight against the hardwood door and strode into the entrance hall, Maggie bobbing along behind her. At the sight of them, the cluster of spirits that often lingered in Eve's side of Fort Denbury squealed in delight at the base of the stairs.

The sound of rejoicing ghosts drew Eve's mediums into the hall to see what the disturbance was all about. Once everyone saw who had come home, little Jenny joined in, celebrating by waving her arms delightedly at her ghostly elder sister. Cora and Antonia both wiped a tear from their eyes and maintained stoic composure.

"Maggie, Maggie!" little Zofia screamed, lifting her spectral arms in the air, and soon she and Maggie were twirling about in laughter and delight. Even Olga, who usually chose to visit only for a séance, had to greet Maggie's homecoming, wafting in for an embrace.

"I've missed you, my little button!" Maggie declared to Zofia, touching her nose with a fond tap, reaching out to Olga and grasping her hand before turning to Jenny and bopping a luminous finger on the tip of her nose in turn. "And *you*, my bonnie lass!"

Jenny reached out hands to cup the vaporous sides of Maggie's face, whispering a welcome home.

Vera, their oldest spiritual asset, a painter who had spent most of her life in upper Manhattan, was curiously absent. This gave Eve a distinct, disturbed chill. It wasn't like her not to be lingering in the parlor, her bony fingers sketching on the air.

"I've a great deal to catch you up on," Eve explained to her mediums. "I hope, Antonia, you've been so kind as to leave me some dinner?"

"We've already eaten, but of course, I anticipated you'd be late. Come eat and we'll have tea. Tell us how you brought our Maggie home!"

Eve turned to the celebrated ghost. "You rejoice with your colleagues," she said, gesturing to the other spirits. "Catch them up, and I'll do the same with my living darlings."

The ghosts swept into the parlor. Even spectral Cyrus, their resident angel of music, had shown up at the piano, and he was at the keys immediately, with gusto and joy, the ivory faintly moving in a whisper of the full force that a human hand could wield, but it played soft and sweet and bouncing. His dark skin in life was a beautiful deep grey in death, and he was still an expert at the keys.

It was a beautiful scene of so much life from the dead that Eve was reluctant to cross with the living into the dining room, sliding the pocket door shut behind them. Once seated, Eve looked around at her colleagues.

"So?" Cora asked, her arms folded.

Eve explained everything as best she could, from Maggie's reappearance in Union Square Park all the way through the trip to the Sanctuary arch, leaving out the near kiss between her and the detective. But the way little Jenny was staring at her, squinting a bit, she wondered if the little girl intuited it anyway—one of the rare moments she resented the intrusive gifts of a curious Sensitive.

"That's… That's quite an experience," Antonia said softly. Eve nodded.

"Would you like to hear about *our* day?" Cora asked. "Or are you too preoccupied?"

Eve didn't rise to the edge in Cora's tone. It was true her colleagues felt abandoned by her taking off with the detective on various whims, but she couldn't help that. What she would do was be patient with Cora, who in particular didn't want to be displaced.

"Please," Eve entreated. "I would have no precinct without you, dears. Of course, I want to know everything. I always do."

Before any of them could question Eve's loyalties further, little Zofia manifested nearly on top of her, and the smell of smoke that was the cause of her death accosted Eve's nose, a residual sensory trauma.

"It wasn't me," Zofia stated. "Today, at the office… It wasn't me. Or Olga. It was other children."

"We know," Cora said with a sigh. "Go back in with the others. Celebrate the return of your big sister, please. Let us tell Eve what happened."

"I'm sorry," Zofia said, sounding like she wanted to cry. "I'm just worried. Things feel strange, and now we can't find Vera."

"What do you mean?" Eve pressed.

"I think she may be gone like Maggie," the little girl said, floating back to the door. "Maybe Maggie saw her, coming and going." The spirit disappeared through the wall, the precinct colleagues looking after her, baffled.

"I hope not. I don't know that I can go after another missing ghost," Eve said, feeling nauseated at the thought, sitting back heavily in her chair. "Go on, dears, what happened at the office today that has everyone so rattled?"

"We sat down to begin a séance," Cora said, her words as crisp and efficient as her work ethic, "just to see if we could gather information on the threats. To see if we could find out what all that equipment during the abduction was for."

"We started, but soon, it was like the spirit world *blew* open," Antonia explained.

Then the temperature dropped, Jenny signed.

Eve nodded, understanding sign. She'd been taught by her mother who had suffered from the same condition of selective mutism as Jenny did, and Natalie taught Jenny in turn when the ghosts of the Friels brought their surviving child to Eve's door in hopes of safe refuge. Cora and Antonia were trying to learn sign and often were able to intuit what the girl meant and always gave her a moment to communicate as she wished.

"*Then* the file cabinets came open. All at once." Cora took up the narrative, hands shooting out as if to demonstrate. "Flew open or slid gratingly, it was all so startling."

"How is that possible?" Eve asked, sitting back in her chair. "We don't even have all the keys! I've only been able to get one set from the chief, and even that was an argument."

"Has a poltergeist happened in the office before, Eve?" Antonia asked. Eve and Cora, the first to have worked in that office, shook their heads that it hadn't. "After the movement of file cabinets and desk drawers, with no visible forms attached, a swarm of voices begged us to 'come find them.'" Antonia, passed long fingers over her angled face, tapping at her temple as she spoke, her keenly empathic ability to feel the spirits' angst was clear in her rueful tone. "It was very chilling, unlike anything I've experienced, this mass of voices all seeming to beg from the same point of strife."

Another spirit wafted in from the rosewood wall paneling, a face appearing in the flocked wallpaper and manifesting directly behind Cora's high-backed dining room chair.

"*Bonjour, ma cherie,*" a tall, handsome greyscale man said. He wore a fine dark suit, and his light ashen face held the same lovely, distinct lines and Creole heritage as Cora's light brown skin.

"Hello, Uncle Louis," Cora said, her generally stoic face breaking into a beaming smile. "*Ca va?*"

"*Bien.* I've come because I felt a disturbance," Louis replied. "I wanted to be sure of what I sensed. I was enjoying a beautiful ritual along the river, but as I am tied forever to both New Orleans and New York, you won me over." He smiled. "Illuminate me, niece." The spirit reached out a luminous hand toward her kerchief-swathed head. "Why did I feel what I did?" He looked between Cora and Eve with equal weight and expectation.

Eve explained Sanctuary to Louis Dupris, who had fought preternatural foes alongside Gran and the Bishops when Eve was just a baby. He was a source of great wisdom and comfort for the precinct. He nodded and rubbed his chin, thoughtful.

"That's fascinating," Louis said with genuine interest.

Cora hung on her uncle's every word, hovering at the edge of her seat as if trying to be nearer to his plane.

"I wish I'd have known of Sanctuary when I died," the ghost continued with distinct pain. "But then again, I was put right to work solving the crime of how I died, and perhaps that's why. It seems this Sanctuary is only for those who have nowhere else to turn."

"I was also warned that due to this century's increase in séances," Eve began, expressing Sanctuary's concerns, "that the spirit world is being 'polluted' by the energies of the living. It's vulnerable to the baser energies of the living tromping through its spiritual boundaries."

Louis thought a moment and Cora stared at him with a warm, gentle patience Eve knew she reserved for no one else. A strong and stoic young woman whose soul seemed infinitely older than her eighteen years, Cora had a bond with Louis that was radiant and pure, revealing the depths of her spiritual fortitude and capacity. Her hands were folded primly in her lap, atop her immaculate blue calico dress, her wide brown eyes sharply focused.

"I wouldn't worry about it," Louis said gently, "other than to take great care with every séance. Sanctuary must be unduly sensitive. Mortal fears carry more weight in a space designed for the dead by the dead. They're guarding their own walls without any thought to the benefits of what séances offer the living."

"But what if I can't undo damage done inside?" Eve said, feeling an enormous responsibility not to make a delicate place dangerous.

"Then it may be up to ghosts to clean up," Louis said with a shrug. "I'll ask your spectral assets. There are some things only ghosts can talk about. Some things only we understand."

Eve frowned, hating being left out even if it wasn't her place to help or fix. Ghosts had always made everything her business. They'd always made her feel desperately important to them, so it was baffling to her to hear that there were some things she couldn't be privy to.

"It's best that everyone maintains their own worlds sometimes, Eve, and holds close to their own divine mysteries," Antonia reassured. With a knowing smile, she added, "You can't be responsible for everything."

Dark-haired, angular and statuesque, decked in muslin and lace, Antonia spoke with a cultivated softness that, like her peers, was older than her seventeen years. Of them all, Antonia had lived the most difficult life, coming to the precinct in search of refuge. Expert at reading energy and emotions, Antonia wielded unmatched empathy and intuition as the heart of the group.

"Uncle," Cora asked quietly, reaching out a hand to the ghost, "will you sit by the fire with me and tell me how Mama and Papa are faring? Then when I retire to sleep, you can talk to Maggie all about the Sanctuary. She's reuniting with her little sisters, but if anyone could help the Sanctuary if it needs help, it's you," she said.

The ghost beamed with pride. "With pleasure."

"Will you look out for Vera?" Eve added.

"We hope she hasn't disappeared as Maggie did. Perhaps she found Sanctuary too," Antonia clarified.

Louis Dupris nodded and gestured to his niece to follow him fireside.

Cora looked at Eve. "Good night," she stated, and walked away. Jenny and Antonia followed suit, bidding a warmer good-night.

Boundaries had been hard to set in a house filled with psychics and Sensitives. Doors had to be shut. Eve sensed she'd just been given a taste of what Cora might have felt, being tied to Eve before Eve had gone off with the detective. There was a constant dance of energies—and very often, if Eve wasn't careful, when a ghost or a colleague would leave her, it would feel like they were pulling on her skin, or the corner of her shawl, tugging on a lock of hair. She had to remind herself to detach. At the core of the precinct, she was the center of a wheel, but she needed not to be constantly spinning.

Her legs felt extremely heavy as she ascended the stairs and turned a few paces down the hall to her second-floor room.

As she undressed and hung her skirt and jacket, she absently brushed her hand along the hem to wipe off lingering traces of pine needles. From a peg inside her tall wardrobe, she withdrew her nightgown, a beautiful, layered confection in soft muslin, lace, and satin. She wasn't one for frills or fanciness, but she allowed this indulgence in her nightclothes, her private romanticism. As she slid into the nightdress and tied it closed, then slowly shut the wardrobe, her reflected form in the door's interior mirror moved, the image looking for all the world like a ghost.

She glanced across at her vanity; that reflection too was another specter in the rising moonlight. Wisps of ghosts were always visible out of the corner of her eye, so she often mistook reflections of herself—pallid complexion, dark circles below glassy eyes—as just another ghost. She wondered if anyone else who saw ghosts as much as she did appeared so haunted.

Moving to her bed, floorboards creaking below the plush runner between the bed and wardrobe, she crawled under the quilt of roses made by her mother. Restless, she lay awake for hours, listening to the whole house settle in for the night, ghosts and all, until only the sounds of sleepless New York were heard far beyond her window. Her eyes must have drooped into a half sleep, because they fluttered open in a sequence of flashes before focusing on the small, delicate glass light fixture above her bed, its bulbs of fluted flowers in need of a good dusting.

A distinct prickle of unease swept up her arms and raised her hair beneath the thin muslin gathers of her nightdress. Looking at her tin-stamped ceiling and the concentric patterns of geometry and tracery that made the surface decorative, her mind played cruel tricks, shifting the circles into faces with teeth.

A dark spot at the corner of her eye had her turn to the window. The raised hairs went ice-cold. Terror swept her body.

She clapped her hand over her mouth, stifling a scream. Scrambling back against her headboard, with her knees clutched to her chest, she closed her eyes and opened them again, hoping what she'd seen outside her second-floor window was a trick of the trees outside.

It wasn't.

A man hovered at her window as if he were standing on a platform outside. But there was no such ledge.

This man was not a ghost. At least not as Eve had ever experienced one in her nineteen years of life, sixteen of which had been beset by haunting. One of her first memories was of playing with a child and crying when her hand passed through theirs. Ghosts had always been luminous silver and made of gorgeous mist. This apparition had none of the luminous, greyscale transparency she had come to expect of spirits that showed themselves to her. He was solid. Impenetrable shadow, dressed in a long, black coat.

The wide brim of his hat shaded his eyes from view, but light glinted through the corner of thin, wire-rimmed spectacles. A clean-shaven, clenched jaw was illuminated by the moon. He looked slightly familiar, but Eve couldn't place the section of face. Lips turned half down into a serious frown.

But as Eve stared, those lips shifted and curved. As if forcibly bent, his mouth twisted into a smile. Her stomach plummeted. A frisson of disgust raced over her before settling into her hands, which clenched into fists.

That was the worst of it, that smile. A bloodcurdling smile. A smug smirk, bent and cruel. Eve was haunted, of course; she had been forever, and that fact didn't trouble her. But this… This was new.

Finally, her body seemed to come back to itself, and she mostly found her legs. Throwing aside her bed of roses, she lurched to her feet, legs fully finding her as she hit the top of the stairs. She turned, fear seizing her muscles in a painful freeze as she registered what she saw. The figure floated from one window to the next, from her bedroom now to the hall window, keeping effortless pace.

Running down the stairs, she dreaded glancing out the parlor windows.

But there he was. As she moved, so did he. Still there, out the next window. Thank God he didn't cross the threshold. For now.

Run but you can't hide, said a whisper, as cruel in sound as the smirk was in sight. *Not anymore.*

"Begone," Eve hissed, remembering what her mother had told her to say whenever something frightened her, something that was beyond the melancholy pity of a ghost—a rule for anything darker. "I renounce thee..."

Almost as if summoned to her side, Maggie, her stalwart warrior, appeared through the wall and floated before her.

"What, what is it?" she asked. "Eve..." Maggie floated down to look into her eyes. "What happened?"

"I saw..."

Eve looked through Maggie's eyes to see if the figure was anywhere else to be seen.

"Something..." She could no longer see a form but also couldn't be sure he was gone. "Unfamiliar,"

Not anymore, the whisper sounded.

"Did you hear that?" Eve asked.

"What, a voice?" Maggie asked.

"A voice just said 'not anymore.'"

"I'm sorry, no." Maggie shook her head. "All I heard was you using a renunciation. I'm not sure I've ever heard one of those out of *your* lips. I was floating in the dining room as I tend to do overnight—it's where I can get the best view of the block—when I heard you come down."

"You didn't see anything out the windows?" Eve asked. The ghost shook her head. Eve described what she'd seen, how the man had followed her, and what he had said.

"Well *that's* disturbing," Maggie whispered.

"If you didn't hear it, then was it just in my head?"

Maggie lifted her hands in a questioning gesture. "You know better than anyone that not everyone hears ghosts, and never in the exact same way. Even your own colleagues who usually can hear our voices don't every time."

"It wasn't a ghost," Eve insisted. "He was absolutely corporeal. But that's impossible, because of how he appeared at my window then followed. I saw him from the waist up at the window, eye level to me."

"If not a ghost, then perhaps an astral projection, sent from someone who wishes to unsettle you."

Eve nodded absently. She wondered what change could have initiated this new paranormal threat. "Could this have come because of the Sanctuary?"

Maggie shook her head. "There isn't anything like that there."

"We were threatened, the precinct and I," Eve explained. "Nasty notes decrying our association with the dead as 'unholy.' This must be part of the ongoing threat."

Maggie made a face, trying to parse the logic. "Someone who shames your connection to the paranormal then uses paranormal means to threaten you at your own house?"

"Hypocrisy at its finest," Eve grumbled. She'd have taken another severed finger sent to her office any day over this presence at her window. "Are the other spirits resting?"

Maggie nodded.

"Then you should rest too, please. I can't have you blinking out on me again. I need you, Maggie, especially with new things happening. I don't know what to make of them. And I don't mind you seeing me scared. But I can't appear scared to my girls. To my precinct."

"You can always be vulnerable with them, they'd understand—"

Eve shook her head. "No. I don't like to. It isn't good for morale."

The grandfather clock, a lovely old melodic treasure Gran had gifted her upon moving in, chimed softly in the parlor. Gran had owned the clock since her first husband bought the Fifth Avenue townhouse and his father, the elder Mr. Northe, stepped in as a father figure for Gran and gifted them "useful things to pass down to your children." Its musicality and soft tone, Gran said, were good "for sensitive souls who don't sleep well through any given night." The chimes denoted three in the morning.

Eve groaned. "And my morale will be even worse with no rest, so let's get to it."

"I know you've your rules and your boundaries, but would you like it if I came to your room?" Maggie asked quietly.

"Yes, please. Thank you." Eve closed her watering eyes. The terror of the moment, of the look of that man, his confident cruelty… "Thank you for offering and not making me ask."

"It's why we're best friends," the ghost said proudly.

"It is, my dear," Eve said, and cupped the ghost's face fondly. Maggie put a ghostly hand to Eve's, and her skin froze on both sides. Eve didn't mind. For her, the cold of the dead was a small price to pay for their comforts. "Just don't tell Zofia I've let you in, otherwise she'll make excuses to stay up late and be my watchdog," Eve added.

Maggie chuckled. The two ascended the stair, soft footfalls and icy draft.

"Zofia winked right out to sleep after our reunion, poor thing," Maggie said. "She must have used so much energy staying visible."

"She didn't rest after you disappeared. I think she was afraid she'd blink and miss you," Eve replied.

Maggie smiled fondly, a glistening tear forming at the side of her transparent eye.

Ghosts manifested so much energy to stay visible that it wasn't always practical or possible to take form, certainly not at all times. They needed to fade out into a sleep-like state in order to stay present to the mortal world for long-term haunts.

The two women stopped talking lest their chatter wake or bring any other spirits to their side. Once Maggie had floated past the threshold of Eve's door, Eve shut it behind her and crawled into bed.

"I'll be right here," Maggie murmured, and even though Eve hadn't told her where, she floated right to the center of the window where the figure had appeared. Moonlight shone through the trees and through the spirit's outline onto the hand-embroidered quilt, an item that Eve used to comfort her, because even though her relationship with her mother had its strain, the quilt contained so much loving energy in every stitch that Eve could feel it like a hug every night, tucking in her aching body.

"Promise me you'll rest, though," Eve whispered.

"Promise. But I'll be right here." The ghost blew her a kiss before her luminosity faded into invisibility. Eve's trained eye, however, could make out the slight waver of the air and a sliver of light where the presence remained. Eve closed her eyes, comforted by the surety that no soul, if connected to their own purpose and tethered to the heartbeat of others, ever entirely disappeared.

Chapter Three

The next morning, the four mediums left for their office at the same time, Eve taking a striding lead, gnawing tension driving her onward.

She actively forced herself not to think about the figure at her window. It was good practice for psychics not to dwell on things they found frightening or distasteful, as it inevitably created a channel between the subject and the problem. Shoving the sight from her mind, she focused on the children who were asking her precinct for help.

Surely, with the recent poltergeists, there were clues in the open file cabinets—cases yawning open, begging to be set to rest.

When their department had been founded, one of their missions had been to examine stalled cases that had gone cold. The spirits, cold indeed, expressed a great interest in all that was unfinished.

The dead outnumbered the living, and life was full of unanswered pain. Eve tried not to think of the daunting enormity of her task were she to open herself fully to all of it. She couldn't. One thread at a time, with so many loose ends still dangling.

As the group turned the corner onto Mercer Street in the Fifteenth Ward, Cora gestured ahead at a man who crossed in front of their plain red brick building, dressed in a dark blue uniform just as another came into closer view. "They've increased a patrol on each corner."

Two beat officers wandered their street. They all bobbed their heads at one another in acknowledgment but said nothing. If they resented being put on this watch, neither young man seemed to show it. After the threats that had befallen Eve, Cora, Detective Horowitz, and his associate Fitton, arrangements had been made that there would be a guard watching out for the precinct.

Those threats had come from someone thinking Spiritualism akin to some kind of devil worship, never mind that Eve considered herself vaguely Episcopalian—following Gran's tradition but with personal beliefs of her own that encompassed all peaceful faiths. Working with the dead was often misunderstood. The threats, however, no one took lightly.

When the mediums got to the front door of their building, Eve was relieved to see that electricity had been restored after a blowout during one of her intense spiritual connections. Eve let her team in with the turn of a hefty key. Ascending a flight of stairs toward their office door, the four stopped in unison.

The gilt lettering on the frosted glass door of their precinct office had been erased. The text *had* proclaimed that this was the office of The Ghost Precinct, Evelyn H. Whitby, Supervisor. At present, there was no longer anything written there.

McDonnell, their oft-insufferable matron at an exterior desk, was nowhere to be seen. Their door was cracked just slightly.

"What on earth..." Fresh dread overtook Eve.

Antonia gasped as Cora drew her small pistol from a holster concealed in her vest. "Really, Cora, is that necessary?"

"Eve and I were drugged and held captive, lest you forget," Cora replied in a whisper. "If someone has come trying to remove all traces of us..."

Eve threw open the door.

Inside, wreathed in cigar smoke, leaning on their round séance table, was Governor Theodore Roosevelt.

Eve stood dumbfounded in the doorway. Cora quickly holstered her pistol as Antonia coughed. Jenny grabbed Antonia's hand, and Eve fumbled for words.

"Sir! Why, I... Hello, Governor! What brings you here, and... I'm sorry, but do you have any idea of what happened to our door?"

He gestured them to enter and close the door behind them. Eve reached out to the light switch to brighten the interior lights, which buzzed too loudly for her comfort, an irritation that had increased since her incidents. Perhaps with the erasure of their door, they were already being dismantled as a failure—"an abomination," as those threatening notes had claimed. Eve tried not to look crushed, but she felt it.

"I heard all about what happened," the governor said. "Nasty business."

Eve shot Cora a look, and she offered Roosevelt a questioning expression, as if what he was referring to was anyone's guess.

"All of you, gone stone-cold in a warehouse full of mourning weeds?" the man cried. "Why, it's utterly ridiculous! Like something out of a torrid

Gothic novel! I'd not have believed it had your grandmother and two *priests* not been involved. How on earth did you get into such a mess?"

How could he have found out about all that when their precinct had agreed not to make any outcry? Gran had gone missing. When Eve's team and Gran's exorcist friends converged to find her, everyone was knocked unconscious in a funereal supply warehouse by an airborne chemical. Strange tests were done on Gran, Eve, and Cora. No one was very hurt, but they were left with threatening notes to stop the "unholy association with the dead." Of course, the whole incident didn't look good for anyone in the department. Perhaps that was why Roosevelt was shutting them down.

"I'm sorry, sir," Eve said ruefully. "It should never have come to that."

"You're darn right it shouldn't have. You ought to have been given every respect, and yet cowards come and try to scare the daylights out of you? But I know you won't be scared, Whitby, nor you, Dupris, nor any of you, even the littlest of you, there." He winked at Jenny, who smiled at him with all her inherent charm. His words had Eve cocking her head to the side. Was he championing them rather than chastising?

"I despise cowards!" the governor declared, brandishing his cigar, which shook ash across the floor. "However, we are doing something unprecedented with you girls, and that's bound to attract detractors. If I act as though there's a redistribution of the department, hopefully whoever had been too busy in your business will think they had some effect they haven't. Do you follow me, Whitby?"

"I'm sorry, sir, I'm not sure I do."

"You still have a department, Whitby, but *for show* it will seem as though it has been closed down. Not to make them think they've won, but I have to keep you safe, and this buys you time to figure out who is responsible. I felt horrible after what happened."

"Oh, sir." Eve bobbed on her feet, resisting the urge to dart forward and embrace him. The sudden joy at being vindicated and supported made her feel like she could levitate. "Thank you. Thank you for giving us another chance."

"It isn't your fault you were targeted unjustly, Whitby. I know how much you girls want to help this city; I see it clear as day. I feel it. Would half my men have had half that drive when I was commissioner."

"We do want to help," Eve agreed. "With all our souls, spirits and all."

"How, if I may ask, sir, did you hear about what happened?" Cora asked.

"Why the detective, Lieutenant Horowitz, told me all about the ordeal and suggested a full protective detail. I called Ambassador Bishop to make sure no one was pulling my leg, as the whole thing with the funerary warehouse seemed outrageous. You noticed an extra patrol down the block?"

"Yes," Eve said quickly, feeling heat rise to her cheeks at the mention of the detective. "Yes, well—"

"While I'd like to say we can look out for ourselves," Cora interrupted, "we do appreciate the patrol."

"I certainly feel better," Antonia said, looking at Cora pointedly. "For all our sakes."

Roosevelt pushed his wire-rimmed glasses up his nose and slapped his hand upon the nearest wooden desk, making Jenny jump. "Well then, now that you know you're even *further* off the books but not erased from mine, I must be off. Do what you can to bring your assailants to light, girls. Evelyn Northe-Stewart is a treasure of this city, and I'll be damned if anyone thinks they can get the better of her or her family." He punctuated his declaration with a huff of smoke.

"We shall do our best, sir, most certainly," Eve promised, straightening her shoulders.

"I wish you could solve the case of who keeps disappearing my budget money in Albany, but sadly that's an all too living problem," he muttered. "Take care of yourselves, girls. Keep your chins up!"

"Yes, sir," the women chorused. Jenny saluted the governor, and he saluted back to her with a chortle, patting her on the head as he went to the door.

Once he'd gone and the door had closed behind him, Eve turned to her cohorts.

"Well," she said, letting out a long breath she seemed to have had kept for the entire encounter.

"It isn't like anyone would give us credit for anything if we *were* public," Cora stated. "It's best this way." She gestured toward Eve's desk near the front of the room, which held notebooks full of insight into a ghost-filled life. "You can clear the record with your eventual book about all this."

Eve nodded.

We're called by higher forces anyway, Jenny signed. *No matter what.*

Eve brushed a hand fondly down the young girl's loose braid.

"It is good to have a champion in the governor, and that's that," Antonia said, punctuating the moment. "Now let's champion these children."

No one argued.

Having steered clear of Roosevelt for safety's sake, Maggie and Zofia appeared through the walls hand in hand and hung back by the file cabinets, drawing Eve's eye.

Several file cabinets were still yawning open in the aftermath of their poltergeist movement. Eve went to peruse them more closely.

In each of the open file cabinets, one file was slightly ajar, slid upward as if caught in the act of being plucked from the stack.

Eve hesitated before pulling all of them and leafing through incomplete notes and entirely unsatisfactory material for solving a case. That must have been why they were relegated to these sad files, failures of a police department still trying to organize itself after Roosevelt's most strident efforts. But Eve thought, with a breath of hope that gave her strength and purpose, the spirits could help fill in all of the blanks, if given time. What did these files have in common? Why were they the ones targeted?

The lights surged and flickered. The mediums looked up warily.

"What do you see, Eve?" Cora asked. "We... We didn't take a look inside the cabinets after they opened; we wanted the scene to be undisturbed for you."

"Cora's being charitable," Antonia retorted. "If I'm being honest, I was scared."

Me too, Jenny signed.

Eve rifled through. Nothing of names or reports of complaints were the same, but they were all files regarding children. Missing children, dead ones, troubled ones. The kinds of lost, vulnerable souls that had become the Ghost Precinct's prime purview.

Before Eve could make further connections in the scraps of unresolved issues, there was a commotion on the exterior landing, two men arguing.

"There's nothing for anyone here," one of the patrolmen called. "This floor is closed."

"I'm here, on behalf of Evelyn Northe-Stewart, on important business!" the man cried. That name was enough to make Eve open her door no matter what. Even when absent, Gran dominated so much of her world.

"Yes?" Eve called hesitantly at the threshold. One of the patrol officers stepped aside, looking at the man warily.

A small, wiry man in an ill-fitting suit stood at their open door. He was...smoking. Not a cigarette or cigar; his clothes were smoking, as if he'd been singed. Eve squinted. Were his eyes *sparking*?

In his hands was a strange box: metal, about the length of his forearms, with cylinders, wires, and some sort of ticker tape inside.

"I found this outside," the man said flatly. Eve noticed his mousy brown hair, shorn a bit unevenly, seemed to be standing on end. It was as if he were, himself, a live wire. "I was asked to come by and examine your wiring. I'm an inspector." He stared at them. They stared back. "This..."

He lifted the box. "This is no electrical circuit. This is something else entirely, and it's interfering."

"Interfering…" Eve replied, confused.

The singed man pointed to his head and made a wobbling, woozy gesture. "May I set this down? It's heavy."

"Yes, I'm sorry, come in." Eve withdrew from the threshold, and he charged through it. "Please remind me, who are you exactly?" Eve pressed. "And are you in need of medical attention? We can call someone—"

"I'm a friend of your grandmother's, Miss Whitby," he insisted. It was disturbing that he knew her name and she had no idea of his. "Well, not necessarily friend," he clarified, tossing the strange box down on a desk, where it fell with a crashing, burst spring sort of sound. Jenny jumped at the clatter. "I don't have friends, really," he added. "I exist to pay penance for my sins. So perhaps I should refer to Evelyn Northe-Stewart as a cohort in purgatory, rather."

The mediums stared at him, blinking as they took in his words. He was perhaps their age, young, gaunt, but those eyes spoke of ages… He was terribly unsettling, but then again, Gran had collected some interesting acquaintances in her seventy years. If he was a colleague from Gran's former days in the field, then he was older than he appeared.

"Tell your grandmother that Mosley came round to see about the electric as she'd asked, thank you. This thing here"—he gestured to the smoking box—"let's be clear, it was already damaged when I got here, but I sent it irreversibly to its deathbed. But from what I can see, this may be more up your alley than mine." He tapped at his temple, then the center of his forehead, as if poking at a third eye. "It isn't monitoring the electric. I think it's been monitoring you." Then he walked away. As he crossed their second-floor landing, Eve heard him call out, "I'm out of your hair, Officer, sorry for any trouble!"

All was silent for a moment.

"Everything all right?" the patrol officer called from the landing, sounding just as stunned as Eve felt.

Eve went to the open door and smiled at the ruddy-faced young man who, after seeing her smile, seemed able to find the ordeal bemusing. "All is well, thank you, sir," she said. "Let me offer my apologies. This place gets a little strange sometimes."

"That was a far more interesting turn than just pacing a sidewalk, miss," he said with a small laugh and turned back to his beat. Eve closed their now-innocuous door.

"This is the strangest day," Cora murmured. "And I thought that yesterday."

Antonia was the first to walk over and begin inspecting the device, whatever it was.

Her colleagues crowded behind her. Jenny peeked around her side as if something might jump out of the box at her lower eye level.

The box had two spools, a lever, and some sort of device that turned a bar along the spool within. Everything appeared singed. Whatever explosion had engulfed the device—and seemingly, the mysterious Mr. Mosley—had occurred in one fell swoop.

Something about the device struck Eve and Cora, and they looked at one another, both reflexively putting a shaking fingertip to their temple. Cora coughed. Eve tasted the bitterness of poisonous air, memory accosting them.

Antonia glanced at both of them, intuiting the moment. "Does this have something to do with the abduction?" she asked, her generally breathy, pleasant voice a distressed whisper.

"I…" Cora trailed off, her expression blank.

"Think so?" Eve finished.

"How can we find out more?" Antonia pressed. "I want to find out who rendered my dearest, beloved friends unconscious to experiment upon." Her angled face, usually so graceful, and her manner and expression so poised, was suddenly ferocious, protective.

"Gran," Cora and Eve chorused.

Eve went to the telephone, asked to be connected to Gran's number, and waited. Once routed, Eve waited quite a few rattling rings before a familiar voice answered.

"Gran… It's Eve."

"Of course it is, dear," Gran said. "Who else would ever call me?"

"Well…" Eve laughed. "Any number of New York's elite?"

"But I don't give them my *number*, dear. The last thing any woman does who is known to be philanthropically generous is give out her telephone number. What's going on? You don't usually call from the office unless you need something."

Something about her answer struck Eve, a weariness in Gran's tone, as if a routine had worn out its welcome. Eve felt her stomach twist in the way it did when she feared she was letting someone down.

"I…" Eve listened to the hiss on the line.

"It's all right, dear, what do you need?"

There was a definitive shift. When Gran had been abducted, Eve had truly considered the woman's age for the first time, as if the idea that she wasn't immortal hadn't ever occurred to her. When one had an intimate relationship with the dead in full understanding of spirits living on, the finality of death was a formality, a change of logistics and corporeal law. But the idea that Gran might weaken in body as she never would in spirit was a slow, dawning reality.

"Are you…all right?" Eve asked. "I sense you're tired, and I never want to trouble you."

"What troubles you in turn troubles me, dear heart, but you are never the trouble."

"A man came to the office…. He was…on fire? Mr. Mosley."

"Ah, yes," Gran chuckled. "Mosley did an inspection, did he?"

"Yes? He found a box. Not electrical, though, some sort of monitor. He wanted you to know. There are spools. Like what you described on the device used during the abduction."

"Ah…" Gran trailed off, the hiss on the line seeming to roar in a contemplative silence.

The trauma of those strange moments had not fully been worked through. Certainly not solved. There had been no closure for any of them.

"Perhaps I should come see the thing," Gran stated. "Hold the line a moment, dear, let me see if Gareth minds my stepping out. I should ask his opinion every now and then."

"Of course. Give Grandpa my love."

The hiss again as Gran set aside the receiver, a roar of technology and nerves. Eve glanced at her colleagues.

"Everything all right?" Cora asked, gesturing to the phone.

Eve shrugged. "I think we're all still shaken up about what happened to us and we need to be aware of that. Like Roosevelt said, we need to take care."

Cora glanced at the box, the faintest wisp of smoke still wafting up from one corner, and back to Eve. "Indeed."

Eve had not properly put her fury to rest about the iniquity of what had happened to Gran, to all of her colleagues—the bitter helplessness of losing consciousness when loved ones were in clear danger. She'd leapt from that night and its mixture of open threats, jumping to the next tasks without healing, telling herself she was fine as though she were rushing to reset a broken bone and doing it incorrectly, at an aching angle.

She needed time to cry; to talk with Cora, who had been there with her; to parse out their instincts; to discern together the legitimate threats from what was posturing. She needed to sit with herself to see how much of what had happened was threatening to unsettle her foundations by exacerbating little fissures of fear, ready to crack her open if she wasn't careful. All while trying to shove aside the new threat of the man at her window so she might listen to the pleading of ghosts.

"You still there, Eve?" Gran asked loudly into the bell, startling Eve with the volume.

"Yes, Gran," Eve replied. "You should come see the device, and we'll hold a séance about it." The echo of the migraine that accosted her when opening to the spirit world thudded at the back of her skull, distant thunder preceding a storm. "I'd say bring Grandpa if he wouldn't be frightened."

Gran laughed as if the thought of her second husband attending a séance was absurd. She was a Sensitive with keen talents, so anyone who loved Gran had to love her, spirits and all, even if they didn't share her gift. Eve's grandparents' worlds were joined at art and hearts while Gran's spirit was saved up all for Eve.

"I'll see you soon, then, Gran?" Eve prompted.

"Yes, dear. I'll see you soon."

Whenever there was something new, unexpected, and strange, Eve couldn't imagine her world without Gran to make sense of it. Jenny trotted over to the tea tray and began preparing for company as Antonia readied water. Gran was everyone's favorite relative, whether actually related or no; she treated everyone like family, and it had a profound effect. The fact that she was en route appeared an immediate balm to everyone's frayed nerves.

They turned to straightening everything up, Eve setting the protruding files at the center of her séance table. There would be questions. They busied themselves with action.

"What's this?" Gran said, alerting them to her presence by tapping on the glass of the front door they'd left open after Mosley's departure. "No longer a precinct? Is this Roosevelt's idea of 'protecting' you, to just cover you up?"

The picture of elegance, she was dressed in a blue riding habit trimmed in silver ribbon accents, her silver hair swept immaculately under a smart felt hat sporting a sprig of modest feathers. Under one arm she carried a planter with a beautiful little seedling of a plant.

Eve shrugged. "Hello, Gran. Yes. I hope it's all for show; the threats had to result from someone who knew or found out about us. I don't know how it will play out. The governor didn't ask us to vacate the building. I assume you saw the extra patrol officer outside."

Gran nodded. "That's good. I'd have demanded more otherwise." She proffered the little plant. "Here, put this in your window. I just received a care package from my favorite green witch in England. A plant from Lord Black isn't just any plant—it's a force of nature."

"What is it?" Antonia asked, and Eve gestured she take it. Antonia had the greatest affinity for plants of any of them and the best knowledge of their powers.

"An ash."

"Ah," Antonia replied with a smile, lovingly taking the small ceramic pot and placing it in the best light on the sill of one of their lancet windows. "For healing and protection, good for smoothing out internal strife."

"Precisely," Gran said proudly. "Well said!"

"I've been studying the green traditions," Antonia added, drinking in Gran's pride, beaming. They all wanted to make Gran proud, but for Antonia it held more weight, in lieu of a family that couldn't accept her. She'd become their resident esoteric scholar on every type of augury, craft, and practice.

"Very fitting," Eve replied. "Thank you, Gran. You always know what's needed."

"Once it's large enough to be transplanted, you might put it out your window there to shade your little patch of green." Gran unpinned her hat, set it on a peg by the door, and removed her gloves. "So. Our séance concerns that monitor box and all those lost children, yes?"

Eve stared. She hadn't told Gran anything about the children.

"I can hear them too, dear," Gran admonished, reading Eve's expression.

"Well? Shall we?" She turned to Jenny, who had come forward with her tea, setting it carefully on the table before pulling out Gran's special seat at their séance table. "Thank you, my dear."

There was an element of hosting royalty whenever Gran came to the office.

Everyone took to their designated positions, preferring a certain seat in the circle. They often brought elements of their practice—paper and pencil, pendulum, sketchbook, or the occasional scrying glass—to the table. But none of Eve's colleagues had anything in their hands today. Their palms were upturned on the wooden table, ready to receive input by channeling only.

Whenever Gran attended, she was to Eve's right with her back to the door. While this wasn't a tactically advantageous position in any environment that might prove a threat, Gran insisted that she sit with her back to the door where the living came and went, to close herself off to the ways of the living world and open her spiritual door against the grain of present time.

Each of them had clairvoyant and clairaudient talents, and they varied methods of input. Eve, the one most prone to automatic writing, set her notepad before the candle. Cora, to her left, would help bring the séance to order.

Jenny usually sketched, but today she already had her eyes closed, as if all she wanted to do was be meditative. Antonia watched Cora patiently before taking Jenny's small, outstretched hand in her larger one.

The table's array was sparsely elegant: a plain burgundy tablecloth was adorned by a silver candlestick sporting a tallow candle, a painted box of matches at its base, and a palm-sized brass bell with a slender handle cast in the shape of a holly leaf. Eve remembered the detective noting how simple it all was. She'd replied that anything much more complicated indicated a performance, not a practitioner.

Cora picked up the matchbox, exquisitely painted, featuring a bright red heart with a plume of fire leaping up, the edges trimmed in golden paint—a religious icon gifted by a New Orleans relative as a reminder of traditions of generations. Cora did not follow exactly in the practices of her Creole family but honored them as the core animating force of her gifts. Once the wick was lit, Cora carefully passed the lit match to Eve, who then let the smoke unfurl once she'd shook it free of its flame, drawing out every moment as an elemental call to prayer.

Eve placed the charred nub of the match upon the base ridge of the candlestick. A few of the bits had accrued now, so it was time to deposit them as if she were sprinkling someone's ashes. The ash tree would do well for this purpose. Eve deemed that any organic item used in prayer or meditation should be returned to the earth in ritual continuity.

The call to séance was completed by Eve picking up the holly-trimmed bell, ringing it with one sure flick of her wrist, and holding it upright until the clear tone that reverberated in the room faded. Its echoes blended with the general milieu of city noise, an aural tapestry of constant movement—trolley car bells, horse hooves and carriage wheels clattering along cobbles, the occasional shout or laugh from passersby. Tucking her finger into the bell to silence it, she set it down on the tablecloth and pressed her palms together.

"Spirits," Eve began, speaking clearly to the room. "Those known and dear to us and those who newly hear us. We ask for your calm presence. For answers to our questions. Come, friendly folk from beyond the veil, make yourselves known." Eve opened her hands in supplication.

As she did, she heard a rush of wind, a gasp, an opening, a breath. The spirit world turning a key, opening a door.

The spirit world felt like it was right at their fingertips. As if it had never been so open to them. Murmurs swarmed around them, and they reveled in the sound. It was so much better than the silence they'd been coming up against recently. None of them were used to spiritual quiet.

Something was always talking. Absolute silence was terrifying. The rush was a sweet surrender to the power of eternal life.

"Tell us, spirits," Eve demanded, her voice strong and clear. "You opened our file cabinets, yes?"

"*Yessss...*" came a resounding whisper that rattled, sighed, and hissed.

"The files are all of children. Disturbances, either at home or at graves. Is that what you want us to see?"

"Yes..."

"Why?"

"Disrespect..." came the chorus. Not just one voice, but a unified group.

"Shake loose the ties that bind us," said a young voice, disembodied, sounding right over their heads. The drawers of the file cabinets, still opened as the spirits had left them, creaked on their hinges and tracks. Papers rustled within files.

"How do you want us to do that?" Eve asked.

In response, a sullen-faced girl of thirteen or so years appeared. The rest of the spirits, whispering voices urging her on, seemed to be designating her to speak for them all. Pain and frustration emanated from her bony, luminous form.

"We want you to stop the false sanctimony." The gaunt form in a simple dress floated between Eve and Gran.

"Ours?" Eve pressed, the spirit's proximity giving her gooseflesh.

"No." The girl shook her head. "His. You've seen his work. Really *see* it."

"Whose?"

"The undertaker," the spirit insisted. "Makes a display of us. We don't want to be a show."

A sea of voices rose around the room, and the girl vanished before they could get her name. Only the sounds of the others now held sway.

"Draw the curtain," another voice insisted. "Put our pieces together."

"Tell me what pieces to find and where," Eve implored.

"Start with the graves," another child murmured. "Start with the lion."

"The lion. The Lion of Gramercy? That undertaker?" Eve asked. "Mr. Dupont?" There was a rattling hiss. It wasn't even a vocalized yes; it was an affirmation voiced in sibilant disdain and anger. "Is he causing trouble for you? Like what happened with Ingrid Schwerin, her body laid out like a saint?" Another rattle, as if all of autumn's dried leaves were being kicked up by the dead. "Tell us more," Eve demanded.

Silence. That was all they could say on the matter. Eve scribbled notes. Cora shifted tack.

"Who is against us?" Cora asked. "The device placed outside this building. We need to be safe in order to help you. Who is against us?"

There was a murmuring, but no specific name could be made out.

"All who aren't with us are against us," came a ghostly hiss right at Eve's neck, a cold draft blowing into her ear and making her cringe and shudder from the temperature.

Asking spirits direct questions often got indirect answers. Being a medium in this capacity, trying to be investigative about channeling the dead, was a practice in ultimate patience and reading between lines for the truth.

"Can you tell us where to look to find answers to who attacked us?"

"We couldn't get in," one child said mournfully, a partial outline of a small body and a tattered cap. "Had to push so hard we opened all the cabinets. We've been pushing…"

"The device placed outside sought to neutralize you," Maggie said, breaking free from an amassing mist of spirits to make her form more visible. "That much seems clear. Someone has been trying unprecedented methods to block your talents."

"Make those in comfort uncomfortable," said a young voice, the body not fully manifest, just a hazy, lit outline over the table.

"All the world *shouldn't* be a stage," came the frustrated voice of a young woman, her form darting past the table as the candle guttered.

A sound reverberated through the room like the closing of a great door.

Chapter Four

There was a long silence after the séance ended. Clasping her hands together, Eve rose and bowed her head, thanked the spirits, and rang the bell again, closing the channel on their living side.

Eve collected the small nubs of the matches used to strike the séance candle and sprinkled their remains into the base of their new ash, offering thanks to their new little start of healing green life. Nothing of ceremony, large or small, she felt should ever be wasted. There was energy in everything, the chance for a benediction in the least of things.

"Dupont," Eve said, turning to her team. "We're going to have to find a way to get a warrant and search his viewing parlor—by the book or we'll lose our chance—and I'd rather not involve Greta or her sister."

"What did the spirits mean, making those 'in comfort uncomfortable'?" Antonia asked.

"I think that's about your monitoring box," Gran replied. "The experiments upon us were done by someone with means. That related case is the Prenze family."

"Is there any direct correlation between Prenze and Dupont?" Antonia asked.

I think so. I don't know how I know...but I feel it, Jenny signed. Eve and Gran, who both understood sign, nodded.

"Jenny feels a connection, and her instinct is rarely wrong," Eve stated to her team.

"When I corral the Prenze I met at the soiree for a chat in my parlor, you girls won't have any problem posing as my help?" Gran asked the mediums. "Each of you could play a critical role."

The four colleagues agreed to whatever Gran would ask of them.

"Prenze will come for tea, and we'll have to determine any role in this mess. Now, it's time to go home. I won't have you exhausting yourself."

It was true. As much as Eve wanted to press forward, to dive in deeper into a séance, to the point of a trance, pushing herself only made her ill and her colleagues more vulnerable.

"That isn't an option, Eve Whitby," Gran said with a gentle smile, her own psychic sense picking up on her direct thoughts. "I know that look of yours. Nothing can be solved all at once. Let's take what the spirits gave us and look deeper tomorrow. We've got inquiries to make."

Rising from the séance table, Eve went to a long wooden table by the front of the room that they used as a repository for evidence, where the curious box sat. Lifting a wooden milk crate from the floor below, she placed the monitor inside, brushed the soot off her hands from its edges, and stood by the door. "Whatever this is Mosley detached needs to go with us."

Gran made a face but didn't argue. Eve took the device with her as she carefully descended the stairs, maneuvering so her petticoat wouldn't catch on her boot—it needed mending, and she hadn't had time or interest. Hailing the largest carriage available at the corner, Gran had it brought round and ushered everyone to it. Eve hung back with the box.

"You be careful with that," Gran cautioned, gesturing to the box as the driver came around to take it, lashing it to the back ledge.

"It's…inert Gran," Eve countered, "unhooked from the electric that powered it. I doubt it can do anything to us in this state, not after Mosley was done with it." As Eve climbed up into the carriage and gathered her skirts close, Gran doing the same with help from the driver, she added in a murmur, "Please tell me he never did whatever he did to *people*. The box was blackened and smoking, even *he* was, wisps curling off him when he brought it in." Eve and Gran sat together on one bench. Cora and Antonia took the opposite. Jenny was all too happy to sit on Gran's lap for the journey back, eager for the chance to be close and indulge in their guardian angel's care.

"Your 'friend' Mr. Mosley mentioned doing his work as paying penance," Cora added, closing the carriage door behind her. "What does that mean? Was he ever a killer?"

"Mosley is an electrical inspector," Gran said carefully. "Hired by Ambassador Bishop. Suffice to say he's handy when needed. The Bishops and I are quite glad he's on our side."

Eve suppressed further questions, shuddering when she thought about Mosley's sparking eyes. It made her think of the shadowy man at her window, unnerving, unwelcome. She wanted to ask Gran about it, but she couldn't bring herself to speak of it, as if doing so would summon him. Hoping the visitation had been just a nightmarish projection from her own tired, worried mind, she kept silent. One terror at a time.

It wasn't long until the carriage turned onto Waverly, and Eve and her colleagues disembarked. Gran remained in the cab, which would take her up Fifth Avenue. Eve waited for the driver to unlash the crate holding the device, which he handed to her while her colleagues went up to unlock their door.

"Talk soon, love. Pace yourself," Gran instructed from the open carriage window, wagging a finger at Eve, who nodded.

Once everyone had settled in at Fort Denbury, Eve knocked on the large arched door at the side of her entrance hall. That door connected her residence to her parents' home. No immediate answer, so she rang the bell.

Her mother answered and gestured her in with a smile. Eve leaned in and kissed her on the cheek. "What brings you to our side, love?" Natalie asked, glancing around her, out of habit, to be sure no spirits had followed Eve across despite the meticulous warding of the threshold.

When Eve turned sixteen and the spirits were the most unruly they'd ever been, insisting that Eve work on their behalf, it had so troubled their family that Gran suggested Eve have her own space, insisting that Maggie would be there to help. Separate spaces had improved family relations immeasurably, and their living daughter was always welcome. The Ghost Precinct spirits knew Eve's parents had been plagued by supernatural traumas and the ghosts respected the boundaries her parents set. Maggie once mused it was good that spirits be subject to some limitations.

"Is Father here?"

"Yes, he's going over case studies in the library. Did you happen to hear his news?" Natalie asked, her green eyes alight with excitement.

"What? Did he get the position?" Eve whispered.

Her father had been trying to get a position at Bellevue Hospital for some time now, but despite his incredible accomplishments founding clinics in London and New York, the competitive leading hospital in the country hadn't had a general practitioner opening for years, certainly not one that paid well. Eve had stopped asking about it because she didn't want to bring him pain if he still had to say no. Her sense of pride and calling in her own work came from his example.

"Yes, he did!" her mother said, tears in her eyes, and Eve threw her arms around her.

"Oh, thank God, finally!"

This was bigger than the prestige of the institution; this was about survival. Her father being a British lord meant nothing beyond pomp and circumstance back in England and was of little use here. All of his holdings had been liquidated by villains, his estate overtaken and burned to the ground. New York valued money over titles. Their family had had very little when Eve was born, but thanks to Gran's help and the hard work of Eve's father, not to mention her mother's tutoring of American Sign Language, they'd gotten by. It was another reason Eve had taken work as soon as the opportunity presented itself; she knew she could help keep roofs over loved ones' heads and food on her own table.

"Would you like coffee or tea?" her mother asked, drawing back and moving toward a small rear kitchen designed for quick refreshments rather than full meals.

"Coffee, please, thank you! Father!" she called. "Congratulations!" Eve cried, running to the library and embracing him as he stood and strode out from behind his desk. "It's about time they took you on!"

He lifted her up in a huge hug, laughing. The relief was palpable, and the dark circles that she remembered so often beneath his eyes from late nights and constant house calls were gone. He looked years younger; his piercing blue eyes danced and his handsome face beamed.

"We should throw you a party for your new position!" Eve said. "Have you told Gran? She can plan it. We can invite all of the city's greatest talents—"

"No, no, none of that," her father said, his cheeks reddening.

Jonathon Whitby, Lord Denbury, was an earnest, modest man who was born wanting to help people. The fact that he had hardly any ego was for the best; considering that every person Eve had ever met exclaimed how good-looking he was, he'd have been a holy terror otherwise.

"I want no fuss," her father continued. "I'm just very glad to be with the premiere medical institution in this country, finally."

"As you've always deserved," Eve said proudly.

Her father placed his hand on a stack of medical journals.

"As you asked, I've been sorting these to give you the relevant articles." He shifted the stack toward Eve. "What I've been able to find so far in the sparse wilderness of early brain mapping theory. I'll continue sharing anything else I find."

"Perfect, thank you. That's exactly what I want to discuss with you." She leaned in and spoke more quietly. "Remember during Gran's abduction, the tests we thought were being performed on all of us? Remember Gran mentioned a device?"

"Of course." Her father shuddered.

"I'd like to ask you to take a look at something we think is related. Would you be so kind as to come to my parlor?"

Just then her mother brought in cups of coffee for them both. "What's in your parlor that can't be discussed here?" she asked, with a distinct edge to her tone.

"A device," Eve replied. "Found outside my office. It's a possible monitor."

Regarding any evidence or an item relating to a case or query, Eve wished to have it examined on her side of the fort, out of respect for the boundaries her mother tried so hard to erect. Her father was less strict about what he would and wouldn't entertain and promised her she could come to him anytime. Her parents refused to talk about their haunted past, to Eve's ongoing chagrin. Her mother had kept a diary in the early days of her parents' unconventional courtship. Every year Eve had asked to read it, and every year she was told "when you're older." She'd given up.

Still, despite her discomfort, her mother strode across the threshold to Eve's side with her husband, looking around warily as Eve held open the hefty wooden door. Her mother crossed into the entrance hall adorned in dark wood paneling, jewel-tone wallpapers, and burgundy upholsteries. While her mother didn't like seeing or interacting with ghosts, she hated it more when her father involved himself on his own. For as long as Eve could remember, her mother had been overprotective of her father to a point Eve found maddening, but Gran quietly explained that if she hadn't been so careful and so strident, her father's mind would have been irrevocably lost years ago, insisting that Natalie had been his only reliable tether to sanity.

Early in Eve's life, her mother had asked Eve to make a choice. It was either her parents or the ghosts. Gran had played diplomat, explaining to Natalie the error in her ways; Eve's mediumship was too powerful to turn off, and that was an unfair, impossible request.

But Eve could still feel that question hanging in the air, that eternal hope of taking sides, as if her mother were still trying to take her hand and draw her away from everything supernatural. The fierce look in her mother's green eyes seemed eternally to ask her to choose them for once. Just once? It was there even now, a glimmer of hope on her lovely face as Eve put her hand on her mother's shoulder. She couldn't. If she did shut out her gift, then it would be she who would be irrevocably lost, her sanity torn to bits by the spirits demanding to be noticed and heard.

"Where is the implement in question?" her father asked, stepping farther into the main hallway.

"In that box," Eve replied, gesturing across the threshold of the open parlor doors toward her séance table, where the box sat at the edge.

Glancing about, none of her colleagues were downstairs so she assumed the rest of the precinct mediums were taking personal, quiet time in their rooms upstairs.

Eve entered the dim parlor and turned the knob of the gas lamps, intricate glass sconces leaping to warm life, her parents following close behind. "This was planted outside our offices. When Gran disappeared, we found her with tabs and wires attached to her temples leading to a cabinet with cylinders like these. As for the ticker tape, I'm not sure what it's trying to record."

Her father came closer and peered at it.

"Don't touch it, Jonathon," her mother warned.

"Wasn't planning to," he replied. "This whole thing looks like it was burned in a fire."

"Well, I'm not sure if that was the device's fault or Mr. Mosley. Do you know him? He seemed, well, a bit…electrified. *Odd* man."

"Oh, Lord," her mother muttered under her breath.

"What, do you know him?" Eve asked.

"Your father did, once," her mother replied wearily, "but good riddance. I'll never forgive the Bishop family for putting your father in such danger and in such volatile company!"

It was a comment Eve had heard before. The fact that Eve deeply admired the Bishops and their psychic talents wasn't a fight she wanted to pick at the moment. Clara and Rupert Bishop had moved north to Tarrytown when Clara's ability to harness and interpret energy made the city too 'loud' for her Sensitivities. When Gran had gone missing, Clara found Gran via Eve's memories and tracing her present location. It was like nothing Eve had ever seen. But she couldn't convince her mother to trust Ambassador Bishop and his talented wife. She'd tried, and lost, before.

"I'll take this box to the department at Bellevue," her father said, with clear excitement. "Their mental studies department is unmatched. They'll know what to do—"

"No, you're not taking that anywhere," her mother countered. "You don't know what it does and if it is, in fact, inert—"

"But we need to know what it was *doing*, Natalie. If this relates, as it very well might, to early brain studies, perhaps even brain mapping, why, this is critical research, and it shouldn't be utilized by villains. We need to know far more than they do."

"I want you to destroy that thing," her mother declared. "I don't want it in either of your hands."

Her parents began to quibble about the fate of the box and the cylinders therein.

"All right, don't fight about it, you two!" Eve pleaded. "Please," she added, trying to maintain a gentle tone. "We have to make sure no one else is made a lab experiment or being somehow controlled."

An idea occurred to Eve that could serve multiple purposes and excuse another moment with Horowitz.

"I'll have this thing taken to whomever you recommend, Father, by someone else in the police department. The findings can be shared with all of us, but I'll have the device returned to an evidence room rather than my office— Nne of our hands on it anymore. I'll even set it outside overnight, on the balcony. All right? I'll have a pickup arranged tomorrow afternoon. Father, please think of who at Bellevue should examine it. And Mother, if you could please have some tea ready for whomever I bring by?"

"Thank you, I will," her mother said, breathing a little easier.

The idea of bringing Detective Horowitz by to take this box, serving as a helpful party, was the best way, in Eve's mind, to introduce him to her family. This way they would see him in a capacity that showcased their foremost relationship as a business one while hopefully noting him as likeable enough that they'd not pressure her to take on other suitors. She had every confidence in the detective's ability to be charming. Just thinking of him made her smile.

The solution Eve offered seemed to defuse the tension, and she gestured that they return to her parents' side of the fort.

"If you'd like to look over any of the articles I gathered, I can decipher some of the medical jargon for you," her father offered eagerly.

"I would love that, thank you, Father. Let's finish that coffee—and I want to hear *all* about Bellevue and their innovations. I daresay you can teach them a thing or two!"

Eve put her arms around each of her parents as she ushered them back to their side of the fort, the tension in her mother's shoulders easing the moment they crossed from Eve's darker threshold into the brighter lit, pastel décor. Night and day. If Eve kept her house like her mother's, she wouldn't be able to see any of her ghosts against all of the brightly lit rooms filled with whites, lavenders, and powdered blues. But the contrast did lift her mood.

Later that night, after sating herself on fascinating theories about brain activity, likening it to a sort of radio transmission, Eve returned to her wing and heard a soft voice reading a lilting Irish tale. Antonia was reading a bedtime story to Jenny upstairs and affecting a brilliant Irish accent.

Perhaps Jenny's loving parents, who had orphaned her when they died in a church boating accident, were helping the story along; Antonia was the best of them at channeling voices and vivid details. Eve listened at the base of the stairs, a smile on her face as Antonia spoke of fairy transformations.

After a long moment, Eve decided she would gather her thoughts by journaling. Taking a seat on a brocade divan, she wrote by the light of a stained-glass parlor lamp. Cora came into the room.

"Notes for your book about the precinct?" Cora asked.

One of the chief reasons Eve had wanted to create the precinct was to improve the relationship between the living and the dead, to make ghosts less frightening to the average person. She was writing a book detailing what the dead taught her about a good life. But she hadn't been inspired to write lately. Her channel had been so muddied.

"I doubt this will end up in the book." Eve gestured to the pages. "It's very personal. I'm trying to write down details about Gran's disappearance and everything that happened with us at that warehouse. I don't trust the vagaries of memories. I should've done it right away."

"To be fair," Cora replied gently, "you blacked out after a migraine was going to tear you apart. You couldn't have done it in the instant."

"We haven't even processed what happened to us in that warehouse, Cora, and what that box outside our office might be. Everything today brought up a wave of nerves and nausea."

Cora nodded. "You've let Detective Horowitz distract you. I can't say I blame you; if I had someone to distract me…"

Eve sighed irritably. "I know you're skeptical about him, but honestly, we've been following up on case leads of mutual interest. I don't know how else that reads to you."

"I came here to work with *you*, Eve. Visions told me to come and be with you. So just as you're protective of your purpose with this precinct, so am I. I'm not here to just be an assistant. I'm here to be a powerful Sensitive."

"And you *are*," Eve said, reaching out to clasp Cora's hand. "You amaze me. Not to mention the force of your psychometry. Don't you know by now I could do nothing without you and your strength?"

There was something indiscernible in Cora's dark eyes, and Eve wished she understood how to be a better friend and colleague to her.

"I think I've put too much on you," Cora stated. "I need to be more my own person, not to live solely for this precinct, here in your house. You're a very strong personality, Eve, and I think I need to find my own way a bit."

Eve gulped. "Do you…wish to resign?"

"Heavens, no. I want to just give you and myself more room rather than resenting you for not being my everything. I don't mean to say that in a way that makes you uncomfortable."

"You've never made me uncomfortable, Cora. You are, I'm ashamed to admit, wiser than me. You're my equal, and I consider this department yours as much as mine, do you know that?"

"You've never said as much, as you've insisted you be the one standing in the way of any criticism. But I appreciate hearing your confidence in my leadership."

"It's getting late," Eve said, rising and moving to embrace Cora, who held on tightly for a moment before slowly letting go.

"And I promised my parents I would leave this outside," Eve said, gesturing to the milk crate with the device inside. "It's like my mother thinks things will get possessed or something."

"Well, maybe for her things did."

"I've given up trying to figure it out, but I suppose one can't be too careful. Good night, my friend."

Eve ascended the stairs, Cora a few steps behind her, the two of them taking opposite directions at the top landing. Moving to a set of small French glass doors, Eve turned a latch and opened one of the doors, peering at the cylinders again before setting the crate down against the exterior railing.

Her gaze darted around in a fearful sweep, afraid she'd see the cruel jaw and the shadowed face of that eerie man again. But nothing.

Crossing to her room, she noticed a note on the small writing desk against the window that looked out onto that balcony beyond, the paper catching a glow in the moonlight. She didn't remember setting anything out, but when she got closer, her blood chilled again.

"Margaret Hathorn," she murmured to the sky.

A cold chill answered at her back. "Evelyn Whitby," the ghost replied. Whenever Eve called Maggie by her full name it was a summoning, and the resulting chill was a comfort.

"Look at this." Eve gestured to the paper. "I'd nearly forgotten about it in all the tumult. When you went missing, I went into a trance. This is what I wrote, trying to find a trace of you."

She showed Maggie a portion of what she'd taken down in a fit of automatic writing when the ghost had first disappeared.

Whispers and cold, whispers and cold.

All there is. Drawn in, something was wrong, I was found, now am lost.

Someone is very wrong. The children know. Don't let anything in, not the monstrous hum.

"This last line is what struck me most, then and still."
Don't play God lest you play the Devil instead.

"My God, Eve. You captured my thoughts in the darkness, what I thought and felt when I was blinded in the Prenze mansion. There was something about that man that felt like he was playing God with me, with others, in that death photography too. I wish I could untangle it, but it's all a mess. I'm so sorry—"

"No, dear, you're sifting through trauma, as we all are. You were taken, just as I was, as Gran was—violence against us. It's a mess, it hurts, and it's terrifying."

"Thank you for understanding." The spirit stared at the paper. "Having this validates that I existed, even in darkness. I know you don't know this yet, but the hardest thing about being a ghost is proving you exist. It's demoralizing."

"I empathize, my friend. I will always seek to keep you tethered here for as long as you wish. But…just as Cora seems to be needing to define herself beyond me, beyond this demanding life, if you"— Eve blinked back tears—"do need to go, I don't want to stand in the way of your peace." The idea of losing any of them was painful, but the idea that she could demand too much of those she loved and in doing so possibly hurt them was also humbling. Her heart felt wide open and raw.

"Heavens, no, not yet. We've more divine mysteries to discover together, dear one, before I go on to my undiscovered country!"

"But you'll tell me?" Eve pleaded. "You won't stay on just for me—"

"When this soul is tired, you'll see that it's tired. I'm not tired. But *you*, in that mortal body, should rest."

Eve tried, but she kept glancing out the window for fear of moving shadows.

Chapter Five

The next morning, Eve dressed in the finest of her uniforms, remade in black in the manner of a police matron's dress and left early to be down at the Mulberry Street offices, hoping to catch Horowitz checking in for his day before he was off to further untangle the uncooperative Dr. Font case. As luck would have it, they came around different corners—and the moment the detective caught sight of Eve, he smiled.

"Well, hello, Eve, what has you at headquarters first thing in the morning?" he asked, forgoing ascending the front steps and instead crossing to her at the intersection, hands in the pockets of his modest but perfectly tailored black frock coat. "I dare not be presumptuous to think it would be me."

She chuckled and inclined her head. "It is, in fact, you, Detective."

He took a step closer, leaning in with a bemused expression. He didn't seem to be one for wearing hats, and the autumn wind took his brown curls at a gamesome bounce.

"You really refuse to call me Jacob, don't you?" he asked, maintaining a partial smile, an inviting, curious expression, and furrowing his brow as if by looking at her more closely he might figure her out.

"I don't refuse…Jacob." A surge of panic rose in Eve and she set her jaw to keep her tongue from betraying her in a tumult of unrefined words. "I just… It…" Blushing, she found she could focus on only the neat knot of his white linen cravat, entirely at a loss.

"It reminds us we're all *business* at the heart of it," he said carefully, relieving her from further embarrassment. "Have it your way, *Whitby.*"

Eve pursed her lips. She didn't like the formality; it just...felt safer. "Well, I am here to ask you if you'd be willing to meet my parents. Today. Now, in fact."

"Why the rush? Do they have some stodgy British aristocrat lined up for you, and you need me to stand in the way?"

Eve couldn't help but bark a loud, inelegant laugh, the sound so jarring a few passersby jumped and turned to her in disdain, which only made the detective join in.

"God, I hope not another one," Eve exclaimed. "I was threatened by it once; that's when I asked you to court me in the first place, and they haven't pressed me since. But they do wish to thank you for helping Gran and me. They were very sorry they didn't meet you the night of the abduction."

"It wouldn't have been the best of circumstances to have been presented. And ruse of courtship or no, I think we'd all like to be on good terms."

"Absolutely," Eve agreed. "That's why I need you to come by and collect a device taken from our offices and take it to Bellevue. Please."

"The hospital?"

"Yes, Father has just been accepted as a practitioner there. He's been after a position for ages; we're all very excited for him."

"That's wonderful. How can I help?"

"Can I tell you about it as we walk?"

"Lead on, Whitby." Offering another charming smile, he gestured toward the busy street ahead, filled with carts and passersby and they wove between the workday tumult at a fair clip.

"I'm not keeping you from something, am I?" Eve asked, edging too close around a whitewashing cart. A trace of lime smeared her forearm and she brushed her glove along the black wool to flake it away.

"Oh, just a dressing-down by a few incompetent higher-ups who want to keep me 'in my place' regarding my persistence on the Font case, so no, you've come to my rescue."

"While I'm so sorry to hear that, I'm happy to come to your rescue," Eve said, feeling a surge of distinct pleasure at the idea of being a knight in shining armor for such a good man.

They turned and continued north along Broadway's gentle angle— Manhattan's great artery, walking along the busy valley whose walls were cast-iron storefronts and elaborate brick and brownstone edifices, every year climbing stories higher.

"So, what am I taking and where?" the detective asked.

"Father will be arranging for a contact in the mental pavilion to take a look at a strange box that was taken off our offices. We think it was created after our abduction, relating to whatever tests were being done on Gran, Cora, and I at the warehouse. It may have something to do with brain study—an informal and tangential theory, but it's all we have to work with. I think it was placed at our offices to interfere with our gifts."

"So you'd like me to liaise with a Bellevue clinician or with your father?"

"Both. You see… I know I've mentioned my parents don't like anything to do with the paranormal, which makes my life an incessant parade of frustration."

"Indeed."

"My father truly wants to help, but my mother is overprotective."

"Don't I know the feeling," the detective offered with a little laugh.

A gaggle of women and their lace parasols were clogging the sidewalk at a textile shop window and so Eve stepped into the street.

"Mother doesn't want Father to even *touch* the device in question," she continued, lifting her skirts to dodge a construction site's splay of steel beams. The detective matched her every step, looking for open spaces to move freely as she did. "And Mother doesn't want me handling it either. Not that it's a present danger." Eve hoped the thing was just as inert as it seemed thanks to Mosley's explosion. "I wouldn't drag you in the middle if I thought it was. But as a way to stop them quibbling and as a way to introduce you, if you show up and take it as the chivalrous hero, you'll be seen as the charming and helpful man I know you to be."

"I'm charming, am I?" he asked, looking at her, his tone not sly. He seemed genuinely touched.

"Yes, Jacob, you're charming," Eve replied with a nervous chuckle, looking away toward a copse of trees ahead to hide the color that had become a common accent of late on her usually pallid cheeks. "I've no doubt you can unseat any of their plans for some boorish Brit to come claim a wayward American cousin."

The detective joined her in a laugh, less nervous this time, more simply an expression of enjoying themselves despite themselves, which they'd done from the first with uncanny ease. They turned off Broadway onto Washington Place in comfortable silence, pleased by the brisk activity.

They walked along the side of Washington Square Park and continued west along a row of townhouses on Waverly until Eve stopped before a brick and sandstone façade that neatly matched the one beside. "Welcome to Fort Denbury," Eve said. The white lace curtains on the right were open to the day, and window boxes showcased autumnal blossoms. The one on the left featured thick crimson brocade curtains, closed at the bay window, with a black wreath on the door in honor of the dead.

Horowitz glanced at Eve's dress, always in mourning on account of her precinct, and motioned toward the lighter side. "This way to your parents."

"How could you tell?" she asked with a chuckle, ascending the stoop. She lifted the ornate brass door knocker, let it go, and waited a moment. "The device out on a ledge, we'll take care of that once we're settled."

Her mother opened the door, smiling primly, her father standing behind. Mrs. Whitby gestured them into the entrance hall.

"This is Detective Horowitz." Eve began the introduction as she closed the door behind her. "And this is Mr. and Mrs. Whitby."

"Milord, milady." Horowitz bowed his head.

Eve's father batted a hand in the air. "Oh, none of that aristocratic nonsense please, Detective." Eve's father extended a hand for a shake, and her mother did the same. Horowitz shook each firmly.

"Please come make yourselves comfortable," Natalie said, leading the way toward the open pocket parlor doors. She was dressed in a pretty lavender lace day dress, her auburn hair pinned in an immaculate knot atop her head. "I've both tea and coffee, whichever you prefer." Eve was pleased her mother was good on her word and so amenable.

"Coffee would be grand, Mrs. Whitby, thank you."

"I haven't had a single cup yet," Eve said to her mother dramatically, as if she were withering away. "I'll take *two*, thank you."

"My usual, love," her father said, reaching out to squeeze his wife on the shoulder. Eve knew that meant his favorite Earl Grey tea, to which he was addicted. The house always had the pleasant scent of bergamot on the air. Her father wore a fine charcoal suit and the piercing quality of his ice-blue eyes was complemented by his pleasant expression, framed by shoulder-length jet-black hair.

"If you'll excuse me, I'll go and get the item in question," Eve offered, going to the door that joined the houses, ascending the stairs toward the top floor and the balcony where the box remained as Eve had left it.

She wasn't sure what pleasantries she missed but as she returned, she heard her mother speaking softly.

"I can't thank you enough for coming to take this thing away, Detective, whatever it is. "I'm sure Eve has told you that I—"

"Have a hard time with the profession," Eve finished gently as she re-entered the parlor with the milk crate. A bit of ash from the side of the device floated to the decorative carpet, sooty flakes dotting the petals of pale blue flowers. Eve set the box on the console table behind the divan, wiping her hands free of dust and grime on a cloth napkin by the tea tray.

"That's all right, I'm a disappointment to my parents, who wanted me to follow after my father in academia," Horowitz said with a smile. "I don't expect anyone else to like what I do; I simply content myself knowing what we do helps. It makes a difference and eases suffering."

"That's...that's nice to hear, and to think of it that way," her mother said, and for the first time, Eve thought she might be trying to bridge what had been a heretofore impossible gulf.

"Am I to understand you know my darling Rachel?" Natalie asked, pouring cups of coffee from a silver urn into small, simple china mugs. "My dearest friend from school?"

"She's a second cousin," Horowitz replied eagerly. "We'd lost track of her after her guardian passed, then after her move to Chicago. You can imagine my delight when your daughter mentioned your family connection, bringing her back to us."

"When she visits, sometimes she'll stay with us; you're welcome to join us at any time," her mother said and added, after a moment, "Shabbos included."

"Rachel always let me light the candles," Eve said, "writing out the prayers so I could read them. It was my favorite part of the week."

Horowitz appeared quite touched. "I'd love to, thank you, that's very kind."

"In fact," Natalie said brightly, "I recently heard from Rachel that she plans to come to town soon, so I'm glad we've all met."

Eve looked pointedly at her father, who nodded with a smile.

She'd certainly never experienced any aversion to Jewish people coming from any member of her family, but she was glad she didn't have to press the issue. She'd passionately defend her right to consider anyone she chose, but thankfully there seemed to be no immediate discomfort from her family—and that was something she wanted Horowitz to see, a crucial matter of trust in an oft intolerant world.

If anything, Eve thought, it wouldn't be Horowitz's beliefs they'd worry about but that Eve would be too steeped in her profession, too surrounded by death and danger, unable to separate work from the rest of life's pursuits.

But at least his willingness to help was a clear mark in his favor. That was, presuming, of course, the ruse went forward as a truth. Eve didn't let further thoughts run away from her but instead let the taste of coffee on her tongue ground her in the present moment.

"I've written out my colleague's name," Jonathon Whitby said, handing Horowitz a paper. "I don't know him well, but we've had a few enthusiastic conversations about innovation and I know he's a good man. He won't likely be able to give you any certainty, but you'll have an opinion, at least."

Horowitz took the paper and examined it. "Thank you, this is very useful. In my line of work, knowing open-minded doctors on the cutting edge of new thought keeps us one step ahead of criminals—at least, that's the hope." The detective smiled, and her father nodded. "Why medicine, Mr. Whitby, if I may ask? It's impressive to me that considering your background you chose this work. Medicine, investigation"—he turned to Eve—"mediumship, it all seems a calling. What called to you?"

Her father's bright blue eyes lit. "Why medicine?" was his favorite question, and Eve couldn't have prepared Horowitz better if she'd tried. His gentle inclusion of her work as a calling too was sheer brilliance of navigation.

"I saw disease take terrible tolls across England," Jonathon replied. "There were several epidemics near me as a child that indiscriminately put friends, family members, and too many good people in early graves. I simply wanted to ease suffering, and that single purpose seemed to be the only thing that made life bearable until I met Natalie."

Her mother beamed proudly.

"And now, being here in New York," he added, "a city that has more hospitals than anywhere else in this country, I couldn't imagine being anywhere else."

"And you, Mrs. Whitby," Horowitz set down his coffee cup and turned to Natalie. "Eve tells me you tutor in American Sign. That's a wonderful service."

"Having suffered from Selective Mutism as a child," she replied, still smiling, "I didn't want my recovery, my ability to speak later in life thanks to Jonathon's help, to distance me from the ostracism I saw and that I still see in those who can't communicate. There is nothing so lonely as that."

Eve's heart felt so full. "My noble parents and my noble friend!" she exclaimed, reaching out a hand and, without thinking, brushing her fingertips across Horowitz's sleeve. He noticed and did not draw away, simply looked at her, intent on her words. "The detective tells me that following in family footsteps as an academic didn't give him the feeling of direct action and satisfaction of bringing justice. I find that beautiful, and I feel the same—utilizing whatever we can, all of us, to ease suffering, in any form."

"But your parents worry for you, I'm sure," her mother said softly. "There is a…danger in what you do. It isn't always an easy time for us."

"No different, I'm sure, than treating the ill," Horowitz countered in the same quiet tone, glancing at Lord Denbury, who nodded solemnly.

"Everything in life has risks," her father added, his accent making the sentiment sound sweeter; a certain charming elegance offsetting harsh reality.

"I won't keep you any longer, Mr. and Mrs. Whitby. Thank you for the coffee; it was delicious and will fortify me through the day." The detective rose, and Eve followed suit. "I'll go to your Bellevue contact straightaway, and any findings, I'll share. I'd also like to take it to another name recommended to me at Mount Sinai, the Jewish hospital uptown. Any inquiries will remain utterly discreet. We don't want this item to attract interest we can't contain."

"The more minds the better," her father stated, "especially at such a prestigious institution as Mount Sinai. Incredible work is being done there."

"And I should get to the office," Eve added. "There are children with unfinished business, and they deserve being paid attention to."

Eve kept the word spirits out of it, but there was no hiding the truth.

"Thank you again for your help," Eve's mother said to Horowitz. "I'm very glad an implement used against my girls is being taken away from here, and I hope, whatever it is, it's understood so it can't be done again. The lost lambs who were directed by the heavens to Eve's doorstep to form their precinct, they're all my girls now, especially little Jenny, as I've taught her to sign. I do worry, it's in my nature, but I suppose the only thing for worry is action, so thank you, Detective. Call anytime."

Eve was struck that her mother said all of that out loud to a stranger. It was to Horowitz's credit that his kind nature made her usually stoic mother so open.

The detective took the box in hand, and they descended the stoop.

Looking back as they turned onto the street, she saw her mother watching from the bay window of the parlor. Catching her eye, she waved. There was a smile on her face.

As they walked together in the direction of Eve's offices, the detective holding the box carefully, she asked if he wanted her to hail a hansom or hack, or take the trolley, and he shook his head. "I like walking with you," he stated. Eve blushed.

"You were amazing with my parents. Genius. You've gained me precious time free from pressures and men forced on me. I daresay you made the exact impression I'd hoped. Thanks to you, my mother was more at ease than I've perhaps ever seen her." She didn't know how else to express her thanks to Horowitz without sounding overly sentimental, and she didn't want to put undue pressure on him, so she didn't belabor anything, but her heart was grateful.

"Pleasant enough, helpful, not too overzealous?" he asked with a smile.

"Precisely."

"Good."

They were quiet for a long moment, and Eve realized they had just stopped to stare at one another, not knowing what to say but not wanting to look away. The sharp whinny of a nearby horse, as if it were laughing at their awkwardness, broke the moment, and the detective began walking again at his usual brisk pace. Eve kept up.

"Why is there a separate Jewish hospital?" Eve asked. "Are there such different practices of care that require a separate building?"

"In some cases of orthodoxy, yes, there are preferences, and of course access to a synagogue in the building, but you really don't know the answer about why?" He eyed her. Eve stared at him, feeling sheepish and at a loss. "Because," he continued carefully, his words edged, "we haven't been allowed to train in the general medical schools. So we had to start our own."

"I'm sorry."

"The city desperately needs the extra care, personnel, and facilities at this point, and Mount Sinai takes on loads of patients who can't afford to pay—without, might I add, additional discrimination. It's now famous and lauded with prestige, but it was founded because of exclusion. That's something that shouldn't be forgotten."

"I certainly won't."

"Mount Sinai was also the first hospital in the city to allow women on its house staff," he added for good measure.

"May it continue to lead by example," Eve said. "By openness."

They walked in silence and watched the city, an endless source of movement and distraction; the constant, striving pace of it across every class and culture, everyone a distinct character, every varied building housing myriad stories and Eve was curious about them all.

"Speaking of openness," the detective continued carefully, "you know, I'm not used to…folks from your background…being open, willing. Lighting Shabbos candles with Rachel… I'm…trying to trust it. I know that must sound terrible to say—"

"No, I was just now oblivious to a point of prejudice in institutional history, so I understand being wary. Even someone's best intentions can be unhelpful, or ill informed. I'm just sorry that openness has been unusual," Eve replied. "Rachel and my mother were 'unfortunates' deemed second-class citizens because of their disabilities. My mother clung to Rachel and she to her, ports in a storm. Just because my mother regained her voice from Selective Mutism doesn't mean she turned her back on her best friend. When they met at the Connecticut Asylum, it seems they fell in like long-lost sisters, and that only grew through time. Found family comes from many traditions."

"Indeed."

"Not to mention Rachel helped make sense of Mother's world when it all turned topsy-turvy and violent."

"That's right." Horowitz rubbed his chin. "Didn't Rachel help solve the case of the villains that targeted your father?"

"Yes. Rachel is as gifted a medium as I am, though I think she may deem it more a curse than I do. I don't know much about those days. I've been getting 'we'll tell you all about that when you're older' all my life. I'm not holding my breath."

"I'm sure they think they're protecting you by not discussing it."

Eve rolled her eyes. "I'm sure. Thankfully Gran fills in enough that I'm prepared for a paranormal life, and I understand the forces that were in play then no longer are. If I didn't have Gran..." Eve shuddered. "I don't know how Rachel managed it, all on her own."

"I don't either, really; she never talked about it—well—wrote notes about it, that's how she communicated. I should have learned to sign. I had no idea she was like you," he said with a bit of wonder. "How much of the world do those of us who don't see like you do miss?"

"Even if you're never certain, you've already begun to open yourself. Think of the bridge you began to cross with Maggie. It's such a process."

They turned toward Mercer. "Oh!" Eve stopped suddenly, putting a hand to her face. "I didn't mean to lead you in an opposite direction from where you needed to be."

"It seemed a suitor's thing to do, walking you back," he said, offering a smile that made Eve shift on her feet so she didn't appear weak-kneed.

He turned closer to her, the box between them. Eve had a mind to toss the damn thing aside and embrace him.

"Do you think they, your parents, want us to continue to court, then?" he asked quietly. "Have we crossed beyond merely tolerating the idea?"

"I... Well..." Eve felt a nervous sweat break out at the hollow of her throat, a blush working its way up her neck. Was he asking? Did he want to? Truly?

"I suppose they'll tell you their mind," he said, rescuing her from panicked fumbling. "It seems they've no trouble at that."

Eve chuckled. "That's the truth. I hope I can somehow endear myself the same to your family, should that be helpful, should you be pressured, I mean..." Eve looked away, grasping her own hand so tightly she thought she might leave herself a bruise, trying to force herself back toward cool composure.

"We'll keep finding ways to carve out our own lives as we see fit and play our field together accordingly," he said assuredly. Goodness, what a balm he was.

"I shouldn't keep you any further; carrying that thing must be a bother. I hope the contacts are fruitful and lead to something fascinating, at least."

Horowitz nodded, bowed his head, and turned toward the direction of an uptown trolley line. "Until soon," he called.

She stared after him. He didn't look back, but he seemed to walk with a happy surety, a confidence, perhaps a breath of possibility on his lips…

"You lost, Miss Whitby?" called the patrol officer with a little laugh from across the street. Eve shook her head, coming to.

"It's a dangerous profession, that of a daydreamer, Officer. Thank you for retrieving me from God knows where," she replied with a smile, waiting for a delivery cart to cross the street and darting behind, carefully avoiding a pile of manure on the cobblestones.

She knew exactly where her mind had gone, rapt with the possibility of an endless courtship of unspoken delight, forever hanging on the edge of "what if," professional colleagues orbiting until one day they'd be forced to collide in a mess of delicious tension and—

The front door almost hit her in the face. McDonnell was striding out, a cigarette in her hand, arguing with the other patrol officer about whose turn it was to buy lunch. Evidently she'd won, as the young man grumbled down the steps, fumbling in his pockets for change. The burly woman leaned on the railing of the outside landing, a newspaper under her arm.

"Milady," she said with a forced smile. "I'm back. They've put me downstairs for reception now rather than up on your landing."

Eve in particular had a prickly relationship with the police matron that had only just begun to warm. She smiled and tried to seem happy to see her.

"Good to see you, ma'am," Eve said, bobbing her head.

"And you, my girl. I'm glad they didn't end up transferring me, just rearranging the desks."

"You mean you like being here after all?" Eve asked in disbelief.

"Well someone's got to be looking out for you *hapless* things," the woman declared. She flipped open the paper tucked under her arm and began reading.

Eve sighed heavily. She supposed that was meant as a fondness, but the woman was as kind as a piece of sandpaper.

Ascending the stairs and striding to open her office, Eve noticed Maggie and Zofia floating outside. Eve glanced at the clock on the wall.

The meeting with the remaining Prenze brother wouldn't be until the late afternoon; there was work to be done before.

"You can always go in," Eve said with a smile.

"I'm not about to start doing work in there before you do," Maggie said, then clucked her tongue, a soft, echoing sound in the air. "We may not be on the clock in the ways the living are, but if we're not careful, we'll be taken advantage of! We should have a ghost union in *addition* to ghost suffrage," she said, entirely seriously.

"Have you seen Vera?" Eve asked.

"We still can't find her," Maggie replied ruefully.

"Keep looking. I don't want her to suffer as you did," Eve said fearfully. "She's quite old, and while I've told her repeatedly she's welcome to rest, she's been insistent to stay. She was very worried about Ingrid Schwerin and the goings-on at Gramercy Park and Irving Place."

"I'll haunt Vera's haunts," Maggie suggested and saluted Eve before wafting out the side windows and disappearing into the bright day.

Inside, Jenny was dusting all of the surfaces and staring above at two floating specters. Her parents had come to visit and were singing to her softly as she worked.

Antonia, not wishing to disturb the touching family picture, came to Eve at the door and spoke in an undertone. "Cora wanted me to tell you she's gone to gather psychometric evidence at some of the graves listed on the files. She'll meet us at Gran's at the appointed time."

"Very good, thank you."

"What's the order of business before we go to Fifth Avenue?" Antonia asked as Eve entered and closed the door behind her.

"We continue with the children," Eve said, gesturing to the files at the center of their table. "As many as we can try to get through. One by one."

As Eve approached the séance table, Jenny waved to her parents and watched them float away before bringing her sketchbook and sitting down. The three mediums went through their séance rituals, and Eve called for the name atop the stack of notes.

"We summon upon the spirit of Giacomo Fiarini," Eve said clearly. "Did you call for us to see your case?" Eve placed her hands on either side of the case file filled with yellowed, midcentury paper.

Soon there was a child floating before them, round-cheeked and dark-haired. Ten, maybe eleven years old, in a fine little suit that was likely a funerary garment.

"What can you tell us about your life, and how can we help you in death?" Eve asked clearly. The little boy bobbed back and forth as if trying to decide on an answer.

"It's my sister. I'm here on her behalf. Just like I went to the police on her behalf because something was wrong with her grave."

"Go on, please, Giacomo," Eve said gently.

"All I know is she was always an argument in the family. I mean it wasn't her fault she was born. I didn't care why; she was my sister and I loved her. She died of the fever. Mum wanted her laid out, but the rest of the family didn't want her laid out, didn't want to see her, said she'd cause too much trouble, just like she had in life. So Mum gathered everything she had and arranged for her to be laid out with the casket man at his place."

"At a...viewing parlor?" Eve prompted.

Dupont's parlor. She needed proof of foul play or something criminal to be able to get a warrant for the place.

"Yes. I was there as she was laid out. But after *I* died, now I'm kept out," the little boy said. "We're all kept out; a door we can't go through."

"You died young as well?" Antonia asked gently.

The boy nodded. "Everyone was always fighting. Of the blows that came my way, one sent me against a fireplace, cracked my skull, that was that. Frankly, being a spirit's much better than it was in life. So many of us suffer in life, you know."

"I know," Eve said, her heart aching for this child and all others who suffered abuses with so few champions for their battles.

"So, see, I just want my sister with me, so she can have a better afterlife here too. I thought at first when I went to the police about a disturbed grave that's why her spirit went missing, why I can't find her. Maybe something to do with the grave. They didn't do a thing about it."

"The police?"

"Nothing. They didn't care. And a month later I was dead. But now, I wonder if something from that parlor hasn't even let her become a spirit. Something wasn't right about that place—"

McDonnell knocked on the door with a sharp rap, calling for Eve. Eve sighed. She should have let the matron know not to interrupt them.

"I'm sorry, Giacomo." Eve reached out a hand to the air.

"Something's always more important," the spirit said sadly and disappeared.

"No, please, please don't think that, dear boy," Eve called, to no avail.

There was a whooshing sound like a gust of wind. Spiritual disturbance. The files rustled on the table. The candle guttered. A torrent of whispers, different spirits trying to get through to the mediums, but one desperate voice rose above them all.

"Mama!" came a scream from the spirit world. The voice sounded familiar to Eve's ear.

A resounding boom like a clap of thunder and spirit channel was slammed shut.

The three mediums jumped at the sound of another loud rap on the office door.

"Miss Whitby, it's urgent!" McDonnell insisted from outside.

Eve went to the door and opened it just slightly, enough to see a distressed woman in a threadbare coat pacing outside, a woman she recognized. Susan Keller. Greta Schwerin's sister, Ingrid's aunt. There again, Dupont wrapped up in all of it.

"Miss," McDonnell explained, "this woman *refused* to wait, she said it was—"

"An emergency," Susan exclaimed.

Eve opened the door wide. "Thank you, McDonnell, we're acquainted. Hello, Susan. Come in. What is it? What's wrong?"

Eve closed the door behind them as Antonia and Jenny darted closer. Each of them had questioned her, had tried to help, and she looked at each of the precinct girls pleadingly.

"It's Greta," Susan said in a hoarse whisper. "She's gone."

Antonia gasped. Eve took a step forward.

"When?" Eve asked.

"Three days ago."

"Why didn't you come to me immediately?" Eve tried to keep her tone level; chastising would do no good, but the delay would make everyone's job searching for her that much harder. "Have you alerted any other authority?"

Susan wrung her hands. "I lost your card. I'm sorry, it's terrible of me, I wanted this all behind me—when I went into the local precinct nearest me, they didn't seem interested. When I asked them if they could contact you, they acted like you didn't exist. When I arrived here, the door—"

"Of course, I'm so sorry," Eve said, running a nervous hand over her mouth. Damn the critics and all the threats against them. The people who needed the precinct couldn't *find* it.

"There have been some changes for our protection," Antonia clarified, keeping her tone warm, bidding Susan sit in an empty chair while Jenny fetched her tea.

Each member of the precinct had found the whole family's situation heartbreaking and, in the end, Ingrid was dead of tuberculosis. It had been difficult for anyone to find peace, especially the way the body had been dealt with.

"Are we *all* in danger?" Susan asked fearfully, her eyes falling worriedly on Jenny, latching on to the girl Ingrid's age, murmuring thanks for the tea and cupping it with shaking hands. Fresh tears pooled in the woman's tired, red eyes.

"I hope not," Eve said. But these days she could promise nothing. In a world where women weren't believed or trusted, she would not engage in false assurances, only in vigilance. "Tell me what happened before she disappeared."

"Greta had been going on about Ingrid, of course," Susan said, her words coming in bursts, her German accent strong. "Wondering why she'd been lied to about the body, the absurd arrangement. If she'd once loved Dupont when she worked there, well, she began obsessing about him again—and I wonder if she didn't try to seek him out. If her husband Heinrich was…" She gestured to her head. "Didn't you say someone had hurt him when you found him in the asylum? Made it so he couldn't speak?" Eve nodded grimly, and Susan's next question was a terrified whisper. "What if that happens to my sister?"

It hit Eve like a blow. The cry, during their séance, of "Mama" from a voice she recognized. Ingrid. She'd been trying to alert them.

"I don't know where to look," Susan continued, sinking wearily back into her chair. "I've coursed Gramercy Park so many times people must think I'm mad. I've asked everyone I've seen if they know a Dupont, and all they do is point to an empty house across the park and say 'they were odd' or 'I haven't seen them for a week.' The building they were pointing to looks entirely empty. So, no use." She looked between them, eyes wide and desperate. "Maybe you, then, with your gifts, maybe you'll know and find something, care enough to do something…"

"We'll go and see, and look into all of it," Eve promised. "We've much unfinished business with Dupont. You go back home and rest. You look like you haven't slept in days. We'll come to you with anything."

Eve turned to Antonia. "We've only got a few hours before Gran needs us. We must go to Gramercy now, take a look around the house and the viewing parlor. I wish Cora were here; her gifts could help us track—"

"Would you like me to go find her?" little Zofia asked, hovering in the corner. The young ghost had been quite invested in Ingrid and was staring at Susan with empathy and sorrow.

Eve nodded, gesturing her thanks. The spirit vanished through the wall. Turning back to the troubled woman, Eve placed a hand on her shoulder and made a pledge she had no idea if she could keep. "We'll recover your sister."

Chapter Six

With the Prenze appointment looming, time was of the essence, so Eve hired a cab waiting at the corner. In a few jostling minutes, the three were turning toward the small enclave that was Gramercy Park. A gated park with townhouses facing the rectangular green, Gramercy was a small patch that the progress roaring toward the twentieth century seemed to forget, a slice of old wealth with keys to a spot of green at the center. Eve alighted at the north corner, helping Jenny out as Antonia was first down.

"First the house, then the parlor?" Eve asked. The girls nodded.

The landing light of the Dupont townhouse was dark, and the front curtain of the door was missing, revealing a vacant hall beyond.

Spirits floated about all aspects of the park, sometimes diving in and out of buildings, but all of them steered clear of the plain white stone façade before them. Just as before when they'd paid the undertaker's wife, Mrs. Dupont, a visit asking after Greta and Ingrid, the spirits seemed to avoid, or were perhaps kept from, this particular address.

Their spirit operative Vera had gotten into this address and caused a stir, but perhaps because of that incident, she hadn't been able to get back in—and now that she had vanished, Eve couldn't ask her latest opinion. Maybe it was this empty house that had somehow banished her to the darkness as the Prenze mansion had done to Maggie.

Eve ascended the stoop just as she heard a voice call her name from the street.

She turned to see Cora running up to her, Zofia floating behind.

"She was already on her way," Zofia said proudly.

"The first grave I visited today," Cora explained, breathless, "psychometry revealed an image of this place. There's something here we missed, or something terrible that's hidden."

"Greta Schwerin has disappeared," Eve stated. Cora's eyes widened. Eve grabbed her cohort's gloved hand in a supportive squeeze. As Cora's psychometry sharpened, so did her need to wear gloves more often than not. "I'm glad you're here."

"My God," Cora murmured, peering at the house. "Roads keep leading back to Dupont."

Cora rang the bell. Antonia and Jenny took to the perimeter of the park for a read on the attendant spirits, Jenny writing impressions in a notebook and gesturing to spirits hovering above the gated park, to whom Antonia would then speak, provided no other passersby were near enough to deem her a problem.

No one came to the door, and everything within remained dark, but Eve tried the bell a few more times. A lock clicked nearby, and hinges squealed.

"You won't get anyone," a voice declared in a distinct Irish brogue. A maid poked her white-bonneted head out from the front door next door. Little red ringlets of hair were visible from the edges of her lace bonnet. Her freckled face looked tired.

"Hello," Eve said brightly. "I'm looking for the Duponts?"

"Ring all you like, no one is home," she insisted. "And won't be back. The missus went out with her help, and no one said a word. Suspicious if you ask me, but then again, what family around this park doesn't have secrets?"

"Is that so?" Eve asked, trying to be gamesome and nonchalant. She'd learned from her work thus far that if a person was pressed about a haunting, it often magnified their already prevalent discomfort.

"Don't mind me," the woman said hurriedly, looking down. "All I know is you won't find 'em, so don't waste your time ringing that bell. I think it calls the ghosts."

"What ghosts?" Eve asked gently, moving to the edge of the stoop and sitting on it, nearly within reaching distance of the maid. "I believe you. I work with ghosts; it's why I'm here."

That seemed to unnerve the woman, and she shrank back, almost hiding behind the partially open door, not daring to step out fully.

"Ghosts like the park, but they don't like it there," the maid called. "So, just...tell them all to go away. Just because I see them doesn't mean I want to," she said, an aching misery in her words. She looked around, fearful of being overheard.

"I understand," Eve offered. "Truly I do."

"When you get overwhelmed, demand they let you be and give you peace," Cora offered, stepping toward the skittish woman. "They're not here to trouble you."

"Some trouble has gone on around here, it's true, but it's not yours to hold," Eve added. "And I'm hoping we can broker peace."

"That…that would be nice," the maid replied.

"Do you know any place the Duponts usually travel?" Eve asked. "Did they ever mention a vacation house or perhaps the wife's family?"

"Irvington, I think. I heard mention of that, once. The gentleman made a crack once about the headless horseman. It just…" she shuddered. "Wasn't funny. Stuck in my mind."

"That's very helpful, thank you," Eve said eagerly. "Anyplace else?"

"No, just talk of gettin' out of the city," the maid replied. "But then, folks who can always do." Eve registered the sadness in this woman's soul like the note of a dirge.

"If there's anything you can think of," Eve continued gently, "*anything*, no matter how trivial, about the Duponts or anything to do with their business of the viewing parlor, please come by."

Eve plucked out her thin metal card case and handed a card across the railings. The maid was hesitant but finally opened the door wide enough to come around and snatch the card.

"My title there," Eve explained, "you won't find that written on the door, they've changed it, but I'm still there. And I always want to help. What's your name?"

"Brenda," she replied. She turned toward the park, and her eyes followed a floating spirit that paused, hovering in the tallest tree. "This city. It's so full of the dead. A spectral city, 'tis."

Eve and Cora looked at one another. Cora posited a gentle question.

"Was one of the ghosts you ever saw here an old woman, tall and pleasant? A floral shawl around her shoulders?" Cora asked, looking for information about Vera's last sighting.

Brenda thought a moment. "Maybe. I think so. Yes, I remember because she looked kind. Her shawl was pretty; I could make out the roses on it, even through her mist."

"When was this? That spirit is very special to us," Eve said.

"Maybe a few days go, but she seemed sad, and then I didn't see her again." Brenda looked uncomfortable, glancing at the green then back at Eve. "Do set some spirits rest, if you can, so that we can rest… Good day to ye." She disappeared behind the door.

Eve stood looking at the park; its strolling ghosts had all paused to look at them.

"Well, then." Eve turned to Cora.

"Poor thing," Cora said. "Since the spirits were blocked out of Dupont's house, I bet they haunted hers by proxy. Something must have attacked Vera here, same as Maggie. I wish we knew why."

As Eve and Cora descended the stoop to street level, Antonia and Jenny completed their stroll around the park perimeter and joined them at the corner. The quartet walked together up Irving Place.

"What did the spirits tell you?" Eve asked Antonia.

"They were eager to gossip," Antonia replied with a little laugh. "Mrs. Dupont was gone in a swift minute; movers had their things out within a day. They said they only saw her and her two help."

"So no Dupont, then. Any sense of the mood?"

"Grim. Resigned."

"She wasn't a warm lady, but I pity her, especially if her husband was as unfaithful as all of Greta's letters seemed to indicate."

As the group paused before the viewing parlor, the sign—declaring Dupont and Montmartre, Undertakers, Funeral Arrangements, Viewing Parlor—was still there, but like the house, everything else looked abandoned.

"Wait, where did Jenny go?" Antonia asked. Their smallest charge was nowhere to be seen.

They started as the front door opened and Jenny stood on the threshold.

"What… How did you?" Eve whispered loudly. Jenny gestured to the gate around the side of the building.

I climbed up and opened a back window, she signed nonchalantly, waving them in.

Eve couldn't help but grin as the girls ascended and shut the door behind them, throwing a latch lest anyone from the outside come ask what they were doing. They didn't have a warrant, the cover of uniforms, or any technically open case. They were, in all honesty, trespassing. But if anything deserved an inspection, it was this viewing parlor. Eve cupped Jenny's face in her hand before signing *my brave, clever girl*.

The first floor was empty. When they'd first made an inquiry, there had been furniture, seats, and a dais. The dais remained, but the curtains were down, chairs and cabinetry gone.

Antonia made for the stairs leading up. "Be careful, let's all go," Eve called. Antonia turned from the partial landing between the floors. "It's empty. I can feel that it's empty. You see what you can glean here while I see upstairs. We've not much time—let Cora do her magic."

"Yes, I'd better get to it," Cora said with a deep breath.

"You say what you see," Eve instructed, "and I'll write it down." Eve turned to Jenny. "You've your notebook?" The girl patted her pinafore and nodded. "Then please write down anything you sense. I know you can't see what Cora sees, but—"

I feel it, Jenny signed, gesturing around her, adding, *This place holds a lot.*

Cora took off her gloves with simple ceremony, murmuring a prayer in French honoring her connection to *Les Mystères*, the higher, intercessor beings Uncle Louis had taught her to value from his Voudon beliefs. She incorporated several practices and traditions, the finishing touch of crossing herself evidence of the syncretism. Turning to Eve, she nodded.

Beginning her psychometric read in the main space, Cora placed her hand against the wall. As she closed her eyes, a shudder went down her spine and her breathing became sharp. The physical part of the process always seemed to hurt, and Eve's own head took on a sympathetic pain. All psychic gifts took various tolls.

"I see bodies," Cora began. "Laid out on the dais, as one would expect. Audiences. Speeches. Eulogies. Tears. Flowers." Cora rattled off words, and Eve ticked them down in her notebook. Once the images had run their course, Cora shifted areas. Moving into the entrance hall, she did the same against that wall, moving close to the base of the upstairs stairwell, her face turned upward as if she were listening for something from the next floor.

"Dupont going up and down the stairs," Cora reported. She furrowed her brow. "Constantly. Ritualistically."

"I see a body dressed as a saint. Yes. Dear little Ingrid was here. Heinrich bending over her. A fight between him and Dupont." Cora wobbled on her feet and sank to her knees in the hall.

Jenny had been right about the building feeling a lot.

"Pace yourself, Cora," Eve said gently. "This is more than you usually gather."

"I'm fine," Cora barked as Eve placed a hand on her shoulder. Eve withdrew. "Ah! Greta!" Cora's head sank low. "She's crying and yelling. Now she's fallen into his arms. He's comforting her. Kissing her forehead. Murmuring sweetly to her."

Cora shifted and slid her hand. "Damn," she muttered, opening her eyes. "It will give me nothing more here."

"Could she...have gone willingly with Dupont?" Eve asked.

"Greta was in love with him, if the letters she wrote her sister were to be believed," Antonia said from halfway up the stairs, peering at an inset on the wall at the partial landing. "There is reason to believe Ingrid was their child together. He had said once he'd run away with her...."

"He could have done so now," Eve countered. "What, then, about the wife?"

"Separate arrangements as many philanderers do?" Antonia posited. "Getting everyone out of town when there are too many inquiries? First hobbling Heinrich from telling the truth, then clearing Greta out?"

"All to keep an affair out of the public eye?" Eve wondered. "Why move everything here too? What all was suspect here?"

"Come." Cora began ascending the stairs. "There's more."

The women went upstairs to a carpeted room with wide, bare windows bearing a glimpse of Fourteenth Street and the roof of a shorter building next door. Cora was drawn to a tall metal cabinet against the rear wall with its doors open. Slowly she touched an interior shelf and hissed. "Cylinders inside. Music. No. Not the old wax phonograph cylinders. Modified."

"Like the machines used against us in the warehouse?" Eve asked.

Cora removed her hand. She opened her eyes. "From what Gran described, likely so. They do resemble what was in the box taken off our office."

"Then it was Dupont who did it to us, the experimentation."

"Perhaps," Cora said. "I saw another man putting a cylinder onto the shelf. It was dark, and he was in a black hat, low over his eyes. Nice frock coat, dressed well."

"Montmartre, the unseen partner in this parlor?" Antonia supplied.

Jenny tugged on Antonia's skirt, gesturing outside. Eve turned as Antonia did, and the mediums started again at the sight.

Ghosts. A whole host. Outside, looking in, a transparent, sullen group. Most were young, children to young adults, their clothes fine enough to suggest merchant, middle class, their families well-off enough to hire the new concept of a funeral parlor to express their grief. The cluster of them together made a mass of luminous forms, and the details were hard to pick out.

"Still?" Antonia commented. "Even empty? What are they staring at, and why can't they get in?"

"What haunts the haunted?" Eve asked. "Tell us," she begged the spirits.

A spirit with wispy, long hair dressed in a floor-length robe pointed to the corner of the room, toward the floor. Antonia followed the spectral finger's aim.

Gliding to the corner of the room, Antonia bent her tall body and examined the area in question. Even with her lanky form, she had perfected a precision grace, a fluidity of movement and a lilting quality about her that followed into her careful speech and a constant awareness of the world around her. Part of it had been forged in the struggle to live and be seen as the woman she was, but it had made her the most graceful of them by far.

Gently pushing back the lace cuffs of her crisp white shirtwaist, she peered down between the carpet and the baseboard. Scraping a pointed fingernail between the edges, she plucked out a long brown strand of something.

Rocking back and standing up, Antonia brought the thing closer, pinned between thumb and finger. It was a thin, braided lock of hair, like one would press beneath glass to make a memento mori token of hair jewelry.

A little girl at the fore of the spirit cluster mouthed something, staring hard at Jenny, floating as close as she could to the window without wafting through.

Jenny gestured that she come in, but the girl shook her head. She kept mouthing words, but Eve couldn't make them out. Finally, Jenny took a sharp intake of breath. She turned to Eve and signed.

That isn't all he took, Jenny signed. *She's saying hair isn't all he took.*

"Oh God, that's right…" Cora turned to point at a wide, squat oak cabinet with its doors open. "Heinrich Schwerin's mind, when I touched him in the asylum, he showed me that cabinet. It…" She shuddered. "Held canisters. Containers. Jars. Each with something inside. A finger. A tooth. Locks of hair, all braided neatly. Nails. Fingernails, toenails. An eye. A small heart, floating in a solution. Hair *wasn't* all he took."

Jenny whipped a handkerchief from her dress sleeve, choking bile into it. Antonia grabbed her and held her against her hip.

"Why can't you come in, spirits?" Antonia begged softly.

The girl put her hands up as if to indicate a wall the dead could not pass through.

Antonia held up the lock of hair and spoke to the child. "Will you tell us where you'd like us to take this?" The ghost nodded. "For now, I'll place it carefully here." She tucked it into a pocket of her skirt and patted it. "Safe and respected. Just as all of us should be. We'll call a séance so you can tell us where it should rest."

The little girl nodded eagerly, looking curiously at Jenny, who had regained her composure. The girls smiled at one another.

Eve withdrew her pocket watch and clucked her tongue, snapping it closed. "I'm sorry to cut this short, but for now, friends and spirits, that's all we can examine. If we don't make our way uptown now, we won't have time to change and be in our places when our *next* man of the hour arrives. Come, darlings, we've parts to play."

A thought occurred to her, and she grasped Cora by the shoulder. "You've done too much—I fear we've overtaxed you already," Eve said ruefully.

Cora straightened her shoulders. "We need every scrap of information across all of our messy loose ends," she said. "Our safety depends on anything Gran can glean from Prenze, and none of it can be gained by normal channels. Besides, the more I practice my gift, the stronger I am. This is steeling me," she declared. And that was that.

Chapter Seven

In the downstairs kitchen of the Northe-Stewart townhouse on Fifth Avenue, just northeast of the lower corner of Central Park, the girls were readying themselves for reconnaissance. The man Gran had charmed at his own soiree had agreed to discuss philanthropic possibilities, and the whole precinct would be on hand to see what could be gathered surreptitiously.

Eve, Antonia, and Cora put on maid's attire while Jenny was given a bright new smock to go over her calico dress; she was to portray a visiting niece and sit unobtrusively in a corner.

"Everyone ready?" Gran asked, gesturing them close. "Now, darlings," she began, rallying her troops, "we don't know how this is going to go. I'll be intuiting, reading signals, taking opportunities. So please just—"

"Follow your lead," Eve finished with a smile. "Always, Gran."

Gran led them to a small rear preparatory kitchen reserved for basic refreshments. "Your station, dear," Gran said to Antonia, and she quickly set about making herself comfortable and aware of anything she might be asked to prepare, moving with grace and flair, setting the finest of Gran's tea trays. Eve knew well that kitchens were Antonia's favorite places, the only safe haven she'd been loath to leave when she left those who rejected her.

"Cora, you'll be stationed closest in the hall, first on hand to help with his things. Eve, further back. We can't risk him identifying you, since you were at his gala."

Eve shifted her lace bonnet to shade her face.

"Be advised," Gran continued sternly, "I've stationed a reinforcement upstairs. She doesn't want to be bothered; she's got a headache, poor thing. And for her that could turn into an epileptic event, so she needs to use every last bit of her energy probing Prenze's life force. Nothing more."

"Mrs. Bishop?" Eve asked with hope and excitement.

"Who else indeed?" Gran replied with a smile. "Clara told me her social graces always fail her first if she's about to have a seizure, so we'll leave her be. For the moment she's ensconced comfortably upstairs, her powers attuned to everything below."

Eve empathized. Her work often caused her migraines too. "There is always a cost to these powers", Clara had told her the day she'd requested her help in finding Gran. Glancing around at her colleagues, Eve could feel such magic around her. Such careful, delicate brilliance.

They jumped at the sound of the bell.

"Ease and insight, darlings," Gran declared, rallying her troops. Cora clasped her hands, receiving the words like a prayer, and went to open the door with a pleasant greeting, ushering the man into the entrance hall.

"Good evening, Mr. Prenze," she said softly, beaming a smile. "May I take your coat and things?" She reached out and took his greatcoat, walking stick, hat, and scarf. Eve stood at attention, similarly smiling, from the opposite end of the hall.

Eve watched as Cora took a careful moment to balance all of his things—in doing so, her ungloved palm grazed his forearm, and she let his hand press upon hers as she took his hat. Bobbing her head, she stepped aside to place the things in the wardrobe by the door and on the rack beside.

A subtle shudder shook Cora's strong body, and it took everything in Eve not to rush to her side to support her. Cora was overtaxing herself with so much psychometry without a respite, but Eve knew better than to tell her she shouldn't do it. Cora and she were forever trading who could push their own limits to the most unwise length.

Their charge was now hesitating in the hallway, and Eve needed to pick up the next cue.

Mr. Prenze—tall, thin, and sallow—faced Eve at the end of the hall. Dressed in a fine dark brown suit that augmented the dark red of his hair, he wore a cream waistcoat and matching neckwear, a glimmering jewel tacked in the folds of the voluminous off-white silk. He was the picture of elegant wealth, not nearly as ostentatious as his house, but to Eve's eye he appeared bewildered. Her first instinct was to feel sorry for a lost, tired soul who was hardly the life of the party Eve had glimpsed at the ball in his opulent mansion. But then she remembered he might be the man who had tried to send Maggie away forever, and her heart hardened.

Eve stepped forward and bowed. "Mrs. Northe-Stewart will see you now, sir, just this way into the parlor." Eve spoke with forced cheer and gestured ahead, trying to betray none of what she was thinking.

"Thank you," he replied with a small smile and turned toward the elaborately carved wooden pocket parlor doors opened wide enough for entry.

As agreed, Maggie had been floating atop the stair, invisible to him from the beginning, slowly floating her way down as he disappeared behind the pocket doors. "I think he's ill."

"Is that the man who hurt you? Who sent you into the outer darkness?" Eve whispered.

"I...I don't know. He looks like him, yes, but...something's off..." The ghost met Eve's whisper. "Something's not right...."

"Hello, Mr. Prenze, thank you for coming!" Gran said from inside the parlor.

"Delighted, madame, thank you for the invitation."

Cora took her leave from the hall, nodding to Eve. Cora would take a downstairs service set of stairs and re-enter above from a passage that connected to two panels on either side of the parlor. From there she could watch intently from behind a service screen without making him aware he was a subject of study.

Jenny, sketching, would take down any words or images psychically projected from Prenze or anything the spirits might say about him. The spirits, in a clear directive, had been instructed by Gran to hang back on the outermost periphery of the room.

If Prenze was indeed the one who had blinded Maggie into an inert state and had any part in the threats made against Eve's department, he obviously wouldn't want to see supernatural involvement in his midst.

Eve's next duty was upon her. She adjusted the lace cap even farther forward to shade her face, as she would be getting very close to him. Prenze wouldn't recognize her from the ball at his mansion; they hadn't spoken. And no one noticed the help. Such inequity was a curse, but in this case, it was of use.

She lifted the vase of flowers she was to bring into the parlor as they settled in.

"You wanted these in here, ma'am?" Eve had to bite her tongue, having nearly slipped and said "Gran."

"Yes, dear, do set them by the window, if you would. I think little Jennifer would like to sketch them. She is such a talent."

Gran signed to Jenny to show her sketchbook. She lifted up the bound volume of sketch pages. Eve set down the vase as directed, taking time to arrange the boughs artfully. With her back to Prenze, she winked at Jenny, who returned a small smirk.

"When one cannot speak," Gran said to Prenze with severity, "one must communicate somehow. Jennifer does with pencil what an eloquent speaker would do at a podium."

"Indeed, poor thing, what a tragedy."

"Tragedy is in the eye of the beholder," Gran cautioned. "And God makes no mistakes."

"Of course," Prenze said deferentially. "I meant no offense. You...know how to..."

"To speak in sign? Yes. I love learning languages, and decades ago, when it was first being codified, I thought learning a *physical* language would be a wonderful skill. Then God granted me my stepdaughter, Natalie, who suffered from Selective Mutism, and our world was made brighter for our ability to communicate. That it can now extend to more family members is yet another reason why one should never shy away from a challenge—and one should never stop trying to build bridges."

"That's...wonderful," Prenze said, leaning in, clasping his hands as if wanting to truly connect with Gran. "Family is...such a gift."

"It is," Gran agreed. During the pause that followed, Eve could feel Prenze wanted to say more but didn't. He shifted back in his seat again, as if closing a door. She left before her lingering presence became suspect. She returned a few moments later with a few pieces of mail with key names visible, the makers and movers of New York, passing them along to Gran, who set them aside, but the names were noted as they crossed the tea table where Gran and Prenze sat. A reminder not to take Gran or her associates lightly.

Eve exited again and hurried around through a narrow corridor to her next position. There were two small service doors on either side of the parlor, each blocked by elaborate carved wooden screens inlaid with rich rococo details and mother-of-pearl accents. Eve took to the back one and stood watching through the cut patterns in the wood while Antonia and Cora stood behind the one at the front of the room to serve and clear. All would read him.

The position of the tea table had been arranged so that Prenze's face would be tilted within at least profile view of the hidden girls, Gran's back to them. Jenny, who sat across the room near the bay window, could give them looks or cues when Prenze wasn't looking.

"Now. To business!" Gran stated warmly. "I know your time is valuable. A dear friend of yours, Mrs. Sweeney, is helping me host a ball, the proceeds of which will be donated to the American Society for the Prevention of Cruelty to Animals. The admirable Mr. Henry Bergh himself will be in attendance. I've been one of his most ardent supporters since my youth. Some of my earliest activism involved his first laws in '66. I would love for you to sponsor the event. I am sure the…loss of your brother has dealt a blow to your company, and I can assure you charitable ventures are as good as gold in press and confidence as any effort in cost."

"Agreed."

"The Astors have taken to the libraries; let us help the animals," Gran declared with a bright smile that seemed to be contagious as Prenze tried to mirror it.

"Give me a moment to think on it," he said amiably.

He looked around, his smile fading, as if he still considered his surroundings and wondered what to make of them. Did he sense all of the supernatural stops Gran had pulled out for this, the many gifted people watching him? Eve couldn't tell whether he appeared nervous and culpable or simply tired. As Maggie had said, perhaps ill. Worried. Preoccupied. Guilty?

His gaze flicked periodically to Jenny, preoccupied in her sketchbook. Eve knew that while the little one was very good at pretending to look unobtrusive and uninterested, her sharp mind was probing her surroundings and what the spirits had to say about present company, the results of which she would decode for them from her sketchbook afterward.

While not having fully committed yet to Gran's suggestion, Prenze started in on niceties and details about the families they knew in common, little things, sharing others' good news, testing waters. Eve wasn't one for small talk, but she understood it was necessary in taking a certain temperature.

He soon forgot Jenny was even there, which Gran had counted on. Eve knew from her mother's Selective Mutism in her youth that once someone thought a person couldn't speak, a host of other inappropriate assumptions followed. They might assume she couldn't hear or was slow; a litany of injustices. Women had great practice at this unfortunate art and Jenny was a quick study at making underestimation work to her advantage.

Gran had posited a question about a Prenze relative's European season when he turned to stare out the window at a passerby. Allowing the interruption to sit, Gran simply sipped her cup of tea rather than pressing. In silences and strains, there were distinct clues. Sensitives let them go on, reading between lines and words, intuiting the inner workings of the mind they were studying.

To Eve's mind, the moment Gran said "Europe," there was a distinct tension. Prenze's jaw had clenched reflexively, and he had turned to the window. Likely his brother's death or the presumption of his death. The length of the silence on Prenze's part seemed to catch up to him.

"I'm so sorry, Mrs. Northe-Stewart, I must seem addled. I know from my friends that you are an insightful woman, to say the very least. I've… I've not been well. For a man who made his fortune in tonics, I'm sure that doesn't bode as good advertising." He chuckled mordantly. And there it was. Ill.

"Your friends do me credit," Gran said softly, "but I am indeed sorry to hear this. Is there anything I could do to help?"

There was an awkward silence.

"I… Have you ever experienced periods of…well, *absence*? It seems I have these episodes where something had come over me and I am bid to go rest, but then sometimes, much later, I am told I said and did things I do not recall doing."

That struck Eve as an answer, and she saw Jenny sit up straighter, as if a light had gone off for all of them. A fugue state or other manipulation would explain why this man, or someone who appeared just like this man, had been so cruel to Maggie. Gran leaned in toward her subject.

"Hmm. The mind is a mystery, is it not?" Gran said sweetly. "Is there an example you would feel comfortable sharing?"

"I… Well, it's all hazy." Prenze passed a hand over his face. "I've been told it's sleepwalking, but even during the day? I must sound like a fool," he muttered. "Never mind me. We don't know one another well enough for me to impose like this."

"Nonsense. Everyone of note in this city knows me as a sort of… counselor. I take pride in the title."

Prenze half smiled again. "A cleric in a fine satin day dress."

"I think I'd make a fine priest," she said proudly. "I'm trying to get my Episcopalian brethren to ordain women. If I have any say, they'll be the first denomination to do so!" She knocked the marble counter of her tea table with a sharp rap for emphasis.

"You…you are so unique, Mrs. Northe-Stewart," Prenze said, with genuine admiration. Eve couldn't hold back a smile. There she went, Gran, making all the world fall in love with her just by the sheer quality of being so very much herself.

"Why thank you!" Gran said brightly.

Antonia entered the room with a tray of refreshments on an elegant wooden cart, and the next few moments were taken up by lemon cake and fresh tea.

"Ask him about the pictures, Auntie," Maggie urged. "However you can."

"Tell me something, Mr. Prenze," Gran said, gesturing to an art magazine she'd laid out with a standing camera on the cover. "As many of our mutual friends are heavily invested in the arts and new technologies, are you a fan of photography? I've been thinking about gifting Jennifer photography lessons."

"What a wonderful invention of our century," he exclaimed, suddenly beaming.

"Yes," Gran said. "To capture life. And death."

His smile soon faded. "I read somewhere recently that sometimes, due to expense, the only photograph a family has is one of a family member in death. Can you imagine?"

"Yes," Gran said gently. "I can always imagine the circumstances of the less fortunate. Because I was unfortunate, once. That's why you're here, to imagine such circumstances with me, and see what can be done about it."

"Yes...of course..." He looked out the window again, far away. "It's just so terribly sad to me that one would only have an image of death.... So static and still."

From the angled side of her screen, open enough to face the back wall, Eve watched Antonia and Cora, from the opposite side of the room, lean in from behind their screen as Maggie wafted even closer and Jenny stopped drawing to listen in.

Perhaps their collective psychic powers were leading him forward a bit, with Gran being the best lure. She was the world's best confidante. But Eve, glancing at her best ghostly asset, wondered what was wrong. Maggie seemed as flustered as she was engaged.

"Postmortem photography, then, do you find it important or troubling?" Gran asked, pressing gently.

"I...I know it has its uses for those who want an image to remember someone by, which is important...." He trailed off, as if he wanted to remember something

"Then why did you have a *collection* on your mantel?" Maggie hissed from the doorway and then clapped a transparent hand over her mouth, wafting back, to be sure not to be seen. If Prenze had been aware of Maggie in his house, he didn't seem aware or alert to ghosts here and now, but no one wanted to test the theory.

"There was a man I counseled once," Prenze continued, as if prompted by the ghost's outburst. "I don't know if you know this about me, Mrs. Northe-Stewart, but I too have gotten a reputation among many for being a... counselor of sorts to my peers—to men who have done well for themselves who don't always feel comfortable going to the church."

"How good of you," Gran said, encouraging him to elaborate.

"A man came to me once, years ago. He said he'd been sent by a friend...." Prenze trailed off, deep in thought, and Gran let him go on. "Never did find out who. He had an unseemly collection of postmortem photography, of children. Children that were of no relation to him. He'd been collecting them, and at some point, he seemed ashamed. He gave me his collection, asking if I would pray over those children. He didn't want to get rid of the portraits, saying that would be disrespectful, but he needed to be rid of them."

"What was his name?"

"Hmm. French, I think. Began with a D? I can't recall."

"Dupont?" Maggie whispered, and the mediums echoed the word in their minds, as if to nudge him, but Eve didn't want to lead the witness. He said no name, and Gran didn't prompt him with one, as it would seem suspicious.

"Part of what brings people to me is that I don't press," Prenze continued. "I am like the priest in the booth, ready to take confession without judgment. He brought them to one of my parties last year and asked if I could take them. I did, and he asked me to pray with him. I don't believe I ever saw him again."

"Did you? Pray over the pictures of the children?"

"It's the strangest thing—I did in the moment; I prayed quite hard, and I placed them next to a cross on my mantel. I confess, I forgot about them. But then the box went missing. I don't remember anything more about it." He shook his head as if he were coming to after a trance. "I...I ended up unburdening myself far more than I had intended."

"I have that effect on people," Gran said with a charming smile. "Just as you have for those who need counsel."

"Who counsels the counselors, then, I suppose?" he said with a weary laugh.

"Who indeed? I'm happy to, at any point. That is, unless you disapprove of my methods."

"Whatever do you mean?"

"May I be bluntly honest with you, Mr. Prenze?"

He blinked a moment, stiffening. "Why, yes."

"We were threatened, recently. Myself, my family, my associates. For 'unholy association with the dead' and associating us with the likes of devilry and devil worship."

"My God, why?" Prenze gasped.

"I am a Spiritualist, Mr. Prenze, as are members of my family, and we help others by receiving messages from the beyond. This is too often misunderstood. Someone who thinks of our sacred communion as sacrilege targeted me. I was taken from my home. I was held hostage, and so was my granddaughter, who is more sensitive than I am, as well as several of our colleagues in spiritual arms."

Eve was stunned by this direct line of inquiry. Antonia and Cora had their hands over their mouths across the room, the patterns of the cut wood screens making lace-like shadows on their faces. Forcing Prenze to confront their truth, Gran likely thought his discomfort or the results of his response would prove whether he had anything to do with the threats and abduction.

"While I didn't know your family was involved in such work, what happened is terrible," he exclaimed. Eve narrowed her eyes, sharpening her senses on his veracity. Generally speaking, the spirit world would rustle and whisper if one lied to a Sensitive. There was no response here. His surprise and horror appeared genuine. "You went to the police about it, I hope?"

"Quietly," Gran replied carefully. "We've only spoken with those I trust. You can imagine the fuss if we'd gone public about it. While séances are all the rage in parlor tricks, when one does them accurately, when one is truly a Spiritualist, it's another story—and one the public is less likely to love. It is more convenient if our movement is one of charlatans and wild women. Isn't that how poor Victoria Woodhull was painted, pilloried as she ran for the presidency twenty-seven years ago? Have we not progressed—"

"Well," Prenze said with a dismissive laugh. "But she was a radical—"

"Be that as it may, in my opinion no one gave her fair credit, and ever since, I've been cautious of keeping any public profile beyond philanthropy. To bring my story forward would only paint more of a target on my family." Gran squared her shoulders. "Do you remember a spectral incident in your house?"

Prenze blinked glassy eyes. "I'm sorry, what?"

"I'm trying to rule out that your family had some hand in this."

"Why…on *earth*…" Prenze seemed genuinely aghast. Eve admitted she had not expected Gran to come right out with the accusation and continue pressing. She expected coy and clever, not direct. This was bold. Even Jenny, whose eyes had widened in shock, had to remind herself she wasn't supposed to be hearing this. She turned back to her sketchbook, but with her head cocked to the side as if she wasn't believing her ears.

Gran went further. "There was a spectral incident in your house, Mr. Prenze, involving the postmortem photographs you happened to mention."

"I…I recall no such thing. But, as I said, the photographs went missing."

"Could that have been during one of your 'ailments'?" she asked, sounding genuinely curious and keeping her tone clear of judgment.

"Perhaps. I'm very sorry to not be of more help. If I think of anything…I'll tell you."

Even though Eve didn't want to believe it, this man was telling the truth.

"May I ask something additionally related to my family?" Gran continued without waiting to be granted permission. "Why would a Sergeant Mahoney have such a keen interest in protecting you?"

"Ah." Prenze sighed. "Sergeant Mahoney is…overprotective of my family, more so since my brother's death. We hired him as a guard to supplement his police salary; his brother was a clergyman near our first shop. Why do you ask?"

"He filed a complaint against my granddaughter for meddling in your business when she had not authorized any such thing. He just jumped to some sort of conclusion."

Maggie glanced back at Eve. No need to mention Maggie was part of the same department; the truth was, she hadn't authorized anything. Maggie had gone in of her own accord. Still, one had to be careful in the realms of their Preventative Protocol.

"Mahoney means well, and I'm sure he was just rattled by the idea of spirits meddling with the family, though that I can't corroborate, as I've seen no such thing."

"Would he abduct and threaten?"

"Never!" Prenze said, aghast. "You don't really think what happened to you and your family had anything to do with mine, do you? Mahoney would never threaten anyone, and I can't imagine these incidents had anything to do with him. I'll confront him directly, but…"

Gran was all warmth. She'd gotten her window in, and they could all work to open it further. "Think no more of it. My granddaughter and I will seek answers, just as you will, for your ailments."

His furrowed brow eased a bit. Eve understood. Time with Gran was indeed like a confessional, and she agreed that her mentor would make an incredible priest.

"I am a man who likes to be of help," Prenze said, offering a genuine, if not a bit tired, smile. "So, if there's a way I can help get to the bottom of any of this, I'll try."

"I am grateful to hear it."

"Thank you for letting me be the face behind your venture; I'm glad of it," he said earnestly. "I may be back to seek your counsel."

"Please do," Gran replied. "I can tell you're troubled, and I'd like to help."

Prenze nodded as if he knew she was right but wasn't sure why. What were his *ailments*, really? Eve, watching him so closely, with such psychic and visual scrutiny her eyes watered, found herself torn in wanting to pity him—even to like him.

Cora was at the door awaiting him, giving him back his things. Eve noted a similar baffled look on Cora's face, mirroring what she was feeling.

He paused at the door. "You know, there is one thing." He crossed back toward Gran a step. "Before my twin brother, Albert died, he said he and a colleague were working on something that would 'rid the world of the troublesome dead. He hated ghosts, you see. I was never troubled by them, but he claimed he was terribly haunted by the spirit of our mother. Truth was, I was the favorite. He must have taken that too much to heart, and her 'haunting and taunting' him from the grave was a reaction his grieving mind couldn't take. He could never reconcile being second in her favor, and he clung to that misery and rivalry. He did once go on a hateful rant about Spiritualists being a plague upon the earth."

Alfred Prenze glanced at Gran, his face ashen. "I wonder if a colleague of Albert's didn't follow through with some sort of plan, and that's who or what came after you and yours?"

"Who could that have been?" Gran inquired, her voice a gentle lead.

Prenze shook his head. "I'm sorry, I don't know. There was so much about my brother that was secretive. I thought that was for the best. If not for my sweet sister, there would have been open war. But now I see I was in error not knowing his circle, his goings-on, his colleagues. I wish he and I could have reconciled before his death. It is my greatest regret. My living haunt."

The man bid Gran good day and walked out. From the open parlor doors, Eve watched Cora usher him out the door.

Once Prenze left, there was a long silence. Eve came out from behind the screen and took a seat on a cushioned chair opposite Gran's tea table. Cora entered the parlor with a furrowed brow and sat slowly on the divan, and Antonia came around to sit on it next to her. Jenny sat on a pouf nearest to Gran, reaching up for a tea cookie. The only sounds were Jenny crunching the snack, the tick of the clock, and the slight, eerie whistle of wind that could be heard on the air next to a spirit. Maggie descended from the stairs to hover closest to Eve.

"Well... That was something," Gran said finally, trying to parse what had unfolded. "Whose instincts first?"

"It was him, but he wasn't him," Maggie insisted, bobbing up and down, unnerved. "The man who..." She struggled for words to describe what had happened to her. "Who blinked me out in his mansion. It looked like him, but it wasn't that man. Are we dealing with a Jekyll and Hyde?"

"Remember the bottle," Eve began quietly, "in the possession of Dr. Font, the man who signed off on Prenze's death certificate? The label of that Prenze tonic had writing on the other side that said 'isn't dead.'"

"The twin, Albert," Gran said, nodding.

"It would *have* to be the twin acting out to make any sense of this," Eve continued, "assuming the role of his brother in spurts. But what accounts for this Prenze, Alfred, during? What brings on his 'spells'? Wouldn't the staff know the difference between the two men?"

"Their persona seems so distinct." Maggie floated in a circle around the women as she spoke. "But the cruel one, Albert, if what we're saying is true, dropped a façade at the party once he ushered everyone out and turned to me. He may put on a show to mask their differences, but in just simple logistics, wouldn't the staff know one of them slept while another walked about?"

"Unless the sister is somehow vouching for him," Eve stated. "The one who was trying to keep the peace. Perhaps the resurrected twin, keeping the fact that he's still alive from his brother, has power over her."

"Yes, there is a third energy at the center of this spinning wheel," came a voice from upstairs, and a luminous figure followed. Not a ghost, but the arriving lady was a powerful creature that had almost transcended the quality of womanhood and become a force of nature. Something the Greeks would have wondered and warned about.

Mrs. Clara Templeton Bishop descended in a gauzy white gown, dark-gold hair up in a braided bun atop her head, her gold-green eyes wide and glassy. She hesitated at the pocket doors, looking around curiously at her audience.

"Mrs. Bishop," Eve said deferentially, bowing her head.

"These days, with my Sensitivities so acute, it's healthiest if I work from at least a room away so I don't trigger a seizure," Clara explained, gliding to the opposite side of the room between two potted ferns and reaching out to caress the fronds. "Walls are almost like skin to me now. But don't worry about me; worry about this man and his complications. There are three entities entwined."

"You believe that the twin isn't dead as well," Gran prompted.

"I can't tell what I'm sensing. With twins, if they are connected, and only if, there can be a feeling of a second soul present even if they are nowhere in the physical vicinity. But where people mistake twins, and often prove offensive, is in assuming that a psychic or mystical bond is always true. Twins are two distinct and separate human beings. If Albert is actually dead, his energy might be strongly connected as a ghost. But a ghost doesn't explain the absences Alfred described. That, I think, must be filled and acted by the twin, as Maggie has described."

The ghost nodded from the corner where she had shifted. Out of care and respect, Maggie had hung back against the wall behind Gran since the moment Mrs. Bishop entered. Proximity to too many spirits was another seizure trigger for Clara, and the ghosts of the precinct had been instructed to give her plenty of space.

Clara turned her unsettling eyes toward Eve, who had always felt this woman had the capacity to see past her skin and bones and directly into her soul.

"And you, Eve, I hear you learned of a new spiritual plane recently—Tell me about it."

"Oh, that? I don't want to trouble you—"

"Tell me. I think it will prove very important," she said matter-of-factly.

Eve glanced at Maggie, and the ghost gestured her on. Eve carefully shared what she knew about Sanctuary. She also mentioned that Sensitives should be sure no negative energies polluted the place. Explaining this, she felt an inelegant, graceless child compared to Clara's expertise, and in her nervousness, she jumped in with an addition: "Cora's Uncle Louis said not to trouble—"

At the name Louis, Gran flashed Eve a deadly look. Eve felt the color drain from her face.

Gran's eyes, boring into Eve, were all fury. When Eve had first met the Bishops, years ago, Gran had explained that there was a very painful past that Mrs. Bishop wouldn't want to discuss. She and Louis Dupris had been a couple long ago, and his ghost had assisted in Clara's work even after death, but their souls had agreed to part. When Cora came to work for the department, Gran had requested that Eve and her team not bring up the connection so as not to subject Clara to further pain.

"Uncle… Louis…" Clara repeated the name quietly. She turned slowly toward Cora. "Cora, dear, you're…the daughter of Andre Dupris, yes?"

"Yes, Mrs. Bishop," Cora said quietly. "Eve didn't mean to—"

"I'm so sorry—" Eve blurted.

Mrs. Bishop raised a hand. Her face was expressionless, but her words were careful, clipped. "Louis Dupris speaks to you, Cora?"

"Yes. Yes, he does," Cora said. Unlike Eve, she had no reason to apologize. Cora was very proud of her uncle and the spiritual channel they cultivated together, all the more powerful for Cora having left her parents behind in New Orleans. "He is a loving uncle, and I am so very blessed to have him as family."

Some deaths never quite healed. Even when an offer came out of Eve's mouth, she knew she was only making things worse. "You're always welcome to come join us—"

"I think communing with my former lover would be an affront to my husband, Miss Whitby," Clara said icily. That she reverted from using Eve's familiar name was an additional cut direct.

"Yes, of course." Eve glanced at Gran, but there was no help there; she'd plowed right in and mentioned the one thing Gran had asked her not to.

"I appreciate your concern, but Evelyn, dear, you must have made me out to these girls as too fragile." Clara eyed Gran before turning to the window, speaking quietly but firmly. "Mr. Dupris and I said our heartfelt goodbyes seventeen years ago. While the spirit never ends, Mr. Dickens was correct in his observation that life is 'full of meetings and partings.' Louis and I met; we parted. My heart will always skip a beat at the mention of him. It would be my wish that every woman understood love, deeply, twice as I have done. How fortunate I have been."

Eve had no idea what to say.

"No, there isn't anything to say," Clara responded, picking up on Eve's exact thought. "Leave it be. I should return home to Rupert. I'm feeling well enough to stand, and my carriage is around the corner. Tell me if anything changes, and if I can get a more distinct read on the Prenze situation, I will update you."

"Thank you, Clara," Gran stated, and the precinct mediums echoed the same sentiment.

She nodded and saw herself out. Gran turned to Eve, folding her arms.

"For God's sake, Eve, I'm trying to make sure all of our assets are in best form. Clara already feels abandoned by me, because in stepping up to help you from childhood on, she was left in the cold with few friends other than her dear husband. You could try not alienating her further."

Eve hung her head. Mrs. Bishop's powers were unique and priceless. Eve couldn't afford to create distance with any ally; she needed every one she could get.

"Don't mope; eat something. Let's discuss what else came to mind during the discussion with Alfred Prenze." Gran moved to a console table against the wall and removed fabric draped over a plate of sandwiches. The mediums took to the spread eagerly, removing lace bonnets and aprons to return to their regular clothes.

"You were quite forthcoming," Antonia stated. "That surprised all of us."

"Indeed. Well, I run on instinct, and that seemed the thing to do."

"It did give me a sense he was telling the truth," Antonia said. Jenny nodded.

"We've not seen Vera in days now," Eve said. "But she was drawn into the Dupont house by the spirit of a child, and asked, just as Maggie was, to throw a postmortem photograph into the hall to make a scene. I wonder if somehow Vera was 'blinked out' like Maggie and if Dupont is the one who gave the images to Prenze, trying to get anything that could be used as evidence of malpractice out of his viewing parlor?"

The women nodded at this plausible circumstance.

"Could Dupont also be the twin's unnamed colleague Mr. Prenze mentioned? Working on something to eliminate the dead?" Cora asked.

"To draw two disparate threads together, pointing in one direction, that would be convenient," Eve said, "but it may be too convenient."

Jenny made a twirling motion and signed *ghosts*.

"Jenny's right, however," Eve added. "Ghosts were parading outside Dupont's parlor; they were insistent that they were being kept out. Maggie got into the Prenze mansion, but there were no ghosts anywhere near when Gran, the detective, and I went to a ball. The fact that Albert Prenze hated ghosts and Spiritualists is the most concrete lead on abductors and the devices."

"I promise to continue working on *Alfred* Prenze, and as long as we proceed with care," Gran began, "we'll make progress. If Albert is alive, I doubt he wants his secret known. When one has a high-profile individual in one's sights, especially after your departmental trials with the family name, everything has to be done with the greatest delicacy. If we come on too strong, we'll scare Alfred. I breached his comfort today; we dare not push it."

En route home, Gran making sure her driver took the girls back in her finest cab that could seat them all comfortably, Cora leaned in to Eve, worrying her lip between words as she spoke.

"A word has been ringing in my ears during psychometry. At the graveyard, at the parlor, it keeps repeating. Remember when I touched Mr. Schwerin's trepanned head, back at the men's asylum?

Eve thought about that dreary day and that sad man. "You heard the word 'magic.'"

"Yes. *Magic*." Cora nodded. "Another wrinkle. What does that mean?"

"We need a bit of magic to find Greta's whereabouts," Eve said. "I hate trying to call back her daughter Ingrid to help, not after I saw her soul go to rest."

The scream during our séance... We have to make this right, Jenny signed.

"Let me try another graveyard tomorrow," Cora offered, "one of the locations mentioned in the disturbances in the files. If any child retained a connection to Dupont, perhaps they can help us locate him, and then, hopefully, Greta."

Once home in their entrance hall, as they were hanging up coats and cloaks, Antonia offered the grim souvenir of the lock of hair from Dupont's viewing parlor to Cora. "You should take this when you go to the graveyards, in case you can find the girl it belongs to." Cora nodded and placed the lock carefully between the lid and glass of her pocket watch.

Antonia turned to Eve. "Why don't you ask Detective Horowitz if he can make calls for us? Other precincts won't listen to us, but they'll respond to one of their own. The neighbor said Irvington, so we've got to try to get somewhere."

Eve nodded. It had started as a little tickle during the Prenze encounter, but the sound and pressure were growing. It felt as though the spirit world were pounding on her skull. A thousand little fingers. Pointing. Pressing. "Damn migraine. This one will be bad if I'm not careful."

"Go rest, you look ill," Cora stated, turning her and giving her a push toward the stairs.

"You've worked just as hard, and you look fresh as spring," Eve said, looking at her lovely colleague, who never appeared as drained as she did.

"The benefits of a beautiful, warm brown hue," she said with a smile. Eve returned it.

Eve reached toward her, nearly stumbling on the first step. "If you need anything—"

"I know," Cora said, shooing her upstairs, still smiling. "I'll be out early for the trolley, then a ferry. I've graveyard rounds in Queens, so we'll see you back home tomorrow night. Sleep deeply. You're no good to anyone if a migraine guts you—not to mention you're miserable company."

"Yes, Mother," Eve said with a chuckle and blew a kiss from the top of the stairs.

Eve took two aspirin from a bottle next to her bed, the brand-new tablet such a great blessing, a vastly improved departure from more sedative, opiate-based measures. She lay down, pressing her eyes shut, blocking out the pain, and not even the fear of a face outside her window could pry her from the spirits' grip. Too tired for blocking specters, she let the whispers and murmurs of the dead become a sea, thinking she was merely on a cot by the crashing waves of an eternal ocean.

Come find us, they begged.

Chapter Eight

The next morning Eve checked her office early, not wanting to be disturbed as she looked for any mail or messages. But who was waiting for her, pacing back and forth by the patch of green beside their offices, but Greta's sister, Susan. As Eve approached, the weary woman looked up, a note in hand, her brow knit with worry.

Eve ushered her inside and prepared a cup of tea over the small coal stove at the rear of their room. She was glad she'd worn one of her nicest matronly mourning uniforms of the several she'd commissioned, as she felt more official in tending to this poor soul. Susan took the tea eagerly.

"We'll be contacting a precinct in Irvington to see if there are any leads on Dupont—" Eve was cut off as the woman brandished an envelope.

"She wrote me. It came in yesterday's post, posted a day before."

"Oh, thank goodness," Eve said. "If it's only a day, she can't be far."

"And it is her handwriting. I even compared it to her letters just to trust my own eyes."

"That was very smart of you," Eve reassured and took the note she was handed.

Sister Dearest,

Do not fear.

I am not being hurt. I am here willingly. Please do not come find me.

Eve sat with it, tried to discern, to listen to see if the spirit world had a response about it. She had none of Cora's psychometry, so she couldn't gain any sense of where it had been written or images around it, but while Eve heard a rustle from the spirit world, she didn't hear it reject the note as a lie.

"Do you believe her?" Eve asked.

The sister shook her head. "At first, no. But then again, if she did still love him, with Heinrich incapacitated, if she and her 'Lion' did run away together, like he'd promised when she worked for him, if she's happy..." The sister sighed, her shoulders falling as she folded her arms. Eve noted the threadbare elbows of her shirtwaist, how many times the cuff at her wrist had been carefully mended. "Who am I to stand in their way? Just because I am lonely doesn't mean she has to be."

Eve wanted to put her arm around the woman but sensed that would not be welcome. Instead, Eve spoke carefully through sips of tea, wanting not to worry the poor woman further.

"I...I think there's more going on with Dupont than we know. His being an undertaker isn't the issue; it's that I doubt he's entirely...balanced. I'm not saying Greta's in danger, but I do think we should still try to find her."

Susan nodded. It seemed to Eve like the woman has lost weight since she'd last seen her, as if she were hollowing out.

Antonia had recently baked small loaves of nut bread to have on hand in the office for long days without lunches, so Eve rose and wrapped one in a thin piece of butcher's paper. "Here," she said, sliding it across her desk. "We've more than we can go through, and we'll be out of the office all day."

The woman hesitated, proud.

"Please." Eve could tell the woman needed just a bit of help to regain energy and momentum. Being alone and impoverished in this city, relying on the piecemeal lacework that Eve knew was her sole income was a difficult living.

Susan murmured thanks.

"We'll keep thinking of anything we can, and trying through all our channels, traditional and...not," Eve reassured. "If you hear anything more, or if you have any other ideas, we want to know."

Susan nodded and left, a soundless, sorrowful woman lost in the city. Even the ghosts didn't dare make a noise during their entire encounter. Sometimes the living became ghosts too soon.

The precinct each had their own tasks and free rein to follow wherever clues led. Eve had begun to feel like there was constantly something behind her, watching her.

Like a man outside her window.

In the time since she'd seen him, she'd felt he was there even if he wasn't. Something terrible had gotten into her head. A driving ache still pounded at the back of her skull, and she put her dark glasses on before striding back out onto the street.

At least she looked forward to her next errand. Detective Horowitz instilled an electrifying sense of hope within her. She prayed she could keep her temperature and awkwardness in check. Along with hope came severe nerves, but Eve found the butterflies were too intoxicating not to indulge them.

It hadn't been exactly arranged that Eve would call upon the detective the next day at Mulberry Street headquarters, but he didn't seem surprised to see her stride through his open office door in the rear guts of the building, knocking on the doorframe as she entered his small, dim room lit by one lamp at his desk, shining a light onto his brown, curly head as he glanced up from an open notebook. His frown upturned at the sight of her.

"A lot has happened since yesterday," she declared, removing her dark glasses and standing before his desk. Glancing down, she saw he'd been writing neatly in a casebook.

"Busy day for you too, then?" He gestured to the seat opposite. "Tell me all about it—then I'll tell you about the hospitals and an exsanguinated corpse."

Eve grimaced as she took the battered chair across from the detective's desk. The exterior of Mulberry Street looked grand and imposing enough, but the interior was as worn and tired as its workforce.

He went to a narrow table by the wall and poured a dark substance from a tin carafe into a small ceramic mug and offered it to her. "It's gone a bit cold, but knowing you—"

"My hero," she said, taking the cup eagerly. "I've run out at home, and I've had a migraine since last night." She lifted the cup. "*L'chaim.*"

He looked at her and smiled, lifting the remains of his own chipped mug. "To life!"

They sipped cool coffee and stared at one another. The detective finally looked away, noise from down the hall breaking a sort of reverie. He set his cup down and frowned.

"Which grisly detail should we start with?" he asked.

"Well, for my part, we've a missing person, and I'm hoping I can ask your help in access and contacts. Greta Schwerin may be with Mr. Dupont, her former employer, possibly being held by force or coercion even though she seems to have sent a note saying otherwise. Greta did say they had been lovers, and her sister thinks that in the grief about Ingrid and her body, details Dupont may have lied about drove her to confront him. She's been gone a few days."

"Dupont is the undertaker with the viewing parlor?" the detective clarified.

"Yes, and he's gone missing too. The whole Dupont family. Vanished from Gramercy Park, from the parlor too, everything in it just gone. Possibly to Irvington, thanks to a next-door neighbor. It seems the wife cleared out the house and left with the help—two young maids. No one saw Dupont go, but he hasn't been seen there. Both his home and parlor buildings are bare, as if they're not planning on coming back. So, if there's any Dupont property, or the wife's family—"

"I'll call the Irvington precinct," the detective said. "The poor Schwerins."

"There was a little hole drilled in Heinrich Schwerin's head when Cora and I saw him at the asylum. Someone didn't want him talking about Ingrid, or other things. And..." Eve winced, hearing the sad sound again in recollection. "I think I heard Ingrid's voice screaming for her mother. That child should be at peace. Nothing should wrench a resting soul into pain."

The detective shuddered. "It must be awful, the bits and pieces you get. I mean"—he gestured to stacks of paper on his battered desk and the table against the wall—"all of these are bits and pieces, but what *you* see and hear... If unanswered paperwork is maddening, I can only imagine..."

"Thank you, truly, for that empathy, Detective; that's very kind of you." Eve took another sip of coffee. It was helping with her headache. "I will appreciate if you can find out if there's any truth to the Irvington connection. Otherwise I don't know where to look. About the strange box, I'm hoping to hear Father's contact at Bellevue was helpful?"

"Very much so. Doctor Newstead at Bellevue didn't know what to make of it, but they'll take a look; they didn't want to make a judgment right away. When I said you thought it might have something to do with the mind, the brain, he was very surprised, having thought at first it was perhaps trying to record a pulse or other vital functions. Then at Mount Sinai, Doctor Levi was similarly rapt at the possibilities. 'The brain,' Levi said, 'is the most vital function of all, but we don't know its beat, we don't know its voice. Perhaps something is trying to hear the mind's distinct voice.'" The detective shook his head in wonder. "There was a poetry to him, and in these doctors' excitement; I'm hoping this odd state we all found ourselves in actually leads to some sort of medical breakthrough."

Eve nodded. "It would help me feel less angry and helpless. The abductors are still out there." She voiced just a small bit of the large fear she felt, a sentiment she didn't dare show to her girls.

"But you are strong and not to be intimidated," the detective declared, "and you have the eager help of myself, my friend and colleague Sergeant Fitton, and a *host* of far more influential characters your Gran likes to parade about." The detective's smile widened as Eve chuckled.

"So." The detective placed his hands on the table. "The bloodless body. Remember that one? Mr. Zinne?"

"What, the case where we first met?" Eve asked. She'd never get the sight of the entirely drained body from months ago out of her mind. "Is there a new development?"

"Well, we've already established we don't believe in vampires… and considering all you do believe in, it's comforting you draw the line somewhere," he joked before leaning closer across the desk. "But, now hear me out on this, what if the blood was being used, somehow? Zinne's estranged sister was clearing out his boardinghouse room and found things that may shed light on what happened."

He passed a notebook across the desk with a pamphlet lying on the open page, a letter beneath it.

"She brought this into the precinct, along with some letters, insisting she talk only to me. That riled the leading investigator on that case, I'll tell you, but she insisted I was the only one who listened to her when she came in to identify the body. Zinne's last words to her before their estrangement was that he wanted to 'give himself over entirely to beauty.' She didn't know what that meant, but once she found this, she wanted me to see it."

Eve perused a pamphlet stating *Arte Uber Alles*! "Art above everything?"

"That's how I'd translate the German," he said, "give or take a bit of nuance."

The cover bore an illustration of an ecstatic, half-naked woman wrapped in diaphanous fabric with her arms upraised, her head thrown back. The text was an overwrought ode on art for art's sake, but this took aestheticism to a fanatical level of subordinating oneself for something beautiful, positing artistic expression as the only divine act. The last line chilled Eve. *Use the body and all its possible capacity in the interest of art. Then you are like an angel, more than mortal.*

Eve examined the letters, torrents of excitement about leaving flesh behind.

"This discussion of transcending flesh," Eve began, glancing down the missive, "to me, sounds like Zinne was ready for death. Perhaps an assisted suicide? The rest of the note looks like curated lines from Milton and the *Divine Comedy*. All of it has to do with the body."

"Or with blood," the detective added. "There's not much sense in the letters sent to Zinne; the sister brought me everything she could find, but it's mostly raving. But there are many mentions of blood, of capturing and using it. Not consuming it, but considering it as an object. A supply."

She arched an eyebrow at the detective. "You're saying the blood could have been removed somehow and used, then, as…what?"

"Well, if it's for the sake of art… The letters mention the words 'decorative' and 'bathing surfaces' with blood."

"What?" Eve breathed. "As *paint*?"

Horowitz grimaced, as if it had sounded better in an unvoiced theory. "It does sound utterly inane."

"As plausible a theory as any, especially considering this whole macabre premise, but I'm not sure anyone"—she gestured around her, at the headquarters beyond—"will support you in that leap."

"Not without further evidence," the detective agreed. "It seems this"—he tapped the pamphlet—"was a bit of a club."

"Have you been able to track down other club members? Where they meet?"

"Of course no one uses a real name, and there doesn't appear to be a meeting place— More that someone simply wanted these ideas to live out in the world, and a small set picked up on it. There are a few names mentioned in the letters to and from Zinne, so I made a list."

Eve scanned the list of names printed in the detective's impeccable script. Her finger stopped and so did her heart as she ran across Montmartre. "I know that name."

"Well, it *is* a grand Paris graveyard—"

"*And* the name of Dupont's partner at the viewing parlor. Where Ingrid was taken and her body made into a little saint."

"Well, let's question Montmartre, then," the detective declared, rising to his feet.

"I don't know where to find him, and there's nothing at that parlor anymore."

"I'll see if I can dig up anything on him, if it's a real name, if he's been practicing as an undertaker anywhere else."

Eve perused the list of the ten or so names. Mostly they were famed locations, a few Shakespearean kings and Greek philosophers, but when her eye fell upon Dr. Font, she gasped.

"The presiding doctor on Prenze's death, the man who relatives claim was 'scared to death' before he was found dead in an empty apartment?" Eve clarified. "He was involved in this…interest group?"

The detective nodded. "His name came up in a letter discussing moving their 'group' to New York."

"From?"

"It would seem letters making their way between the names I listed came from England or Germany, with at least three different handwriting styles, each interested in science as well as art—but everything has that same rhapsodic almost mania to it that sounds a bit unhinged."

Another name caught Eve's eye: Mulciber. She wasn't sure what it was a reference to, but something itched at her, and the spirit world seemed to enflame the irritation, like a rustling of leaves picking up inside her ears. Perhaps her faraway thoughts prompted the detective's next question.

"What might the spirits be able to tell you?" he asked. "I assume you've tried gaining information about Dupont from the beyond, what about the partner?"

That he was jumping to her and her precinct's methods so quickly after having been such a confirmed skeptic was heartening, if not a bit surprising.

The surprise must have registered on her face, for he added, "Any line of inquiry when one is left flat-footed *must* be taken up. Your ghosts have proved useful. I'd be a fool to deny that."

Eve smiled. She hadn't realized how much his warming to her methods would affect her. All her life she'd been walking a careful tightrope with her family, never being able to share the love of her work, never being able to rejoice in the belief, in the certainties and wonderful divine mysteries of her calling.

Here, her gifts were being celebrated in earnest by someone she'd thought she'd have to maintain her guard around. So often women weren't believed, compounded by Spiritualism's vagaries, so just this simple invitation for her to take a lead, for him to listen, was a gift she wasn't sure she could fully articulate to him. He tilted his head slightly with a look on his face that seemed to ask why she'd fallen silent or her eyes watered.

With a little nervous chuckle, she broke the silence. "I'm just…I'm just very moved that you…believe in the possibilities of my gifts even if you don't understand them."

"No one ever solved anything by believing only one thing."

She smiled at him. "That's a very wise thing to say."

"Have a séance here," Maggie said, materializing to Eve's right. "You know you don't need any of your trappings."

Horowitz blinked, and his eyes flickered toward the movement next to Eve.

"Maggie is saying I should just have a séance right here, with you."

"You don't need to be in your offices, at your table, with your peers?" he asked.

"There is so much that needs investigating," Eve exclaimed, overwhelmed. "I haven't even gotten to tell you about Mr. Prenze."

"Or poor 'scared to death' Dr. Font," the detective added. "There's more on him too."

"Then we must try," Eve stated, rubbing the back of her neck. The pressure of her recent headache remained, ready to build, but listening to the dead might prove a bit of release. The only way to make progress was to keep asking questions. "I should ask the spirits about these names and any new connection. A séance right here, if you don't mind."

"Go on, then, how can I help?"

Eve downed the last of her coffee, sighed, and took a deep breath as the detective rummaged in a desk drawer. "You don't happen to have a—" She stopped abruptly, chuckling as he pulled out the exact thing she needed: a small candle on a brass holder and a box of matches. "Are you *sure* you're not psychic and withholding your talents from me?"

The detective laughed, rose, and went to the door. "I assume you'd like this closed. I don't mean to suggest any impropriety—"

"You're the perfect gentleman. Please close it, thank you. Let's see what the spirits have to say, shall we?"

He returned to his side of the desk. Eve poised a match on the side of the box and paused.

"Would you like to say a...*berakhot*?" she asked, hoping she pronounced it right. The detective stared, clearly surprised that she knew the word for a blessing. "It's always more successful when one brings their own thoughts and traditions into this practice," she explained.

He nodded and said something softly in Hebrew, translating in a murmur.

"*Baruch Ata Adonai, Eloheinu Melech Haolam, shehechiyanu, v'kiy'manu, v'higianu lazman hazeh.* Blessed are You, Eternal Spirit who has given us life, sustained us, and allowed us to arrive in this moment."

"Amen," Eve whispered, striking the match and lighting the candle. "Dear spirits, heed this call, arriving in this moment. We are here to help you find justice. We are here to listen." She blew out the match and set it gently against the side of the candle.

"Take his hands, Eve," Maggie said from the corner. Eve swallowed.

"I'm sorry, if you don't mind," she whispered, reaching her hands across the desk. "It's best if we..." The detective didn't hesitate in taking her hands.

Instinctively, they threaded their fingers together, as if it were the most natural thing; rather than a simple touch of palm to palm, this was an entwining. The resulting shudder up their spines, visible and in tandem, Eve tried to convince herself was just the fault of the ghosts.

She closed her eyes and opened herself to the spirit world, inviting the external noise closer, putting what was constantly in the background at her mental and physical foreground.

"Dear spirits, you who are so tied to me, especially the children of late, all those named in our files and all those unnamed, can you help us with the names Montmartre, Dupont? How can we find them? Where have they gone, and is Greta Schwerin with them?"

"Pieces, pieces," replied a sequence of voices. Eve narrated to the detective what she was hearing, disembodied voices, no visible forms, just murmurs, but the words were clear.

"We know all the information is in pieces; how do we put it together?" Eve asked patiently.

"*We're* not put together," came one voice. The rest of the spirits in the murk seemed to be repeating only pieces.

"You must give us something specific. Please don't talk in riddles," she pleaded. "I know Dupont took tokens— Give us someplace to look, my dears."

When dealing with the ghosts of children especially, she found that endearments helped. She had to remain patient with them. Being dead addled the brain; no soul was entirely linear. That Maggie had retained such clarity and focus was unusual, matched only by Cora's uncle Louis, but to him Cora credited his spiritual beliefs and practice; to Maggie, Eve credited love and seeing justice through. For these children, they didn't know what their purpose was—they didn't even know most of the time why they were unsettled. It was why their cases had languished in file cabinets.

"Where do we start with Montmartre or Dupont? Mulciber?"

"*Magic!*" cried a voice of collected children, and Eve repeated their cry.

Then the spiritual door shut, as if it was slammed, sending with it an abnormal force. Eve was shoved, thrown forward against the edge of the desk, and with a gasp she came to, lurching forward, her torso folded on their still entwined hands, her forehead inches from the detective's.

The force of the movement had blown out the candle, sending droplets of wax onto the scratched wood as smoke wafted between their close faces. A dab of wax had fallen on the back of Eve's hand, and she barely noticed it; all she saw was her white-knuckled hands clenching his, as if he were the last thing holding her to this earth before she floated away into some distant corner of the spirit world.

She turned her head and cleared her throat, letting go of his hands, using the table to right herself. "I'm sorry," she murmured. "To have taken your hands so tightly."

He studied his hands, still white-knuckled, a curved mark where a fingernail had dug in, a growing redness where her fingers had pressed so urgently against his palms.

"I'm not sorry," he replied, staring at her unflinchingly.

Eve forgot to breathe.

"*Magic*, you said," he whispered.

Yes, this moment most certainly was.

"The spirits said 'magic,'" he prompted. "I'm sure that's a clue."

Eve coughed. "Yes, right. Let's take a walk." She whirled in the chair, rising to her feet, desperate for fresh air to cool her cheeks. "Diving into the edge of life and death on my own makes me particularly woozy." She tried to cover the increasingly unavoidable truth that it was the detective's presence and closeness that made her world spin. Snatching her dark glasses, she slid them unevenly onto her nose and turned unsteadily toward the door.

"Are you in pain?" he asked, stopping her with gentle hands on her shoulders, turning her back around to face him. "I…didn't mean to ask you to use your gifts if they cause you pain. I shouldn't ask that of you lightly, I'm sorry…."

Eve lowered her head a bit, looking at this dear man over the top of her dark shades, the desk lamp backlighting his brown curls to give him a subtle halo, the shadows of the dim room casting his sharp features into a further, striking contrast.

"Mrs. Bishop is right when she says 'there's always a cost to these powers.' The thing is, if I don't let the spirits in, at least a few of the constant whispers, they beat down the walls of my head and tear my mind open, forcing me to listen. No matter which way, there is always pain. It *always* hurts. What makes it bearable is listening so that we can do some good, together," she said.

The detective's brown eyes ringed in blue widened in awe. "Eve Whitby… If I may say so, you are such"—he raised his hands as if he were going to cup her face—"an *inspiration*." He took a step closer. His hands, which had remained hovering on either side of her head as if he were ready to scoop her up, slowly went to her glasses. He withdrew them from her nose, carefully unhooking them from behind her ear. His eyes kept hers, searching, perhaps asking permission. She let her gaze fall to his lips and tilted imperceptibly closer.

Perhaps he would finish what they'd very nearly started in Union Square, before Maggie returned, that perfect moment where time stopped.

A clanging bell rang out from the front of the station, making both of them jump.

"Street brawl on Mott!" an officer yelled down the hall, and a series of mutterings, laughs, and a stampede of footsteps filled the hall as those on site poured toward the front door.

Maggie brandished a transparent fist toward the door and the noise. "You bastards, they were just about to kiss!" The ghost hissed as she went through the closed door. Eve's cheeks went scarlet as she felt herself slapped out of another reverie—she'd forgotten her dear spirit was still there.

The detective seemed to come out of a spell too, shaking loose of the grip that tightened around them when they were too close.

"So, what was that again about magic, as we take that walk?" he said sheepishly. He must have realized he still had her glasses in his hands as he hastily offered them back to her, and she slid them on, eager to hide behind them.

"There isn't any case of yours, or anything odd of late, that has to do with magic?" Eve asked as they filed through a sea of uniforms. "Whatever that may mean, stage magic, the concept of a 'spell,' whatever comes to mind? 'Magic' keeps coming up in our findings."

"We should walk by the magicians' row, then," he offered. "The district is full of performers; something might ring a bell."

"What's this, Has-no-wits," a red-faced officer sneered as they walked toward the exit, jabbing a thumb at Eve, "they assign you a police matron to mind you?"

Eve whirled on the beat cop.

"Actually, I'm a secretary assigned to help with new information because he's running *circles* around all of you as the only person victims trust. You might want to start working on useful communication instead of infantile bullying. You may one day catch up to him."

The man's jaw dropped, stunned as she whirled back to Horowitz, who didn't acknowledge the officer further. They stormed out the door in tandem, turning away from the mass heading in the direction of the infamous Five Points.

"You didn't have to say you were a secretary," Horowitz said as they crossed the busy street, narrowly missing the whipping flick of a dirty horse's tail as a cart careened behind them.

"But I am now, technically, as Roosevelt demoted us to anyone looking. They scrubbed my title off my door."

"That's not fair!" the detective exclaimed.

"If it keeps my girls safe, for now, that's all I care about. Roosevelt knows our title, and we do—that's all that matters. You know, bluster back there aside, it is a beautiful gift of trust when victims come to you because you've listened, in Zinne's case and others. It's the mark of quality and the fact you're resented for it tells me everything I need to know about the politics here."

"We're not in it for the politics, madam secretary."

"Sure aren't," she retorted.

"Still, thank you."

"We are allies."

"I couldn't ask for better."

They walked in a comfortable silence for a few blocks, Eve feeling fresh air on her face—well, as fresh as Manhattan could get: a heady mixture of smoke, autumn leaves, a belch of coal dust, roasted nuts from street vendors, and horse droppings.

"It's funny that we're heading this direction"—the detective gestured ahead—"into my father's old haunts, long before I was born."

"Oh?"

"My parents met, actually, in the theatre community. Father was a mediocre magician while in school for his higher degrees, and he needed an assistant. My great aunt played yenta and roped my mother in for the task, knowing they'd be perfect for one another. Once he got his first of three degrees, they married and left the circuit, but the love of it never quite left their hearts."

"That's wonderful and makes your family story even more interesting," Eve said as they turned onto Broadway, south of Astor Place.

Once Eve turned the corner, she stopped dead, holding out her arm, and the detective ran right into it. A devilish looking figure was surrounded by images of the macabre and the divine at war, devils pitted against angels, with an imperious figure between. The huge bill outside the theatre in front of them read:

THE AMAZING MULCIBER!

"*Mulciber*, from Zinne's letters," the detective and Eve chorused, turning to one another with excitement.

Eve glanced at the theatrical bill then withdrew a small golden watch and chain from the breast pocket she'd insisted be sewn into her uniform for convenience. "And we're just in time for the matinee!"

"It's like there's order in the chaos," Horowitz said triumphantly and approached the ticket counter without missing a beat.

Magic. Eve could feel the word pressing on the back of her skull, the spirits searing their bidding into her ears, begging her not to miss patchwork clues finally leading somewhere.

She closed her eyes, pressing the bridge of her nose, trying to reroute the building tension. When she opened her eyes again, Horowitz was standing before her with tickets in one hand and two fresh pretzels in the other—an angel of practical things.

"*You're* the inspiration," she declared, realizing when she looked at the treat how hungry she was. She seized the pretzel as if she were a raptor, bits of salt flying onto the cobblestones.

Once inside the narrow building, patrons milling about in the lobby with its vaulted ceiling awash in red lighting, Eve considered the theatrical poster hung at the fore. A bright lithograph sported The Great Mulciber in a flowing robe, arms outstretched, shoulder-length dark hair billowing in a dramatic wind, an angelic host behind him. His beard was trimmed to a sharp point, bushy eyebrows swept back to heighten the effect of his bulging eyes. At the edges of the poster, lightning bolts came down from a thundering sky.

The text of the poster was typical overindulgence and exaggeration:

A guided journey through the vast Inferno! Only the Great Mulciber can protect you!

Come see choirs of angels! Witness the magnificence of heaven and hell! To which kingdom will YOU be sent??

Other than the fear of hell or the promise of heaven, Eve wasn't sure what Mulciber's trick was. What kind of magician or faux spiritualist was he? A mentalist? An escape artist? Cards? Levitations? Swords? No real Spiritualist would boast such divine extremes.

"Any idea what we're in for?" Eve asked the detective as she finished the last of her pretzel and they entered the back of the house.

"Was just going to ask you the same thing. My parents aren't in touch with the new generation of talents, and I've never heard of this one. But it looks to have Dante's bent. Inferno imagery was rife in those letters to Zinne."

The curtain lifted, and the audience gasped at the spectacle. Instead of starting with the poet Virgil leading Dante first through Hell, then Purgatory, then Paradise, they were starting with Heaven first.

The stage was filled with a heavenly, three-dimensional assembly clearly inspired by the engravings of Gustave Dore in his illustrated edition of the *Divine Comedy*. Wax figures of cherubim and seraphim in rich robes of spectacular color, heads crowned with spiking metal halos, their fabricated forms posed on graduated risers from foreground to background of the stage, all leaned in toward a golden arch. Lighting, presumably electric given the steadiness of the small bulbs, lit the arch in an almost painfully bright arc.

Some of the angelic figures carried musical instruments, some papers upon which proclamations were writ; others bore impressive, fully outstretched wingspans, and still others had wings hidden behind close-pressed forms. All gave attention to the vacant center stage. The backdrop was of a blue sky with painted clouds; other clouds were hung from scrims at varying distances to heighten depth and perspective. Everything had a circular arc reminiscent of Dore's vision of concentric rings of angels leading toward God. A trumpet blast blared.

A small wax figure of a winged cherubim, rendered in quite remarkable detail, was lowered from the rafters, and a catch was released, allowing the scroll the cherubim carried to unfurl, revealing a written proclamation:

"Hark! Ye who stand at the gates of Heaven! Will you applaud to gain entrance?"

A roar of applause came in response.

Timpani drums offstage rumbled. Cymbals crashed. The golden arch on stage brightened. Eve had to nearly turn away, sliding her tinted glasses more tightly up her nose in protection.

The Great Mulciber appeared from an explosion of yellow-and-white smoke, garnering a gasp and round of applause as he stepped out of the colored mist and into the glow of the footlights in a flowing white garment, his head bedecked with laurels.

"Welcome, fellow travelers!" the man said in a booming voice, a crisp London accent. The performer did have a certain compelling presence.

"I am your guide on this journey," he continued, his voice echoing through the hall in a keen use of acoustics. "Through *me* all things are possible."

"How aggrandizing," the detective muttered. "I thought that was God's purview." It was clear from the detective's frown that he found something disturbing about the man.

But the sheer spectacle of it couldn't be denied.

"O the troubled state of man," Mulciber opined. "Sinners, all, we yearn for heaven. Each of us, coming here tonight to partake of this journey, thinks we're going here when we die. We ache for the angels to welcome us. There is not just a hope of heaven, but a *promise…*"

Mulciber stalked the stage floor, drinking in the angelic host around him. He stopped. He whirled on the audience, those bushy-browed eyes bulging as in his poster.

"Should. You. Be. So. Lucky."

His booming voice of welcome turned threatening. Suddenly the lights shifted to red and another smoky explosion surrounded Mulciber. The angels' feathery wings turned to those of a bat or gargoyle, some trick of released fabric or a projection from the lighting, Eve couldn't be sure, but she couldn't blame the many audience members who screamed at the admittedly dizzying, frightening turn. The man stepped out from the smoke again, his white cape exchanged for a black one.

"At any time, in any place, we may take one wrong step, one wrong turn, and find ourselves DAMNED." The word echoed through the rafters and back.

Why so many of the spiritualist acts were so popular was that so many of them focused on the macabre, demons alighting around the presenter, offering the crowd a titillation, not a spiritual experience. Mulciber was exploiting the drama and draw of the beyond, preying on the human need to feel safe even when flirting with terror.

"Travel with me through the hellfires as we experience unknowable depths," Mulciber said alluringly, and with a wave of his hand, the stage again transformed. "See here the frozen lake as reported by great Dante...." The set became an icy pass, and the angels appeared to fly away into wings and upper rails, leaving Mulciber nearly alone on stage save for the set's interior proscenium, whose bright lights had gone a dimmer setting.

"The careless may fall into the mouth of Lucifer himself, presiding over this miserable void...." He opened his wide flowing robes as if it were a great flap of wings as another plume of smoke engulfed him and he turned away from the stage. He jumped and seemed to fall through the floor. The audience screamed and cymbals crashed. The lights flickered as if embroiled in a lightning storm.

A figure stepped out into what appeared to be midair from the other edge of the stage. Mulciber, arms upraised triumphantly.

"But I am no match for the devil himself; I shall pass."

Riotous applause. Admittedly, that was an incredible illusion, and she didn't know how he managed it.

Another few changes of scenery focused on various hellscapes. Mulciber offered no Purgatory as Dante had posited, only Heaven or Hell, a binary afterworld of contrast presented purely for the effect of diametric poles, and he, floating up and down the extremes.

There was a return to Heaven, the magic of shifting sets, structures disappearing and reappearing. It was easy to lose oneself in the wonder of it. Eve glanced at the detective, who remained engaged but with his brow furrowed, as if he were running everything the act was doing through a sequence of questions and a bitter taste came with the answer.

As she turned back to the stage where Mulciber was attempting an ascension to a different divine level, quoting Dante as he went, something occurred to her. Eve had been so focused on the constant and overwhelming change of spectacle and scenery that she could not immediately pinpoint what else was wrong.

None of it was *haunted*. A show like this was bound to gather spirits, if nothing else but as spectators. But nothing within stirred. Something like this would have half of haunted New York weighing in about the realities of the afterworld. Something was flat, stale, dead. The performance, or possibly not even that, but the *setting* was terribly off, and she had no idea how to articulate it. Her Sensitivities deemed the whole thing sour but with no proof of why.

The next part of the show was a distinct departure, a set of psychic and mesmerist stunts.

He went around to people in the audience and told them something about themselves. In each case, there were screams, shouts, fainting, or joyous laughter. The reactions appeared genuine, especially from the patrons' companions, who seemed equally flabbergasted.

A few volunteers were then brought up from the audience to the stage and bid to stand in the front, far from the clawing reaches of the devils behind them.

"Now," Mulciber bellowed. "Resist my mesmerism! Try to refuse my demand!"

Turning to the audience, he added, "I will overcome them."

Standing to the side, Mulciber lowered a staff as if it were a lever pressing them down. He drove every volunteer to their knees as if pushing them down himself.

"Within the fires the spirits are; each swathes himself with that wherewith he burns," Mulciber quoted from the *Inferno*, adding eerily, "But no, friends, we cannot let you burn...."

If Eve wasn't mistaken, two of the audience members brought to the stage for this display were actually reduced to tears. It seemed cruel. In his final moment, Mulciber quoted instead from the *Paradiso*, asking of the audience as if it were the heavens:

"O soldiery of heaven, whom I contemplate, Implore for those who are upon the arth!"

The audience uneasily clapped for those who were on their knees. With another explosion of smoke, the entire affair disappeared behind the red house curtain as it fell dramatically. The audience was left gasping, turning to riotous applause as no one seemed sure what else to do.

The curtain rose with a trumpet blast, revealing the set of the heavens once more. Applause crested as the participants returned, dazed, to their seats. After a number of bows, Mulciber retreated and the red house curtain closed once more.

There was no way for Eve to prove what he was doing one way or another, but it was indeed an elaborate production.

After the house lights returned the orchestra level to a warm glow, Horowitz and Eve sat staring at the red curtain. Patrons around them rose and exited, murmuring amazement all the while.

"I can't put my finger on what made my skin crawl," Eve finally declared with a shudder, "other than the fact that I keep thinking of Ingrid's 'canonized' body. She'd have made a perfect addition to that stage set; she wouldn't have looked remotely out of place."

"I was thinking the same thing," the detective replied.

"The power of a theatrical display can be haunting. But—" Eve glanced around. "Why wasn't this haunted? It should have been. Just like Dupont's viewing parlor and the Prenze mansion, the absence of spirits is noteworthy. In each case, something doesn't want spirits in."

"I kept wondering about the connection to that pamphlet and what it espoused," Horowitz added, rubbing his chin thoughtfully. "With Mulciber's name related, makes me wonder about the purpose of the whole show."

There wasn't a distinct takeaway other than being deeply disturbed, harrowed in a way she still couldn't articulate. Eve hated such vagaries. Something about it made her soul crawl as much as her skin.

Outside, Eve and the detective turned south to head downtown, and at the corner of the next block Eve nearly walked right through Maggie, but the ghost kept her pace and floated ahead of her.

"Hello, Maggie," she said quietly, loud enough for only the detective to hear. "Didn't have any interest in the theatre?"

"I tried to follow you but was pushed back," the ghost exclaimed. "The air around me flickered, and I was so terrified of being blinked out of existence that I flew up Broadway. I found a suffrage march in Union Square. A sea of white dresses and sashes. The spiritual tumult there, a sea of ghostly whitecaps cresting above the crowd, what a sight it was! You, more than anyone I've ever known," Maggie began excitedly, "champion the rights of the spirit world. But have you considered taking that even further? What if we could gain truly *universal* suffrage?"

Eve blinked at the spirit, glad to cleanse her palate of Mulciber's act. "Votes for ghosts?"

"Precisely!" Maggie clapped phantom hands. "We are *of* the universe, and we remain with you mortals to help in your limited sphere. What affects you affects us. We should be able to vote on what world we choose to remain in."

Eve turned to the detective. "After today's suffrage demonstration she saw in Union Square, Maggie suggests votes for ghosts," she explained before turning back to the phantom. "You realize there has been voting fraud involving the names of the dead in rosters already. This would face fierce opposition. How do we account for legitimate mediums and not paid frauds on the payroll of corrupt regimes to uphold an accurate count?"

"That's for your mortal mind to work out. We outnumber you, many to one, remember. Votes for ghosts!" Maggie declared and flew back up toward the rallying crowd, whose shouts Eve could hear many blocks away.

Maggie seemed so delighted by the prospect that Eve didn't want to crush her enthusiasm. But the suffrage movement's shortcoming remained that it placed needs of *some* women above the rights of others, telling the rest "in due time" while disenfranchising them. For Eve, it was all women or it wasn't a win. And yes, ghosts too, if her work could change minds.

Eve chuckled. "Votes for ghosts. I admire her optimism, of course. The reason Maggie is so potent, why her spirit acts as close to a living being as I've yet encountered, is that she is so vitally concerned with and interested in the present moment. It keeps her vibrant and alive."

"Then I say votes for ghosts, to keep your friend at her best," Horowitz said with a smile. "And I've been a supporter of votes for *all* people from the beginning, just so we're clear."

"Good to hear. *Universal* suffrage," Eve said wistfully. "The whole possibilities of the universe; free to make its word its bond and its voice its vote is beautiful in theory."

Once they'd gone westward a few blocks, Eve gestured toward Washington Square Park ahead. "I should get back home for dinner; my colleagues will still be out, and it would be good of me to make food for a change. We try to have an even division of labor, but Antonia's such a good cook, the rest of us are so reluctant."

"She's…had a difficult life, to get to this point? There's something about her, an expression, it speaks of a deep loss. Was she orphaned?"

"In a manner of speaking. Do I have your complete confidence?"

"Of course."

Eve explained to the detective how Antonia had joined the precinct after appearing on her doorstep one night, having been led there by spirits she communed with for the sake of her safety. Her sex as assigned had been unreflective of her person, and she had needed to leave a hostile place before further damage was done.

"I see," Horowitz replied. "I didn't know she had ever been considered otherwise; one is who they are, after all."

"Thank you, Detective, we are agreed and you are a balm. Shall we meet again soon?"

"Any new news, I'd like to hear it. Whoever has it first, be the first to come calling."

"Thank you for today, Jacob, truly, I…" She lingered on the corner, hesitant to turn away, wanting to tell him just how much she enjoyed every moment in his company.

"And you, Eve. I…find the time passes quickly with you. Too quickly."

"Until *soon*, then," she said and forced herself to turn away and not look back, casting her blushing cheeks and schoolgirl smile down at the ground, biting her lip lest she giggle like a fool.

That night the team filled one another in, conversing over a bland soup Eve had made that everyone was too gracious to complain about.

Eve discussed everything she'd seen, including the Mulciber show and how it unnerved her. Her three mediums shared their experiences with the families and at the gravesites. In nearly every case, something was off about the grave or about the body that left all of them ill at ease, and in each case, family members—usually siblings and fellow children—had brought it to police attention but nothing had either been followed through on or found as any evidence of mistreatment, desecration, or foul play. In most cases, it was the age-old injustice of children not being heard.

It was clear that Dupont's harvesting of souvenirs had created a terrible rift in the spirit world—it just wasn't clear why, or what, if anything, the unseen Montmartre had to do with it. The children were of no help locating Greta Schwerin.

Eve dreamt that night of plummeting from Heaven to Hell, with small children's hands tearing at her skin until she bled red paint.

Chapter Nine

Sergeant Mahoney, the man who had taken the liberty to lodge complaints against their department on behalf of the Prenze family, was at their precinct door the next morning, waiting for them, hat in hand. He'd been an initial architect of their trouble.

Eve stiffened upon sight of him, her fists clenched and raised slightly, as if bracing for a physical fight. Her colleagues stopped short a pace behind her out of respect for the precedent she had set at the beginning of their precinct: Eve had demanded all complaints or confrontations went through her first. She insisted it was her duty and mission, and she was adamant about taking the full brunt of any heat, as she wielded the best advantage of privilege to do so.

"Hello, sir," she said calmly. "What can I do for you?"

"Miss Whitby, ladies." He bobbed his head, acknowledging their quartet. "You can listen, if you will, to something I have to say. I have been sent to offer you an apology."

"Oh?" Eve strode forward and turned the key in the lock of her office door. Reaching in to turn on the electric lights, she waited for their flicker and buzz to illuminate the space, glancing in to see if the room was as it should be. The recent spate of poltergeists gave her pause. All was in place. Eve stepped back to wave him inside. "Being 'sent to offer an apology' doesn't bode well for you *wanting* to give one."

"I had a long chat with Mr. Prenze, Miss Whitby. And I do owe you"— he turned to the rest of the team—"and you, young ladies, an apology."

"Ah," Eve said crisply. Alfred Prenze had had a talk with him after all.

As they entered, the usual precinct ghosts, minus Vera, were present, but they wafted to their corners and between the file cabinets, inserting themselves as part of the furniture until they were called forth into service. That was their custom whenever a visitor came to their office.

Jenny went to the coal stove, started a fire, and put on a kettle.

"Well then, we're listening," Eve prompted, gesturing the sergeant to sit in a chair opposite her desk at the fore of the room. She perched on the edge of the desk, keeping herself elevated above him, refusing to be intimidated, no matter if he had been part of the plot to abduct and test her or not.

"I am sorry for…making trouble for you," he said quietly.

Eve leaned forward. "Why, besides the fact that we're women, don't you like us?" She gestured to the unmarked door that had previously borne her title and the gilded letters of The Ghost Precinct before being wiped clean to throw people off their tracks. "We've been demoted merely to secretarial work, so I hope you're happy."

Mahoney squirmed in his chair. "It isn't that I don't want you to have work…I was being overprotective."

"What is it, then?"

"You have to understand, I…I was out of work, I was drinking myself to death. Prenze found me outside his mansion one night, and I don't know what made him take me in rather than call the cops on me, but he must have seen the pain in my eyes. I got right with myself, God, my family, and set out to help his."

Eve let this sit a beat. "So that's why you're so loyal to that family."

"Yes, to Alfred Prenze specifically."

"You filed a complaint first, but then it escalated," Eve said bitterly. The sergeant cocked his head to the side as if unsure what she meant. "You think our precinct a sacrilege, worth threats and violence?"

"I think it's highly questionable, but I wouldn't go threatening anyone about it."

Eve showed him the notes that had been left with her after Gran's abduction and their group unconsciousness, sliding the screaming threats in bold type across the desk. "Do you know anything about these?" She pressed them into his hands. "Are they familiar?"

Mahoney's eyes widened, and he shook his head, setting the notes down and shoving them across to her side. "Again, I've a…certain thought about some folks who claim to be Spiritualists. They robbed my wife before she… Well, that's no one's business but hers, but I wouldn't go threatening you like this. If I wanted to shut you down, I'd continue with complaints and put you to rout through the system." His fierce face softened. "But I won't trouble you further—"

"What about a finger sent to my office?" Eve quipped. "A severed finger in a box I assume was also a warning. That came in before the abduction."

Mahoney sputtered and crossed himself. "No. That certainly wasn't me! Heavens."

"You made a complaint that I was meddling with Prenze," Eve pressed. "However, please understand, I never authorized any of my ghosts to go into Prenze's mansion. I learned after the fact that one of them did go there, but not on my orders. However, when they were there, they were treated very poorly. In fact, Prenze tried to kill her. Again."

"I…I don't understand."

"It's hard to explain when it comes to ghosts. But there's something going on with that family that is…more complicated than you might know. I want the best for everyone, please understand that. Do you think there's something dangerous surrounding the family? Because I do. And your favorite Mr. Prenze might think so too, even if he can't articulate it."

Mahoney's expression went distant in recollection. "Mr. Prenze, during one of his troubled moments, mentioned there had been something unsettling, an actual spectral visitation. He very much wasn't himself. He was about to throw a party and said he wouldn't be needing me, so I went along to join my superior at a function. That was the very night I learned about your precinct at that to-do with the governor when you were announced at the club. So I just put those things together. The Prenzes don't like ghosts, you see. Albert in particular was terribly haunted by his mother. The stuff to give anyone nightmares, that."

Albert's passionate dislike of specters, as the living Prenze had mentioned, was certainly motive enough to try to stop Eve and her department—and the ghosts working for them.

"I admit," Mahoney continued sheepishly, "when I learned about you, I was not fond of the idea. So naturally I assumed the visitation at the Prenze mansion and the opening of your precinct was related. The Prenze family did some questionable dealings in their early days, I found out, through another rival company that wanted to do them harm. It's why I was taken on as extra security. There have been extant threats in play for years now, but they'd finally died off when the Prenze twin went to Europe. But then…"

He paused as Jenny brought him a cup of coffee, her personal one, with lucky four-leaf clovers on it. "Thank you, little one," he said warmly, looking at the cup and smiling. "Luck of the Irish, even." An unexpected tear in his eye. When the man spoke to Jenny, any sourness he'd ever had vanished into thin air.

"But then?" Cora prompted.

Mahoney's face reddened. "No, I'm gossipin'. It's wrong to speak ill of the dead."

"Not if the living are being treated ill," Eve countered gently. "And I do believe many are. *We* have been treated ill. It might continue if we're not careful. I also fear for Alfred Prenze. I'd love to clear it all up, so thank you for any insights you can share."

The sergeant sighed. "Mr. Prenze, Alfred, was worried when his brother went to Europe. Alfred told me Albert was developing interests he feared weren't in the common good. Science that bordered on sacrilege and art that bordered on the profane. But when he died in the industrial accident... No one was the same after that, it seems."

"Do you have any idea what happened? Regarding the accident?"

Mahoney shrugged. "It was said there was a chemical reaction. A building exploded. A charred body was found within."

Which could easily, Eve thought, have been another body planted therein to specifically throw off any case. The undead twin remained the heart of the problem.

"Was there any police inquiry into the death?"

"That would've been under Scotland Yard's oversight. It happened in London. The family was devastated, especially Miss Prenze, who has always been devoutly religious, doting on her brothers. She went into deep, inconsolable mourning. I heard nothing more about Alfred's concern for Albert's pursuits. Their recent ball was the only time I've seen Miss Prenze happy since Albert died. I will admit, there have been some confusing moments."

"With the family?"

The sergeant nodded. "I'll think I have a certain marching order, and then it will change. I was sure Prenze wanted me to pressure you, and now he seems horrified as if he never said the thing in the first place, but he did."

"Has he been in his right mind?" Eve pressed.

"He's had episodes. Fainting spells. If you ask me, I think sometimes they rely too much on the tonics. All of them did."

Eve glanced at her girls. Jenny squinted her right eye; code for telling the truth, as Eve sensed too, but she never took her own instinct as gospel. Being psychic in a precinct capacity meant she needed multiple confirmations to count as empirical evidence. In this moment of vulnerability and tepid trust, Eve shifted a bit closer to the man and dropped her voice.

"As a fellow police employee, may I enlist you in a bit of surveillance that I *promise* is for Alfred and Arielle Prenze's own good?" He looked at her with a complex, anxious expression. He wanted to trust her, but he wasn't sure. "We have very good reason to suspect someone is manipulating the surviving Mr. Prenze. There's a possibility it could be someone from within the family."

"Well not Miss Prenze; she's an absolute angel."

"I'm sure she is, but we have to keep all options open," Eve insisted

"You can count on me as an additional eye lookin' out for these concerns *and* for you. That's what I promised Mr. Alfred Prenze as a way to make up for bein' hard on ye in the beginning."

"Thank you," Eve said earnestly. "To have someone willing to make amends in a place that I don't generally feel welcome, it means a lot."

"The force is full of proud men reluctant to change. I know I have been. Mr. Prenze allowed me to see that. Women in the force, near the force, it's a change. The idea of the supernatural, no less? Change. I'm not saying take any guff from any of 'em, but I say keep being yourself. Be proud in turn and refuse to budge."

"We will," Cora said with steeled calm.

Eve was aware there were other charged aspects here for her colleagues. Antonia had kept herself poised and stoic in the corner, reading a historic case log pulled from the cabinets. Mahoney hadn't paid her any mind.

"Going forward," Eve stated, "if you agree Mr. Prenze is being manipulated and his 'episodes' are in fact being brought on by an oppressor, we can help. My spirit assets are willing to be additional sources of information, but ghosts are curiously blocked from Mr. Prenze's house."

"Ah, no, it would be best if Mr. Prenze doesn't feel haunted," Mahoney cautioned. "But I will let you know if there's something I can untangle. Just promise you won't go after the man."

"You are a police officer," Eve countered. "If you found out he had broken the law, wouldn't you do everything in your power to ensure justice?"

"Of course."

"Thank you for your help," Eve stated, putting out her hand, which he shook. "Go in peace."

Mahoney bobbed his head. "And you, ladies." He offered a lingering glance at Jenny before he turned away. At the door, he spoke in a pained voice, not looking at any of them. "I…I had a little girl. She died. It's…why I took to drinking and why my wife ended her life. The idea of contacting spirits in a séance is a balm, but in reality…"

Ah, Eve thought with new understanding as he trailed off. Charlatans only exacerbated the pain of death, and he'd clearly had no good experiences with real Sensitives.

"I...I was trying to follow them both to the end," Mahoney continued sadly, "through the drink, until Prenze made me feel there was something to this miserable world again."

"I'm sorry for your loss," Eve said as he paused at the door. He nodded and walked out.

We could hold a séance for them, Jenny signed to Eve, gesturing that she could run after him and offer. Tears of empathy were in the little girl's eyes, but Eve shook her head.

"It would be too much now, love. Perhaps once a better bridge is built," Eve said.

Cora was staring ahead, arms folded. The fact that Cora didn't trust easily was a great help to Eve, whose blind spots sometimes had to be pointed out to her. She was trying to read a greater perspective in the moods and the words of her colleagues, who had all suffered to get to her and lived lives of struggle outside of their camaraderie in ways she hadn't known or experienced directly.

Eve turned to her séance table. The stack of file folders had been opened and shifted, the interior of the files scattered. It wasn't the way they'd been left.

"Who did that?" Eve asked her colleagues. They all shook their heads.

"Dear spirits," Eve said to the room. "We haven't forgotten you. Please bear with us."

"Not every name here correlated with our graveyard search," Cora stated, gesturing to the files. "There are many names we could not yet make connections to."

Some file folders flapped shut of their own accord. This unexpected and incorporeal action caused the women to jump back. Just because one worked with ghosts didn't mean they didn't startle regularly.

A sharp knock at the door made them jump again. McDonnell came in with a note.

"Relay from Irvington," she said, handing the folded slip over, giving Eve a little mock curtsy as she exited again.

Eve set her jaw, taking the paper. Because Eve was the daughter of a British lord, McDonnell always acted like Eve put on airs, when as far as she knew, she didn't. But she tolerated the caustic matron's teasing because she was trying to "toughen the girls up." The term matron had been established when the first women were allowed into the force in 1880, as a way to keep women in their place, to remind them what they *should* be. McDonnell's odd bullying had been defined as preparation to handle the rest of the force. They all, in their way, chafed against expectation, and Eve tried to see that as a backward sort of care, but she just scowled.

As Eve read the note, she rose and began gathering supplies. "Darlings, a lead. Come, we've a Hudson River train to catch! The Irvington precinct has found Mrs. Dupont's maiden family—the Vree residence. We must make inquiries."

Eve gathered up a canvas bag with a few provisions, took some bills out of her desk, and waited patiently for everyone to put on capelets, jackets, hats, and gloves.

The trolley to Grand Central Depot was swift.

"In each file," Cora explained as they boarded a northbound train and took their seats, "something went wrong with a child's funeral or burial. Either a disturbance or an irregularity." She pulled out her notebook as the team settled in on either side of her, tapping a page scrawled with notes as she thought. "Dupont's name wasn't necessarily in each file, but his name was noted as having done at least a part of the funerary arrangements in several. We have to find out what they seek from us now. Even they don't know. I can't make any better sense of it than the pieces they keep saying they're in. It's maddening."

Eve had neither felt nor seen her team quite so frustrated, a solution just out of reach. Cora, out of everyone Eve knew, liked to be a step ahead, and this situation was her worst nightmare.

"Keep Dupont in focus," Eve bolstered her team. "Despite Greta declining help or rescue, we must try. The dynamic is dangerous, and Greta isn't in her right mind. This is the first living lead we've had, so we've got to get something out of Mrs. Dupont."

"Let's just hope the wife is nicer to you than last time," Antonia added.

"Oh, I highly doubt that—she'll likely be worse." Eve braced her team for the encounter.

Jenny signed an unpleasant word for the lady, and Eve sputtered a laugh.

The team fell quiet as they stared out the lace-curtained windows. The steam billowed from the depot, and the train screamed along. As the city changed around them, spreading out from its clusters to open lots and grassy knolls, Eve unpacked her bag, and the colleagues partook of the bread that Antonia had made while Cora went to the dining car and brought them back a round of seasonal spiced apple cider in small paper cups.

When the train came around a bend, soaring above the Hudson River Valley, the four colleagues gasped. The autumn splendor of New York, in its varied and spectacular colors, was on full, dramatic display:

an unrivaled landscape. Eve had just seen it with Maggie, but it was breathtaking every time.

"Heaven," Antonia murmured, and everyone nodded. There wasn't a better word for it. The bright golden leaves against the flaming crimson, with burgundy and evergreens, the depth of field, the wending river, and the sheer scope of dramatic land was ceaselessly stunning. Even the fellow passengers on what was usually a lively, talkative line were all staring out the window, transfixed by late autumn splendor and intoxicated by spiced cinnamon on the air.

Reluctant to get off the train as each turn and widening, multicolored vista of the Hudson winding on was a new delight, Eve wanted to keep drinking in the beauty until sundown. But there were much-needed clues ahead, and her body ached for progress: something to ease the painful pressure of the restless dead that made her skull feel as addled and untethered as their transparent forms.

Wincing at the squeal of the train whistle at the Irvington station, Eve glanced at the instructions handed over from the relay that described turning off Main and toward the river. She led the way along a lane curving away from the small station, and it was only a convenient few minutes' walk until a charming, picturesque lane and a two-story house with Tudor timbers appeared before them, *Vree* posted prominently on an ornate brass mailbox in the front lawn.

Antonia noticed a children's playing area at the end of the block, a wooden merry-go-round, with a group of girls in pinafores and mothers or minders in day dresses and parasols.

Jenny gestured to the area, signing back to Eve. *There may be clues only I can get, there.*

Without a word needing to be said, Jenny pulled on Antonia's hand, their bond as surrogate sisters replacing what had been ripped away unbreakable, and Antonia accompanied the girl down the block, glancing back to Eve with a smile as she tapped her ear, signaling that she'd be listening spiritually, psychically as well as materially—mothers gossiped while watching children play.

The routine that had developed was quite helpful, as it was too much for four investigators to expect a comfortable welcome in an interview, and it had become custom for Eve and Cora to take the lead while Antonia and Jenny assessed the surroundings. And perhaps Jenny just wanted to play with little girls her own age for a moment and forget that circumstances had forced her to become an adult far too soon. Antonia, expert at the art of care, enjoyed tending to everyone's emotional health.

Eve lifted a hefty doorknocker and let it fall, echoing into the hall within. Cora hung back until she had a better read of safety and openness. Cora was light skinned and didn't often face the most direct vitriol, but there were often indirect cruelties and countless little cuts of aggression. Eve would always stand in the way to nip those in the bud, and Cora never backed down, but one had to be *en garde*.

A petite brunette maid in a black dress with a starched white apron and bonnet that was tucked low on her forehead to shade weary-looking eyes came to the door, anxiously recognizing them immediately from their first inquiry back at Gramercy.

"Why are you here?" she whispered.

Not the response of a place that had nothing to hide.

"We're here to speak to Mrs. Dupont," Eve said.

"She's not feeling well; she can't take visitors—"

"We won't be but a moment," Eve reassured with a smile. "Please tell her we must speak with her." Eve leaned in, matching the maid's murmur. "We'd really prefer not to involve the *actual* police in the matter."

The maid swallowed, gestured them in to wait, and scurried away.

The entrance hall was nice and wide, with light coming in from rooms accessible in either direction. Wood timbers and paneling were prominent features; plain burgundy carpet ran the length of the entrance hall toward back stairs and a large, arched window.

Framed photographs in the hall featured family standing before fine homes—modest but stately, a family that had done well enough for itself but didn't feel the need to boast it. Interspersed between the family portraits were framed catalogue covers featuring Vree family wood products: cabinets, paneling, features and more. Evidently Mrs. Dupont's maiden family was associated with logging, building, and décor.

The maid scurried back toward Eve and Cora, motioning them forward. "Through the parlor, in the atrium just beyond. I'll bring tea." She disappeared behind the stairs.

"Still so nervous. Hardly a good sign," Cora whispered near Eve's ear, and she nodded.

The parlor was open and sparse, but green fronds poking out from the archway beyond proved more dynamic. The adjoining atrium was a bright oasis of ferns and small hibiscus trees, potted ivy hung from decorative wrought iron rafters of the glass room, a cushioned bench stationed on each side of the long, conservatory room.

When Cora and Eve had first met Mrs. Dupont while making inquiries in Gramercy Park, the woman had been unwelcoming to say the least. This time, when she looked up from her knitting, she seemed tired, fragile, and a bit scared. The steely exterior was cracked.

"Please sit," she bid them. They did so on the bench opposite her.

"Mrs. Dupont, you may remember us—"

"Yes, you came to my house," she replied, cutting Eve off, "inquiring about one of my staff. Did they ever find the girl? The child?"

"They did," Eve said, bowing her head. "She died of tuberculosis."

"How sad," Mrs. Dupont said with a frown. "What brings you here? How did you find me?"

"We went to the house and the viewing parlor again, as we wanted to ask your husband some questions."

"About what?"

"A few…sensitive case materials. Nothing that would concern you, I'm sure, unless you noticed him with anyone lately or you were aware of any problems with funerals."

She sighed, waving a languid hand. "I don't know where he's gone. I haven't seen him in some time. When he shifted his work over to the viewing parlor, I saw him less and less—check there."

"That's empty too, so where is he operating out of now?" Upon Eve's question, the wife rocked back, her careful mask slipping to reveal shock. This was clearly news to her.

"I…I don't know. He told me we needed a change, that I should stay here with my family, and I made arrangements accordingly. My mother is here alone after the death of my father and this is…for the best. My husband and I have been…" She stared intently at fern fronds as she fought for words. "Distant for some time, so this is better for me." She reached out a trembling hand toward a hibiscus blossom, caressing it gently. "Less cold. Doesn't feel like I'm being watched all the time even though there's no one at the windows."

Eve glanced at Cora. There had indeed been ghostly eyes looking through the windows outside that Gramercy home. Waiting. Clearly they hadn't been waiting for Mrs. Dupont. Nothing haunted this place. Not even the precinct's spirit operatives had come along, since there was nothing to be gleaned that the living couldn't do themselves.

"Has my husband done something wrong?" Mrs. Dupont asked, turning away from the plants and staring down at her teacup.

Her tone of resignation gave Eve the confidence to continue gently. "You tell me."

"I…I don't know. Perhaps, but nothing I could put my finger on. Besides…"

"Besides what?"

"The girls," she muttered. There was a long silence. "A wife knows, of course. And…" There were sudden tears in her eyes. "I suppose I couldn't blame him. I couldn't conceive. I offered to raise one, from our first maid, years ago, as my own, but she left and took the child away."

"He had mentioned one of his children was grown," Cora said.

Mrs. Dupont laughed hollowly, waving a trembling hand. "Well, they would be at this point. Maybe he even visited it— I don't know if it was a boy or a girl."

"I'm sorry to be all indelicate—"

"This is an indelicate topic," Mrs. Dupont interrupted Cora crisply and took a sip of tea.

"Yes, and I wish it were otherwise," Eve took up the inquiry. "Was there any indication that your husband and Greta Schwerin…?"

Mrs. Dupont narrowed her eyes. "Oh, probably."

An uncomfortable silence was broken only when Eve cleared her throat.

"I'm very sorry to press. But Greta has gone missing, and we have reason to believe she may be with him."

Mrs. Dupont snorted. "Finally giving one of those poor things the runaway they were looking for? Then good riddance. I managed to set enough aside through the years that I could live on it entirely if I had to, if he abandoned me without another cent. I was wise enough with finances to set some aside in my family's accounts."

"We don't know for certain where they are," Eve offered. "That's why we're asking—"

"I don't know for certain either, so I'm sorry I can't be of any help." She rose and placed her teacup on a mahogany tea tray at the side of the room.

Eve knew they had only another moment before her welcome was revoked, so she pressed rapid-fire questions. "Montmartre. The partner at Irving Place, what can you tell us—"

"Never met him," Mrs. Dupont replied, fussing with the tray, not looking at them.

"Any idea where he lived?"

"At Irving, from what I understood, upper floors."

"Didn't you find it odd you'd never met?"

Mrs. Dupont turned to Eve with a frown. "My husband said Montmartre was a secretive man, but he paid in handsomely to the firm, so we didn't care. And once my husband moved the business to the parlor, I felt far more at peace, and so I simply didn't feel the need to be sociable if Montmartre didn't. Women aren't allowed into a man's business arrangements; my husband made that quite clear."

The woman's venom was palpable. Eve had to tread carefully. She noticed Cora trying to get a psychometric read on the house; her ungloved hand brushed across the bench.

"So, you've no idea where Montmartre could have gone either?"

"Back to Europe, I suppose? That's where they'd met, at an undertakers' conference in Belgium. Then he continued on to London, sharing the latest in chemicals," she said and shuddered. "Fill you with poison while you live and poison when you die," she muttered with a bitter chuckle. "That conference was sponsored by Prenze tonics, as I recall, right before the poor man died there in London. It was a whole to-do, that industry fire. My husband was sent home with an enormous case of the foul tonics— I told him to get them out of the house, sell them off to the grieving."

Eve and Cora shared a look.

Mrs. Dupont strode to the atrium threshold. "I'm tired and not feeling my best. That's all I know about any of this, which is to say, nothing more, so if you'll excuse me—"

"Does your husband have any other property?" Eve continued, rising along with Cora. They followed Mrs. Dupont into the sitting room.

"He was looking to establish a smaller parlor up the river line another fifteen minutes or so. He bought a scrap of land, but as far as I know he never built on it. But then again, I stopped paying attention." She turned toward the rear stairs in the entrance hall.

"See our guests out, Bette," Mrs. Dupont called to the maid sharply and disappeared up the stairs.

"Yes, ma'am." Bette waited until her employer was fully clear of earshot before she gathered Cora and Eve close and spoke in a hurried whisper as she ushered them out. "Don't tell the Mrs. I said this, as I'll get into a heap of trouble, but about Montmartre— I saw Dupont writing him a note a week before we came here. I'd accidentally spilled his tea as he was writing, and I dabbed across his blotter before he snatched the note away. I saw something like, 'A chapel in the woods holds half my treasures. I am assembling heaven.' Good luck on whatever you're doing, he always frightened me." She closed the door on them.

The nerves, fear, and bitterness of everyone involved spoke volumes about Dupont, Eve thought: a toxic environment.

They strode up the walk just as Antonia and Jenny, sensing them, had begun walking up the lane. All waited to speak until they turned back to Main Street and toward the station.

Cora and Eve shared what they had learned inside, about the children he had been having with maids—coerced most of them, surely, save perhaps Greta, who might have cared for him.

"Ingrid likely was Dupont's child?" Antonia asked.

Eve nodded. "And the European conference where Dupont met Montmartre was sponsored by Prenze tonics, right before Albert 'died.' So, the question is, who was that poor burned body in Albert's stead?"

Cora shared what the maid had said about Dupont's chapel, treasures, and assembling heaven. Everyone shuddered.

Antonia reached out and straightened Jenny's haphazard hair, retying the ribbon at the base of her braid as she spoke. "I looked after Jenny. The two women watching the other children didn't seem too concerned about me; they were talking about an old ghost story they'd heard as children, about spirits in the northern woods. One of them said they heard that recently the woods had become more haunted. That the ghosts were all looking for lost children."

"We can't just wander forested New York looking for a chapel," Eve grumbled. "If the ghosts knew where to look, they'd already have told us. All of us, still blocked."

Jenny signed to Eve that there were ghosts who came to spin with her on the merry-go-round, two little girls.

They said the undertaker took from them too, Jenny explained in sign.

"The common denominator in this spate of restless children is that Dupont took something?"

Jenny nodded.

"Did they happen to say where we could find Dupont, or any of their missing items?" Eve asked. Jenny shook her head. "That would have been too much to ask," she muttered, stepping up to the ticket counter at the station to procure tickets before returning to the group, speaking quietly so as not to arouse any curiosity from passersby.

"I'll send an inquiry about land holdings north of here and see if Dupont's name comes up. See if I can get a list of any chapels."

"Building heavens... So is this all a sort of religion for him?" Cora asked.

Eve nodded. "I think so, and Heinrich was following in his vein, offering up his own child. Just as I'd told the sisters at the Foundling Hospital where Ingrid's body was found, it wasn't meant as a horror but a tribute—but these men don't see how terrible it all is and how the spirits don't give their permission."

They kept mulling over details on the train ride back. It was that precarious part of ongoing investigations solely focused on gathering more and more information, a reactive stage that made Eve itch with restless anxiety, pent-up energy desperate to rush toward justice. But if rushed out of order or propelled in the wrong direction, she did no one, alive or dead, any good.

Chapter Ten

There was light and time enough after they returned to the city for Eve to update Horowitz. His perspective was different from Eve's, his contacts and context varied, and at this point, he deserved to know the nuances of any case he'd had a part in. Even if Eve couldn't be visible within the police department, Horowitz was, and he represented the best of what the force could be.

The moment she turned the corner of the rear hallway and saw his open office door, his head bent over his desk, his features half-lit by the lamp, she felt the little flutter that had become so consistent and so telling whenever she laid eyes on him. It was so pure a feeling that she was helpless to stop it; the dance of butterflies becoming addictive.

Pausing outside in the hall, she considered the fact that every time they'd been together of late, there had been a physical gesture that made her heart skip innumerable beats. What would it be next? She cautioned herself to keep a level head and to pace any action or sentiment.

His desk was littered with papers he was trying to sort into an organized stack as she knocked on the frame of his office door.

"Why do you keep the door open with such racket out here?" Eve asked, stepping in as he gestured her forward, grimacing at a howl down the hall. She took a seat opposite him.

"I make these men nervous, in every tired stereotype, so I'll not play into their paranoia of secreting things away. I keep myself and my door open because I have nothing to hide."

"Such nonsense shouldn't be borne." Another raucous yell from another corridor. She made a face. "It sounds like a zoo."

"Well, it is." He proffered a note and a newspaper. Eve reached out to take them. "After examining the empty apartment where Dr. Font was found dead and drowned in poison, I wrote Scotland Yard about it—he was a British citizen after all—and I finally managed to get a response."

Noting the seal, Eve read the brief note from a sergeant saying their force would look into the signing-off on the Prenze death, which had been verified in London, and any correlation to names of interest.

"Good work," Eve said eagerly. "If this stalls and you need an additional push, Gran knows someone there. At the very top."

Horowitz smiled. "Of course she does. How's the spectral front?"

Eve relayed Mahoney's odd turnabout and the results of the Irvington trip. Her frustration at not knowing the location of Dupont's "chapel of treasures" was evident, she couldn't keep it from her tone.

"This fresh connection of Montmartre, Dupont, and Prenze at a meeting before his 'death,' with Prenze as a sponsor, is noteworthy," Horowitz declared. "I'll add that to my next Scotland Yard query. And in terms of the larger pattern, I haven't been able to stop thinking about the Mulciber act and how it may relate to the sadistic side of this collection. I need to know how he fits in and what about that act got under our skin."

"I should write Houdini about it," Eve mused. "I want to keep in touch with him as a resource, and I want to know if he's seen the act and what he thinks. And the fact that Mulciber's name was in those letters connected to all these other men can't be a coincidence."

"While you await a response from the great escape artist, why don't you come and ask performers their thoughts tomorrow?" the detective asked. "I'm sorry— Asking you to an event tomorrow is sudden, but it entirely snuck up on me. My parents are helping host a soiree for the Yiddish theatre community down at the Thalia Theatre. The proceeds will benefit a community organization standing against discrimination and defamation. The guest list will include a host of magicians and personalities, entertaining and talented people…." He paused and leaned in, his expression sheepish. "And, I confess, my mother is giving me some…grief for not having met the woman I'm ostensibly courting, so it would give an opportunity—"

"Of course, I'd love to go and support such a magnificent cause, and I'd love to meet your family." She tamped down on her nerves. "I don't want to be a burden. I don't want our ruse to become a trouble for you with your family rather than a freedom—"

"You're hardly a burden." Looking away, he continued with halting, careful words. "And I want them to like you, and ruse or no…"

He seemed to want to go on. Eve felt her breath catch. Every time they spoke of their pretense it was as if they were discussing a delectable secret. Could either of them pretend the ruse in and of itself was the only thing that was attractive anymore? A flimsy veil shrouded a growing desire taking indelible root in Eve's body, her mind, her heart.

A sobering thought occurred to her. "I wonder if I should have a chaperone in this instance?"

"You're head of a department," he replied, as if such a societal formality for someone in her position shouldn't even need to be in question.

"On certain casework, yes—that's different. In society, I'm still beholden to being a virtuous, well-bred young lady. I must consider how everything appears from the standpoint of my age, position and expectations...."

The detective shrugged. "Open cases and perpetrators at large should offer us all the legitimacy we ever need to be seen together, beyond the courtship we've put into play. However, let's see if Rachel could join us. I've heard, thanks to the reconnection of our family due to your prompting, that she'll be in town for this event."

"That's a lovely idea; I mean, I can't wait to see her, I just—" She stopped herself from finishing the sentence with "want to be alone with you", not knowing what else to say in its place that wouldn't sound equally damning. She snapped her mouth shut and rocked on her feet.

"If there are any other performers you know," said Horowitz, always brilliant at coming to her aid in an awkward moment, "my mother has said 'more the merrier' for the cause."

"How about the Veil family?" Eve asked eagerly. "I don't know if they're back from England yet, but they're an asset to any performance." Nathaniel and Lavinia Veil were more than just Eve's godparents; they were soul guides. Their obsession with all things Gothic and eerie helped Eve understand her paranormal life as something to be celebrated, not feared.

"The Veils are already invited," the detective replied with a smile. "Nathaniel Veil has been instrumental in helping support a network of anti-discrimination alliances in England and here in New York. This gala represents a merger to form a better network."

Eve clapped her hands together in excitement. "The Veils have always been an inspiration to me. They don't want anyone to feel abandoned or oppressed, especially not the oft misunderstood eccentrics of the world." Eve smiled. "It was Lavinia Veil who said I should dress in black, not only to be fashionably Gothic, as she always does, but as a mark of respect for the ghosts—and she's right, it's helped my relationship with them. The

Veils and Gran helped me feel like I wasn't alone or out of place in this world. Was this gala your parents' idea?"

"No, just helping those they know on the circuit. My parents left performance long ago, but they do believe that the art is vital for social growth, community, and education."

Forcing bravado lest the butterflies in her stomach actually lift her body off her chair, Eve smiled. "I couldn't agree more. Your parents sound very interesting and agreeable."

"My father certainly is, always. My mother—she is a loving, dear woman who is fiercely protective of me. I have to keep reminding her I am a man of my own mind and vision."

"I understand, truly."

As nervous as his parents would make her, at least she could show genuine affection for their son. Before a voice within her could insist there was more than affection, she tamped down any such words. More would threaten her very existence.

Women were fine in the workplace unmarried. Once married, their place was then housewife and mother. That was the way of it. She couldn't play at any more than this slight flirting; nothing could come before the profession she was born to do. The thought of trading the spirits for a bit of worldly affection felt like a betrayal, and it sobered her.

"What is it?" he asked quietly. He was so attentive.

"Nothing." She couldn't be honest about where her affections were bending or her struggle; both were too much of a risk to reveal. "I just… hope I remember how to dance. It isn't my strong suit."

"You'll be fine in a good waltz, surely," he prompted. "You must give me at least that." He curved his mouth into an inviting smile. There was a beautiful hope that sparked in his brown eyes ringed with blue, such lovely gems that ignited emotions in her she'd never experienced. They kept staring at one another.

After the weight of their stare grew deeper and hotter, she let out an inelegant breath and he turned away with a cough. None of this was helping her resolve to remain detached.

"I will…give you that waltz," she said haltingly.

"In further news, the Font family has been more forthcoming," the detective said abruptly, shaking off the spell they'd put themselves in. "The cousin I initially spoke with had quite the reckoning with his family, and it yielded results. Font's brother came in from Connecticut—stopped by the precinct yesterday and gave me a full statement."

"Good for you. It's impressive that you get people to talk to you."

"I just try to relate to them. When you're not out acting like you're trying to win and leverage power over everyone at every turn, it's amazing the admissions people will trust you with." He passed pamphlets across the desk to Eve. "It seems Font became involved with two groups overseas before he came to New York after Prenze's presumed death. The brother found these in Font's London apartment."

Eve looked at the pamphlets. The first of the two pictured a diagram of a phrenology skull, a dubious and racially unjust pseudoscience, but the tract diverted into discussing the powers of the mind and asked what if the mind's inner workings could be recorded.

"The early studies are trying to map the brain," Eve said, "trying to tap into it like one might try to intercept a telegraph transmission. And I think that's related to the experiments done on Gran, Cora, and me, and to those boxes attached to my office, and likely other places of interest, that blocked gifts and spirits."

Eve perused the next tract, a familiar one. *Arte Uber Alles.* "Art over everything, again." The same tract found in Zinne's things. "I'm an enormous supporter of art. My grandfather is a cornerstone of the Metropolitan Museum, but I don't think *everything* is valid for the sake of art, without limit, without law, without balance or possible thought toward effect…. There has to be a limit."

"People make an art of cruelty all the time," the detective stated, and Eve nodded. "This seems to celebrate an abdication of personal responsibility that sets me on edge."

"Exactly."

"Font became obsessed with funerary art, his brother said. Memento mori and the like. He became close friends with undertakers and funeral directors, and the brother said that the last time he went to Dr. Font's flat, it looked like a graveyard. The brother mentioned a few names that Dr. Font was close with. I don't suppose you've a guess."

"Dupont and Montmartre," Eve stated.

Horowitz nodded. "The very ones. And our circle closes in."

Scared to death was what the spirits had said when they tried to get Dr. Font's spirit to engage with them in a séance, the first the detective had experienced. Font had gone too far, and it had caught up to him. It was all entwined. Of course. The spirits wouldn't have gotten them into this otherwise. Spirits, their eyes on flocks of sparrows, saw patterns the living missed.

The detective passed Eve a bound journal detailing the Font conversation. She perused his notes. One item in particular, written in the detective's beautifully neat script, struck her. *Possessive and possession.* "What do you mean by that?" she asked, pointing to the words.

"I think Font was trying to get too close to Dupont, and it made him and Montmartre nervous. I think Font wanted access to something Dupont had and was unwilling to share."

"What?"

"I don't know if it would be chemicals or something else."

"Access to bodies?" Eve posited with a frown. "Test subjects for the brain theory?"

"His brother said that the good doctor would go on and on about the human body being a work of art at every stage of its existence. Birth to death. And beyond, decay being an art too... In that crypt of a London apartment, Mr. Font said he saw countless daguerreotypes and photographs of decaying bodies set among flowers and beautiful sculptures of seraphs. He said the juxtaposition was dizzying. When the doctor 'fled' to New York, he sold everything in the apartment. As far as the family could tell, he took nothing with him but some bottles of tonic, his doctor's bag, and a change of clothes. Seems he'd burned some things in a metal tub."

Eve bit back a curse. "What a shame. Cora and her psychometry might have been able to make something from some of that."

As Eve frowned, the detective smiled suddenly. "Tomorrow at six, be ready for the event. I can officially call upon you at your parents' house, if you like?"

"Let's not involve them this time. Meet me at the southeast corner of Washington Square and we can hail something there. Ordinarily I'd say we could walk the, what, twenty blocks or so? But not if I'm in silk, trapped by finery."

Horowitz chuckled. "Noted. We can catch up on any news while winding our way down to the corner of Canal and Bowery. I'll have Rachel await us outside; then we can go in together, appearing as if you've been chaperoned all the while."

Eve offered a prim smile as she thrilled at the idea that he might, just the same, want a moment alone with her too. Carefully arranged, his cue—subtle. A slow unwinding. She wanted to revel in their affinity, but the lingering questions of the strange cases and the unsettled children didn't allow her such an indulgence or enjoyment. Nerves ate away at her mind and body. The detective was a welcome respite, but purpose and unfinished business ruled her.

"Until then, Detective," she said quietly, rising to her feet.

He bowed his head. "Until then, Whitby."

Once home, Eve found her colleagues around the séance table. The candle at the center was smoking. The spiritual door had just been closed as she entered. Her team looked up at her as she stood at the open threshold of the parlor.

"What have I missed?" Eve asked.

"We still can't find Vera," Cora stated. "She was drawn into Dupont's house in Gramercy, by presumably little Ingrid's spirit, yes?"

"Yes. She threw Ingrid's death portrait into the hall, where it was picked up by Mrs. Dupont, who recognized it as another person's child. An unraveling of trust and truth."

"Do you think Vera's trying to help Greta and has some idea where she's gone? Maybe has gone after her and doesn't dare leave her?" Antonia asked.

"Maybe," Eve said, trying to rally in that hope even though the growing unease made her feel sick to her stomach. "I hope she reappears with something specific. A location. A trail."

Zofia was circling the sides of the parlor: spiritual pacing.

"There must be some kind of a device on all of the buildings spirits have been kept from," Maggie stated. "I should ferret them out. Then you should get Gran's electrical friend to dismantle them. Maybe something zapped Vera out as it tried to do to me."

"Maggie, what about checking the Sanctuary for Vera?" Eve asked with a sudden excitement.

The ghost's eyes widened. "I shouldn't. Remember, Eve, it's not a place one just comes and goes from."

Eve didn't press; instead, she withdrew the pamphlet from Font's things and placed it on the séance table. "*Arte Uber Alles*, ring a bell to anyone?" The spirits and mediums shook their heads. "Can you try to ask around, gain any kind of insight about it for me?"

The spirits nodded, and Cora fluttered her hand toward the tract. "I can do a psychometric read on the paper, but tomorrow, if you don't mind, leave it there and I'll attend to it after I return from Jersey. Time to rest after a long day."

"There's stew for you in the kitchen, Eve," Antonia said. "We went ahead and ate because we didn't know how long you'd be."

"Of course. Thank you."

The girls said good night, and Eve ate leftover stew, brewed herself a cup of tea with herbs and roots known to aid in sleeping, and lay down to do a bit of automatic writing, picking up on phrases from the spirit world, but was out before she knew it.

Chapter Eleven

A sharp pain radiating down her neck woke Eve, and she came to the next day with it already being early afternoon, her cheek on a notebook. She rubbed the crease that had been imprinted there and rolled her stiff shoulders.

Eve had slept so deeply she remembered nothing, but there was one phrase she'd managed to parse out from the constant murmurs emanating from the spirit world before the effects of the tea took her. She had managed a sloppy scrawl on her journal page.

Pieces. Put our pieces together. In heaven and hell.

And never forget; don't let anything in.

The pieces were clear enough; that had to mean the bits and tokens Dupont had stolen. They had to be recovered. She was chilled by the latter caution, a direct repetition of spiritual warnings from the first moments Maggie had disappeared had returned to haunt her again. She couldn't help but think of the figure outside her window, that terrible shadow. What if it tried to get in? If it was in her mind, it already was....

She shook herself loose from the grip of the words and listened to the sounds of the house. It was very quiet.

Cora was out visiting an ill relative and had taken Jenny with her, who had never seen New Jersey and was curious. Eve tried never to work her colleagues on weekends unless there was an emergency, and with no clear picture on Greta, it made no sense to keep anyone. Considering the precinct spent so much time together, it had been agreed that everyone would go their separate ways if a breath was needed.

Antonia was in the parlor with a new deck of tarot cards when Eve came down for breakfast, frying herself eggs and preparing a steaming mug of coffee. She didn't want to disturb Antonia, so she nearly slipped by her once she was finished.

"What's on your docket for today?" Antonia asked as Eve passed in the hall.

Thinking about the night ahead, Eve paused at the threshold and realized she had no idea what to wear. Nerves flooded her in a mixture of exhilaration and terror. "Family friends are in town, and I'm very much looking forward to seeing them at a charity function."

"That's nice!"

"And you?"

"I've been invited to do a reading for some artists near the university this evening. I'm hoping that if they don't know about *Arte Uber Alles* they might know someone who does. I'll be sure not to encourage anyone to it, that's certain."

"Brilliant. Are you advertising your services?" Eve took a step closer, narrowing her eyes. "How did they know to contact you?"

Antonia laughed. "You're delightful when you're overprotective!"

Eve thought a moment about how she must have come across. "I'm sorry," she began, contrite. "You're your own woman, and I want you to have a life outside of our work. I'm just—"

"I left a note on a community poster-board in one of the commons last week," Antonia reassured her with a gentle smile. "That was before you brought in that pamphlet, but the timing's just too perfect. I must get better at readings, and I can't just use you three as subjects." She waved a hand in playful disdain. "I feel like I know everything about you, and that's not good for progress."

"Fair. Just—"

"Be careful, I know, I always am. You too, dear. Now go get ready. You look green, and I can't say that will go well with any of your gowns."

"Do I? Oh God."

Glancing into the oval mirror in the hall, she made a sour expression. Her black hair was haphazard atop her head, and her face was indeed a pale, sallow green. Though thankfully the dark circles usually under her eyes were just a slight shadow. Sighing, she harrumphed up the stairs. In addition to getting ready, there was something else she needed to do, but it slipped her mind. Addled. That's what she was. She needed to pull herself together, for everyone's sake.

Perhaps that realization was what summoned little Zofia into the hallway. The young shade wavered, her white dress with its singed hem buffeted in the slight breeze wafting off all spirits—the eternal chill. The girl's mother had perished in the same shop fire and her father had died in Warsaw

long before that, but her parents' souls had gone on to peace. Zofia chose
to stay in the city to help other children find ways out of desperate ends.

Zofia had met Eve on her first case, haunting the same place a child
was in need. In some cases, Zofia would appear to point a child toward
an exit in an emergency; in others she'd try to inspire escape from myriad
torments. Eve tried never to pin Zofia down to one mission. The child
fiercely chose her own. But right now, it seemed Zofia just wanted a friend.

"Hello, dear," Eve said, taking her time washing up in front of a basin
and mirror in the large upstairs water closet. The cool water helped her
nerves and pallor. "What's on your mind? You've that thoughtful expression
you take on when you're trying to solve some difficult problem."

"I feel the same worry I felt when Maggie disappeared," the child
replied, wringing her small hands. "About Vera. I want to go find her,
and I feel…like I'm being pulled. I feel we haven't done enough for Vera."

"I know, love. I trust you. Whatever you think to do, just don't put
yourself at risk. Don't go chasing after people who can see and who
might want to hurt you. What happened to Maggie is a warning to us
all that some people who don't want ghosts around may have discovered
ways to hurt them."

"Do you think Vera got hurt too?"

"I don't know," Eve replied, "but we'll keep searching for her however
we can. We've all reached out with no luck. Remember, she is old. She
might want rest."

"But she's like Maggie— I can't imagine she didn't want to say goodbye."

"I agree. But then again, I can't always fathom your spirit ways, your
needs or sense of time."

Trying to reassure the little girl helped Eve calm the nerves that threatened
to shake her off every surface she sat on or stood upon. Thoroughly combing
her hair, she managed to work out a few tangles.

"I know we're not supposed to be in your room," Zofia murmured, "but…
can I watch you get ready?" The child looked pained. "I will never experience
going to a ball. Having a suitor. Trying to make myself beautiful…"

Her plea hit Eve like a blow, and she blinked back tears. "Of course,
dear. We can experience all this together, then."

Opening the tall wooden wardrobe in her room, she stared at the dresses
therein. There were only a few, nothing ostentatious, a couple of ball gowns
Gran insisted she have ready for moments like these where work would
be accomplished while socializing. Other area performers might know
about Mulciber, and she needed to know why his name had rotated into
their notice. Staying on task helped Eve counterbalance the butterflies that

threatened inelegantly to topple her over. There was waltzing to worry about too. The aerial flips her stomach had been doing now plummeted. She dreaded dancing; she wasn't any good at it.

"Zofia, come here, practice a waltz with me. I'm hopeless."

She hummed some Strauss and practiced the box step in her room with the little girl, thankful there were no corporeal feet to trip upon, laughing with the child until Eve felt she had made herself safe for contact.

"Who will you be dancing with, the detective?" Zofia asked excitedly. Almost too excitedly, as if it were a foregone conclusion. Eve pursed her lips.

"Perhaps. And if the detective demands a waltz, I can't step on his feet, or worse, trip the poor man."

"He'd be a good sport about it even if you did," Zofia posited. "He's very nice."

"Yes, yes he is," Eve said. "Now I have to choose a dress. I'm a disaster at this."

Back to the wardrobe again. Nothing gaudy. This was a working-class theatre circuit. But she couldn't wear her black uniforms. There was a simple royal-blue evening dress, nice taffeta with elegant gathers. When she put her hand on it, Zofia nodded her approval. Starched lace along a high bodice line provided modesty, and that would be wise. She was meeting his parents, after all.

There went the stomach again. She removed her outer layers, keeping on her chemise, bloomers, and petticoat, and lifted a long-waisted whalebone corset around her, cinching it tighter to accommodate the dress, an act that didn't help her stomach in the least. She slipped into the body of the dress, folding her arms into it, double checking all of the hooks and eyes on the side that kept her swathed. When Gran had insisted Eve own a few fine dresses, Eve had said she wasn't interested in wearing "a thousand ties and tribulations" and agreed to be fitted only on the condition that she could get into an outfit entirely on her own.

Dashing rosewater about herself, she carefully swept up her hair in her favorite marcasite hair combs and debated about a necklace. A tiny sapphire on a whisper-thin silver chain, a gift from her father, completed her ensemble. The stone was an important one.

Powder, a faint dash of rouge, and a slight tint of lip balm made her less green. She stared in the mirror and tried to bolster herself. For someone who was so confident about her work, she felt terribly awkward being a lady in polite society. Zofia wafted her little hand over Eve's temple and utilized the cold breeze generated by her spirit to brush a stray wisp of hair back in place.

"You look beautiful," Zofia commented. "Thank you for not minding me."

Eve's eyes watered as she smiled at the girl, wishing she knew what to say when the ache of a life cut short was an unmitigated melancholy. "As if I could ever mind you," she murmured, a lump in her throat.

"It all seems a bit magical," the child continued, wistful romance in her voice.

Magical. In all Eve's daydreaming, she'd forgotten a critical task.

"Damn," Eve muttered. "I forgot to write to Harry Houdini!"

Rushing to her writing desk, she took out a few sheets of writing paper and began a note to the man she'd met a few weeks prior, a man whose fame was widening as he traveled through Europe. She'd try to match his performance schedule and send it ahead to where he'd be next.

Mr. Houdini,

I hope this note finds you well and charming audiences in Europe as much as you charmed our police precinct a few weeks prior as you managed to escape an old cell. We had a wonderful conversation about Spiritualism after the fact, and I hope you meant it when you said we could keep in touch.

I recently saw Mulciber, a levitation, psychic, and mesmerism act in one of the Astor theatres. I've no doubt you've many ideas about how the man got up to all that, and I'm sure it's all very clever, but that's not why I'm writing. There's just something off about the whole thing. I wish I could describe why I was so unsettled, but I can't.

The second act shifted focus onto mind reading and mesmerism. There was a level to his mesmerism that was domineering to the point of troubling, going so far as to literally drive people to their knees.

So, he's either a very talented psychic and gifted Spiritualist in ways I'm not, or there's a new brand of tricks on a level I've never seen. Any thoughts would be a boon to my investigation. I have a hunch this performance is somehow wrapped up in my current cases and that something sinister lurks behind the curtain. I've no wish to know the secrets of the trade, per se, but I would love to know what I'm dealing with.

Sincerely,

Eve H. Whitby, formerly of the now-shuttered Ghost Precinct, wrapping up final case material.

She supposed she'd better cover her tracks about the department being closed, especially to someone of prominence, but she knew he'd be disappointed seeing it. Perhaps she could tell him in confidence what had occurred and why they were keeping an even lower profile. She sealed and stamped the envelope, gestured to Zofia to accompany her, and wandered down to the parlor, where Antonia had shifted from reading tarot to reading newspapers.

"Antonia, my dear, since you're in the papers, could you check London and Paris to note Houdini's schedule? I've a letter for him. I'd love his insight on that Mulciber fellow."

"Of course. Shall I address the letter to an appropriate place when I find out the schedule? Do we know where he's staying?"

"He's got a booking agent in London. Call Ambassador Bishop. I've got to run out."

"Will do. Have fun with the detective," she said with a smirk.

"How did you—"

Antonia laughed. Her laughter was often a lovely, tinkling sound, but this one was a deeper, more resonant amusement. "It's abundantly clear you're unused to courtship. I'd have thought you'd have gotten better at blocking your energies and intentions from gifted psychics. Once one gets to know you, you're not terribly hard to read. That, and the rosy blush on your previously green cheeks, and the extra effort you put into your appearance— You never spend that much time if it's *only* family." Antonia clicked her tongue a glint in her dark eyes. "It's all very telling."

Zofia giggled, and Eve shot her a warning look. "Not you too. Cora will admonish me as well," Eve grumbled. "She already thinks I make too much effort to spend time with him."

"We're all scared new people will unseat us, especially when you're treasured." Antonia reached out from her chair, patting Eve's hand. "And you're treasured, Eve."

"As are you all, please don't forget that," Eve said, looking both at Antonia and her youngest ghostly asset. "I'm forsaking none of you—"

"I begrudge you none of this. Cora, I'm not so sure." As Eve must have appeared uneasy, Antonia smiled and reached out in a reassuring gesture. "But I can ease the edges, I promise. At least, I'll try."

"Forever my diplomat." Eve bent to kiss Antonia on her high forehead. This made her giggle, that tinkling laugh the echo of some ancient fey land.

"If I've any trouble tracking down Mr. Houdini," Antonia added, "I'll let you know if the escape artist also eludes the mail."

"Bless you." Eve paused. "Zofia here remains worried about Vera."

Antonia turned to the spirit. "Would you like to call her via a séance tonight, you and me, once I'm back from my reading?"

Zofia put her hands together, darting to and fro as she answered. "Yes, but first I want to see a ball, and Eve promised me I could watch."

"As long as you stay out of the way and safe, dear," Eve countered, putting on her best cloak at the door, black velvet with lace trim. "I can't have any trouble or awkward moments."

"I know," Zofia said to Eve, then turned to Antonia. "But after, yes, please."

"See you later." Eve waved to Antonia, and Zofia wafted out the closed door after her. "Now, if you don't mind," Eve said, striding toward Washington Square Park, "I'd like…"

The little girl intuited her and gave her space, disappearing from sight.

Eve continued ahead until she saw a distinct figure. For the next moment, the man before her at the corner of the park and the sudden race of her pulse were all that existed in her world. She smiled to see him looking dapper in a fine black suit with a burgundy waistcoat and black silk ascot, sitting on a bench with two cups of something savory and steaming in hand. Once she approached, he handed her the small paper cup of cider, augmenting autumn's rich scent.

"Hello, Detective."

"*Still* averse to calling me Jacob?" he asked with a smile. "Even on a soiree night?"

"I…" She thought about it a moment. "I don't know. I suppose I am. Perhaps I'm trying to reinforce a certain distance, for our safety."

"Our safety? Am I endangering you?" he asked with sincere curiosity and slight hurt.

Eve stared at her steaming cup, not sure she read him correctly. *Only my heart, but—* "No…"

Horowitz chuckled. "You don't sound convinced. Have it your way, *Whitby*, but if you don't want my mother hounding me about why on earth you keep calling me 'detective' and not the cherished name she gave me, written in the book of life itself, well—"

"I'm sorry, Jacob," Eve said, blushing. "I don't mean to be difficult."

"I know the work comes first," he said gently. "I'm not here to challenge that. In fact, that's the whole premise here, that we, together, won't challenge that. But we do have to act like there's a closeness."

"Well, there is, I mean, a closeness here, with us, of course, only if you think so too, I think—" Eve stammered and gestured too boldly, spilling cider on the detective's black coat. "Oh, goodness." She looked down at the leaves at her feet. "I'm a disaster. Sorry."

The detective laughed heartily. "Who doesn't need a splash of spiced cologne? And to be clear, I don't think I've ever had such a good time with a disaster before."

Eve glanced at him sheepishly and chuckled. "You're too kind."

Once they finished their cider, he carried their empty cups to a bin and went to the corner to hail an enclosed carriage. Helping her up, he grasped her hand and steadied her before climbing in across.

"Rachel has agreed to meet you and I outside the Thalia," he said. "We exchanged a letter ahead of the event."

"I can't wait to see her. It's been too long."

"And she you. She told me endearing things about you as a child," he added.

Eve groaned. "Embarrassing, I'm sure."

"No, she wrote that you were the most passionate, driven little girl she'd ever met, a force of nature, and I can't say I'd disagree."

"I've had to be so, for survival," Eve said graciously. "And so did she."

"I'm ashamed she and I were never closer. She's such a brave person."

"There's always time. It feels destined for us all to be reunited," Eve said, and gazed out the window, not wanting to look into his eyes for any further talk of destiny.

The carriage slowed and the detective hopped out, paid the driver, and helped Eve down. She wasn't used to so many layers or quite so much constriction, so she leaned a bit more on the detective than she'd planned descending from the step, but he sturdily and patiently held her.

Within view, the event was held in the colonnaded Thalia Theatre—called the Bowery Theatre in rowdier days—just down Bowery from Canal. More recent theatre communities like the Yiddish theatre and Italian immigrant productions sought to elevate the intellectual offerings.

Even just approaching the grand Corinthian columns gave Eve a thrill that raced along her spine, though this was mostly due to the detective's close stride. Her cloak, open and billowing to the side, meant his hand absently landed on her back, his palm grazing a triangle of bare skin where the back of her dress plunged.

As she paused to navigate a cluster of pedestrians and the trestles of the elevated rail line grating and squeaking above them, she was jostled, and his hand darted around her waist to nimbly steady her. Once they regained their stride, he returned his hand to that spot on her back, and this time his thumb traced her back in the subtlest of caresses. It was the most exquisite sensation Eve had ever experienced, and she had to bite her tongue not to gasp.

As she turned to stare at him, he remained entirely focused ahead, but she saw the angles of his face curve into a brilliant smile.

Ascending the wide steps to the front door, Eve followed his gaze until her eyes fell upon Rachel Horowitz, beloved friend of her mother's, standing in a lovely powder-blue dress, a charcoal cape over her shoulders and her brown hair up in a small feathered hat.

"Thank you for waiting for us!" the detective declared, holding out his arms for his long-lost second cousin. He said while embracing her, "It's been how long, cousin?"

Rachel gently pushed him back and pointed to his mouth and then to her eyes, reminding him that she could understand him only if she could see his mouth so she could lip-read.

"Ah, right, yes, so sorry." He blushed. Careful to make sure he had her eyes, he continued. "I'm *so* happy to see you. My family was very worried when you disappeared."

If you work with Eve now, I'm sure you understand why, Rachel signed and Eve translated. *I had to get out of this frenetic city and I wanted to start a new, fresh life.*

"He's warming to Spiritualist talent," Eve said to Rachel. "He's not fully won over yet. He's still a skeptic, and I wouldn't change that for the world. Keeps my ghosts and I on our toes." At this, the women shared a smile.

"Shall we?" the detective said, gesturing to the open front doors.

Glancing behind her, Eve noticed Zofia had reappeared, and she subtly gestured that the little girl go on ahead. Excitedly, Zofia flew through one of the grand first-floor windows.

The living trio entered and took in the spectacle of happy people in finery, drinks in hand, with quiet chamber music wafting in a pleasant ambience.

A banner that hung across a back wall above a small dais read:
Welcome, all ye who seek to lift thy lamp!

Eve thought this was a reference to Emma Lazarus's poem "The New Colossus," which had been written to raise money for the pedestal for the Statue of Liberty after the great fight to put her up in the first place. There was talk of putting the poem on the statue itself, but that too was controversial.

A gentleman in a suit and tails welcomed them and whisked champagne flutes into their hands.

Bells sounded somewhere from the recesses of the building, quieting the chatter into a dull murmur. A russet-haired man with a neatly trimmed mustache, in a tailcoat and a tall top hat, took to a dais overlooking the wide room.

"Thank you all for coming tonight! I'm Benjamin Heifitz, social chair of Artists Against Intolerance, and I'm very grateful you've come out to support our cause. Throughout the night, our colleagues will be making rounds with hats; donations of any amount are welcome as we create educational programs, opportunities, and safe havens for new New Yorkers and lifelong residents alike."

Polite applause followed. Heifitz was handed a piece of paper.

"Ah! The Great Houdini sends his regards and wishes he could be with us tonight!" the toastmaster declared. A cheer went up from the crowd. "He wrote this note to all of you." He began to read:

"The joy of magic and entertainment brings us all together tonight, as it has since the dawn of time, but there is something far greater that binds all people at all times: our common humanity and better selves. May we all stand proud of building community, strength, and hope for all people in the beautiful city of New York, a haven and refuge, a shining light."

Heifitz lifted his glass. "To the noble cause of a fair world. *L'chaim!* To life!"

The crowd lifted their glasses and repeated the toast, Eve chiming in enthusiastically.

Horowitz leaned over. "Your Hebrew isn't half bad," he said with a smile. "At least, one word in."

Have you told him we lit Shabbos candles together? Rachel signed to Eve, who nodded. *It meant a lot to me to sit, to share that with you,* Rachel continued. *That your family became an extension of my lost immediate family, proving tradition can live vibrantly with new friends who are willing to learn.*

The detective watched his cousin closely. Eve supplied Rachel's poetry and care as best she could.

"That's a lovely thing to share," the detective said as his smile widened. "And I want to learn to sign. I don't want to miss anything." Eve believed that; he was so invested in the world around him that he didn't want to miss a single expression that might otherwise be lost in translation.

Rachel signed that she'd be willing to teach him, and they shook hands on the proposal. She then turned to Eve and signed, *And Eve can help you. Not to mention, her sign isn't half bad either.*

Eve laughed and signed her thanks. "Yes," she added for the detective's benefit. "I can help."

"You always do," he replied with the simple, clear kindness that shone like a beautiful light.

On cue, warmth flooded her cheeks, and she turned to her champagne glass. Rachel eyed them carefully and pursed her lips, holding back a smile of delight.

Well, at least Rachel wouldn't object to their close acquaintance, Eve surmised, ruse or no. Rachel made her way over to a couple Eve assumed were Jacob's parents, and there was embracing, happy reunions, and "where on earth did you go" questions. While Rachel could read lips and hear their fondness, as they didn't know sign language, the exchange stilled. Eve wanted to rush up and help facilitate conversation as a translator, but she didn't want to appear overbearing. She needed to wait her turn and be introduced.

Mr. Horowitz glanced over and caught his son's eye. The tall, dark-haired man with a black goatee turning partly grey was dapper and magnetic as he broke into a wide grin. Radiating geniality, he gestured them over with enthusiasm. At his side stood an elegant, stoic looking woman: Mrs. Horowitz.

"Well now, the moment of reckoning," the detective said ominously. Eve must have looked startled, for he laughed and added, "Oh, come now, they'll be nice to you; I made them promise."

He placed that gentle hand on her lower back again, and they stepped forward. Rachel beamed, watching them.

"Mother, Father, I'd like you to meet Miss Evelyn Whitby," the detective said, and everyone bobbed heads.

Eve didn't want to seem too forthright, so she didn't present her hand and demand handshakes, but she was glad that everyone seemed to be genuinely smiling. Perhaps this wouldn't be as strained as she had feared.

"A sincere pleasure, Mr. and Mrs. Horowitz," Eve stated. "Your son has been an incredible colleague and one of the best men I've ever had the pleasure to know."

"Well, we tried our best," Mr. Horowitz said, his big grin infectious.

"I am glad the force is employing women," Mrs. Horowitz said carefully. She wasn't as tall as her husband, but she had an imposing air that added inches just in power. "And Jacob has told me you've been very helpful in his cases, not to mention stood up for him. That is very good of you."

"It's infuriating that anyone should have to bear the brunt of prejudice," Eve replied. "Your son has stood up for me the same. And I'll never back down should I have to make a defense again. This cause of yours tonight honors everything I believe in. Strength, education, and safe havens."

Mrs. Horowitz looked at her son and then at Eve. "Good," she said after a long moment, her expression warm. "That is very good, thank you."

"Don't I know you?" An elderly, bearded gentleman who had clearly already taken to the punch tables and had a few too many clapped a hand on Mr. Horowitz's shoulder.

"I was the Amazing Antoine, once," Mr. Horowitz said, wincing. "I hope that's not how you remember me. I've done many better things since."

"Why on earth did you give up the stage?" the gentleman asked Mr. Horowitz.

"You ask as if the world shouldn't be grateful that I chose another career. I was so amazing I set myself on fire. I've the scars on my leg to prove it."

"Surely you exaggerate," the man declared.

"I was a terrible magician," Mr. Horowitz retorted bluntly. "If I'd have gone on, how many watches taken from trusting audiences would have gone missing, unrecoverable? Rabbits maimed, doves trapped—and my poor assistant, now wife, I might have *actually* cut her in half. Believe me, my turn into academia saved lives."

Eve laughed heartily. Seeing that she was enjoying him, Mr. Horowitz turned to her with that delightful grin as the old man grumbled and walked away to accost another failed performer.

"I'm glad *someone* finds me entertaining," he said to Eve conspiratorially, gesturing to his wife and son on either side of him. "I've grown tiresome to these two."

Mrs. Horowitz pursed her lips and batted a hand at him.

"I'm so glad the Veil family was invited tonight," Eve offered. "It's lovely we've all these wonderful connections of dear family friends between us!" At this Rachel nodded.

"The Veils have always been supportive of any network for good; they're notoriously generous and inclusive," Mr. Horowitz said. "I leave the grand theatrics to folks like them, to be mastheads for education and philanthropy. I'm better off behind the scenes making sure the paperwork is sound. Back in the days of performing, I never could quite close the distances between my ideas and audience."

Nodding, Mrs. Horowitz drily punctuated the moment. "He's better in theory."

Everyone laughed at her academic dig.

Rachel touched Eve on the shoulder, gesturing toward a beaming man at the side of the stage who waved at them. *Would you explain to everyone that I've a friend from my days at the Connecticut Asylum who works the prop department here and would like to give me a backstage tour? I don't want to seem rude going off.* Eve signed back that she'd be happy to and turned to the company to explain as Rachel darted off.

"It's truly wonderful that you know American Sign, Miss Whitby," Mr. Horowitz said. "The Connecticut school, that's how your family knows Rachel, yes?"

"Yes. My mother spent her whole life, up until she was nearly my age, unable to speak due to Selective Mutism from a childhood trauma. But she made sure I learned to sign. She said finding ways to communicate and making friends like Rachel saved her life."

"*L'chaim.*" Mr. Horowitz raised his glass to that, and all toasted.

"I want to learn too," Jacob said. "Rachel and Miss Whitby said she'd help. Thank you, Eve," he added.

"You're welcome, Jacob," Eve replied, bowing her head. "I am here to help."

"That's simply fantastic," Mr. Horowitz said enthusiastically.

Mrs. Horowitz exclaimed at something Eve couldn't see, and the woman turned away for a moment before turning back to her son.

"Jacob, I've brought you a surprise all the way from Paris," she said and stepped aside. Behind her stood a breathtakingly beautiful young woman.

"Sophie? Is that you?" the detective asked incredulously, his lovely eyes widening. The young woman was a vision: fair and rosy cheeked with red-blond hair and a dazzling smile.

"*Oui! Bonjour,* Jacob! Surprise!"

"Oh, my goodness, look at you!" he exclaimed and gave the stunning woman an enormous hug as they kissed one cheek then the other.

Eve felt something sharp pierce her insides.

"Our families have long been keen on one another, and on our children," Mrs. Horowitz explained matter-of-factly to Eve before turning to her son. "I'll leave you all to chat. Jacob, I promised Sophie you'd save her a dance. I'm sure Miss Whitby won't mind, will you, dear?"

Eve swallowed hard and rallied a smile. "Of course not, Mrs. Horowitz. How lovely to see so many old friends reunited!"

She smiled and scrutinized Eve for an uncomfortable moment before gliding away with her husband, who was laughing beside another comedian. Jacob was asking Sophie how long she'd been back in the city.

This was clearly deliberate, Eve thought, but there was no time to feel hurt or accusatory; this was all to be expected. She couldn't blame Jacob's mother for wanting him to continue tradition, for their families to have had a history, regardless of his new circumstances. Besides, everyone was just friends, yes?

Jacob seemed to suddenly have remembered Eve and whirled around to make introductions.

"Eve! Meet Sophie! Sophie and I were childhood sweethearts, you could say, before her family whisked her off to relatives in Paris. Sophie Perlman, this is my departmental colleague and *dear* lady friend, Miss Evelyn Whitby."

"*Enchantée, mademoiselle,*" Eve said, bobbing her head. Miss Perlman beamed and replied the same. The music changed to a tune Sophie was clearly enamored of; her already bright face lit even further, and she gestured to the floor with a graceful hand.

"Ah, I am obliged," Jacob declared, "and we've much to catch up on. If you'll permit me, Eve?" He offered his arm to Sophie, whose radiance was undeniable.

All Eve could do was nod, and they were off.

Childhood sweethearts versus a "dear lady friend." She was outmatched. Everything was against her. The sudden, sharp pain of this turn widened its scope.

She blinked a few times as she was left alone. Watching them, she wasn't sure how much of their beaming smiles at one another she could take, so she searched for some sight of comfort.

Little Zofia was over by the dessert table, glancing in awe alternately at the cakes and at the dresses of elegant ladies she would never get the chance to become. Another aching sight, that, and Eve let the child be. Tears stung the corner of her eyes, and she looked up, forcing them back.

The heavens were merciful in granting Eve a respite. At that moment, who should enter but the Veils. No one ever forgot a Veil family entrance.

A little cheer went up when attendees recognized the Veils. Nathaniel Veil wore a voluminous black cape, black brocade suit, and an onyx helmet bearing open raven's wings on either side. Long black hair trailed out from under the helmet, and his dark eyes pierced the crowd, his lips in a smirk. The ensemble made him appear a sort of mischievous divinity from some yet unnamed religion.

He made his name and infamy as a Gothic performer of literary works adapted for the stage, with a generous helping of Poe, monologues from Minerva Press novels, and traditional staples, from the seminal *Castle of Otronto* to Wilde's recent *Dorian Gray.* As he strode in, the cape billowed as if there were a wind-device positioned somewhere. Perhaps there was.

Lavinia Veil, Nathaniel's red-headed wife of seventeen years, strode in at his side, herself a fantastical queen in a huge period gown of deep burgundy and black brocade and a tall standing black collar embellished with jet beading: a Gothic Queen Elizabeth.

Nathaniel Veil had befriended Eve's father when they were young men in England. Eve's father had run a health clinic for those in need, and Nathaniel had founded a society to help melancholiacs, celebrating darkness rather than letting it rule them. Her Majesty's Society of Melancholy Bastards, he'd called his witty, self-effacing club. The two of them had managed to avert quite a few suicides during their time running the clinic, one of them being Lavinia's. They'd all spent a great deal of time in America but traveled back and forth to their native England.

The Veils's son Daniel, now seventeen and devastatingly handsome, trailed behind them in a subdued black suit with red neckwear. The blush on his pale cheeks made it abundantly clear he'd rather no one be looking at him. Danny had not inherited his parents' theatricality. He was a gentle, shy soul, and this sort of entrance mortified him as much as it delighted his parents. Eve rushed up to her old friend. It had been several years since she'd seen him, and he'd grown up beautifully.

"Danny, dear!"

He turned at the sound of his familiar name. Only family could call him Danny. At the sight of Eve, his discomfort vanished.

"Eve!" he cried, rushing into her arms for a tight embrace and happy laughter.

"I can't *tell* you how good it is to see you," she exclaimed. "You've rescued me."

"I'll say the same of you, dear one. I wish they'd let me slip in a side door," Danny said. Eve laughed. "But from what have I rescued you, Eve? You're the knight in shining armor sort—I thought you never need to be rescued!"

"Ah, well, remind me of that. Keep me strong," Eve begged, sliding her arm through his.

The young man had inherited both of his parents' ethereal beauty; his father's long black hair combined with his mother's flame-red locks made a rich auburn, kept long and down around his shoulders in waves. He was the very picture of a Raphaelite angel.

"Shall we dance?" Eve asked, eyeing the floor where Jacob and Sophie were taking yet another turn. She may not like dancing but she needed to keep an eye on them and she'd be damned if she was going to be a wallflower disappearing from Jacob's sight.

"We shall," Danny agreed.

"How are you, dear? It's been too long. What now, three years?"

"I am well," he replied. "No, two years and five months."

"You've a better memory than I." she smiled. "It's sentimental of you to have counted the months."

"You're the only friend in the city I miss."

Eve squeezed the hand he held as they danced. "Ah, but you've been remiss," she chided gently.

"In what?" He appeared horrified.

"You've not sent me any poetry in ages."

"Oh…" He blushed and looked at the floor. "I've been so busy with school."

"I know, of course, and your schooling is tantamount. I'm only teasing. I just don't want you to ever forget how gifted you are. Your parents might have a gift for the stage, but you, my dear, are a poet of the ages."

His blush widened to the tips of his ears. They enjoyed their dance in comfortable quiet until Danny broached a new topic, his voice hesitant.

"Do you remember once, when I last visited and we took a walk around the park, that you understood me? That you understood what I meant about *who* I was…"

Eve thought back. When he'd last visited, he'd seemed haunted. Withdrawn and worried, and that wasn't like him; a quiet soul, he'd always been a vibrant one. When they'd taken a walk, Eve had pressed him to be honest about what troubled him. He had asked for her confidence, terrified about that year's trial of Oscar Wilde, his imprisonment, and the injustice of it all.

"When you asked me if I could keep your secret?" Eve asked gently. Danny nodded. Eve remembered that he had been so scared that what had happened to Wilde could then happen to him, too. Eve had taken his hand and reassured him, though she could not speak for the world but only for herself, that he had nothing to fear from her or anyone they held dear. "Yes, my dear, of course I do. I remember and I understand."

"Well." He blushed again. "I've met someone. A schoolmate. I'm very much in love, and it seems he is too. The kind of love that…well, is the stuff of poetry. That's why I haven't written you. All of my work has been about him, and I… Well, I wasn't sure what you'd think, and I didn't want anyone to find the poems." He bit his lip.

"Oh, my dear heart. Danny, you are an incredible poet, and if you have fallen into an epic love for the poetic ages, then what could I possibly do but wish you all the best?"

He smiled. "It is very complicated. But we'll find a way."

"Yes, you will," Eve encouraged.

"I'm so glad I have you," Danny gushed. "That you understand."

"I take it you've not mentioned this to your parents?"

"Perhaps I will, someday. But they don't know now. They might suspect, but they've never asked. You know how sometimes you can think you know someone, and know they love you, but they still can't accept your truths, and sometimes even the things they do out of love for you, that you know are out of love, end up harming anyway?"

"Yes…I do," Eve murmured. "Nothing about my paranormal life has been anything but a curse, in my parents' eyes, when to me it is a gift. It is not the same as your situation—"

"But it is a certain parallel. You can at least empathize."

"Your dear, beautiful heart that loves so big and so strong, who could ever deny that?"

"Oh, plenty could," he said mordantly. "The world is cruel. But this event tonight gives me hope. I… There may be others like me here who take refuge in the arts as I do. I know my parents have friends who are… like me; they just don't ever make it an issue."

"Which is heartening, in an age that seems too curious about people's private lives. It isn't anyone's business but one's own. I believe your parents will be good to you. If they are not, you have refuge in me. And in Gran, I promise. If things ever get bad, I even have room in my townhouse. And it's *my* townhouse, which I pay for with my salary, so I get to say who comes and goes. You, and your love, will always be welcome there."

Danny was overcome and kissed Eve on the cheek. "My angel," he said. "That is generous of you, and it is a comfort."

"It is part of my calling—doing what's best for loved ones."

"I love you too, my shining-armored princess."

Eve laughed and spun beneath Danny's arm in an artful turn. As they spun, Eve nearly stumbled when she caught another glance at the detective, who seemed to have made Sophie laugh as she tossed her head back in glee. Another few steps brought Eve within view of the Veils, who had taken up a lively dance themselves not far from her. They waved and blew kisses.

"How can I be here for you in turn?" Danny asked Eve. "I can tell many things are on your mind and in your heart. You're always thinking, but you're not usually so distracted. For one, I can tell that attractive man you keep eyeing over there is troubling you."

Eve loosed a pained chuckle. "Ah. You think he is? Attractive?"

"Don't you?"

"Well, yes, I… He's a dear friend, a colleague. And, yes, he is a suitor of mine," she said. "Well, at least…we have been… It's hard to explain."

Danny furrowed his brow and looked at the man in question with a flash of consternation. "If he is a suitor of yours, then why aren't you dancing with him?"

"Because I've missed you!" Eve exclaimed. "I'd never miss an opportunity to spend time with you."

"You're a darling. But you mustn't let me take away from a work in progress," Danny said, nodding toward the detective.

"He is clearly preoccupied," Eve said with a bit of vitriol. "And has been for a while now."

Danny watched them a moment. "Ah. Yes. Well, one can have many suitors, and they may call upon many. She's very pretty, but so are you. You're young— And besides, I thought you didn't want to settle in with anyone."

Eve squared her shoulders. "I don't."

"So then play *games*, darling. Isn't half the fun of attraction the game of flirtation? A good chase?"

Eve arched an eyebrow at him. "You're too young to be so experienced a sportsman."

"I'm only two years behind you—and *volumes* of poetry ahead of you," Danny replied loftily. Eve laughed. Danny leaned in. "Maybe you both could do with a bit of a push."

"We need no such thing," Eve said with a sputtering chuckle. "It was my idea, his being my suitor, to push back against family pressure to take on callers. This was our solution to bide time and continue as professionals in our fields."

"So you figured he could be a cover, masking the truth that your true lover is your work," Danny supposed, almost as if he didn't entirely believe it.

"In a way," Eve said, squirming a bit. Danny could read her too well. "Nothing is going on. He is a convenience. A ruse, we've said."

"Eve, before everyone fussed over our entrance, I swept the place from the back, looking for you specifically, and I *saw* you two standing together. You're terribly awkward. Knowing you, and guessing about the detective, that means something is, in fact, going on—"

"We are dear friends," Eve declared before tossing her head in their direction. "What that is between *them*... I don't know. She's a childhood sweetheart. Evidently. A relationship his parents seem very keen on maintaining."

Eve felt deeply hurt and knew she had no right to. She had no legitimate claim to him other than the pretense they'd been playing at. She couldn't expect him to keep himself from someone he truly cared about.... The pain twisted again.

"He's at ease with her because he's known her," Danny surmised, watching and murmuring his assessment. "Like you've known me. I confess, I've been staring at him from the moment I saw him because I found him so striking. All angles and sweet elegance. He seems so earnest. Reminds me very much of my love."

Queasy, Eve was glad for the subject to shift to someone else. "I'd like to meet him, your dear one."

"You will, someday," Danny said wistfully.

Mr. Veil appeared as if from nowhere and lifted his son up by the waist, deposited him neatly to the side, and picked up Eve and continued dancing without even missing a beat.

"*Dad!*" Danny pouted, folding his arms at the side of the dance floor. But there was no circumventing the force of nature that was Nathaniel Veil; one simply had to get out of the way or be pummeled by capes and melodrama until relenting.

"Uncle Nat!" Eve cried joyously.

"My Little Bat!" Nathaniel Veil cried in turn.

One of her earliest memories, a purely happy one amidst constant night terrors, was a rhyme Nathaniel had made up when her father shared his concerns about her state. As Mr. Veil whirled Eve around, they recited it together:

"Uncle Nat and his Little Bat
Befriended spooky this and that
When they found a little spider
Nearing harm they rushed to hide her
When they found a starving snake
They fed it bugs from off the lake
When they found a crying ghost
They cheered it up with jam and toast!
Uncle Nat and his Little Bat
Were loved by spooky this and that!"

Eve threw her head back in a little girl's giggle, transported to the time he'd made the poem up to help her; her godparents had reframed what was scary into something lovable and gave her things to celebrate instead. It helped Eve deal with the ghosts and infinitely more.

"How are you, Little Bat?" he asked.

"I'm…very busy with work."

He narrowed his dark eyes. "Is there enough play involved in this work? You're too young to be such a serious businesswoman."

"Uncle Nat, tell me, are you familiar with the magician Mulciber?"

As Nathaniel bounced her about in a quadrille, he thought a moment. "Can't say I am. I admit, I'm a bit rusty on the upcoming talents; I've been very involved in my society's educational ventures." His voice was very nearly like her father's crisp upper-class London accent, but occasionally the merchant-class sound of his upbringing slipped through. "I've had to step everything up— Sending Daniel to the best school hasn't come cheap."

Veil hadn't come from much, and the fact that actors weren't a respected class had been hard on their family. But they were the picture of grace, charity, and having fun with hard work.

"I wish I could have seen you and Father in your early days at the clinic," Eve exclaimed. "I'd have been so proud! Did you hear he finally got the job at Bellevue?"

"No! Goodness. I'm so thrilled. Give him my regards; I wish he were here."

"I certainly will. I ask about Mulciber because there's something wrong with the show and I can't put my finger on it. It uses a *Divine Comedy* theme; the extremes of Heaven and Hell. The first act is all levitation."

"Levitation relies on tricks of the eye and carefully placed plates for the performer to stand on," Veil explained. "Raising and lowering is hidden by fabric, sets, black wing curtains, and smoke effects."

Eve nodded, recalling that there had been many effects present. She explained the second act of psychic recall.

"*That's* likely someone planted out in the house," Veil explained. "Someone innocuous who takes cues from people as they're coming in. Might rifle in the pockets of coats, ask questions in the lobby, eavesdrop on everything. It's never just one person, these things."

"Do you think Mulciber could have a legitimate psychic gift?"

"If it's as decisive as you say, then no, can't be. There's at least a second person in the house, working it over. Generally, in my opinion, the real psychics, the real Spiritualists, aren't the ones out performing. Ask the Bishops, ask your Gran, ask yourself—you all know."

"I'm...trying to keep Gran out of this one. She got too close to a case recently, and she became a target. Abducted. Hurt. I don't want her left out, but she's getting too old to be the soldier she was."

"Good God!"

"I'm trying to keep a low profile myself and trying to distance her."

"And you think you'll have any luck with that?" Nathaniel chuckled.

"There was a mesmerism sequence where he drove volunteers to their knees. It was...discomfiting to watch."

"That sounds like someone's vain fantasy of power and dominance," Veil declared. "Likely paid plants in the audience."

Eve frowned. The control had seemed very real.

"Does a group or a philosophy known as *Arte Uber Alles* mean anything to you?" she asked next.

"*Arte Uber Alles*?" Nathaniel made a face. "From what I understand, folks gravitated to that notion are troubled extremists. I've had a few devotees rotate through the society and try to give me one of their pamphlets. Taking one look at it, I deterred them and said never to contact me or my society again. Art saves lives, but one shouldn't live solely for it. Nor should one give their life entirely over to art without sparing care for oneself."

"We've a couple of cases, the detective and I...." Eve made the mistake of looking over at him. He and Sophie were laughing, and she raked her hand through his curls fondly. Eve had yearned to do that same fond gesture to him, and Sophie's intimacy hit her like a punch to the gut. Nathaniel followed her eyes. Eve coughed and stumbled a step in the dance. He righted her, and she continued. "We've reason to believe the group has led to at least one death if not others in related tragedy. Mulciber was a name mentioned in the notes of one of the deceased."

"Then it bears looking into, but keep an eye out for those behind the scenes. They're the ones making the magic happen while you're focused on the spectacle."

"Noted, thank you."

"Now what was that about?" Nathaniel asked, nodding his head in the detective's direction. "You looked over at that man and it's as if you were a kicked dog. I've never seen a single thing ruffle your feathers once you truly embraced your gifts, and if that man—"

Eve stopped his protective rant with a chuckle. "I'm all right, Uncle Nat. He's a colleague, we're close, it's... We're..." Panicked, she had to recover herself. She had to maintain the ruse of courtship to keep her parents from forcing anyone on her, and anything said to Nat could be fodder for discussion with her father. "We're courting."

"Well then he'd better come dance with you if you're courting," Nathaniel declared.

"We'll get there," Eve said, trying to remain hopeful.

Veil whirled her back to Danny, who waited, admittedly bemused, with his arms still folded.

"In the meantime, take care of my boy, Little Bat," Veil exclaimed. He vanished into the crowd in a billow of black satin, disappearing as suddenly as he'd arrived.

"You got to be the Little Bat," Danny opined. "I had to be the Wee Warlock."

"A wee warlock is far more powerful than a little bat, Danny."

"But I *love* bats," Danny whined.

"And this little bat loves you," Eve said, kissing him on the head, which made him grin.

"See, don't you feel better?" he asked with an eager smile. Eve made a motion to see where the detective had gone, but Danny reached out and shifted her face back toward him again. "Pay him no mind."

"I...can't help it." Eve's heart spasmed. Out of the corner of her eye, she saw the detective still staring at Sophie, still dancing—and from what Eve could tell, clearly enamored. The pain she was felt was distinct, utterly foreign and wholly dreadful.

"Oh, dear heart. You're truly a goner for him, aren't you?" Danny smiled. Eve scrunched her face up, blocking back sudden tears. "I understand. We can't control who we fall for—"

"I have not *fallen*—"

Maddeningly, Danny just giggled at her. "He's handsome and seems charming. Play the game. I believe in you."

Kissing her hand in an exaggerated fashion, her childhood friend twirled her away and toward the punch bowls, perhaps as a hint. Eve realized she could use a bit of cordial to take the edge off her unease. She downed a glass more quickly than she should have.

A voice behind her made her jump.

"It would appear nearly the whole night has gone by and we've not even had a dance," came a familiar, gamesome voice at her ear. Jacob's voice so close and soft had an unmistakable effect on her. "That's terribly unseemly for a 'courting' couple."

Eve turned to his playful half smile, raised her head, and squared her shoulders. "Well, you were dancing."

"So were you. Every time I looked over, you were entirely preoccupied."

"So were you."

"Well, now, may I?" He offered his hand. Eve gave it.

"You did demand a waltz," she said.

"I did, and I intend to take it," he replied confidently.

He placed his hand upon her back, there in that spot that had felt so exquisite. His commandeering of this moment at any moment until now would have thrilled Eve, but having seen him so lively and at such delighted ease with another woman, it didn't feel so special anymore.

"You seemed to be enjoying yourself," Eve said, trying to keep an edge out of her tone and failing miserably.

"As did you," the detective countered.

"Childhood friends," Eve stated.

"Is that why you were so friendly?" he queried, trying to search her face. She kept her expression blank.

"Is that why you were?" she countered. "You did refer to yourselves as childhood *sweethearts*."

"Childhood friends carry a great deal of weight in one's heart, do they not?" he asked. She couldn't tell if he was making a declaration or gauging her. Their verbal fencing had a distinct bite.

"I should introduce you to Daniel Veil," she said. "He's a brilliant poet. I've so many poems he wrote to me."

"Ah, I see. Well, very good then," the detective said. There was something detached about his response. It was almost as if they were back to a first conversation, an alien and cold one at that. Perhaps she shouldn't have tried to be coy, to use Danny as a foil to Sophie. She wasn't good at games. Not when it actually mattered. She didn't know what to do next, afraid she'd already made mistakes.

"Your family seems kind. Jovial. I...I wish they liked me as much as they like Sophie."

"Well, Sophie has the advantage of time and—"

"Being Jewish, I know," Eve murmured. "I don't begrudge your mother wanting you two together. I should just get out of the way—"

"You should just what, be so easily put off the pursuit?" he asked, a bit sharply. "A convenient excuse?"

"This isn't a game. I don't want games," Eve said, almost numb. She felt all energy leaving her; the entire experience had deflated her, and she wanted to crawl away.

The music stopped. Everyone bowed as they withdrew. The detective slowly put his hands down, as if still trying to grasp something, looking at her with a furrowed brow.

"Eve, I don't—" Jacob was cut off by the host of the night's festivities. The man rang a bell and thanked everyone for coming, saying that distribution buckets would be coming around again for any donations for the cause of a just and caring city, and he encouraged everyone to have a safe trip home.

"Shall I call a carriage and escort you back?" the detective asked. Whatever he'd been about to say, he must have thought better of it. Eve had no idea if she'd have wanted to hear it or not. She couldn't meet his eyes.

"No, I... I'll be all right. I'll call one from outside; there are several lined up."

"Suit yourself," he said with a smile that appeared forced.

"Please give your parents my warmest regards."

"I will. Until next time, Whitby." He waved. She waited for him to reach for her hand, to regain even a moment of the heated, breathless physical brushes they'd had amidst their work. There was none. There was a hesitation in his eyes. Still searching her. She didn't know what he wanted to find.

Squaring her shoulders, Eve held her head high. "Until next time, Detective."

Eve got out the door and hurried down the steps before anyone could see the tears stinging her eyes.

Chapter Twelve

Eve's mind was beset with two torments as she stepped into the first enclosed carriage she could find for hire, throwing herself into the compartment and closing the curtains so no one could make note of her conduct therein. The first trial was the host of children's voices accosting her, as if a door had been thrown wide open and only cries lay on the other side.

"How much closer are you?" the chorus asked.

"To what? To *where*?" Eve asked, exasperated, railing against the unseen horde.

"To helping us," a single small voice cried. Others took up the rest: *"We can't get* in *to see where we* are. *There's a woman far away in the woods; she's with part of us in the gilded ways, and then everything else is a blur."*

"I don't know what that means. In the gilded ways?"

"We've been gilded. Some of us. In pieces. We've been blocked, you see."

"If you could tell me where," Eve pleaded.

"We're lost. In your world and in time."

Their roaring chaos faded as a brass band on a street corner blared a modern tune. The carriage rolled by, sickening lurches on uneven cobblestones.

"Keep trying," Eve and the spirits chorused all at once, demanding each take responsibility for their vagaries.

Zofia appeared next to her in the carriage in a blast of cold air. Eve shuddered involuntarily.

"All we've been doing is trying to help you." Zofia, quick to defend Eve to the spirit children, admonished them colorfully in Polish before shifting again to English. "Give us a way *in*—otherwise, stop the torment!"

The young spirit examined Eve as the rest of the spectral chorus subsided, as if taking a collective step back from pounding on the walls of

Eve's brain. "What's wrong?" Zofia asked. "Did you not enjoy the party? It was overwhelming and amazing!"

"Yes, it was, and that's all I'll say about it. Go on home, please. I'd like a moment to myself." Eve tried to sound tired rather than sharp, but she couldn't manage it.

Frowning and confused, the spirit flew out of the carriage, leaving Eve alone again.

The secondary torment grew throughout the carriage ride home; Eve relived the distress that was Jacob and Sophie. Her mind replayed the excruciating moment when he had turned to that lovely woman, and she replayed with a growing bitterness the warmth they shared. The familiarity of the childhood sweethearts and how his family beamed at them. Over and over again, she torturously relived the way he touched Sophie, happy and fond. Closing her eyes, she leaned back against the leather cushion of the carriage interior to keep from retching.

Once home, Eve went straight to her room, ignoring the ghosts who said hello. Her eyes and Sensitivities raw, she kept the gas lantern dim by her bedside and collapsed onto her pillow and quietly wept.

The ghosts let her be. Ghosts didn't have to obey walls or doors, and for most of her life she'd had no privacy. All that changed when she began the precinct. Making peace with the ghosts meant they had to allow her autonomy. This room was the only place she could be alone.

However, when one lived with Sensitives who were in tune with the peaks and valleys of one another's state, the boundaries of emotional privacy were another porous threshold. But she couldn't worry about what her colleagues might pick up on. The truth of her heart, her mind, her resolve: it all felt like it was crumbling before her. She hadn't admitted how much she'd come to care for the detective, and she didn't know if she could possibly overcome these new barriers to assert some kind of claim on him, especially not after tonight.

Even though ghosts weren't allowed in her room, the murmurs of the spirit world, increasingly loud voices that were constantly behind the doors of her psychic shields, were building pressure at the base of her skull. A migraine through the night and into the morning was inevitable. The pain of it already made her feel dizzy.

Failed. Failed us. Failed all of us. The dead children continued to chant their far-flung damnation.

It only made her tears flow more freely.

After she had dried her eyes, there was a quiet knock on her door. Eve panicked, not wanting to be seen in a disheveled state. Being a leader meant presenting unwavering strength.

"Eve," came a murmur beyond the door. Cora.

"Yes?" Eve turned the gas lantern by her bed even lower so Cora wouldn't see the redness of her eyes or face.

Cora opened the door a crack. "Are you all right?"

"Yes, just tired," she lied. There was so much emotion within her, roiling and crashing against her crumbling interior walls.

"I know it's more than that. And you know I know that. If you don't want to say anything, that's fine. But I can't turn being in tune with you off. If I do, my gift suffers."

Eve nodded and patted the end of her bed, reaching out a hand. Cora came and took it.

"I take it something happened at the soiree," Cora prompted.

With as much detachment as she could muster, Eve relayed her night. She failed to keep her recounting of the detective and his long-lost childhood sweetheart a dispassionate one. She went into the excruciating description of the way they looked at one another, how his family acted about them, and how there was a distinct distance between Eve and the detective afterward. Tears were fresh in her eyes again. "I…I feel pain and my body aches in an odd way I've never felt before," Eve gasped, reeling.

"Eve, may I be honest with you?" Cora asked gently.

"Yes?" While she wanted to be open and ready for anything, she wasn't sure she had the strength to withstand criticism.

"You like being the center of attention."

"I do not—"

"Not in a crowd, necessarily, but in a group. Among friends. You are a leader. You're an only child. And a bit spoiled. Well, a lot spoiled."

Eve's mouth dropped open, and she made a small, squeaking sound of protest, but Cora continued.

"It isn't your fault; it's been circumstance. You've had to maintain that center of attention; otherwise, you'd never have lived. With all the pressures on your head, you'd have psychologically become a ghost. You'd have floated away had you not bolstered and grounded yourself with pride. But there's been no one close to you enough to counterbalance that. You're now fairly set in your ways," Cora said with a smile.

"When my parents adopted my sister Lottie, I was fuming mad about it, because I wanted to be a princess. But Lottie opened my eyes and toughened me up. And I needed that for my coming north, because goodness knows the north has different cruelties for people of color, and I needed to understand the world didn't revolve around me. I needed to learn how to function when the world doesn't make me feel like it wants me in it—"

"*I* want you in it," Eve pleaded, grasping at her foremost colleague, wondering if she'd failed everyone she cared for. "I hope you always know I love you—"

"Oh, stop it, you big baby," Cora said with a laugh. "This moment isn't about me. I'm making a point about perspective. Your heart is so full that it doesn't know what to do with itself sometimes. You don't like to acknowledge vulnerability, especially if it feels that your emotions, your care, or your attention isn't being matched. Requited. Centered back on you. Tonight, you weren't completely at the center, and that was painful."

"Am I unbearable?" Eve murmured in horror.

Cora laughed again. "No, darling, I'd have left already if you were. I've little patience for the unbearable. But this man is forcing you to face different things than you ever have before. He's the only one you've ever truly fancied—"

"I do not fancy—"

Cora placed a finger gently on the end of Eve's nose and tapped out the next words. "Doth. Protest. Too. Much. I don't dare claim you're in love with him because I'm not sure you know what that *is*—any more than you know how to share something that interests you. You have to admit he interests you; you've said that much, at least."

"What do I do?" Eve begged.

"Give it space. Let him be the ruse you claim. If he breaks that off, he'll still be a useful colleague who can give us contacts and access within the NYPD we wouldn't have otherwise. That's the worst-case scenario. We can't afford to lose a friend."

The idea of the detective being solely a contact, just a useful transaction, a mere reference, seemed cold, bleak, and tragic. Eve wanted to cry again.

"Protect yourself," Cora urged. "Don't pin your whole heart on him. I can't speak to him and this childhood sweetheart, but be cautious."

"Of course. I...I'm having a bit of trouble with perspective."

"It's hard when so much is on your shoulders. But please remember, so much remains unanswered."

"I promise I haven't forgotten that. I was attentive to the spirits; they've been speaking, no, *shouting* at me. They've been unbearable—"

"And we were here with them the same. They are *so* loud. Tomorrow we must try even harder."

Eve put her face in her hands. "I don't feel well. I've failed everything."

"That's drastic and untrue."

"The pressure." Eve pressed her temples. "All the children. All the files. They keep shouting that I've failed them all."

"Maybe you had too much cordial? Rest. Tomorrow, we find Greta. And Vera. We have to."

"Poor Greta, darling Vera, I can't fail them too!"

"None of us can. Get some rest, Eve." Cora shut the door behind her, and Eve turned to her pillow.

Next came tears of failure; she'd not been a good detective, putting the failure of not being closer to resolutions solely on herself. She could hear Maggie murmuring at her from the threshold, trying to respect Eve's boundaries between the dead and the living, begging her to calm herself, to rest, but she shook her head, her sorrow immense.

Her thoughts kept circling back to the detective smiling at Sophie; the image wouldn't leave her mind. Here she thought that smile had been reserved just for her. How naïve and arrogant. What a fool she'd been.

After another hour of tossing about, Eve took a bit of sedative in her tea, reserved only for the nights when her mind would otherwise have been a horror.

It was the middle of the night when Eve began walking within worlds.

I'm dreaming, surely, Eve thought, as the darkness around her became impenetrable save for slivers of silvery, glowing light down a dark hall. But it was also her upstairs hall.

Here she was searching for a weeping young spirit that nagged at the edge of her mind, one of the lost children, showing up as ghosts so maddeningly did, at the corner of an eye, glimpsed as a glanced refection in a window or mirror. An aberration in the shadows that might be seen if one squinted. A sound, a cry edging just above the disquiet of the city, and a scent of long-forgotten memories—a ghost nudged in their sixth sense just above the living five. She worried it was little Ingrid Schwerin, whom she'd put to rest, perhaps now worried for the fate of her missing mother, with no leads as to where to find her. What if she were the cause of Ingrid's fall from peace to unrest?

"Why do you weep, spirit?" Eve called. "Let me help you. It's what I do. I help little lost souls like yours. Tell me how to help."

"We've tried. But you're not listening," came the voice from up ahead, remaining out of sight. *"You're not seeing."* It did sound like little Ingrid.

"Then help me again," Eve begged to the dark, the spirit's words cutting her to the core. "I'm sorry. It isn't for lack of care, but we don't always speak the same language, living and dead," Eve said, meekly adding, "I've devoted my life to all of you...."

This wasn't a trance she'd put herself into, because she floated along as if on water in this long, dark hall lit only by the occasional eerie glow of an orb, an afterimage of a spirit. It was also her staircase, and she felt herself float down it, stepping weightless like a spirit.

The hem of her nightgown seemed to be edged in mire. Darkness was seeping into her spiritual gift. She kept moving forward, toward the voice ahead, but it seemed to be retreating as she tried moving forward.

"*It's all there, in the bits and pieces,*" said the spirit, now invisible, just a voice. "*That's all we are, scrap. Bits and pieces. All that's left.*"

She turned to the walls around her, flocked wallpaper like her own walls, though in the center of the detailing, the empty sockets of little skulls stared back at her instead of her usual rosebuds. The tiny details of her own house were transforming into a horror. Ahead, a light brightened, a cool, expanding orb before her.

Groggily she realized the light was the brightening sky. She'd sleepwalked down her own stairs and stood in her parlor at the break of dawn.

"Show me more," Eve begged to the spirit world. "I want to understand. I don't want to *fail.*"

"*But you have failed us, you have failed him....*" The murmurs were merciless, and the light of spirits dove around her. She was freezing cold and assaulted; spectral light was upon her, transparent hands open, reaching for her face. Ghosts weren't just pressing in against her mind—they were floating over her in a mass of silvery light, reaching out, their icy fingers clawing her arms, skin, hair, cheeks. Their collected force sliced a tiny cut across her forehead. She hissed and waved them off.

Squeezing her eyes shut, she tried a shielding technique Gran had taught her in her youth, spreading her energy out like a wall. The chill of the spirits eased back, giving her a slight circumference in which to breathe. She was in both places, as if she stood in the Corridors between life and death as she stood in her own home, her body and mind torn between worlds as she always had been, but the visual representation of it had never been this disconcerting.

Wavering in the parlor, she found herself staring at the telephone receiver in her dressing gown, standing right before the wooden box mounted on the wall as if she were expecting a call.

The phone rang. But it didn't. At least, it sounded like a distant bell. A phantom ring.

She picked up the receiver. There was a distinct hiss on the line. Breathing.

Eve wanted to recoil, to drop the bell in terror, but a familiar voice began speaking as though from a great distance.

"Hello, Eve," said the voice through the bell, soft, barely audible over a static hiss.

"Hello?"

"It's Lily Strand. Remember me?"

Lily Strand was dead. A deaconess who had ushered Ingrid Schwerin's spirit onward to peace, a guardian of children's souls who used to work for the city's vulnerable mothers and children.

"Yes," Eve whispered into the bell. "I remember...."

"Come to the Sanctuary, Eve. I need you to come. For the children. It's the only way to make this right. You've failed them, so you *must* come now."

As if Eve were moving through water, she picked up a pencil on the telephone box and wrote a note on the notepad set on its wooden shelf.

Out of the corner of her eye, something moved. At the rear window of the parlor was a face at the window.

That man's face.

"Come now," Lily Strand begged through the receiver and Eve dropped the bell, shrinking back from that terrible smirk, that terrible shadow. He was back to torment her.

Eve suppressed a scream, rushed to the front hall, threw on a coat, scarf, and boots—and ran.

Chapter Thirteen

A quiet voice sounded from downstairs and woke Cora from a deep sleep. She rubbed her eyes, rose, and put on a nightgown, sliding slippers on her feet and padding into the hall. Peeking to the side, she noticed Eve's door was open and the covers tossed aside, her bed empty.

Cora trotted down the stairs. "Eve?"

Movement against the wall drew her eye to the telephone bell, swinging on its cord, off its handle. She replaced it and looked out the window. Turning the corner, about to disappear down the next block was Eve. Her hair up with a few dangling locks, a bonnet in hand, and her bootlaces undone. Her long black coat, billowing out around her, had been thrown over her voluminous white silk and satin dressing gown. She looked like the madwoman from Rochester's attic.

"Oh no, no, no!" Maggie appeared at the window.

"What's happening? Where is Eve going?" Cora asked, horrified. "And like that?"

"I've a suspicion. Look at this." The ghost pointed to a note. Cora picked it up. "And if I'm right, we're going to have to assemble an army to keep her safe."

"Go after her," Cora commanded, running upstairs to get dressed. "Tell her to close her coat, at least; she'll get arrested as raving and indecent! Find out where she's headed."

* * * *

"Evelyn Helen Whitby!" Maggie shrieked, a ghost banshee appearing before Eve in a burst of light and a blast of cold. Eve stopped dead on the street, locks of black hair falling in her eyes. She tried to brush them back and found there was a bonnet in her hand. She placed the bonnet on her head and tucked the errant strands under. "What the hell do you think you're doing!" the ghost continued to shriek. "Close your coat!"

Chastened, Eve looked down and realized her coat was hanging open— and while her dressing gown was thick and layered, it was still recognizably a dressing gown. She buttoned the top buttons of her coat and cinched close the belt. She bent to tie her bootlaces, wondering how she'd gotten so many blocks without tripping.

"I'm going in, Maggie," Eve exclaimed. "I'm going to find that stone, and I'm going to enter the Sanctuary. Nothing else is giving us answers, and Lily Strand said I had to."

"Oh, no you're not— And who is Lily Strand? Didn't I tell you it was dangerous? Didn't I tell you it was *not* for mortals?"

Eve turned away from the ghost, tears in her eyes. Vaguely aware of passersby out and about at dawn who glanced at her in disgust, pity, or horror, she didn't care as they hurried nervously on. "What does it matter? My heart doesn't matter, so maybe I don't, maybe my form doesn't. Perhaps I can do better from inside, like Lily Strand."

"Eve, what are you talking about," Maggie snapped. "What do you mean your heart doesn't matter?"

"It's broken anyway. I'm a damned fool. A naïve fool. And the ghosts won't stop *shouting,* so I've no choice or they'll rip my head open."

"Who broke your heart, Eve?"

"You can't stop me, Maggie." She clutched her head as the ghost chorus swelled again, a torrent of murmurs and pleas. "Shut up," she shouted, accosting the air with a swipe of her hand. "Shut up! I know I failed!"

"Who broke your heart, Eve?" Maggie repeated.

Eve wiped tears on her sleeve and ran up the steps of the nearest uptown trolley, fumbling for tokens in her coat pocket.

Maggie appeared before Cora as she was buttoning up her bodice. They weren't always in uniform, but Eve had had a black version of the police matron dresses made up for each of them for any formal occasions. Cora felt that going to rescue Eve was as good an occasion as any, especially since she didn't know what would be asked of her; she wanted to look as official as she could.

"Well?" Cora asked the ghost.

"She's going to go into the Sanctuary because spirits were shouting and some woman named Lily Strand told her to. And she was going on about a broken heart. I assume the detective? I don't know. She was weeping. To be honest, I've never seen her like this."

Cora nodded. "I've never seen anything like it either."

"What happened at that soiree?" Maggie asked.

"You weren't there lurking?"

"No, actually, I gave Eve some privacy to just be a normal woman. I went prowling about the outside of the Prenze mansion, as I couldn't get in; I was blocked. I couldn't see anyone or find anything new."

"Fair. So how do we do this? With this Sanctuary?"

"I don't know." Maggie wrung her transparent hands. "We assemble the team. I know where the exit point is, but that's *all* I know. I don't know whether she will physically transport somewhere or just her soul will travel. It's too dangerous...."

"One of us should remain here to be a call point for a relay. Likely Jenny, because I can't bear her being put into danger when we don't know what's ahead. Do we involve Gran?"

"No! Not a chance," Maggie exclaimed. "That place is tied too closely to her, and she's not the young spiritual solider she used to be. Knowing Auntie, she'll want to charge into Sanctuary after Eve, and she's too old now to do such tricks and keep her body safe. Only if we can't reach Eve do we involve the elders like Auntie or the Bishops."

"Should we also tell the detective?"

"Oh, certainly, I was going to go there myself and overturn the contents of his desk until he paid attention. Much more productive if you grab him. The Sanctuary is about the heart. And if she's heartbroken, then we need the thing that can mend it."

"If he's worthy," Cora retorted. "If he was courting another woman this whole time, their agreed-upon ruse or no, then he's a cad and I will punch him in the face—"

"No, there must be a misunderstanding," Maggie stated. "I've intruded on them. I've seen the way he looks at her."

"Well, then, the noble detective can *look* to get her out of trouble. I'm going to be at Mulberry the moment it opens. Please alert Antonia to meet me there with a waiting carriage and then go look after our lovely fool, will you?" The ghost nodded and vanished through the wall.

Once Cora had packed a day bag with supplies, she hailed a hack to get to headquarters, strode in, and showed her clearance card to a man in uniform at the front desk.

The card was a new one Roosevelt had sent the girls, and she could feel the judgmental eyes on her from the front reception, as if the officer on hand were weighing the color of her skin against the card itself. She suddenly empathized with the detective and the prejudices he faced.

"Here to see Has-no-wits?" sneered the man. "His office is in the back, where it should be."

Cora stiffened, her fists clenching. "His name is *Horowitz,* and I hear he's due a promotion, so I'd take care with your juvenile—"

"Miss Dupris!" Horowitz bounded up to stand between the admissions officer, who had risen to his feet with a threatening look, and Cora. "So glad you've come. Thank you, please follow me."

The two strode into the hall, Cora holding her head high as they turned the corner. "Friendly place, this," she muttered.

"Northern hospitality," he replied in the same tone. Once they were in his office and he'd turned the lamps up, he partially closed the door. "How can I help you, Miss Dupris? To what do I owe this pleasure?"

"Eve's gone, and you need to help."

She handed over the shakily written note Eve had left by the swinging receiver that Maggie had called her attention to.

"Two paths diverged in a pinewood. I chose the one ghosts traveled. I've failed them and I've lost him.

I have to go to the end of the world to make it right."

"You think this has to do with me?" the detective asked, handing Cora back the note.

"I think you may know where she went."

The detective furrowed his brow. "The pinewood and the ghost travel suggest the Sanctuary, near Sleepy Hollow."

"That's what Maggie thinks. And you've been there," Cora stated.

"Not *into* it; we just went to its…door."

"Still, you shared that special experience with her." Cora took a deep breath and tried to make sure her tone didn't betray the jealousy she felt at being left out of something so important.

"Are you going after her?" he asked, frowning. "Is Maggie with her, at least?"

"Yes, Maggie is trying to monitor her. Ghosts have been unusually hard on her, to the point of screaming at her for unsolved troubles. When Eve doesn't get answers, she pushes herself. Too hard. I'm afraid she's going to venture further than her body or mind can take."

"Then we must prevent that," he said, rising to his feet. "Maggie said Sanctuary might listen to the living at that stone. Depending on what kind of state she's in... I wish for nothing improper—"

"And you will remain a gentleman," Cora stated sternly. "Antonia is outside with a waiting cab to take us to the depot. Jenny will remain at home in case she has to take a call and alert Mrs. Whitby. For now, there's nothing for the average mortal to fear, and I don't like getting Eve's mother or Gran worked up for nothing."

"For the above-average mortal?"

"Something darker than usual was driving Eve out at dawn. It isn't like her to be this vague or reckless. She was sleepwalking and may have spoken with someone on the phone. It's all so odd. She made all of us promise when we began the precinct that none of us would ever embark on a mission alone. But after the party she was... Well, like I've never seen her."

The detective was gathering supplies: a small kit, a glass jar of water, and a paper bag of roasted chestnuts on his desk. He paused and turned to Cora.

"What do you mean?"

Cora sighed. "This is none of my business, Detective, truly, it's just... I've never seen her like she was last night. And for Sensitives, the state of one's mind is crucial to understand."

"What happened last night?"

"You tell me," Cora said and folded her arms. "I know your courtship may be a ruse, but you shouldn't be seen courting two women at the same event."

The detective stared at Cora, confused.

"I...was greeting an old friend, and then when I turned back, Eve was"—he clenched his jaw—"*enraptured* by the young Mr. Veil. They were..." The detective adjusted his collar. "Very close. I...I assumed she was preoccupied."

"Oh!" Cora laughed. "No, it isn't like that. Daniel is like a brother to Eve. From what I understand about you, however, the woman you spent all night dancing with seemed to have held *all* of your favor."

"Oh, what, Sophie? Oh! No, I mean, our parents always joked about us being childhood sweethearts, when we were children. I'm very fond of her, but I don't see her like *that*—"

"Well, that's not what Eve saw."

The detective stood there, slack-jawed and deeply uncomfortable.

Cora took a deep breath. "This is not my place to say, Dectective, and Eve would slap me for being so bold, but when she said in her note that she 'lost him,' I think that means you. I don't think she realized, until last night, how much she cared. I daresay she's begun to think of you as... more than a ruse. I...think her hopes and her heart were dashed last night."

The detective put a hand to his mouth, his eyes widening. His cheeks went scarlet. "Oh... Am I an unwitting cad?"

"I can't answer that for you."

"Well, I certainly didn't mean to be," he exclaimed.

While part of Cora wanted to be warmed by this display, protectiveness surged within her. She might have hit the crux of their trouble—mutual jealousy leading to unnecessary drama—but she needed to set a safe stage for their rescue mission. "Well then, regardless." She gestured forward. "Let's not waste another moment."

"Certainly not."

He locked the door behind them, and they strode back out past the scowling front desk clerk and out to the street corner, where Antonia had held a hack for them. The driver clearly had been told not to dally, for once the door was closed Cora had to hold on to her bonnet lest it fly away in the sudden start of the small, open car. Antonia and Cora sat across from the detective on cushioned benches, the city flying by as they raced to the depot.

"Miss Morelli," the detective said, bowing his head. "What are you two...sensing at this stage? I can tell you're scared for her, which makes me just as worried."

"Danger," Antonia replied. "The spirits have been after her, dogging her hard. I can hear it. The spirits of restless, aimless children have grown impatient to the point of torment. There's a convergence of spiritual energy trying to find resolution. She's been managing it very well, but I think last night"—Antonia looked at the detective pointedly—"something tore down her defenses, and her emotions were left raw and vulnerable."

The detective clenched his fist and looked away ruefully. "I'm no good at this."

"If you mean fancying someone, I assure you Eve's *terrible* at it, so you're in good company," Antonia stated. Cora barked a laugh. That seemed to ease the detective. "Don't tell her I said that."

The hack darted up Fourth Avenue until the street was covered in waves of billowing steam. Before Cora could offer, the detective had stepped up to an open counter and bought three River Line tickets, nearly running to the designated platform.

Once they'd sat on wooden benches facing one another, against a wide window with lace curtains drawn, Antonia spoke carefully. "All joking aside... She truly cares for you, Detective. You should probably be aware of that."

Cora held up a hand to stop Antonia. "The detective and I discussed that. For Eve's sake, let's not continue to betray her confidences. This is unfair—"

"The detective needs to know the full scope if he's trying to get her out of the Sanctuary," Antonia countered. "Working in these matters requires a complete trust and thorough, if not intimate, understanding of the other party. Even, dare I say *especially*, what they're not admitting."

"I'm not as well-versed in spiritual gifts as you two," the detective stated. "Shouldn't either of you go in after her? I'm not averse and I'm not afraid—I just don't want to be a detriment."

"We'll take that as it comes," Cora replied. "But Antonia is right, the best results in a Spiritualist emergency happen with those with whom the concern in question has a strong tie. All we're saying is she...has a strong tie to you."

The detective nodded. "That is an honor, then."

"All I'll add is this: I'll leave any details to be sorted between the two of you," Cora said. "But you might want to clear up last night—"

"Without a doubt. Definite misunderstandings." He passed a hand over his face, clearly overwhelmed if not a bit awestruck. After a long silence of just listening to the train, he asked them in a whisper. "You really think she cares for me? *Truly* cares? It's not some game she's playing? Because I've thought this whole time she's just being coy—"

"Whatever it started as, I assure you it's no longer a game," Cora declared.

"If you ask me, she's *hopeless* for you," Antonia blurted with a wide smile. "But again, don't you *dare* say we said so!"

At this admission, a convulsive, purely joyous laugh escaped him, and he turned to look out the window, surreptitiously plucking a handkerchief from his breast pocket to dab at his eyes.

Cora's heart swelled at his overflow of sentiment, and she glanced at Antonia, who put a hand to her heart to see such a reaction from this open, earnest man. She could see, now, why Eve cared; she didn't begrudge her that. It was just lonely losing someone Cora felt was a partner, a sort of soulmate in her own right. But everything changed in time: partnerships, dynamics, and resources. They were all now in utterly foreign territory with no idea what was next.

Chapter Fourteen

Whether it was sleepwalking or a different kind of mental shift that left her without recourse or control, Eve had no further sense of herself until she was on a train.

The conductor's shout of "Tarrytown" woke Eve from her stupor, and she found Maggie snapping incorporeal fingers before her face.

"What's going on with your mind, Eve?" Maggie asked, concerned. "It's like you're in a trance."

"Perhaps I am," she replied. "We're here."

She stumbled out of the station, ignoring the looks of those concerned with the state of her. Eve was sure she looked bedraggled and distracted, but an otherworldly momentum was carrying her along the path Maggie had first led her down.

"What do you think you're doing, Eve?" the spirit asked. "How will this help?"

"We've made no progress, and we still have no Vera," she said through clenched teeth, trying not to make a spectacle by raving to herself. "So I'm going where I've been told to go. I am answering a call! Lily Strand told me to come, and I trust that she can help. Strand unraveled the mystery of Ingrid, who first appeared to Vera, and so I'm sure someone there can help us with the rest of the children. I'm following spectral bidding, as nothing else is working!"

She made it to the woods, stumbling down the slope toward the solitary, open stone arch that jutted out of the green.

"But how can you make progress here?" Maggie insisted. "You're going to what, talk to the stone and see if it answers?"

"I'm going to go *in*," Eve said. Maggie tried to block her, but Eve stepped right through her, the icy wake of her dearest friend chilling her already cold body to the bone.

Looking around to see if she was alone, with no other living company, and satisfied that she was, Eve placed both hands on the unfinished stone arch.

"Sanctuary, I ask for your blessing, your help. I come with deep respect, on the wishes of Lily Strand. I know I am mortal and beyond your laws, but please let me in."

The sound of the spirit world opening—a distinct, rushing sound of wind and some far-away scrap of gorgeous music—washed over her as if she were taken under by a wave. Eve closed her eyes and wished to give over to something more powerful than herself. It would help take away all of the pain in her head and her heart.

"*I'm here for you, Eve Whitby*," came a voice ahead of her. Lily's voice, as if it were coming through the empty heart of the unfinished stone arch. "*Reach out*."

Eve did so, one hand braced on the arch, the other reaching through it.

"*Take my hand*." A hand grasped hers, soft but strong. "*Give way*."

The sounds around her shifted into an echoing hollowness, and she felt as though the ground indeed gave way beneath her.

"Eve, don't!" she heard Maggie cry before she careened into darkness.

Whatever hand had held her let go, and she fell, spinning, tumbling down a hill, too startled to scream or cry out. She could only gasp inelegantly.

She didn't dare open her eyes; she braced her arms before her face in case of impact, but nothing hit her. There was a resistance around her body like a gale-force wind, but it was light and song, and she felt herself fully upright, felt her feet on solid stone.

"Eve Whitby, it's all right. You made it. Your soul stepped through," Lily Strand said in a gentle voice.

Eve opened her eyes and found herself in a wide, tall, immense stone cathedral with beautiful stained-glass windows. It was an incredible place that was hard to describe, because for one beat of her heart it appeared like an ancient church but in another beat it seemed as made of mist and light as it could possibly be of stone. A space beyond mortal understanding.

The woman next to her was tall and willowy, lovely and serene in a deaconess's habit, dark blue and white, like those at the Grace Memorial house that had taken in sick Ingrid Schwerin and her desperate mother. "Welcome to Sanctuary."

Eve looked around at this new world. A moment ago, she'd been standing in the woods at a half-hewn arch. Now she beheld the likes of

Notre Dame, lit brightly with ethereal, ghostly light—a place of dreams and hope. It, like her, seemed to breathe, its surfaces rippling gently; the luminosity of the place glistened like a star. Eve had journeyed to a plane that was its own entity.

"This place…is incredible," Eve said, examining the windows, whose patterns were intricate designs of interwoven flowers and angels: vibrant, protective things.

And the music. The most hauntingly beautiful music. Medieval-style incantations were sung in sweet, pure tones by women's voices, far away and yet all around her, an impossible trick of the ear—the movement of spirit through sound, as if music were the lungs here.

Tears flowed down Eve's cheeks.

"For those of other beliefs," Lily explained, "Sanctuary shall resemble their houses of worship, or for those of no faith at all, this place appears to them as a beautiful forest glade just like it is in the mortal world, where you remain."

Part of Eve thought that she didn't want to return, but she wasn't sure she should voice that here. It likely broke another rule. Still, her heart ached so badly.

"You poor thing," Lily said, scrutinizing her. "Here you're whole, but out there"—she gestured behind them—"your poor heart, your addled mind."

Eve chuckled mordantly. "Is it that obvious?"

"The spirit world knows and cherishes you," Lily replied warmly. "What weighs on your heart weighs on ours. I've been watching you ever since I came here, knowing you were the best asset any ghost ever had, and you mustn't lose sight of all the good you've done and will continue to do."

"Thank you. Help me understand. I'm…there and here?"

"Yes, you've been…*paused*. Ghosts are watching over you, but we must speak and act quickly. This is not a place for you, and we are on borrowed time. We are breaking every vow I took in becoming a Sister here, and while I trust that the forces here will forgive and understand me, I can't be sure."

"It was you who took Ingrid Schwerin onto peace, rest— Is she all right? You work on behalf of children's spirits; can you help all those presently tormenting me?" Eve asked.

"Yes, on all counts; it's why I called you here. I didn't have enough energy to manifest the ability to tell you all of the details." The spirit smiled conspiratorially. "It takes a deal of energy for a ghost to make a telephone call," she added. "I had to bring you here for Greta and for the sake of the children, to reunite you with your friend who will help you through the next phase. Reconnecting you will help her regain the mortal world again."

From behind Lily stepped an old woman, and Eve gasped in happiness. White hair up in a bun; a colorful shawl patterned in bright, bold red roses draped over a sky-blue dress. Vera in vibrant, full color was a moving sight to behold, as Eve had seen her only muted in greyscale. The wrinkled elder, whose eyes were a bright chestnut, lit up at the sight of her colleague.

"Vera!" Eve cried and embraced her. Solidly. Here, the spirits were tactile. Eve held on and squeezed as Vera laughed. Having left her native Mexico City for Manhattan in the midcentury, she had lived to a ripe old age on the Upper East Side painting beautiful art and loving every ounce of New York as her own, so much so she refused to leave. A soul as bold and colorful as her signature floral shawl. The old woman's ghost had been invested in the cases of children from her first encounter with Eve years ago.

"*Mi amor! Bendiga!*" The specter cried her benediction, patting Eve on the shoulders, stepping back to cup her face in her wrinkled hands. "*Gracias*, I was not sure you could come for me."

"We were so worried about you!" Eve said.

"I followed the troubled children, but I got lost along with them. I don't remember when I blinked out, but I did. There was a terrible darkness, but then I woke up here...."

"Like Maggie!" Eve exclaimed. "She returned to us. This place saved her too; it's how I knew where to go." She turned to her spectral guide. "Miss Strand bid me come, and I trust her." At this, the kind deaconess's gentle expression turned radiant with a smile.

"You went so deeply into your powers," the deaconess explained, "when you sought to set Ingrid to rest that you came all the way to the outskirts of Sanctuary by the sheer, intense scope of your gift. It was unprecedented, and your tie to Maggie allowed her to be pulled back to the mortal world in the wake of your force."

Eve remembered the searing pain of it, but the staggering beauty of seeing Lily Strand usher Ingrid's innocent soul toward peace was a treasure she'd never forget. Maggie had pushed her away from getting too close to the all-encompassing light.

"Ingrid's mother, Greta," Eve said to the spirits, "she's gone missing—"

"I know," Vera said. "I could feel something terribly wrong. I went to Gramercy Park, back to the house that started the whole inquiry with Ingrid, to see if I could determine why. I have no sense of time between standing outside that empty house and here."

"We think Dupont has taken Greta," Eve explained. "Perhaps the same force keeping the spirits out of Dupont's home and parlor shoved you all the way here."

"I don't know, but I do know what's ahead," Vera said grimly. "There's a part of Ingrid that she's detached herself from, something left behind for me to find, but it will lead us forward. I know where to go."

"What do you mean?"

"You'll see."

"*Where* is this place?" Eve asked Lily. "This isn't the Corridors between life and death; the Corridors are Purgatory, but this, this is more like Heaven...."

"It isn't Heaven," Lily clarified. "It was created by the spirits of a sect of nuns centuries ago, women of powerful mysticism. What you call the Corridors between life and death in other places may be called the Whisper-world. While the Whisper-world was created in ancient time by great, divine forces, this place here, in contrast, was entirely built by human souls. This is a human creation, a deep and divine mystery, magnified by the need to provide the act of sanctuary to the lost who aren't yet ready to move on but find themselves trapped."

"Like me. I was in darkness," Vera explained. "I wasn't ready to move on; I hadn't said my goodbyes like we've all promised. If I was in the Corridors between life and death, I'd have at least been somewhere familiar; I'd have tried to get my bearings. But I was in an outer darkness and could gain no sense of either world. Somehow I stumbled here and was given safe harbor."

"Something, in effect, snuffed you," Lily Strand began, choosing her words carefully, "and pardon me that I don't know how to explain this better—it's new to us. Vera's spark was somehow cut to the quick, and while the spirit is eternal, something canceled your ability to manifest," she said gravely. "This is of great concern to the Sanctuary. Whatever did this to Vera and Maggie could do great harm to this place, and that harm would ripple into the Corridors before lashing back out into the world again. Find out what did that to Vera and to Maggie. But first, Eve, tend to all of the lost children confused about their fate, helping Ingrid's mother along the way. Vera can lead you to the pieces. She has been shown the way."

"Good," Eve insisted. "All I've ever wanted to do is help. I don't always know how."

"I believe you. Just please take care," Lily begged. "Too many séances take a toll on us, pull on our stones, weaken our glass."

"I'll try to find ways to fortify this place, if I can," Eve promised.

There was one sharp, reverberate gong of a bell, a huge carillon; the sound rattled in Eve's bones.

Lily ran to the front door of the cathedral, looked out, and ran back, grabbing Eve by the arm and rushing her forward to the entrance nave. "Go, Eve, we've disrupted the rules of this place for too long, and we're now in dangerous territory."

There was a darkness, a shadow that crossed in front of one of the great windows. The floor shook a bit. The angel choir faltered, and an icy hand of dread clamped down on Eve's gut.

Lily opened the great wooden front door of the cathedral. Ahead of her was only bright grey light, like the glare of a foggy day.

"If we're not careful," Lily cautioned, "your continued presence here could tear what keeps the Sanctuary separate from the worlds. Go now. There's a gentleman outside who has come for you, and you should go to him. I can feel that his heart is radiant, and that will do you good. Take a moment with him. The task will hold. You must be at your best, and he can help."

"Who do you mean, Lily? I don't see anything."

"Keep looking," the deaconess demanded. "Let me have a moment with Vera, spirit to spirit, to tell her the way and mend what's been torn. She and I must repair the breach, but you must go on. Keep doing good work, my child, even if it feels thankless. I assure you, you are loved by the dead."

The deaconess gave Eve a push, and she stumbled forward into a blinding shaft of light.

There was another weightless sense, where the physics of time and space were suspended. Her whole being so full of experience and emotion she couldn't begin to process, she felt impossibly heavy with the weight of sentiment, dragging her down out of the sky, falling from heaven by the depths of feeling.

Her name echoed in the distance. Leaves rustled nearby. A chill grazed her skin.

Was that someone familiar, there beyond the shafts of light? A gentleman, yes, in a frock coat, collar undone, mop of dark hair... Familiar, yes, he was calling her Eve. Her heart began to race. She knew him. She cared for him. She wanted to remember him.... Goodness, how this place addled the mind.... She reached out a trembling arm, weary from strain.

"Eve!" Came the desperate cry again. "I see you! Come, come back to us! It's me, Jacob...." He tried to move closer, to move past those bright shafts, but he was coming from another world, unused to the ways in which the Sanctuary operated. "Eve! I'm here for you...."

She felt arms scoop her up, as if she were about to be enveloped in a ravenous embrace, yet she kept falling from that great height. She gasped in fear, but something warm and strong broke her fall.

Her vision snapped back into focus, and she looked down at a handsome face. Wide brown eyes tinged with an entrancing ring of blue glimmered up at her, and soft, perfectly drawn lips parted in a bit of a laugh, a bit of a sigh.

She had fallen on top of Jacob Horowitz, knocking him down, and they now lay in a wooded clearing—and goodness if he didn't look inviting. She smiled, dazed. Then the reality of their compromising position struck them both. Eve felt her cheeks flood with heat just as his went a sudden vibrant rose.

"Hello," they said at the same time, then laughed as they continued in awkward unison, "I'm sorry."

"I didn't mean to—" Eve tried to lift herself, but her body was entirely unresponsive and simply collapsed back on him again. Her lips accidentally grazed his warm cheek; her nose slid against his. "Oh! Still sorry—" Eve blurted, gasping as she tried to adjust, but the gasp sounded more sensual than she'd intended.

Their faces were so close. Too close. Eve had enough strength in her arms to pull back a bit and stare at him again. "I'm having trouble. I can't quite seem to get back up."

"Then don't," he said, his words suddenly soft.

He tucked back an errant lock of black hair behind her ear. Her previously unresponsive body offered up a shudder of delight that triggered his own, a delectable vibration coursing between them. Dangerous, such friction.

A certain raw and visceral hunger twisted deep within her, something at the core she'd never felt when just dipping her toe in the waters of flirting. No matter whom she'd tried to charm, nothing had ever quite awoken her like this. She hoped her eyes didn't betray her. But the good detective didn't miss anything. His eyes glimmered anew.

"You don't need to go anywhere," he continued in that same sweet tone. "Just take a moment; I've got you." His gaze was full of sentiment Eve didn't dare parse. "You're safe," he continued, hypnotic. "You're back, and we were quite worried for you."

"I…I don't really know what happened," Eve said quietly. "I was sleepwalking. The ghosts were after me, and so was a man in the shadows— It's all muddled. But the Sanctuary is beautiful, and it will help us."

"I thought to find you at the stone, but you weren't there. Cora and Antonia are searching down the hill. I found you propped against a tree, your eyes all glazed over. I'm sorry for having grabbed you, for touching you without permission, but you were unresponsive. This is all very improper—"

"Well, *I'm* still lying on top of you—"

"Then *you're* very improper," he said with a grin.

"You don't seem to mind," she teased. But then, like a slap to the face, she remembered how he'd gazed and beamed at another woman, and her smile fell. That was one part of what had driven her out here: the desire to run away, to not feel anymore, to lose herself into a place of spiritual comfort. "But then again," Eve continued sharply, "you don't seem to mind a woman smiling at you, close, laughing, leaning against you. I saw all that—"

"*About* that," Jacob interrupted firmly. "I owe you an apology."

Eve tried to wrestle free from him, feeling her heart constrict and her stomach clench.

"No, Eve, wait," he continued softly; his arms held fast around her. "Let me hold you while I tell you this. Sophie is a friend. A dear, delightful friend, but nothing more. I was surprised and overjoyed to see her, just like you were with your Daniel. It seems we both jumped to the wrong, and admittedly a bit jealous, conclusions."

Eve couldn't look at him. She didn't know if she could trust his words, but his news felt like dawn breaking after an endless night.

"Forgive me for the misunderstandings?" he asked.

Eve bit her lip and nodded. "So…you don't mind our agreement? You're still game to court *me*?"

"I could be persuaded to court you indefinitely, Eve Whitby," he said quietly, reaching up and pressing a finger to her jaw. "If you'll have me…."

She let him turn her face toward his, let him bend his head toward hers, trembling, closing the distance….

"I will," she whispered against his perfect lips.

"Eve?!" A desperate cry from down the hill sounded like Cora crying out through tears. "Eve!"

The detective and Eve sighed in unison, their heads falling to the side.

Forever interrupted. That was perhaps for the best. There were very pressing matters, and a kiss should be saved for a moment when danger wasn't around the corner. A kiss should be saved for plenty of time to enjoy it.

Lily Strand had said to take a moment with this man, this radiant heart, that the task would hold. But there were answers that had to be found, and it would be unseemly to make her friends wait in worry.

Eve arched her body slightly in what she thought was an effort to extricate herself and shift away. In reality, it pressed their bodies firmly together. Heat traveled and blossomed all over, and her breath caught in her throat.

The moan the detective had been trying to contain burst from his lips, and he seized her, clapping his palms wide around her waist and then grasping, ostensibly to help her up as she shifted, but the grasp was possessive and held her more than it moved her. His eyes flashed with hunger before he closed them lest they betray more.

"I *am* sorry," Eve gasped, trying to shift again but able only to press harder. "I'm not trying—"

"To drive me mad?" he said through clenched teeth.

Eve bit her lip, having no idea what to say. That she affected him as he did her... It was overwhelming. The detective lifted her, his wiry body strong as he rose with her now on his lap. His touch felt so raw as she navigated this close physicality without a corset, just layers of muslin, satin, lace, and silk below the wool of her coat. She was without armor, and it heightened everything.

"No, I'm not trying?" Her reply was a question because she was, in truth, pushing the boundaries they'd laid out for one another. It was a delight to flirt, to play, but this was an entirely new game she needed to pace properly. "I mean, I'm sorry, I'm sure this has all been a terrible frustration, having to come find me."

"That's not how I meant you were driving me mad," he said, setting his jaw and staring at her with searing intensity, a look that shot a bolt of desire down her spine. "*But* I would like to maintain my unwavering commitment to being a gentleman."

Eve stared at him, still scared to let his words in, frightened by her own vulnerability. "You're *very* good at your part, Detective."

The detective threw his head back. "Good God, I thought we were moving past everything being an act!"

"Do you want to?"

"Are you going to counter questions with more questions so you can never be held to account for an answer?" he asked, exasperated. When she gaped at him—overwhelmed, addled, and thrilled in equal measure—he chuckled. "Come, Whitby, let's get you presentable. Your friends were terrified for you; let's not worry them any further, and let's establish what's next."

She blinked, nodded, and tried to regain her composure.

"Yes. Next. I have to follow directions from Sanctuary as to where to find Greta and the restless children at their wits' end." Eve looked around at the forest. "Vera should be coming to help, but I don't see her."

"Can you put any weight on your feet?" he asked.

Eve tried moving her legs. She nodded. "I think my soul left my body to go into Sanctuary and the return has left me a bit jumbled."

"I'll help you." Horowitz rose, keeping hold of her arms, lifting her as she found her legs.

Once standing, she wavered, a wave of dizziness sending her back against him, cheek to cheek. The tip of her nose grazed his earlobe, and if she turned her face, she knew she'd impulsively kiss the hollow of his throat—and the very thought sent her roiling again. He smelled of fresh soap and sweet mint. She took a deep breath, inhaling him, wanting every sense filled by his delectable details. His arms fully around her waist, he righted her and stepped back. The moment she didn't have his closeness, she missed it.

"You know, you don't have to go to such great lengths just to be next to me," he said with his most charming smile. "You can just ask."

This offer weakened her knees again. To cover for nearly swooning, she turned away with a nervous laugh and began brushing leaves and pine needles off her coat. "Thank you for coming for me…. You pulled me back from a precipice. How did you know where to find me?"

"Cora came asking for my help." He turned away from her to call in the direction of Cora's shout. "Miss Dupris? Miss Morelli! Up here! We're here and all is well!" the detective called, his voice strong and clear through the forest.

Oh no. Eve's heart pounded. What had Cora told him? Had she revealed how heartbroken Eve had been? How childishly overdramatic? She didn't know how embarrassed she should be. She looked down in a panic. Thankfully, Maggie had demanded she button and cinch closed her coat, lest the detective realize that not only was she uncorseted but she'd been lying atop him in only her nightdress.

A cold chill washed over Eve, and she recognized the distinct, elderly form of Vera floating above, her reds and blues traded for greyscale once more, floral shawl draped over her bony shoulders, her white hair up in a bun with straggling strands floating about her wrinkled face.

"Vera, you made it," Eve exclaimed, holding out her arms as if to give the spirit a hug. Vera bent down and kissed Eve on both cheeks, a peck of ice. "Vera here, floating to my right, is one of our best assets; she's been missing," Eve explained to Jacob. "Thank you for coming back to us—we need your help to navigate! Lily said you'd know where to go."

"I'm here thanks to you, *mi amor*! You are my anchor and now *you're* back!" Vera cried. "But I saw the little children from the pictures and they were my guide. Sanctuary mends broken pieces and helps us see our path. Lily told me to follow your voice back to the living. Come. Greta's not got much time. I know where to go: the chapel of treasures. Hello, Detective! Follow me, all of you."

The detective looked on patiently but raised his eyebrow. Eve relayed what was pertinent. "We're already north of the city," Vera explained, "but Greta is farther; we need to keep going. There's a chapel in the woods, and Greta's there. Along with half the answers to the spirits' needs."

"Where is the other half?" Eve queried.

"Somewhere in Manhattan still."

"I need to alert the local precinct. We will need reinforcements," Horowitz determined.

"I think we're enough," Eve stated. "Not to mention Cora's a good shot, remember?"

"As you wish, but if we find ourselves over our heads—"

"We'll not do anything brash, but we must go now," Eve reassured, hiding her dizziness by leaning against a tree, still trying to get her body to cooperate.

Antonia and Cora appeared from around a bend and rushed up to Eve, embracing her.

"You silly thing," Cora admonished, pulling her canteen from her pack and handing it to Eve, who took to it ravenously.

When Vera became visible to Cora and Antonia, there was further rejoicing in their reunion.

Her heart swelling at the seams, Eve didn't dare look at any of her dear ones lest she burst into tears. Antonia squeezed Eve's shoulder and glanced pointedly between her and the detective.

"Vera alone can lead us forward, to Greta and the children," Eve explained. At this, the old woman nodded. "She's come from another spiritual plane to do so."

"Lead on," Horowitz stated quietly. "We are ready for the next task."

The team made their way back to the Tarrytown platform, thankful not to have to wait long for the next northbound train. When it pulled in, Cora pointed to the dining car. "Coffee and an actual meal, if you please."

"Agreed," everyone chorused.

"Two stops north," Vera declared, looking out the window. Eve relayed the instructions. "Then you'll have to follow me."

Food and refreshments were devoured eagerly in the dining car before anyone pressed for more out of Eve than she dared say.

"Thank you for coming to my aid, friends," Eve said finally, reaching out and squeezing the detective's hand briefly before pulling away. He tried to keep her hand, but she withdrew too quickly. Her cheeks coloring, she rose, coughed, and excused herself to a restroom on the next car.

Once Eve was out of earshot, Cora turned to the detective, who was worriedly watching Eve leave.

"She's nervous," Cora whispered. "And embarrassed. She knows something was said. She's not easy to fool. The trouble with keeping psychics in your close company."

"I'm nervous too," he said quietly, fiddling with his collar. "Isn't that how it usually goes?"

"You're a good man," Cora said.

"This is a good team," he replied.

"Thank you for coming," Cora said. "For trusting us without question."

"I haven't always understood what's gone on in your precinct, or even your methods, but I do know you're worthy of trust and help, and you've been generous with yours in turn."

"I...want to apologize if I was sharp to you in the beginning," Cora stated. "I was wary."

"Of a man coming in and possibly trying to tell you how to do your job? I can't blame you. Most of my colleagues, save the ones I call dear friends, are insufferable," Horowitz stated, and Cora snorted a laugh. "I wish never to intrude, only to be of assistance. If I'm ever in the way, tell me."

"Eve would never say you were in the way," Antonia added.

Eve reappeared, and everyone turned to look out the window in unison, which made her scowl, immediately suspicious.

* * * *

After a lifetime of being hounded by ghosts, talked at mercilessly, Eve didn't like being talked about behind her back, and she knew they were doing it.

She felt raw and vulnerable, and equally ecstatic from her moments of closeness with the man she... Well, she wasn't sure which passionate word she felt, so she didn't choose one, just let sentiment stew within her, disconcerting and exhilarating and nauseating.

It was so hard to stay focused on what was ahead because her mind had been expanded by the mystical beauty that was Sanctuary. She wasn't the same person who had entered, and she understood now why Maggie didn't want her to go in. Sanctuary's ethereal nature defied comprehension and had made Eve feel like her soul was bursting at the seams.

"I know you want to know what happened to get me to the Sanctuary and what happened within," Eve said, breaking the heavy silence. "I'm still making sense of that journey in and what I saw there. It was as beautiful as it was overwhelming. If we're not careful…something awful could come of it, a catastrophe of human error. But I found Vera, and we have a next step."

"We're just, all of us, glad you're all right," Cora said quietly. Everyone nodded.

Before they knew it, their stop was called and the train whistle screamed, piercing the peaceful day. As if the loud sound was Vera's summons, she appeared before them as an even brighter manifestation than when she'd first appeared, luminous and transparent against the picture-perfect autumn panoply of trees and shrubs around the station stop.

Vera flew out from the car before the doors opened. The colleagues rushed to keep up. Eve's residual dizziness still spun her, but she tried not to let herself appear weak.

There was a gravel path leading away from the station that gave way to slate stairs down a hillside.

And then ahead was nothing but forest, evergreens interspersed with flaming colors. Vera's chilled form kept ahead of them, Eve close behind, her bedraggled form trailing the floating, translucent greyscale flag whose form fluttered as falling leaves fell through the elderly spirit's body.

Only a vague trail, wending an undulating course down the valley from a gravel road, made them feel there was any tie to civilization or way in which to orient themselves. It wasn't a terrible distance from the station and yet the way the land and the path sloped away into dense forest, it felt curiously far and instantly remote.

"We'd never have found this without help," Cora exclaimed. Reaching into her pack to draw out a compass, she checked their direction against the upper road.

Soon Vera left even the path itself.

"Are you sure?" Eve murmured, trying to keep up with the spirit, not wanting to seem to others that she was doubting one of her best assets.

"I'm being led by Ingrid Schwerin, so yes," Vera said. The elderly spirit was all business. She'd come back from her time in the Sanctuary with more focus and surety than Eve had ever seen.

"Oh!" Eve exclaimed, a hand flying to her chest. "Is she here? I…I don't see her."

"I didn't ask her to come back into the mortal world, Eve; I knew you wouldn't want that," the spirit replied solemnly. "But she told me what piece of her body lies ahead, and that is the beacon I am following."

Eve swallowed. "I see."

Vera slowed as they came to a bend in their path, nearing the crest of a hill.

"Stop." The elder spirit held up her hand. "You're under my direction now, as bidden by the children. Before you go any further, let me inspect the premises."

The ghost flew forward, and Eve explained to the detective what she and her mediums had heard.

Vera returned a moment later. "I cannot get inside, but through the window, I see only Greta. Alive. Dupont is nowhere to be seen, but he might come back."

Eve relayed this message.

"I really should involve the local precinct," Horowitz stated. "It isn't far; the station is right near the train. I can't afford any animosity between the jurisdiction here and the city. It could interfere with Dupont being charged correctly and to the fullest extent with whatever we can."

"Of course, you're right," Eve said. "Go, then; we'll be fine. I told you, Cora's a good shot."

At that, Eve heard the sound of a cocked and locked chamber. Cora stood at the ready with her small pistol in her calm hand. "I am."

The detective looked at Eve, at her colleagues, then back to Eve. "Take care," he said, reaching out to grasp her hand a moment before running off, disappearing behind the ridge.

"It's just ahead," Vera stated, her luminous body a swath of white against an evergreen and her long, bony fingers pointed. The women strode down the crest and into a clearing. The trees parted to reveal a small, single-room, white wooden building with a steeple and arched Gothic windows. A tiny, eerie chapel in the middle of the woods.

"Thank you, Vera." Eve shuddered.

The team ran to the chapel and threw open the little grey door. Inside, laid out on a cot set upon a dais appointed like an altar and draped in red velvet, lay an ashen-faced Greta.

Pistol out, Cora swept the perimeter and rear, noting to her colleagues that the coast appeared clear. The chapel was only one small room fitted with a coal stove. Icons and religious artwork filled the space, but all of Eve's focus was on the woman they'd been trying to find.

"Greta!" Eve rushed to her. "Wake up, my friend. We're here to help. Wake up."

There was a long, painful moment before her body stirred. An agonized moan began low in her body and escaped chapped lips in a stifled sob. Greta, groggily, began to cry.

"Greta, it's me, Eve Whitby, and my colleagues. We're here to help. You...you do want out of here, yes?"

Greta nodded. She looked like she wanted to speak, but seemed to be having trouble. The empty bottle of tonic next to her seemed to indicate she'd been drugged and sedated.

"Are you expecting Dupont back?" Antonia asked.

"Night," she managed, as if her tongue were numb. "He comes at night."

Cora offered her water and the woman drank. "Let's take a better look at where he's brought you." Eve turned and gasped. "My God."

The small chapel was filled not only with icons and frescoes—one wall had a pyramid of shelves showcasing small, gilded boxes with grand detailing and metal halos spiking out from the items in radiating coronation.

Upon closer inspection, it appeared that the boxes and frames were showcasing specific items. Small, desiccated somethings...

"Reliquaries," Antonia stated.

Cora took a sharp breath. As she did, her nostrils flared. Eve picked up on the scent. It had been a subtler emanation at first, but the overwhelming smell of surrounding pine and residual incense couldn't entirely displace the distinct odor that turned Eve's stomach. Embalming fluid.

"Body parts of saints— At least, that's the idea." Antonia crossed herself.

"Ingrid," Eve murmured. "Presented as a saint. This is Dupont's theme, and Heinrich went along with it, if not fell in with the 'devotion' of it."

Cora nodded. "It matches the images psychometry provided when I touched Heinrich's injured head along with the images from Dupont's empty parlor. The cabinet full of small tokens. He puts pieces from bodies into these."

"No offense to the dead, but I do not believe these are collected from actual saints," Antonia said. "This many, if authentic and stolen, would already have created a world-wide search."

"No, he's made these," Greta said, struggling to sit up. "And something here is keeping the ghosts who those parts belong to away."

Eve made a note to ask Horowitz and any officer he trusted if there were other sacred items taken in recent memory. The things Heinrich Schwerin had taken to prepare Ingrid "as a saint were a curtain from a synagogue, a wooden angel from an orphanage, and garlands from a chapel display. The things here were grander and gilded. Whether they were truly golden or just painted with metallic paint and patina to look aged and valuable, Eve couldn't tell without a closer look—and she wasn't ready to touch them yet.

In examining this tier of parts, Eve noted a closed metal box was affixed to the wooden wall below the lowest shelf; a smaller, different device than what was taken from her office. A thick, encased wire ran along the baseboard and up to the box. The chapel had no fixtures indicating electric lighting. Prayer candles in clear, tall glass votives were sat everywhere. Nothing was lit now but perhaps it was part of Dupont's nighttime ritual.

"Whatever that is, it's likely keeping spirits out," Eve said, gesturing to the metal box.

Antonia suddenly grabbed one of the unlit glass votives, upended it and dashed the side of the glass against the base of the box without breaking the votive. With a loud snap, the wire was dislodged. "Don't touch the exposed end," she warned, pointing at the tip of the wire as it fell to the floor.

Maggie appeared in the instant, manifesting to Eve's right, dousing her in a wave of cold air. "Eve! I'm so sorry…" tears glistened silver in the spirit's eyes. "I didn't mean to leave you again! I was watching and waiting for you, but so close to Sanctuary, I was lost again… I don't know what happened… I couldn't get back to you…"

"That's all right, friend," Eve said calmly, "You're here now and thank goodness. We'll need your help." Eve then turned to Antonia, her eyes wide with wonder. "Whatever you did… How did you know what to do?"

"I've been studying electricity ever since the lights went out and you went unconscious for days," she replied nonchalantly, as if she were a seasoned academic. "Ghosts seem particularly attune to current. Though the wire looked encased, I didn't dare touch it directly. Glass is a low-conductivity material."

Cora and Eve both chorused praise for Antonia's intelligent initiative and her sharp-featured face beamed as Maggie applauded.

Vera was the next to appear before them. She pointed to the center of the pyramid. Surrounded by white satin and framed in a box, was a small, shriveled heart. Gilded edges and adornments had made it into the image of the sacred heart in flames. "This is what led me here and now you've made room for the children to follow. Well done."

Eve stepped back, viscerally affected, her hand flying to her throat. "Please tell me that's not little Ingrid's heart," Eve whispered to the ghost, sudden tears in her eyes. The sweet, forgiving little girl whose soul she had met in the Corridors between life and death did not deserve this odd desecration of her body. No one did.

"It is," Vera said gravely. "But do not fear or despair; she is at peace. You and Lily made sure of it. But her heart was my guide here, the light I followed to find this place. Perhaps she is a little saint after all... But..." the elderly ghost glanced at Greta. "Tend to the living. Greta doesn't know about the heart. Take care."

Eve turned away from the terrible display and sat next to Greta. "Talk to me while we've some time."

The thin, drawn woman coughed. Eve reached for a glass sitting on a dusty side table near the cot that had a bit of liquid in it but put it aside after sniffing foul contents therein. Cora stepped forward with her canteen, and after another drink, Greta was able to clear her throat and speak.

"His life's work. I...I didn't realize... There was so *much*. I knew his interests. It all started with a postmortem photography collection. He'd told me he'd given it up to a friend. I just...didn't think so many of his thoughts had been realized. It didn't start like this," she said fearfully. "I'd never have...indulged his affections if..."

She began to cry. Eve held her hand. "In the beginning"—Greta spoke haltingly, struggling to find the right words in English—"when I first worked for him, I thought it was beautiful, the way he spoke about death. The way he...revered it and made corpses beautiful. He made me less scared of death and made me feel so alive.... So when he asked if I would share the joy of life with him, and have a child with him, since his wife couldn't...I said yes. But then I was seized with shame and fear I'd be thrown out if I started showing. I went and got properly married."

"To Heinrich— But Ingrid was Dupont's child?"

Greta nodded. "When I found out he had lied about Ingrid's body, that he'd been working with Heinrich to make her into a little saint, I flew into a rage. After her funeral I confronted him. But then, somehow, in my shattered state, he wooed me again. I don't know how I let him." Tears of shame poured down her face. "He brought me here so we could make another little saint together. The fulfillment of his art and heart. He said this place would be our haven of the saints and angels. That we would bring Heaven to us here."

"But he worried about you leaving, so he started putting poison in your tonic?"

Greta nodded. "A day after I got here, when I realized this was a prison, when he saw all of these items frightened me instead of making me feel closer to God, he...turned cold and began incapacitating me, locking me in here and going off God knows where. I...I don't know how long I've been here."

Cora carefully removed her gloves. It was true her psychometric powers would be critical to determine which parts went to which child. There were twenty-some examples here. But not now, even though the pressure of the spirit world was at a near boiling point.

"Each one will tax you Cora," Eve warned. "This would be a game of chance and a danger, with no guarantee you could get through them all. Each of these samples needs to be attached to a soul, but it will take time and we need to do so while reinforcements keep watch. Once Greta is out of harm's way, we'll return and the detective can help us catalogue. Gran too."

Cora nodded, but instead of putting her gloves on she placed them over her shoulder.

The image of the file folders on the table all flying open made Eve wonder how many were tied to this fetish.

All of us… The spirits echoed as if in response to her mental query, as if they were listening in to her thoughts. *"For years and years, gone unchecked…. No one would listen!"* The spirits' accusatory voices tumbled toward her like rattling bones.

"Are you hearing their wailing?" Eve gestured to the atmosphere then to the tall bay of reliquaries before pressing her temples. Her colleagues shook their heads.

"I feel spectral weight and hear murmurs. Clearly not as loud as you," Cora said, and Antonia nodded agreement.

"No one is listening!" the children screamed.

"I'm listening now!" Eve declared to the air. "Stop torturing the person who is helping you!" Pressing at her temples and the back of her neck, she tried to relieve some of the pressure, but it was too strong, pain like a hot poker behind her eye and the base of her skull.

Greta looked around her, at the air, as if trying to see what Eve was reacting to.

"I'm sorry," Eve said. "Spirits have been tormenting me about this. I don't mean to seem unhinged."

A river of tears streamed down Greta's face. She gestured to the reliquary showcase. "Do you know… Which…which part is from my daughter? He wouldn't tell me." Moaning, she turned to the side with dry heaves.

Antonia soothed her. No one answered that question.

Be careful, the spirits moaned in chorus.

"Detective Horowitz will be returning with local police to this scene," Eve stated. "Dupont will be met with quite an entourage he won't have expected."

At this Greta offered a wan smile.

"I need...to...go to the outhouse. If you'll excuse me...." Greta stood with the help of Cora, put on a wool cloak, slipped her feet—shod in socks darned so many times they were multi-colored at the toe with so many different stitches—into worn boots, and moved with only slight discomfort toward the door, each step stronger, as if just moving her aching muscles was a relief.

"Indeed, get a breath of fresh air," Eve encouraged. "You're safe now."

"You've been through so much," Cora whispered to the woman, tears in her eyes. Eve realized that in helping Greta up, Cora must have seen with her bare hands images of what led the grieving mother to this moment.

As Greta exited out the front, Eve stepped outside the rear door, another simple Gothic arch with a grey wooden door. Taking a deep, shaking breath, she glanced around the empty, still woods behind the chapel, a grove of birch trees looking tall and elegant in a cluster before her. The back of the chapel was faced in slate, and there was evidence of a fire pit surrounded by a circle of rocks.

She felt that distinct prickle along the back of her neck. She was being watched. As she whipped her head around, a figure separated itself from the trees—something dark coming into view between the bright white birch trunks.

The shadowy man from her window, with his hat and that terrible smile.

"Damn you," she cursed. "*Whatever* you are, I renounce thee."

Antonia had followed her out. "What is it, what do you see?"

"There's something following me. Watching me—and it isn't a ghost. Likely an astral projection, from what I know of it. A living soul trying to send itself as a haunt."

She pressed against the necklace her father had given her, the tiny sapphire given with so much love and charged with her energies, glad that through the tumult she was still wearing it from the soiree. Sapphire enhanced psychic abilities, clarity, and insight. It was a stone of strength and confidence. As she touched the gem, the figure before her flickered—still spectral in part, but not in the way she was accustomed to.

The spectral world was operating in new and untested ways. The thrill and sense of purpose Eve gained in creating the Ghost Precinct was ebbing away, her confidence in her gifts and her own strength faltering. She pressed harder on the small stone around her neck, narrowing her eyes as if by the physical act, her third eye could shove this shadow back where it came from.

It vanished, and Eve breathed a bit easier.

Antonia came up beside her. "I didn't see what you just did. I know you're the most gifted of us, but tell me how I can share in the burden if at all possible."

Eve turned to her colleague, whose elegant, tall forehead was creased with worry, her dark eyes searching for something helpful to do.

"You do, just by being here, gifted as you are. Never undervalue that. You and Cora lend such vital fuel to my endeavors. As soon as I can figure out what's attacking me, we'll banish it together."

A sudden rush of sound knocked Eve and Antonia backward as if they'd been physically pushed.

"*Listen to us,*" came the chorus of children in the air, wailing. It was maddening and heartbreaking, and Eve didn't know how to reassure them. Antonia winced from the force of it.

"We are," Eve said to the children's chorus, trying not to lose her patience. "We can't conduct a séance yet to attach all of you to each part. It will take hours, and we're not yet safe here."

"Don't trust ghosts," Maggie said, her spirit appearing at the door of the chapel, luminous against the Gothic archway. "Not that they'll deliberately try to mislead you, we just... We just don't always know better. We make assumptions as you do. We want and feel as you do. And when we fixate on something or someone... Let's say the lore of obsessions and repetitions in haunting, well..." The ghost looked away, staring out into the forest.

"Lore can originate from certain truths," Antonia offered.

"Yes," Maggie said, turning back to her colleagues; her luminous eyes glittered, spectral tears in those eerie orbs. "The children are speaking their heart. They feel betrayed and abandoned. Iniquities were done— whether at the time of death, during their wake, during their funeral, embalming, any number of moments in the process of death—something from them was taken."

"We'll try to match them with parts as best we can, but we can't do it all here or today. Now that I know the extent of it, I'll need Gran and all hands," Eve said ruefully, grimacing at the thought of so many severed things to sort through.

"You understand why it's so fraught, yes?" Maggie asked. "It isn't that we think if our bodies aren't whole that we can't go toward peace; it's that those children and their families didn't give permission for such a token to be taken. It is about consent."

Eve nodded. "Of course. Permission and intent are everything."

"*There's more,*" the chorus of children's voices cried. They seemed to be huddled right next to Eve's ear, even though she could see no forms.

"Where?" Eve exclaimed. "You must tell us where to set this right!"

"*Magic!*" they cried, and in a burst of light, their forms appeared. A flurry of floating, silvery white bodies flew back inside the chapel. Eve followed them inside, toward the shelves of reliquaries, watching as they stopped and posed as if they were creating a scene.

Eve stared at a tall candlestick, one on either side of the pyramid of offerings. At the top of the pillar, a carved wooden hand curved around to cup the circular iron base holding the thick candle. A spirit floated near it, placing his own little hand right where the carved wooden one curved, a perfect match. Another little girl floated to the other side, mirroring the boy. Where had she seen those candlesticks before? Why did they look so familiar?

"Cora, could I ask you one favor?" Eve asked, gesturing to where that spirit floated.

Cora nodded. "Could you touch that candlestick and see if you can determine any provenance?"

Cora did as requested, stepping back with a gasp. "I saw that child's living face and then a theatre. As if I was on stage, looking out. A staged Hell was all around me...."

"Mulciber!" Eve exclaimed. *Magic.* "I recognize this from the stage set. It was noted Dupont did some stage scenery work, yes? He must have designed that show and... *Parts* are inside!"

A gunshot rang out in the woods. Everyone froze.

"Oh, God, please no," Eve gasped.

Cora led a charge out the front door, weapon drawn, with Vera and Maggie at her side and Eve following as fast as she could. Antonia plucked a liturgical staff from the front of the chapel and held it, ready to swing the eagle-winged tip.

In a clearing they saw a striking sight. Greta stood glowering over a body laid at her feet. Dupont: his white suit bloodied across the breast, splayed with dirt and pine needles. In Greta's fist was the pommel of the gun, and Dupont's unconscious face was bloodied from the nose, a gash across his cheek.

When the girls arrived and paused at the edge of the clearing, Cora aiming her gun at Dupont's supine body, Greta held up a hand.

"I'm all right," she said, the thickness of her tongue finally having fully worn off. "We struggled over his gun, and it went off. I grabbed it and hit him in his insufferable face," Greta said, panting, her eyes full of fury. Cora applauded. "I wasn't going to kill him," Greta added, "because I don't know where all the body parts are. From all the children." She screwed up her face, trying to hold back tears. "There's more. I don't know where, but I know there's more…."

"We'll make this right," Eve promised.

The women gathered around the unconscious, troubled man as Greta added, vehemence heightening her German accent, "Now…would one of you please tie him up?"

Cora was all too willing, pulling a roll of thick twine from her shoulder bag and tying Dupont's hands and feet securely. Greta withdrew a soiled handkerchief from the cuff of her sleeve and wiped the handle of the gun off, then tucked the bloodied rag into the breast pocket of his coat, the soiled fabric another blossom of scarlet to add to his splattered ensemble.

Cora made careful, intentional loops in the knotted twine, asking, "Where do we leave him?"

"Right here, for now. Detective Horowitz can deal with him when he returns with local police."

"I did go with him willingly at first," Greta said ruefully. "I was a fool, but I won't lie to the courts."

"What may have begun willingly became coercion, poisoning, and imprisonment," Eve countered. "Don't blame yourself as the world is all too quick to do."

"There are plenty of counts that will do him in," Cora assured.

Maggie, who was floating at the crest of the ridge, wafted over to Eve's side and bent toward her.

"Your lover is coming," Maggie said softly at Eve's ear. Eve pursed her lips together, leaning into Maggie's coldness to keep from the habitual blushing at such intimations. "At least he's something handsome to look at on such a dreadful day."

"Is everyone all right?" Horowitz cried from atop the crest of the hill a few yards away, running toward the group.

"Yes, Detective, thank you," Eve called.

"I was en route back and heard a gunshot echo all through these woods." He looked down at the man on the ground. "What's this, then?"

"Greta and Dupont struggled over the gun. We rushed out from the chapel to see this incredible sight," Eve said, squeezing Greta on the shoulder. It was only then she felt how much the poor woman was shaking. "She's the hero of the hour," Eve added. "Greta, this is our colleague, Detective Horowitz. He's a great help to our precinct and to the force at large."

"You're indeed impressive, Mrs. Schwerin," the detective agreed. "To have fought so bravely. We need to get all of you someplace warm and safe."

"Thank you." The woman stared at the ground. "I'm…so grateful to you all. I'm so sorry to have brought—"

"None of this was your fault," Eve countered, holding up a hand. "What did the local precinct say, Detective?"

"They've been wary of Dupont for a while; he was evidently a young undertaker in this area when he married into his wife's family, before moving to the city a decade ago. They wanted to get him on something but didn't want to involve the wife."

At the crest of the hill appeared a lanky man in uniform with bushy sideburns and a mustache too big for his young, worried face. Horowitz introduced them as he approached.

"This is Lieutenant Bills, who had the unlucky honor of being the man I ran into," the detective said, gesturing to the uneasy man. "Misses Whitby, Dupris, and Morelli, and Mrs. Schwerin, the subject of our search. That man she bravely leveled on the ground is the suspect."

"Greetings Mr. Bills; thank you for joining us," Eve stated. "To indict Dupont, on what charge I'm not sure, is all ahead. Come." She pointed in the direction of the chapel. "But none of the contents of the place goes anywhere that I can't have access to. I have case files that I have to attach to each piece inside."

"Piece? Of what?" Bills asked in a small squeak.

"Do I even want to know?" Horowitz muttered, and walked toward the chapel anyway.

Bills looked at Dupont's unconscious body and his bindings, noted the man wasn't going anywhere, and only after giving everyone a skeptical eye followed the precinct into the building.

"Detective, Lieutenant, welcome to the world's most disturbing chapel," Cora said, crossing the threshold and gesturing around her. "Do look around, it's quite the collection."

"Good God." Horowitz added something under his breath in Hebrew.

"Dupont likely thinks he honors God." Eve shook her head. "Heinrich was similarly deluded into thinking he was creating holy relics— Indeed, communing with the saints."

"Any religion can be a devil of a drug if taken too far," Horowitz murmured, looking at the shelves of reliquaries with their small, gruesome offerings. "What a unique fetish, this. I take it this was done without the knowledge of the departed or their families?"

Eve nodded. "These are pieces of children whose bodies were disturbed at the end of their funeral or directly as they were interred," she explained to the young lieutenant, who promptly ran outside and vomited. Everyone else grimaced and looked toward the inelegant sound with pity.

"We don't know who shared this fascination with him besides getting Greta's husband involved," Eve said to the detective. "Perhaps *Arte Uber Alles,* but we can't be sure. Greta thinks there may have been others. When she's ready to talk about it—"

"Now that I can talk about it, I'll tell you everything I can," Greta stated, standing at the threshold.

"Nothing like Prenze tonics to tie up the tongue and incapacitate a body?" the detective asked.

"The tonic was mixed with something else," Greta clarified. "Dupont knew how to make poisons."

"Come to the station with us so we can formally process a charge," Horowitz stated.

Bills appeared at the threshold, green, but he managed to speak clearly. "There will have to be an additional team sent to catalogue all of this."

"And like I said," Eve began carefully, "*we* have to be the ones to be sure these items match..." She thought about how to put their needs and not alarm the young officer. "My files should correlate these items with never fully processed incidents back in the city—complaints of disturbances with graves, odd goings-on. Mr. Bills, we *must not* be shut out of this or I promise you, you'll have more on your hands than you know how to deal with."

All of the ghosts dove at the man—and while he didn't look up or see them, he shivered violently at the onslaught of cold. Eve knew Antonia and Cora were aware of the manifest spirits, but they didn't make a scene for the sake of those who couldn't see what was all around them. What had been voices at the beginning had become stable, visible forms during the reveal of the body parts. Eve knew from experience that a more direct channel between her mediums and these children grew stronger every moment, which was good, because they still had a second round of parts to find.

"You work for the force, then?" Bills asked Eve, confused.

"In a...roundabout way." She tried to offer a genial smile. Her head hurt so terribly, the cost of her gifts, but she had to appear competent.

"I promise you access, Miss," Bills said, putting up his hands. "We'll leave it all here and catalogue from here so as not to disturb a crime scene. I'd rather not have anything to do with it, if it were up to me."

"Even better." Eve gestured toward the open door. "Let's discuss the next steps to find the rest of the parts en route to warmth?"

Everyone nodded.

"We'll get the crackpot along the way for questioning, as he's got a lot to answer for," Bills said. "If he's roused yet."

As they walked, Eve explained Greta's situation to Horowitz.

"Greta initially came here willingly. Slightly intoxicated and a bit coerced, but willingly. Dupont will likely make that a case for his own argument. I'm sure he wouldn't hesitate to cast Greta in a poor light. It's possible he might be able to show paperwork that all of these specimens were obtained legally. He likely knows what he's doing is…disturbing, but it might not be illegal, somehow skirting the bone bills."

"*But it* is *wrong*," one of spirits of the little ones insisted, a whooshing swath of white diving near Eve's head. "*We don't like it*," echoed several of the other children. A squabble went up around Eve's head, as if the ghosts were frightened that yet again, they would go unheard and disrespected.

"Pardon me," Eve said to Horowitz, gesturing to the air, lowering her voice. "I need to tell the spirits to quiet down. All this has riled them up a bit."

Horowitz took the cue and led Bills ahead a few paces.

"I know, dears," Eve reassured the air, lest the spirits make the place even more of a scene. "Please. I swear upon my heart of hearts, we'll sort this all out."

Antonia stepped up and took Eve's hand. She gestured to the spirits.

"I swear upon my own life. My living life," she stated.

"My dear, take care with such things," Cora said softly.

"They are our care," Antonia insisted. "When I left my little sister behind when I left my family, I prayed I could help children some other way. The spirits that led me to Eve's welcoming doorstep promised I would, and I then promised them. I can swear upon my life because this is part of it."

At the next clearing, paces ahead, Dupont had roused himself and was struggling with his bindings on the forest floor. Looking up, recognizing Eve and her company from when they had questioned him at his parlor, he scowled and muttered curses at them. Eve remembered that when they'd first interviewed him, he'd come across as a dapper gentleman, albeit a bit off. Now he seemed a man possessed: wide-eyed, sickly, driven by wild obsession.

Greta hung back, her cheeks scarlet. Eve stepped in front of Greta to shield her—and once she did so, he pointedly wouldn't look at either of them.

Bills roughly yanked the man to his feet, thin arms belying serious strength. "Come with me, Dupont," he stated gruffly. "We'll have to undo his feet."

"Ah, allow me," Cora called, rushing up. "I did this with care."

Cora withdrew a pocket knife and made an incision, and suddenly there was a gap of twine. She'd cut the binding, but what remained was a set of twine shackles, enough width for small steps but not enough to run.

"Nice work, Miss," Bills said, looking at the clever bindings approvingly and nodding at Cora as he nudged the scowling, white-faced Dupont ahead.

"I know there are more parts," Eve said to the detective. "They're with Mulciber."

Magic, the children chorused. Somewhere in that theatre lay additional abominations.

"You won't know, because they can't get in," Dupont hissed. "No one can tell you anything."

"Who can't, the ghosts?" Eve asked. Bills shuddered at the word ghosts. Dupont appeared smug.

"The ghosts can't get in because of some kind of device keeping them from the theatre?" Eve pressed. Dupont's smug expression flickered. Eve seized upon a chink in his armor to see if she was right. "The device I'll have the liberty of disarming? I think the ghosts will have a lot to say about Mulciber's 'Heaven and Hell,' Mr. Dupont, when they get the chance to rush in."

He spat her direction. Eve ignored this insult and got closer, grabbing his face as he stumbled, forcing him to look at her as they moved toward the station house.

"Why?" she asked. "I just want to know why."

"I have made a communion of saints," Dupont barked. "And you are sinners for stopping me!"

"Lord have mercy," Bills said, yanking Dupont away from Eve, crossing himself. "None will find that convincing, you dog, least of all the actual saints. You're a sick man."

"My little saints prove the power of the spirit," Dupont said to Eve. "How it can be evoked and how it can be blocked. Someday, the torment of ghosts might even be able to be stopped dead!"

"Why do so? For your own sake? Or for someone else?" Eve pressed.

Dupont said nothing more, but a ghost took the liberty of replying.

"For the shadow man," came the disembodied murmur of a spirit against her ear, and Eve couldn't help but shiver. The litany of injustices done to Eve and her department of late ticked through her mind like a flip-book creating a moving image. The sight of that shadow at her window made her equally furious and scared.

"Who made threats against us? I know you didn't act alone. The severed finger sent to my office back when all this started, who is responsible?" Eve demanded.

Dupont scowled.

Cora stomped toward him, removed her glove again, and shoved her hand on his head. "How have you threatened us?" she demanded. After a long, tense moment, Dupont trying to break contact but Cora not allowing it, her eyes fluttered and she withdrew her hand with a hiss.

"I saw the finger," Cora said, relaying the images her psychometric gifts saw upon touch. "He was told to send it to you by a man in the shadows. It was taken from a dead child."

Eve glared at Dupont, wishing her gaze could start a fire on his pale skin. She'd taken that token to Mrs. Bishop for examination, having been privy to a horrific case involving body parts as tokens, and she'd promised she'd bless it and take care of it. No spirit spoke of it, so the power of Clara's blessing must have removed the owner from the present spiritual discord.

Bills watched the entire exchange in awe and apprehension. Horowitz just stared forward with steeled reserve. Vera and Maggie floated along, silent, grim sentries. The spirits of the children floated along in a luminous, eerie entourage, awaiting their justice in turn.

Dusk was falling when the group arrived at the local precinct, which had been made tactfully aware of the possibilities of the situation thanks to Horowitz's efforts. Staff were ready to greet them; they were ushered in by a quiet matron. No one wanted any to-do about it. This stretch of the Hudson River Line was a nice, lovely place, and Bills seemed to be very interested in keeping it that way, far from the gossip rags.

An area nurse had been called in on account of Greta. Mrs. Henari was a round, golden-skinned woman who was kind and likeable, an exemplar of her profession. Not a hair out of place, a slight stain, or an unraveled thread escaped her wide, dark eyes.

Once Greta was cleared as safe, she turned to Eve and grabbed her hands.

"They're sending me to rest and fully recover my bruises and scrapes in a nearby clinic," Greta explained. "Mrs. Henari, bless her, has promised that if my sister Susan can't come collect me tomorrow, she'll escort me to the city and to Susan's rooms herself." Greta looked at her hands. "I am unused to this sort of kindness and care."

"It shouldn't have been rare for you," Eve said. "I ache for all that has befallen you."

"Take care of those children's remains," Greta begged. "And if…if something there was from Ingrid…"

Eve glanced at Vera, the silent, calm sentry, and the ghost shook her head. Not now. The sacred heart from an innocent child would be discussed later.

"If we can determine something was taken, it will be returned to her grave," Eve reassured. "We can visit it together if you like."

Greta nodded. "I'd like that. You are heaven-sent, Miss Whitby."

"I don't know about that," Eve scoffed, squeezing Greta's hand, "but I'll take divine help any day."

An aide from the clinic approached, bidding Greta follow, with Mrs. Henari promising to check in first thing in the morning. Greta bowed her head and walked away.

The steadfast nurse wanted to examine everyone but was waved off by Eve.

"Mrs. Henari, thank you for your excellent service," Eve stated, gesturing to her team. "Truly, we're fine, and we must get back to the city. There's a time-sensitive issue with our case."

The woman pursed her lips, golden cheeks flushing. "It isn't every day we get a call like what we've gotten here," she said, concerned. "I know you young ladies are strong, otherwise you wouldn't be working"—she leaned in excitedly, keeping the secret Horowitz likely told her to keep to herself when he was preparing the station—"on behalf of the governor, no less! But as a working woman and a mother, I beg you not to be withholding any injury—"

"We promise," Cora said with a warm smile. "There's still work ahead of us."

"But if you've any aspirin, that would help take the edge off my migraine," Eve said. The woman was happy to offer two pills from a bottle in her bag, and she wrapped two more in tissue paper for the trip. "You're an angel."

Eve asked permission to use the precinct phone. The next step required swift planning and supplies. After a moment, Eve was connected to the voice she wanted to hear most. "Gran?"

"Yes, Eve, love, is that you, dear?"

"Yes, Gran."

"Oh, thank God! What happened and where are you?"

"I went to the Sanctuary to find answers to Greta's disappearance. Now I'm—"

"*That's* what I felt, wrenching inside me! You know we're spiritually and psychically tied! Why didn't you *ask* me?"

"I couldn't bring you into that place. I didn't know what it would do to you. Not after your abduction—"

"And so you just barged in on your own—"

"Gran, *please*. Cora, Antonia and the detective are here helping me. It's been an overwhelming day, and we all need *your* help now," Eve said, barreling over Gran's concern. "Can you get Mosley to sweep the theatre where a man going by Mulciber is performing? South of Union Square. I think there's a device blocking the ghosts there, and they need in."

Gran sighed. "Yes, dear, I believe I can. By when?"

"Now? We need to close down that show and inspect everything inside. There's something terrible on that stage. We need the spirits in, but I want the audience out."

"I'll contact Mosley now, but I will be there too. You mustn't do anything further without me."

"I wasn't planning to," Eve assured. "Depending on the trains, it might be in the middle of his evening performance when we arrive. I'll need all of your energy and expertise."

"I'm sure Mosley can create the proper distraction and disarm any device."

"Thank you. We also need notebooks; we've a lot to detail. Jenny will want to be a part of this, so bring her and meet us outside the theatre. She was left behind today because we didn't know if anyone in the woods would be armed. And…also, could you bring me fresh clothes?" She looked down at her battered coat, still covering up her nightdress.

"Yes, dear," Gran sighed, as if she knew Eve had gone full Gothic heroine. "I love you."

Eve hung up and turned to Horowitz, who had come to stand by her side, waiting patiently. "Next up: Mulciber. There's some Spiritualism I don't want the world to see."

"And just what sort is that?" he asked warily.

"The kind that's full of vengeance."

The trip to the train station was spent in quiet, the attendant ghosts bobbed along with them, subdued now that their plight had been seen, but their mere looming presence was an additional drain on Eve. Her rough, tumbled day overwhelmed her body, all aches and heaviness.

After the small bit of food at the train station she could stomach, the moment Eve sat down on a cushioned bench and the lull of the train whisked them off along the winding, darkening river, her eyes began to droop, her body feeling ready to give out from under her. She supposed that leaving her body to enter Sanctuary was a bit like dying, and she was still coming back to life.

"Are you all right?" Horowitz asked, sitting next to her, close enough to reach out.

She responded by falling immediately asleep on his shoulder.

He neither moved nor offered one word of complaint, only shifted to make sure she could be comfortable, tucking an arm around her waist to keep her steady.

The train's screaming whistle as Grand Central Depot loomed woke her awake. She jostled against the detective with a bit of a start, wiping her eyes, looking around sheepishly to see if her colleagues had made a fuss of her leaning on him in such a way. No one seemed bothered, and Jacob simply smiled at her, bracing her and then helping her up to stand and await the train doors.

"Thank you," she said shyly. "For letting me fall asleep on you. I really couldn't help it. Thank you for...*everything.* I've been some terrible company of late, haven't I?"

"Not in the least. But you don't have to push yourself further tonight," he said softly. "You've done enough. I can gather other officers—"

Eve shook her head. "We have to go tonight, all of us, and it needs to be Sensitives taking the lead, because to tell you the truth, we don't know exactly what all we're looking for. I'll never forgive myself if some bit of evidence, something important to one of these attendant children, vanishes. We don't know what could have been set in motion today."

"If you insist. Your fortitude and dedication are exemplary, Eve."

"Thank you, Jacob."

"I *will* be calling Fitton, however, as backup—"

"By all means, and the performer will need to be questioned. There will be a host of us. Mulciber won't know what hit him."

"Dupont is responsible for that stage set?"

"The design is his. And the children are *very* upset by it. We need to know what can bring them peace."

Chapter Fifteen

Mulciber's performance was underway when the team met outside the theatre. Eve, Cora, Antonia, and Horowitz approached the theatre doors to greet Gran and Jenny. Upon their approach, Gran looked up at the sky as Jenny shivered. The ghosts had gathered too.

The scattered retinue of spirits that had manifest at the woodland chapel had attracted the rest of the restless number that must have been affected by Dupont's actions. Thirty-some luminous spirits now clustered ahead of them, many catching Eve's eye so they could gesture her on toward the theatre, waving and beckoning. Eve nodded in acknowledgment. Half the time, that's what a spirit wanted most.

Some of these poor little spirits had suffered in limbo indefinitely, being partially sanctified in ritual, baffled, confused, as nothing was done to bring peace. Torn apart for the sake of a living man's art didn't equate to resolution of a spirit.

"Let's go in and begin. Mr. Mosley is already in place," Gran stated.

"Where?" Eve asked.

"In the lobby," Gran replied. "And here," she added, handing Eve a bag as Jenny drew near. Good on her word, Gran had brought Eve a shirtwaist, shawl, and skirt in a cloth bag. Jenny threw her small arms around Eve's waist.

"Hello, dear," Eve said gently, drawing back and bending to be at the girl's eye level. "Don't you worry any more about me, I'm fine. It's all the spirits of the children we need to keep watch over. You're the best of any of us at getting them focused. Corral them. I know children like talking to you, so give me whatever they give you—names, dates, anything that can tie them to any of the files they've pointed us to."

Jenny nodded and withdrew her notebook from her pinafore. While Jenny's Selective Mutism meant she had trouble talking in public, she'd managed for the past year to whisper to ghosts, and they responded accordingly.

Eve looked up at the assembled ghosts and addressed them quietly. "We'll see what's to be done inside. I know you're blocked, and we hope to disable whatever is doing so. When we do, come in and let us help you." The spectral retinue nodded.

Horowitz held the door for Eve and her company as they entered the lobby, lit with crystal-bedecked sconces and faux marble columns reaching to a vaulted ceiling.

Before anything else, Eve excused herself to a water closet to refresh and change. A quick glance in the mirror had her scowling at her bedraggled appearance, and she tucked fallen black locks back into her braided bun as she smoothed the clean shirtwaist into respectable gathered folds and buttoned her cuffs and lace-covered neckline.

The nightdress she'd been wearing all day beneath her coat was grass-stained and muddied, so she tucked it into the cloth bag, embarrassed by the evidence of her dramatics.

Stepping back out into the lobby, she went to check her coat and nearly jumped at the man staring back at her from behind the coat check's swinging gate.

"Hello again, Miss Whitby," small, wiry, wild-haired Mr. Mosley said, his odd eyes sparking at her.

"Hello, Mr. Mosley," Eve said haltingly.

Mosley stepped aside and gestured to what seemed like a one-by-one-foot-square metal fuse box behind him, mounted to the wall beside cloaks and furs. "I think this is the problem your grandmother asked me to fix."

He opened the lid. Inside, two sets of steel tines with coils on either side nearly touched. In the space between the tines, a thread of bluish lightning lit up across the bars, an electrical spark alternating between, clicking in little zaps like a heartbeat.

"What is it?" Eve asked. "That doesn't look like what you removed from my office but it does look like what Antonia disarmed earlier today."

Mosley shrugged. "Two different things. In your office, that was like a monitor, tracking something. *This* is like a system. A breaker in reverse. It's sending electric shocks into the air, in two currents. Alternating and direct—Tesla's style *and* Edison's. Neither of these is creating a current, but rather, it's as if it's seeking to disrupt one."

"Since the electric lights of this lobby are undisturbed," Eve stated, glancing around, "it has to be what's blocking the ghosts; disrupting the spark of spirit. Being but the echo of life, flickering through time, ghosts and electricity have a tenuous connection."

"Ah." Mosley blinked his brown eyes, where Tesla coils seemed to reside deep in the pupil. "I suppose that makes as much sense as anything. Shall I disarm it for you?"

"Yes, please."

"Everything flammable from this closet should be removed," he replied matter-of-factly.

"But you…"

He waved a languid hand, and Eve noticed his black suit coat was singed at the cuff hem. "All of my clothes are treated with a flame-retardant solution, a necessary precaution. I've spent my life dispensing current, but I've never self-immolated and I don't plan on starting now."

Eve laughed nervously at his nonchalance and gestured for her team to help. Once everything was clear, Gran drew close to see how they were doing.

"Give us a moment before you proceed, if you will, Mr. Mosley," Eve stated. He looked to Gran as if for approval. She smiled at him, and the worried crease of his anxious brow seemed to ease a bit. All the odd world, Eve thought with wonder, waiting for a glimpse of Evelyn Northe-Stewart's pride—a special, unparalleled honor.

Sergeant Fitton arrived, a helpful man who was Horowitz's most trusted friend on the force and who had helped them through Gran's abduction. With Fitton at his side, Horowitz summoned the theatre manager into the lobby—a round, kindly looking man with busy hair and distinct laugh lines that were antithetical to the grave face he wore when talking with the officers.

Horowitz and Fitton showed their badges and quietly discussed some of what had been found at the chapel and the likelihood of something of a similar nature in the theatre. The poor man—in charge of the theatre itself rather than the productions that toured to it—went as white as the detective's notebook paper. Fitton told the manager he should expect a disruption and then clear the audience to safety. The man didn't hesitate to show concern.

"There's something not right here, Detective, Officer," the manager said, "and I hope you find it and put it right."

"Once we clear everyone, we'll need free rein backstage. That includes all of our company." Horowitz gestured to Eve and the mediums. The manager furrowed his brow, looking at the wide range of women and their ages, from Jenny to Gran. "It's a unique task force," Horowitz added. The manager nodded.

The manager stepped closer. "I don't know what you're looking for or what you'll find. But I will say, the whole thing, it just…gives me the creeps."

"What does? Mulciber?" Eve asked.

The manager scoffed. "Ah, 'the Great Mulciber'—he's a hack, his name is Jim Boot, just a face and some posturing. It's his helper who does the real work. But the *set*. That's the trouble, if you ask me."

Eve and her team shared a pointed look.

Setting her jaw, Eve turned to Mosley. "Now, if you would, Mr. Mosley."

At the raise of the man's hand there was a cracking thunderclap and a zap of light, and Eve felt all her hairs raise a bit, then fall again. Eve detected a shift in the air that her psychic senses could only pinpoint as a sort of stone rolled away, allowing the murmurs of the spirit world in.

The theatre manager opened the rear doors of the house. On the stage, Mulciber, cape thrown back, raised his arms theatrically in a demonic caricature.

In a secondary surge, a whining buzz filled the air—then a downstage footlight exploded, a lick of flame leaping from the bulb. At the sight of what could become a potential conflagration, everyone screamed. Mulciber himself stopped dead and stared at the fire as if it were a ghost. He gestured into the wings, and a black curtain swung out from both sides to close on him quickly.

The sparks went no further, the flame died down immediately, and the manager stepped center stage to address the audience.

"Esteemed colleagues," he said in a clear voice. "I regret this technical failure, but we must ask that you exit, quickly and orderly, so we can be sure there is no remaining fire hazard. Ushers will hand you tickets for another show. We apologize for the inconvenience."

The patrons were led calmly out of the theatre. Eve couldn't be sure, but there seemed to be relief on the ushers' faces, as if they were glad to be rid of what was in this space, one way or another. Sold-out run it might be, but it seemed no one thought the price was exactly worth it.

Once most everyone was out, the manager gestured to Eve, Gran, and her colleagues and exited front of house.

"Now, spirits," Eve called out to the empty house.

Descending from the ceiling like a set piece lowering from the fly rails, Vera floated down as if she were a glowing fixture at the head of the proscenium, her elderly face fierce and focused. Maggie floated behind her, bringing up the rear of spectral command. Between them came all of the children.

The curtain that had closed to hide Mulciber parted again, and the man, in a voice full of fear and bluster, yelled at the stagehand to close it.

"Come, spirits, be *seen!*" Vera cried.

The spirits rushed the stage in a silvery flood of mist, and the curtain billowed. Props clattered to the floor.

The great Mulciber began to scream and ran into the wings.

"Exeunt, pursued by the dead," Gran said, and Eve laughed at the Shakespearean pun.

Mulciber, Jim Boot, continued to scream from backstage as Eve and their company walked up the aisle, up the proscenium stairs, and onto the stage. Between the sequence of black wing curtains, Eve saw Sergeant Fitton corralling Mr. Boot, but he'd managed to pick up a bottle of liquor in the tumult and was downing it in gulps.

"Mr. Boot," Eve called. "What do you know about Mr. Montmartre, and where can we find him?"

"I don't know," the man said in a wail. "I never know. I'm just the stupid face," he said, slurring his words. A drunk. The tall, broad-shouldered man who had managed such bluster and vigor on stage curled over and began to weep. He responded to no further questions about Dupont, Montmartre, or any other possible association.

Fitton's patience faltered, and he prodded Boot out a fire exit door where he would be taken to the station for questioning. The real power behind the curtain didn't show himself.

Eve and her company stepped into the wings.

The front set was illuminated by the aptly named ghost light, a single light left on in a theatre for safety—and in folklore for the ghosts, but the Act I finale sets were further awash in the light of the ghost retinue. This was the Heaven set, but Hell awaited them behind black curtains, deeper in.

"Look," the spirits bid Eve. "Really *look* this time…. Find us…."

They pointed at the carved wooden figures and other details in the sets.

"The smell is *potent*," Cora stated.

From the front of the pit, the manager of the theatre, who had hesitantly reentered to join their examination, replied nervously.

"The fire effects," the manager explained. "There are lots of substances I'm told have to be used in this production. I burn a great deal of incense and oils, but it does overwhelm. I confess I'll be glad to be rid of this whole affair, box office draw that it has been."

"Who did these elaborate sets?" Eve asked, needing to confirm Dupont's involvement.

The manager hesitated. "I can look at my ledger. Very secretive— They didn't let anyone in during the build and didn't want any press about or any of the details of the show leaked to the public. All slightly paranoid, if you ask me."

"Any information you have will be very helpful."

"Two French names," he added.

"Montmartre and Dupont?" Eve offered.

"That's it. Montmartre behind the scenes pulling the real strings, and Dupont with the sets." He shuddered suddenly. "Is it…" He gestured before him. "Is it unusually cold in here?"

"It's all the ghosts, sir," Eve stated. The manager's eyes widened.

"All right then," he said, putting up his hands as he walked away. "I'll be in the *less* haunted lobby if you need anything."

The ghosts were all pointing. Each to an image, a face, a hand reaching out from one of Purgatory's layers.

The images were an amalgam, a Frankenstein horror of Gustave Dore–inspired designs made into three-dimensional form.

"Look closely," one of the youngest ghosts, a little girl in a threadbare pinafore, said to Eve, drifting close to tug at the side of her black skirt.

"It will be worse than you think, Eve," Vera murmured. "I wish I could spare all of you, but…"

"Look closely, friends," Eve said, and stepped closer to the sets.

The ghosts wafted close and took up a certain formation. Some turned face out, floating at the same level as a cherubim's face positioned above a reaching hand that another ghost posed before, reaching out the same size hand with the very same mole on its finger.

And piece by piece, everything began to match.

Cora screamed as a protruding eye was ripped from its socket by a frustrated spirit and cast it at the medium's feet where it rolled, glass. But it wasn't the glass that concerned her—it was the socket it had been in.

"This isn't plaster of Paris. This isn't mâché. This isn't wood…." Cora mumbled.

The face floating before her matched the face in the set.

"It's this little girl." Eve choked out the words. It was this child's head.

The assembled company staggered back as if they'd been struck and gained an even fuller picture of the ghastly tableau.

The ghosts who had screamingly sent Eve, maddened, to Sanctuary, the pain that made Lily Strand rush to intervene, sounded in her ear with their terrible truth: *"All we are: scrap. Bits and pieces. All that's left."*

Their bits and pieces. Just like the reliquaries in the woods. More bits and pieces. More desecration for the sake of art...no matter the cost.

Antonia recoiled farthest from the scene, turning and rushing back up the aisle, stifling sobs as she went. "You poor babies," she cried. "I'm sorry we didn't understand. We couldn't have imagined all *this*...." Where Eve's guilt had left off, Antonia's picked up.

"We were banished, but you've set us free," stated the little girl whose head had been used as an angel. "Look closer." The spirit pointed at a patch of the wall that had been painted a deep, brownish red. "You know what you see, don't you?"

Eve closed her eyes and took in a deep breath, her nostrils flaring, her bile rising as she was quickly overwhelmed by the scent of embalming fluid and the distinct, unmistakable smell of copper.

"Dried blood," she whispered to Horowitz, unable to fully voice the horror. "As paint."

"Our worst conclusion, come true," the detective murmured. "Dear God."

Gran put her hand over her mouth. Cora blinked back tears and had her hands up, defensive, as if at any moment this panel of anguish would come alive and she would be ready to fight. Eve wanted to turn and retch, but she forced herself not to, instead closing her eyes to let the chill of the ghosts against her cheeks settle her roiling stomach.

Behind this stage setting were another two stage flats of the changing scenes, the panels just as full of faces, hands, and the occasional full appendage as the rest, real parts exquisitely preserved and assembled seamlessly alongside fabricated sculpture and décor. Ducking into the wings, grateful for a moment's respite from the horrors, Eve went to the appropriate rails and lifted the curtains before the other two layers.

Layer upon layer, the fullness of Hell was revealed.

Everyone had to turn away. Too many layers, too many parts in sum total. It was too much, and the spirits were beginning to vocally scream, matching exactly the screams their lips and hands and arms and mouths all evoked.

"Please stop," Eve begged. "Please quiet down enough so that we may help you!" Maggie and Vera together darted around and cajoled the spirits into quiet once more, Jenny helping from the stage floor with gestures and whispers.

"What do we do next?" Antonia called, partially turned to Eve from halfway up the orchestra level, half asking the spirits.

"Take it all down in notes," Eve said, fumbling toward sense. "Every last little detail." Giving directives helped keep her level when the emotions and empathy caused an inner tornado. "Dear spirits, tell us your names, we want every detail and... God, I'm sorry, there's no way to collect all of this in an evidence room— I should have thought to have called—"

"A photographer?" Horowitz asked. "Well, there you're in luck. I thought ahead at the train station and made a call. Mr. Byrd?" Horowitz called into the wings.

"Brilliant foresight," Eve exclaimed. The detective just nodded before returning a grim expression to the work before them. Byrd came out with his equipment, and Horowitz bid him pay no mind to anyone else or to any other dialogue, to just set up and photograph everything. The man shuddered but set to work.

As if on cue, there was a clatter of chains and a new voice sounded from the wings.

"I have made saints of them all. No matter what you do now, you can't change that."

Dupont stood in a shaft of light. An unnatural one. Striking against the *Divine Comedy*. Wrists in handcuffs, Cora's makeshift twine had been replaced with chain and shackles around his feet.

Lieutenant Bills stood behind him, prodding him forward.

"He insisted that he come here," the policeman explained. "And that if we weren't careful, people would die. I didn't want to humor him but I supposed we couldn't be too careful and I wanted to see this scene for myself."

Eve gestured to the stage, narrowing her eyes at the undertaker and coming forward. "What further dangers have you planted?"

"I didn't kill anyone. Everything here was on its way or already dead, in my care or near to the ground. I know you think you've won," Dupont said sadly. Something that should have sounded ominous sounding sad was just as disconcerting. "If you ever find him... Don't implicate Montmartre; he had nothing to do with this part," Dupont pleaded. "This was my indulgence...."

For the first time, Eve actually saw the man afraid.

"While we shared similar interests, this is beyond his expectation, and I don't know how I managed to keep the breadth of it from him, but I did. Don't tell him what this has come to. He'll kill me."

"Why would he?"

"Because he would deem me unholy.... He and I have very different view of holiness. And because Heinrich and Greta got out of hand, now all of this has come down on my head."

Unholiness was the sort of language utilized in the threats written against the Ghost Precinct. Eve remembered the words of the note that had been left at her feet, screaming up at her: *"You will cease your unholy association with the dead and end your 'Precinct's' courtship of the Devil."*

She and her colleagues had been terribly misunderstood and maligned by the threat's falsehood.

"Make them stop," Dupont whimpered, looking around him. He couldn't see the ghosts, as his eyes didn't focus on any of the forms that stared at him, hard and unforgiving, but he shivered. He could feel them—perhaps their wrath and pain too. "I want it all to stop now...."

"The ghosts, Mr. Dupont, have their own will," Eve said. "Don't blame the living for bringing justice and unraveling you any more than you should blame the dead. The spirits guiding *my* work didn't give their blessing for *yours*. Respect shouldn't stop when the heart does."

Horowitz pressed a step farther. "Mr. Dupont, who is Montmartre? We know this act is more than just Jim Boot."

"Confirm that Montmartre was the one working the crowd to get the 'psychic' answers for his second act," Eve demanded.

Dupont smiled humorlessly. "Montmartre was the mind. The control. I have been the heart. I am a part of Montmartre's great experiment, but this artistic masterpiece"—Dupont gestured to the set before him proudly—"remains all mine. I do not know where Montmartre is. He keeps to himself."

"If you are cooperative with us and tell us more," Eve stated, "we might be able to make your sentencing less dire. I can't promise the spirits won't haunt you, though; they've a right, and I'm not going to take that away from them."

Dupont shuddered. "Montmartre mustn't know what all you've found.... He is the great mesmerist, and I don't know what he'll have me do."

He shut his mouth and, despite prodding, said no other word.

Bills shoved him back toward the door. "If he says anything else, I'll take down a statement," the officer said to Eve. "We've charged him with abduction and desecration. We've got the poisons from the chapel, and we'll need proof from your files as soon as possible. But seeing all this"—the man shuddered—"helps my jurisdiction with the case against him."

"Thank you," Eve replied. "Once this is catalogued here, we'll return to the chapel in the morning to do the same. I didn't want something to go missing here in the meantime."

Bills nodded. "The chapel's guarded. I didn't have to convince anyone to keep out. You won't have anyone wresting this case from you; my men think it's cursed."

"It is," Eve declared and turned to her company to continue the dread catalogue that stood before them.

Chapter Sixteen

Once Eve and her company had thanked Bills for his cooperation, Horowitz saw him and Dupont out and discussed logistics, filling Fitton in on the day.

Now that the spirits' blockade was down and their pieces were recovered, the spirits were now able and eager to tell the mediums everything, and soon, the entire theatre was awash in an on-site séance full of chatter; lively and detailed, about what had happened to each body, where the rest of them could be found, their families, time of death, and other details about why they might have been chosen. Most of it seemed to be opportune moments over the course of funereal work.

That the parts had been taken without permission meant the ghost's narrative had been as scattered an incomplete as their bodies; unable to tell the whole story until the spirits themselves saw the larger picture. One of Spiritualism's great comforts this century was the reassurance that even if a body were torn apart, as in the case of so many thousands during the Civil War, the spirit remained whole and could pass on in peace.

But that didn't mean the living could inappropriately interfere with remains without risking the anger and betrayal of the spirit realm. Respect was sacrosanct and these violations were extreme. The fact that the spirits had been further addled by elaborate obfuscations was another sin to add to Dupont and Montmartre's list.

Eve felt certain about Montmartre's identity, but she had to make sure her instinct wasn't borne of convenience; tying disparate mysteries into a convenient knot. She would await proof.

Each of the mediums, Gran too, had pages worth of notes for the next two hours they spent in open communication: the most massive spiritual effort any of them had undertaken at once. Once every part had been listed and noted, the mediums gathered in a circle, took hands and thanked the spirit world collectively, and shut the door that the ghosts themselves had blown open when the barrier keeping them out was removed.

"Rest, friends," Eve said finally to the mass of children, and gestured to Vera and Maggie to gather them. "Vera and Maggie can bring any further concerns you have to us, but for now we *all* need to rest. Give us peace, give yourselves peace. We'll resume again tomorrow."

Some of the younger ghosts looked to Jenny as if for approval, and she nodded, pointing to Vera and Maggie, who each became a sort of schoolmarm, gathering them up and insisting that they give their ghostly forms some rest and that there was no need to stay manifest through the night. Ghosts didn't sleep, per se, but they weren't always visible in a quasi-restive state. The space warmed as the energy the spirits had collected to be seen dissipated and they were no longer visible to the Sensitive eye.

Odd Mr. Mosley entered from a rear door, trailing smoke and ash, the box from the cloak check in hand. The origin of that blocking device was something Eve had wanted to pry out of Dupont's mouth by force. Perhaps that was part of the "great experiment." Gran intercepted Mosley, and the two disappeared. She returned alone before Eve could worry and go after her.

"Mosley's taking that to your offices in the morning as evidence," Gran explained.

"I'll rendezvous with the doctors at Bellevue and Mount Sinai examining the other device attached to your offices," Horowitz volunteered. "Hopefully, if it is indeed a monitor, they'll have some idea of what it was trying to track."

Eve nodded and had to reach out for the wall as a wave of dizziness accosted her. The detective stepped forward, but she steadied herself.

"I'm all right. I just feel like I could collapse in a theatre seat and sleep for a year."

"It's been quite the endless day," Horowitz agreed.

Glancing at her colleagues, Eve noticed they appeared the same; everyone's shoulders flagged as they moved to the lobby, clearly as eager as she was to leave the unsettling scenes and frozen screams behind.

Horowitz discussed the arrangements of the photographs, plates, and negatives with the photographer, adding a few threats for good measure to keep this out of the press. The manager approached the detective and delicately asked how long all of this would take, how long his theatre would remain dark, and how much of a loss was he in for. Eve stepped up and suggested the Veils take over the rest of the run and wrote down their information.

Fitton offered to keep alternate watch with his beat partner through the night, and Eve shook his hand with hearty thanks for all his help and for his steadfast, good nature.

The manager closed and locked the doors, then hurried away into the night as if he were being chased by all the unpleasantness within. Gran went to the street corner to hail carriages for everyone, a small hack the first to be available for Cora, Antonia, and Jenny.

Gran turned to Eve with a stern look. "I'm taking you to your parents, dear," she said. "It is Sunday after all, and if they don't see you, they'll begin to worry—"

Eve put both hands to her head. Since the beginning of her tenure, she'd promised always to have Sunday dinner across the Fort Denbury aisle. "I totally forgot what day it was. I confess I began the day sleepwalking, so…"

"So, come on then," Gran said, patting Eve on her shoulder before turning to Horowitz. "Detective, your family or ours? You're welcome, especially after all you've done for Eve today; you're a good man and we're grateful," Gran said, reaching out to press his hand in both of hers, a glimmer of tears in her eyes.

"Ah, thank you kindly, but I'd best get home myself. I'm not one to drop in on others unannounced. We'll save it for another day."

"All right, but come with us, and we'll drop you along the way," Gran stated and walked away to tell the next driver the route and rounds.

"Yes, do." Eve glanced down shyly before looking back up at him. "I'd not have lasted today without you. I'd have faltered otherwise. I confess I'm not ready to leave your side just yet."

All the worry and grim intensity of the day seemed to leave his face, and his genuine smile rekindled light and hope in her heart.

"Come now," Gran called out the window of the carriage she'd hired.

Walking her to the waiting cab, Horowitz held out his hand, and Eve placed hers in it. He brought her hand to his lips and kissed it softly, not breaking eye contact with her. Eve felt a jolt of emotion and heat course through her in a delectable surge. He then used the same hand to help her up into the carriage and followed, sitting down next to her across from Gran.

"For a skeptic, Lieutenant, you handle supernatural strife brilliantly," Gran said.

He chuckled. "I think of it this way: I'll deal with the corporeal logistics, and Eve's Ghost Precinct can handle what I can't see or understand. But together, it gets work done."

"That it does," Gran said. "Am I to understand it was you, Detective, who pulled Eve out of Sanctuary, a place she had no business going into, not being a ghost?"

Gran's sharp look at Eve had the detective not wanting to appear to take sides, so his reply was gracious.

"Eve was following clues and so, then, did I follow Eve in hopes of the same— Glad to help ease her out of a difficult moment."

"He was brilliant," Eve stated. The detective just offered them both a warm smile.

"Here I am," the detective stated, gesturing ahead as the carriage slowed at Thompson Street. "I'm just up the block. Ladies, until soon. If you need anything, don't hesitate."

"Thank you," Eve murmured. "For everything."

When he descended and closed the door behind him, he stared up at her, his eyes wide and expressive of more than she could begin to parse. They watched each other until the carriage continued out of sight. Once it did, Eve closed her eyes and leaned back against the cushions.

"Well," Gran stated, that one word containing multitudes.

"It's been quite a day," Eve said, pressing her thumb and forefinger to the bridge of her nose in hopes of easing the unrelenting tension behind her eyes. It felt like the mythic placement of her third eye, the spot at the center of one's forehead thought to be the source of Sensitivity, was sore and bruised. Perhaps psychics could have their third eye blackened just by overuse.

"I want to know everything that happened, but I won't force it now," Gran stated.

"I'll tell some of it. Even to Mother and Father. As much as I can figure. It's best you know what I saw, because somehow, I think I'll be called in there again, or to its gates to help it. I worry the Sanctuary isn't safe. But that's for further meditation and discussion. It's a bit of a jumble. I need time with Maggie and other spirits to help untangle it."

"And how is your heart?" Gran asked with a slight smile in her tone. Eve didn't open her eyes for fear she'd betray too much.

"Full," Eve replied carefully. "I am blessed to have wonderful people in my life."

"Indeed," Gran said. "And..."

"And that's all I'm saying right now if you're angling for anything more about anyone in particular."

Gran laughed as the carriage slowed in front of the lighter of the two sides of Denbury.

"I'll be there with you to help share as much or as little as you like," Gran offered. "I daresay discussing the Sanctuary would be a better tack than anything to do with the children and the parts. Leave all that straight out."

"Thank you for agreeing to run interference if need be."

"Always."

Her parents had gotten worried about the extreme lateness of her hour but thankfully didn't chide as Gran vouched for her work.

When Eve described what had happened in Sanctuary that created for her a literal out-of-body experience when her spirit entered and her body remained in the woods, her parents stared at one another then back at her.

"It's…it's like when your mother came and got my soul out of the painting," her father said after a long moment. She looked at them both. From what Gran had explained to Eve about the days she first knew and helped her parents, her father's soul, in his youth, had been cursed into a painting—and somehow her mother had been the only one who saw and the only one who could get him out. But tonight was the first time Eve truly understood that it had been an actual physical separation of soul and body, not just a period of unconsciousness.

"So…I have a hereditary disposition for my soul and body to be able to exist separately?" Eve asked with a grin.

Her father set his jaw, unamused, and her mother folded her arms.

"I wouldn't go trying it regularly," her mother cautioned.

"Oh, no, I was expressly forbidden; this was an extreme circumstance. But an effort guided by a spirit from within. It was true that, like for you, I needed someone to come help get me out. And for you two, that experience of doing so made you closer?" Eve pressed.

"Yes," they said in unison. That helped illuminate part of what felt like an additional bond created with Jacob.

"It was Detective Horowitz who found me," Eve explained. "We all continue to owe him a debt of gratitude."

"Thank goodness," her mother exclaimed. "What a nice boy."

"He's twenty-four," Eve retorted, "hardly a boy. But I'm glad you approve."

"Yes, and you're a lady," her mother countered, "hardly too young to marry."

Eve set her jaw at their little trap, yet still, a thrill accosted her, even despite herself. The word "marry" had been a dirty one, something damning and imprisoning, until Jacob offered some idea that it might not be a sentence but a partnership. She had no interest in entertaining anyone else, and that should probably be known by all who might wish to interfere.

"You approve of him to the point of accepting should he ever ask for my hand?" She leaned forward to make the next point very clear. "Not *any time soon* but if he were to do so in good time?"

Her parents glanced at one another.

"We want you to be happy," her father stated. "And hope for a reliable, stable, moral man. The detective most certainly fits that bill. We would like to know him better. I would want him to ask permission."

"I like that he's not wrapped up in mediumship or ghost hunting like the rest of your life," her mother stated. "It's good for you."

In this point, Eve didn't argue, even though her mother's dismissal of the paranormal had always hurt her. But she didn't feel the need to defend herself so much anymore; she had given up on her parents ever *liking* the fact that she was a medium. It was simply a matter of acceptance. She didn't need any further approval; thus, no need for additional defense. The detective was a breath of fresh air and a different perspective.

"All right, that's about as much talk of *that* as I can bear," Eve stated. "I've an early morning, so I'd best be getting some rest. Thank you for dinner; sorry I was late."

She kissed her parents and went to her side of Fort Denbury.

"I'll see her up," Gran stated, rising to walk her over. She closed the door on her parents' side of the adjoining townhouses before turning to Eve and continuing with new information.

"Alfred Prenze would like to drop by tomorrow evening," Gran began, "for an after-dinner chat over a cordial. He left a note with my staff after we'd spoken on the phone yesterday. I know there's still work to be done, but could you all make yourselves available to resume your positions? He may want advice again, and I'd like to see how far we can get with him."

"Of course, Gran, wonderful. Let's see if we can tie up another mysterious loose end."

They said good night with a long, tight hug.

All was quiet, for the moment, but Eve felt as though she were being watched. She kept turning, thinking she saw a shadow out of the corner of her eye as she went upstairs, but she convinced herself it was just her tired state and fell immediately into a restless sleep when she collapsed into bed.

Chapter Seventeen

The next morning was an arduous one at the theatre, finishing with the ghostly attachments to the set pieces, double checking that every voice was heard and catalogued. Fitton and Horowitz brought in a tradesman they trusted to be discreet, and together they took the pieces of the sets apart, corralling those that were fabricated synthetic aside from those that were organic and human. Thirty-three pieces total. Thirteen here, twenty in the woods.

Eve enlisted her father's help, and he wrote up a citation on public health regarding human remains that she had on hand in case Dupont tried to challenge their right to take apart his 'art." His signing it on Bellevue stationary furthered the official nature.

Each medium maintained their notebook, and Jenny joined them at the chapel this time, as did Gran, ready to note anything the others were too overworked to hear. Horowitz and Fitton accompanied the team to the chapel in the woods in case anyone tried to disturb them.

En route, Eve, Horowitz, and Cora discussed the next step.

"The great experiment Dupont referred to, when discussing the unseen, unknown Montmartre and his part in all this," Eve stated. "That's what I can't get out of my mind. Of course, I want to link it to the experimentation done on us, but that's my mind trying to make leaps, not steps."

"I'll pry it out of him by touch, then," Cora offered. "Once we're done here, that will be a next step. Bills still has him in custody."

"Yes, brilliant," Eve said.

"We'll need to type up our notes," Cora continued. "Match them with photographs and files."

"I can cross-reference your files, try to put everything together showing pattern and precedent from the first complaints that opened the cases to begin with," Horowitz volunteered. "I'll try to make sure it seems like progress has been made without pointing out too many flaws in follow-up that allowed Dupont to persist. Goodness knows no one at Mulberry likes when I point out where they missed steps, so I'll be politic but clear that these are cases being literally put to rest. Lieutenant Bills will share Greta's statement, the powerful push on the whole package."

"Very good, thank you," Eve said, and Cora nodded. The fact that Cora had warmed to the detective, the fact that they all were working like a cohesive team, was a delightful dose of light in their grim work. "This evening," Eve continued, "Albert Prenze has asked to meet with Gran, so we've got to do these next steps at the chapel quickly. I don't want to miss the chance to see what else we might be able to get out of him."

The cataloguing and dictation of the spirits went far more quickly in the woods—less interference and distraction. The officer standing guard, white-faced outside, seemed all too happy to stand clear and all too reluctant to retake the post.

When Bills saw them enter the station house after the cataloguing, he led Horowitz, Eve, and Cora back to their holding area.

"Has he said anything else?" Horowitz asked. Bills shook his head.

"Has anyone come for him?" Eve asked.

Bills shook his head again. "We notified Mrs. Dupont he was here, had to tell her what happened and that he was being held for further questioning, but no one has been by. Mrs. Henari escorted Greta to her sister in the city."

"Thank you," Eve said. "This has all been unnerving I'm sure, but you've been very kind."

Bills just nodded, his expression uncomfortable.

"Can't blame Mrs. Dupont for not coming," Cora muttered. "But I need to speak with him."

"The key please, Officer?" Eve asked.

"You shouldn't go in there alone—"

"I'll accompany them, Lieutenant Bills, thank you," Horowitz said, holding out his hand and taking the key Bills handed over. The short, wood-paneled hallway behind the central receiving area gave way to damp grey stone walls and floor in the back, where two iron-barred cells faced one another. Horowitz strode toward Dupont's cell; the other was empty.

The undertaker sat on a cot still in his stained white suit, a bandage on his cheek and nose.

Horowitz unlocked the door and stepped in. Cora and Eve followed, and he closed the door behind them.

Dupont was staring forward, dazed and blank. Eve had seen that look on Heinrich Schwerin's face when she and Cora had seen him in the asylum. Cora must have been thinking the same thing as she grasped Eve's forearm in a precautionary gesture.

A dim flicker registered across Dupont's face, but he did not turn toward the new company.

Horowitz turned to the women with a puzzled look. "Have at, if he's able," the detective said quietly.

Cora stepped forward. "Mr. Dupont?" she asked. "I am here to ask about Montmartre and his involvement with you. We need to know who he is, about his 'experiment' and the boxes keeping spirits out of a given place."

No response. Cora leaned closer.

"My God," she whispered. As Cora pointed to his head, Eve could see the small hole and the rivulet of blood trailing behind his ear.

Swallowing hard, Cora removed the glove from her right hand and pressed it to Dupont's forehead. Her eyelids fluttered closed then opened again as she gasped.

"He did it to himself," Cora said a moment later, stepping away in horror, looking down at the floor.

Eve followed her gaze to see a rock and a thin nail tipped in blood. Nausea swept her, and she bit back bile.

Horowitz passed a hand over his face, paling.

"Damn it," Eve murmured. "We have to know more."

The ghost of a little girl in a white pinafore, one Eve recognized from the chapel who had helped her correlate the images of the body parts in the stage set, wafted through the stone.

"The shadow man," the girl whispered. "He's been watching." She pointed to Dupont. "The shadow man made him do it."

"What shadow man?" Eve asked the ghost. The spirit pointed to the window. "At the window, watching. He was saying something, but I couldn't make it out. Then the undertaker picked up the rock and the pin…and…" She made a popping noise, staring at Dupont.

Eve's blood went cold at the mention of a shadowy presence at the window, like the one that had followed along her windows and appeared in the woods, a figure whom she felt might be lurking out of the corner of her eyes even now….

"Why are you here, child?" Cora asked the spirit before them gently. "Have we not brought you peace?"

"I thought if he could see me finally," the girl explained, "rather than having me shut out, he might apologize. To all of us. But he can't.... I suppose this is his eternal torment now. Justice." The spirit turned to Eve and Cora. "Thank you for your help."

Before they could respond, her form brightened and vanished. Eve and Cora looked at one another—and while Eve wanted to take a moment of sentiment for the spirit's passing, there wasn't time.

"What if the 'shadow' appears to Mulciber and convinces him to do the same?" Eve asked. "He's a useless drunk, but he might know Montmartre's whereabouts."

Eve and Cora whirled to Horowitz at once. "Call Fitton," Eve exclaimed. "Tell him he mustn't let Jim Boot out of his sight. These men aren't just trepanning themselves; they're being...convinced to." Eve chose not to say *mesmerized,* but it seemed that was the case.

"Will you two be all right if I—"

"Go," Eve urged, and he raced off to the other side of the station to make the call.

Cora took a deep breath and placed her hand on Dupont's head, closing her eyes as his fluttered, rolling back behind his eyelids. "I want to see Montmartre."

Opening her notebook, Eve took down her words and imagery.

"I see men in a circle with a box between them; there's a current, there are wires." Cora bent over Dupont and asked more directly, pressing her hand harder against his forehead. "Is that where you met Montmartre, Dupont? The great experiment?" She stood back up stiffly, stating what she saw and Eve taking note.

"Now there's a forum, a lecture, 'On the state of the brain at death' the chalkboard reads. He sits down next to a man. Now there's money being transferred. Dupont's looking over his shoulder guiltily, one of his reliquaries in front of him that he's hastily covering up. I see Dupont's viewing parlor, Montmartre's name being added, and him being led to the basement, where there are several wooden boxes like the one in the experiment, like that outside our office and the different kind at the theatre."

Dupont wrested himself away in a lurch, falling back against the cot, and Cora stepped aside, her knees giving out. Eve rushed to catch her, and she propped herself back up, leaning on Eve, who held her fast. "It's all right, my dear friend, I've got you. Brilliant woman, good work."

Cora smiled wanly, trying to recover her breath.

Eve turned to Horowitz when he returned. "We should have Dupont seen by a doctor. I doubt anyone realized he trepanned himself."

Helping Cora back outside the cell, Horowitz locked it behind them.

"Paper," Cora requested. Eve handed over her notebook and pencil, and Cora began to hastily, impressively sketch a likeness, artistic abilities matching her visual gifts, an incredible synergy of talents.

Taking a seat on the bench in the wood-paneled reception area that let in diffuse light past barred windows, Cora finished the sketch and handed it to Eve, who sat back and went cold when she saw it.

A man in a wide-brimmed hat with a half-shadowed face, wire-rimmed glasses, and a cruel half smile.

The shadow man.

She swallowed hard. "Montmartre?"

Cora nodded.

"Remember that shadow I said was chasing me outside the windows?" Eve said, her voice quavering. "The one who appears like a ghost, but unlike any other? That's him."

"Then let's find him and figure out how he got into your head," Horowitz said plainly. "An alert went out to the whole department to look for anything involving his name. I kept yours out of it. I'll check again with my colleagues."

Eve glanced at the clock on the walls. "We've got to get back. Detective, would you like to be a part of our latest endeavor? We're trying to peel open the Prenze family, and we're hoping Gran can work on another layer this evening."

"At your service, friends," he said to the company.

Chapter Eighteen

Racing back to the city and Gran's townhouse, the mediums were offered a bit of quick refreshment before going to the kitchen where fresh maid's clothes hung on pegs. Changing, Eve thought at least their presence allowed Gran's hard-working staff, all of whom were treated like family, another night off.

The same positions were assumed. Clara Bishop was unable to join them, so they'd have to get a read on any differences in his energy and any web of souls he might be tied to on their own.

Jenny was ensconced in the library—too suspect for a "niece" to be positioned in the same place. But with Sensitives, one didn't have to be in a room to get a read, and Maggie, Vera, and Zofia appeared by Jenny's side the moment she entered the library and took up with a book, girl and ghosts ready to listen in. The library had one thin, narrow pocket door to the parlor, which Gran would keep open, dragging a curtain between them to appear shut.

This time, Horowitz was part of the inspection at a vantage point outside to see Prenze coming in, Gran's driver having arranged one of her horses and hack to be out front. Horowitz, donning a top hat and livery coat, would seem busy with feeding the mare. If Prenze then wanted to hire him after the meeting, he'd take the man where he bid and report back. When Eve expressed concern for his safety, he assured that he'd withdrawn a pistol from the Mulberry Street lockers as protection.

A ring of the bell made everyone jump. Why Eve felt so nervous about this visit, she couldn't tell, but before leaving her house, instinct had her tucking the dagger given to her by her mother up her sleeve in a makeshift sheath.

The same dapper figure appeared at the door, though he looked a bit more drawn, tired. Pinched. His mouth seemed harder. Grim.

"Hello, sir, good to see you again," Cora said politely, bobbing her head and reaching out to take his coat, walking stick, and hat.

She allowed her hand to graze his arm as she took the items, curtsied and turned away. Prenze strode into the parlor as Eve waited with a fixed smile at the other end of the hall.

The moment the man disappeared, Cora's eyes went wide as she stared at Eve. She made a wiping gesture as if to illustrate what she had glimpsed. *Nothing*, she seemed to say.

How terrifying.

It was true, Eve thought, trying to get a read on him, on his colors and energies, on his mood and intent. There was nothing.

A grey nothingness.

What had happened to this man, and why was he such a blank slate when he had been vibrant, if tired, several days prior?

Prenze took a step forward to address Gran and bowed his head.

"I've come here to say that I'm sorry, Mrs. Northe-Stewart. I wasn't in my right mind when I came to speak to you about my involvement in your charity function. I must withdraw."

"No soiree after all?" Gran frowned.

"No, I'm afraid not. I must focus on...my health."

His words were warm, and yet there was such a coldness wafting off him—as if he himself were a spirit.

"I'm very sorry to hear it," Gran said slowly, and Eve knew she was trying to get the same read on him they all were, and the mild confusion on her face meant she was facing the same grey slate. "But of course, one's health comes first."

He leaned into Gran, but he looked right at Eve, and her heart began to race.

How did he know where she was when she was hidden, shaded behind a screen?

His eyes were grey, slate *blanks*. His lips shifted into a small bow of a smile, a twisting, revolting expression. Eve knew that smile. If he'd had glasses, if he were in shadow, he'd be the one floating outside her window....

She put a hand over her mouth to stifle a scream.

"That it does," Prenze continued icily. "One's health comes first. You would do well to think on that. Do be *very* careful, ladies, in this dangerous world...."

He looked at every one of them, catching their gazes as they stared at him from behind screens, before striding out of the parlor and out the front door in a few brisk paces. The fact that he acknowledged them, that he recognized them...

That's when it hit Eve, like a blow.

Prenze isn't dead. No, Albert Prenze had been right here. Right now, threatening them in his brother's stead. The shadow man. Montmartre. Albert Prenze. All one terrifying presence.

The door slammed shut when it should have only gently closed, as if he were sucking up all the air after him, in his wake.

A dead man walking who had all the autonomy of a ghost and the resources to make them all into one at any point he pleased.

"It was him," the women chorused.

"He was...blank. Blank. There was *nothing....*" Cora stared at her palm as if when she'd touched him, she'd come back bloody—but there wasn't a single thing to be seen.

Maggie flew into the parlor. "It was him. *He's* the one who hurt me."

Eve rushed to the front door and looked out the glass. She felt a terror within her the likes of which she'd never felt. He could get *in*. A mental, spiritual violator. From the gate at the front of Gran's walk, the man glanced back at her with that terrible smirk, plucking wire-framed glasses from his breast pocket and sliding them on his nose, tucking his hat low to shade his head, and walking away so she wouldn't mistake him. It made her want to vomit.

The shadow man.

Come after me, child, she heard his voice in her mind. Impulsively, surprising even her, her body moved to follow as if it were being pushed forward.

"Eve—" Cora shouted as Eve ran to the door.

"He can't just get away," Eve exclaimed, fury blazing through her body. "Cora, you stay with the girls; you and Gran need to get this house and Fort Denbury secured—you're armed. So is Horowitz— He'll go with me because I have to follow—"

Eve heard shouts behind her as the door slammed at her back, Gran calling after her as she ran, but she was already down the walk and to the street, meeting Horowitz as he'd already jumped down from the carriage and pointed after where the man had gone, racing alongside her toward the next grand property along the notoriously wealthy lane.

"It's Albert Prenze," Eve declared to the detective, breathless.

"Figured it had to be," Horowitz muttered. "He just smirked at me and went this way."

The two darted behind the next building over, the first space between townhouses and a carriage house behind, veering toward the sandstone building when the lower half of a Dutch door swung out and caught them at the waist. Eve and Horowitz fell, knocked onto the cobblestones by the blow. A figure stepped out into the shadows of an arched trellis ahead that led to a rear garden.

"Stop. In the name of the law," Horowitz declared, scrambling to his feet, going for his gun as Eve regained her feet.

"Don't," replied the man, and Horowitz paused the reach for his weapon. Their assailant stood in shadow, but the flash of a knife blade caught what little gaslight filtered into the darkness. "I've very good aim, and Miss Whitby's face is so pretty. I'd hate to cut it wide open."

"You can't keep running," Horowitz countered.

"Oh, you thought I was running from you?" Albert Prenze laughed, a distressing, cruel sound. "No, I bid you *follow* me. To prove how powerless you are...." He stepped forward into the dim angle of light by the dark carriage house door, a few feet before them. Most of his face remained hidden by his black wide-brimmed hat, but the cut of his jaw and the curve of his lips bore the smug, repulsive expression that had haunted Eve from her own window. "And how little choice you have in what's about to unfold."

Eve felt her body twisting against her will as if an invisible hand were forcing her wrist. Suddenly she saw her knife was turned toward the detective and the barrel of his pistol was turned toward her torso. The keen mesmerist behind Mulciber's act was here before them, making Eve and the detective just as uncomfortable as the audience members she'd seen forced to their knees.

"You can't best me, especially when you've no idea what's next," Prenze stated. "You'll just end up hurting one another. Leave a dead man be."

"In the name of all you've wronged," Eve declared, remembering a crucial lesson.

Gran and the Bishops had taught her about mental shielding, for when a psychic wanted to reject a presence that was trying to manipulate her. She clenched her fists and let her righteous anger bubble up within her, fueled by these recurring violations. Narrowing her eyes, she visualized lashing out with the air itself, with energy and intent, cracking her mind like a whip, a reverberate slam from the core of her third eye.

Prenze's ungodly smirk slipped, bringing Eve a distinct measure of relief—the way to fight him. If the unwelcome shoved in, shove back. Eve redirected her knife toward Prenze, and Horowitz stepped forward with his gun aimed at the man's heart.

A small canister was tossed at Eve's feet, and an instant explosion of acrid red smoke engulfed her and the detective. Another magic trick of distraction and disappearance, courtesy of Mulciber and his Purgatory.

When the smoke cleared, Eve coughing and trying to feel her way toward Horowitz, grasping at his shoulder as he braced her against him, Albert Prenze was gone. They briefly searched the rear garden before running back to the street, but the avenue was curiously empty even for the evening hour. Eve clenched her fists and cursed.

"What did you do to make him hesitate like that?" Horowitz asked as they slowly walked back to Gran's townhouse, trying to catch their breath.

"A trick I learned from Gran and the Bishops about shielding and pushing back."

"That was amazing."

"We didn't get him, though, and he's more dangerous than we knew," Eve said glumly. "We'll have to be *very* clever to stop him, proving the dead man isn't dead...."

Horowitz grabbed Eve's arm. "That moment, when it felt like our weapons were being pushed—"

"I'd never have hurt you—" Jacob and Eve said in unison and then smiled, laughing nervously but in the full relief of trust and care.

As they turned up the walk, Eve noticed Gran watching anxiously from the window of her front door. She rushed out onto her grand stoop, eyes blazing with admonishment, but Eve held up her hand. "We're fine, Gran, but he ran away—"

"You shouldn't have—"

"We had to try," Eve countered. "He's a powerful mesmerist, and we'll have to shield relentlessly, but I had a moment where I broke through. Help me get better at the practice, tell the Bishops, teach the girls and the detective here too. Is Cora with Antonia and Jenny?"

"Yes, upstairs, where Jenny is retching over a porcelain tub. When she tried tapping into Prenze's aura and mental field, it made her violently ill. Cora is standing guard while Antonia's tending to her. I called my old security team out of retirement after the abduction, but I've put two more on the rotation now between here and Fort Denbury."

"Thank you," Eve said, reaching out to grasp Gran's wrinkled hand fondly.

"Come inside and get warm," Gran insisted. "I've shuttered all the windows. There's fresh tea in the parlor. Stay here and don't take any more chances tonight." She wagged her finger at them both as she held the door for them.

"We won't," Eve promised.

"I've left Jenny's notebook in the parlor; it's something you should see." Gran withdrew upstairs to check on the girls, leaving the detective and Eve alone for a moment, as if the woman had read Eve's mind.

"Go ahead to the parlor, give me a moment," Eve said to the detective, wanting to get out of her maid accoutrements and take a moment to compose herself.

She didn't want to show Jacob how rattled she really was by what had happened. Rushing to the downstairs water closet, she splashed cold water on her face, taking the lace-covered bonnet off her head, removing the starched white collar and apron, and balling it all up into fists, letting the terror, rage and frustration about these cases be the engine of her ongoing psychic shielding and sending out waves of furious renunciation of anything trying to meddle its way in.

Albert Prenze had astrally projected his energy to become visible outside her house, and she was going to be damned if she let him that close again. Gran had told Eve she was one of the most gifted mediums she'd ever met in her whole life. She needed now to be equally skilled at protecting that gift. Eve stared in the mirror and willed her frightened face to turn steely. Only then would she let herself back out to face the man who represented so much of what was good in this world, a desperately needed contrast to all that had been so terrible of late.

When she entered the parlor, Horowitz stood from the tea table where he'd sat with a cup of steaming Darjeeling, examining Jenny's notes from the evening. There was a simple, elegant ceremony about this man, and the way he looked at her drew her forward as if she were magnetized to his strong, solid presence. He smiled at her, and she felt herself begin to tremble, finally in a way that wasn't out of fear.

"It seems during this visit, the spirit of Dr. Font came to visit Jenny, if I'm reading this correctly," the detective said, gesturing to the notebook, a hasty sketch of a wild-haired, frightened man. "That's him," he said, incredulous. "It's as if this was his moment of death in that Dakota apartment."

The writing beneath was in Jenny's messy script, noted in quotations as was precinct protocol when quoting a ghost directly, not just intuiting but dictation. *Font: "I'm so sorry I didn't stop him when I realized he was getting worse. I signed off on his death and I thought I was rid of him. He was too clever for me by half."*

"Font is saying this, Jenny heard?" the detective clarified.

Eve nodded. "We'll have to call him into a séance again. There's connective tissue between him and everything else."

"I hope England's Met follows up with me about Prenze's 'death.' I'll have to ask your Gran for her contact."

"Ask and it shall be yours," Eve stated, taking a seat at the Turkish suite inlaid with mother-of-pearl. He took his opposite, angling his chair to sit within close reach of her.

"I'm glad to be here," Jacob said with a smile, "and to see that your Gran has such safeties in place. And, I confess, I'm glad to have a moment with you."

"Now that I look presentable."

"Eve Whitby," he scoffed, "you looked just as lovely in a maid's apron. Clothes hardly make the creature." She batted a hand at him, but he continued. "I hope you don't think when I give a compliment"—he leaned toward her—"that it's part of some game. I wonder, sometimes."

"I trust you. I believe you. I…" She trailed off from a number of sentiments she wasn't ready to say aloud; they felt too bold and would make her far too vulnerable. "I am so glad you're in my life," she finished. His smile was a ray of sunlight on her embattled heart.

"And that sentiment is mutual. We are not without recourse," Horowitz stated confidently. "None of us is alone. And you, my dear lady, are not only gifted, but a gift. If anyone can counter the tricks of a man trying to play with minds, it's you. And however you need assistance, I stand ready. Unintimidated."

"Thank you, Detective—Jacob." She reached a hand across the table, and he clasped it eagerly in his. "For everything."

"My pleasure and honor," he replied. "You know, there is a danger, in cases with myriad unraveling loose ends like ours, to not celebrate when something valiant has been done and resolved. You uncovered an enormous irreverence, a blasphemy involving *thirty-three* children, all of whom you were able to finally honor and respect as *they* would wish. You rescued a vulnerable woman from a hellish, warped prison. All because you put yourself in danger to help others. Before we worry about what's next, please celebrate what you have done and solved so far, and bravely."

"Thank you, truly," came a rush of murmurs from the spirit world, glancing softly off her ear. They didn't visually manifest, or with any chill; voices simply whispered in a soothing, peaceful breeze from the Corridors of the dead—a sweet contrast from the gale force that had pummeled her before. The sincerity of this and Jacob's words brought tears to Eve's eyes. The detective shifted his head slightly, searching her, noticing every minuscule change in her expression, following even the slightest of cues.

"I'm grateful for that perspective," she said, her eyes glistening. "I think you encouraged the spirit world to thank me too, which is *so* welcome, after their torrents screaming of failures. I may be psychic but hardly omnipotent; they seem to forget that."

"I hope the spirit world won't be so ungrateful again," he said.

He shifted his grasp, caressing the top of her hand, and then delicately, tantalizing and slow, he threaded his fingers one by one through hers, every single movement a caress of each. Once entwined, he clutched her palm to his. "Regardless, *I* am grateful that a woman so surrounded by death can make me feel so thrillingly *alive*."

Eve's breath caught in her throat. Her emotions surged, and her eyes, which had watered at the onslaught of the spirits, overflowed at this compliment, a tear rolling down each cheek. Impulsively, the detective leaned in and, in two soft gestures, placed his lips on one cheek then the other, drinking in each tear with devastating tenderness. Composure giving way, Eve melted toward him with a passionate sigh.

"I must go," he murmured against her lips, his breath against them causing her mouth to part before he drew back. "I am expected home, and there are things I have to sort out."

He rose and she did with him, wavering, her knees weak, not letting go of his hand. Words failed her, and all she could do was loose a pouting sound of protest.

"We will do our work with diligence and fortitude," he said, his eyes sparkling with delight and promise. "And we will steal quiet moments together. Every one of them a treasure."

He strode toward the door. Eve ran after him, embracing him from behind. Chuckling, he tucked his arms over hers and squeezed before extricating himself.

"I do have to go," he insisted firmly, "as much as I'd rather stay. My family has made some plans, and I need to make sure they're not taking liberties about my future on my behalf."

Eve felt her heart spasm. Surely, they were trying to get him to commit to Sophie. He turned back to her. The worry on her face must have been clear as day, for he shook his head. She remained painfully speechless, and while he wasn't a Sensitive, he intuited her perfectly.

"Fear not, I'll make sure nothing comes between us and our stolen, quiet moments. And someday, during one of those moments, when you've managed, amidst your other powers, to make time stop again, I'll steal something else," he said, reaching out, cupping her cheek in his palm, and grazing a thumb across her lips to declare his intention, making her shudder in delight. "With your permission," he added. She leaned into his palm, and the nod of her assent created a caress upon her cheek. Eyes fluttering closed, she relished every iota of sensation.

He let go and turned back only when the open door was partially between them.

"My darling Whitby," he said at the threshold, "until soon." And he bounded off, turning back to her at the iron gate of Gran's walkway.

She blew him a kiss. He caught it on the air and brought it to his heart before disappearing past a hedgerow. As if it were a firework of sound and sentiment, Eve felt the whole spirit world sigh in delight at their exchange, so much so that it felt like an earthly tremor. A new confidence blossomed in Eve's unnerved soul. When one had the unquestioned blessing of the spirit world, nothing was more powerful. A good position to be in when facing the next unexpected turn.

Epilogue

Albert Prenze walked calmly through a thin gap in the hedgerows toward the back of his mansion, letting himself in a rear entrance he'd had blocked off since before he'd gone to England and everything changed.

He wasn't worried about the girl—he could handle her, but she was going to prove a fight. But in the end, she'd serve his purpose. If she couldn't put up a fight, it would mean she didn't have enough power for what he needed. He'd finally be rid of that which he so reviled.

He descended the damp stone stairs to the cellar level, turned down a narrow passageway, and turned a key in the lock of an unmarked, previously unused storeroom door. A dim overhead light revealed a host of greyscale, floating spirits, all of whom whirled around at the sound of the door opening, the wraiths in fine gowns and suit coats cowering at the presence who stepped in and shut the iron door behind him.

During an extended bout of knocking out his brother and preoccupying his sister, he'd had this room's walls fitted entirely with metal plates and installed one of his devices. The buzz of a constant, low-voltage electrical current made the surfaces of the walls occasionally spark and pop.

A tall, luminous, statuesque spirit, all mist and greyscale, dressed in a grand gown of the midcentury, was pressing her transparent hands against the iron-clad walls of this prison, yelping in pain and confusion at the resultant shock.

The sound delighted Prenze. He'd finally done it, captured and held the one thing he wanted most. The tables of who terrorized whom would finally turn.

Out of the nine trapped spirits, she was the last to turn at the presence on the threshold. The woman's usually fearsome expression transformed into abject horror. At this, Prenze smiled.

"Hello, Mother."

Acknowledgments

Special thanks to my editor Elizabeth May and the whole Kensington team for their enthusiasm and support along the way, especially my fantastic publicist James Akinaka and supreme publicity maven Lauren Jernigan for all the help, facilitating and signal-boosting as well as the amazing art from Lou Malcangi.

Deepest of heartfelt appreciation to my fantastic, thoughtful and incredibly helpful sensitivity readers Elizabeth Kerri Mahon, Sebastian Crane, Brina Starler and Ashley Lauren Rogers. You are stars in my sky.

Endless thanks to my agent Paul Stevens with Donald Maass and to my incredible family, I couldn't have a better support system in all the world. Marijo Farley, that goes double for you.

Empyrean appreciation to my Torch and Arrow business partner Thom Truelove for meticulous, swift and thoughtful research help as well as enlightening brainstorming, you're a wonderful resource to say the least.

Extra spooky thanks to Andrea Janes, founder and CEO of Boroughs of the Dead. I couldn't have a better boss or partner in crime. Not only is it a pleasure to work for Boroughs of the Dead, a fantastic ghost tour company here in our beloved New York City, but I'm so grateful that you seek to honor the dead as I do and can never resist a good haunt and all the history it brings in its wake.

Thank you, spirit world. I feel you. I know you. I will always tell your stories.

Thank you especially, dear reader. Blessings and Happy Haunting!

Meet the Author

Actress, playwright and author **Leanna Renee Hieber** is the award-winning, bestselling writer of gothic Victorian fantasy novels for adults and teens. Her novels such as the Strangely Beautiful saga, and the Eterna Files series have garnered numerous regional genre awards, including four Prism awards, and have been selected as "Indie Next" and national book club picks. She lives in New York City where she is a licensed ghost tour guide and has been featured in film and television shows like Boardwalk Empire and Mysteries at the Museum.

Follow her on Twitter @leannarenee, or visit www.leannareneehieber.com.

Keep reading for an excerpt of the first book in the Spectral City series!

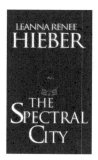

Solving crime isn't only for the living.

In turn-of-the-century New York City, the police have an off-the-books spiritual go-to when it comes to solving puzzling corporal crimes . . .

Her name is Eve Whitby, gifted medium and spearhead of the Ghost Precinct. When most women are traveling in a gilded society that promises only well-appointed marriage, the confident nineteen-year-old Eve navigates a social circle that carries a different kind of chill. Working with the diligent but skeptical Lieutenant Horowitz, as well as a group of fellow psychics and wayward ghosts, Eve holds her own against a host of dangers, detractors, and threats to solve New York's strangest crime as only her precinct can.

But as accustomed as Eve is to ghastly crimes and all matters of the uncanny, even she is unsettled by her department's latest mystery. Her ghostly conduits are starting to disappear one by one as though snatched away by some evil force determined to upset the balance between two realms, and most important—destroy the Ghost Precinct forever. Now Eve must brave the darkness to find the vanished souls. She has no choice. It's her job to make sure no one is ever left for dead.

Prologue

Manhattan dinner parties in the gilded 1890s had become a studied spectacle in opulence for the ruling class of the country's wealthiest city. The bustling, ever striving, never sleeping metropolis's class of most fashionable, up-to-date, technologically accessorized, bejeweled and beholden to no one but themselves were the kinds of company that the Prenze family kept, curating people and their statuses like one might think of assembling a stock portfolio.

That's how it appeared to Margaret Hathorn as she floated into the parlor for light aperitifs and a bit of music and chatter before dinner. She knew the types, their predilections, and their concerns. Margaret had been born into wealth, and during her young life she'd been quite enamored of high society's trappings, dalliances and luxuries, their petty dramas and the consequential ways their decisions affected the city. From her vantage point, she could see the full scope.

She had seen and learned much since those days of carefree and impetuous youth. Not only had she come to understand the tired adage of money not buying happiness, but she realized that Poe had been on to something with *The Masque of the Red Death*. There were dangers in being too shielded, too gilded, too able to make up one's own rules for life, too easily sheltered away from the horrors and cares of the world. She could feel a sense of dread here, as if the Red Death were lurking in the hallway just beyond. Maybe it was, clad in some beautiful House of Worth gown or some finely tailored frock coat with satin lapels.

It should be noted that Margaret Hathorn, herself, was dead. Her perspective was one of two worlds, and for nearly two decades, she had floated between the living and the dead. Once, on the heels of her untimely and harrowing murder, she had nearly decided to seek out the light and go unto that great, sweet Summerland that the legitimate Spiritualists spoke of. Heaven. Peace. Almost… The corridor of light had opened before her and she had almost sought out forgiveness in the oblivion of some great and unknowable thing.

But the spectral city kept drawing her back. New York was a body she felt destined to orbit; an otherworldly magnet. There was so much to *do*. There was so much to learn. There was so much to fix, to reveal, to *fight* for that she now knew had deep meaning; meaning that had been lost to her in a life looking into gilded frames and too many mirrors in which she'd primped lustrous curls.

Looking into the mirror here, gazing into the center of its wide gold frame and etched glass detailing, as she floated in this gaudy and ostentatious mansion she'd been drawn into, she saw a wisp of herself. Nearly entirely transparent, there was just a slight contouring of the air where her figure floated. She was nothing but a slight shade of glowing lines delineating features frozen in youth.

She had agreed to stay a consistent New York City haunt because of the living. Her ongoing work with family and friends gave her a purpose and mission she'd never had as an admittedly vapid socialite whose ill-advised curiosity had killed her like the most inelegant of cats.

But to say she had full command over her immortal coil would be a lie. Take this evening, for example. She'd been drawn into a stranger's mansion and found herself floating about a fine parlor bedecked in marble, velvet, and seemingly unending gold trim, with no idea why.

Spiritualists, as the uniquely American version of the sect had been born of Quakers, would often utter that they spoke "as the spirits moved." Sometimes the spirits too, were moved. By unseen forces and unfathomable hands. She had been moved here for reasons she hoped would reveal themselves. Surveying the room, floating along behind the present company at a sufficient distance so as not to strike up complaints of drafts or chills, offered Maggie the clues of family name and fortune. A few framed images on the parlor walls featured images of beautiful women in frothy day-dresses holding decorative bottles trimmed with golden filigree, boasting the great calming and healing powers of Prenze Tonics.

This is where she was. The Prenze mansion. This family had been on her mind. Something wasn't right about this place. About this family. And the spirit world knew it.

Maggie had followed a series of incidences and instincts to this mansion, all in a rush. There were secrets to be exposed. She now floated by a mantelpiece littered with objets d'art from around the world, and watched the festivities unfold.

There was a medium present, or at least she was costumed as such, with an embroidered set of robes, a turban, and too much eye makeup. The most theatrical ones who appropriated religious aspects of other cultures and muddied the meaning right out of them with fetishistic Orientalism tended to be the most fraudulent ones, so Maggie was certain it wasn't the medium who had summoned her directly into this space.

No. Fellow ghosts had drawn her in. Two of them, children, one dressed in traditional garb of a skirt and vest, and the other in shorts with shoulder straps, straight out of a Bavarian folk tale. Fellow ghosts appeared to Maggie's eyes as fully greyscale figures, their features more solid and clear than any reflections she could see in mirrors.

The Grimm storybook children pointed to the mantel, toward a specific object. There, between a set of candelabras, sat a simple box with a latch; an etching in the wood proclaimed it to be something of smoking supplies.

"Open it," the little girl begged.

"You're a potent spirit," the boy, likely her brother, added hopefully.

"We've been weakened here and nothing responds to our touch. Open it. Show everyone. *Throw* it. This family can't keep hurting all of us."

Maggie knew from working with ghost colleagues and mediums on a spate of recent mysteries that living subjects under possible investigation react in vastly different ways to poltergeist activity. She had no idea what she was about to set in motion, but she also didn't have anything to lose.

Dear Eve, the young lady to whom Maggie had pledged the work and gifts of her spirit, would be cross with her for acting on a hunch without informing her. "There are protocols, paperwork, one can't just *barge* in and begin levitating family belongings," she'd chide gently as if she were a bemused mother and not a nineteen-year-old taskmaster; a brisk old soul in a youthful body.

But every time Maggie had an instinct about this mansion and the people in it, results eluded her. It's why she'd never brought the Prenze name to Eve's attention. She wasn't going to send Eve's new Precinct on a wild goose chase when she was trying to prove herself. Here was the opportunity to engage with an actual object that might be hard evidence and not conjecture. No detective could work with conjecture—she'd learned it was their least favorite word and a liability they couldn't afford.

It was clear that none of the living people in the room saw the three spirits, as there were no indications, no shudders, no looking around as if suddenly unsettled, no brushing down the hackle of small hairs up the backs of their bejeweled or satin-swathed necks. A poltergeist would prove the most surprising, unsettling, and least expected event of the night. The fact that the 'medium' didn't look around or sense any presences when Maggie or the children appeared revealed the woman as a fraud.

The trick would be mustering the energy, the momentum, to move an object. She'd long since forgotten what being corporeal felt like, and that had always been the easiest way, to simply interact with an object just like you would have done in life, feeling a phantom limb in reverse.

Overthinking it was also a curse, so she just allowed herself to rifle through a memory box of every time she'd been humiliated or patronized at an event like this during her corporeal life. Just because she'd been in high society didn't mean it had ever been kind to her. It treated young, eligible women as pretty cattle sold to the highest bidder in the marketplace of social climbing. This surge of frustration was enough. She swatted a weightless hand at the metal box. It went flying and landed in the center of a floral Persian rug, opening and spilling its contents—a stack of photographic images.

Cries went up, everyone, all eight adults in the room, reacted with a jump or a vocal start at the crash of the box. Bodies leaned in, but no one approached the box or its contents—they simply stared.

The photographs were recent, by their finish and the lack of yellowing around the edges.

Maggie took a moment to stare at the pictures she'd revealed to the company. Something bothered her deeply about their nature. They were all posed, with props and scenery, costumes and crowns or halos. There was something too stilted about the figures, something eerie about their features.

Postmortem photography. When it was so common, one learned to tell the difference between images of the living and the photographs of the dead. Often a photograph of a dead loved one was the only picture a family had of them. But these were more elaborately staged than Maggie had ever seen. Far more than was any sort of custom.

Maggie stared at the ghosts of the two young children—six, perhaps seven years old—who had fierce, defiant looks on their faces as they took in the horrified expressions of the living. She saw a photograph lying there of the two of them, in their Bavarian garb, posed with a shepherd's crook and a prop sheep. Their eyes were closed but their eyelids had been painted with eyes as if they were open.

A tall, thin, dour-looking man in a fine umber-brown suitcoat strode forward, his long face elongated in a frown, his auburn hair greying at the temples. The man scooped up the strewn images with an irritated sigh, glaring in the direction of Maggie, but not directly at her. This man, she determined, must be a Prenze patriarch.

"What… What were those…?" a young woman sitting on a velvet settee asked, leaning forward curiously, her blue silk gown pooling around her.

Everyone stared at their host, who offered a thin-lipped smile. "Confiscated property from a recent wayward friend. I have been known to minister to those among my station who are lost. This is a friend's collection. What an unfortunate fetish; to covet deceased who are not his kin. I took them away, lest he be haunted. Perhaps I have brought a haunt upon us instead. What an ungodly thing. Isn't that right, Madame Nightstar?"

Maggie nearly snorted at the unoriginal stage name.

The man turned to the medium, who was white as a sheet. "Oh…of course…Mr. Prenze. Of course."

Maggie wanted to interject that there was nothing inherently 'ungodly' about a spirit in the least, but the man ushered everyone out of the room to go on to dinner, saying he would be right with them all. They did so, looking warily at the upturned box, at their host, and at the 'medium' before obeying and filing out to a feast.

Once the parlor door had closed behind the last guest, the towering man closed the distance between himself and Maggie in two easy strides.

"Ah, naughty girl." The man clucked his tongue, staring at Maggie directly, eye to eye. That answered whether or not she could be seen by him. He hadn't given her any clue before. Wily. "How did you get in?" he pressed.

Maggie turned toward the children. They were gone.

"Just passing by," Maggie replied, unsure if he could hear her.

"Well, now that you're here, stay indefinitely," the man said with a leering grin. He moved to the door, to a switch along the wall that surely controlled the lighting. She had assumed from the opulence of the home that the lighting was electric; it was too bright and had a harsher quality, and the man made it only more so as he turned a knob and the lights grew even brighter. Impossibly so. The room grew blinding. Maggie squinted, raising an incorporeal arm over her eyes as if she could shield herself.

Along with the bright light came a hum, a rising, whining, whirring, grating noise like a mechanical roar. The sound hurt. The light burned. She felt as though she were being torn apart… She opened her mouth to scream….

And then…utter darkness.

Chapter One

Manhattan, 1899

Only the ghosts surrounding Eve Whitby could cool her blushing cheeks as the inimitable Theodore Roosevelt, Governor of New York, stood to toast her before a host of lieutenants, detectives and patrolmen, all of whom found her highly dubious.

Many of these same New York Police Department officers found Roosevelt just as problematic. He wasn't Police Commissioner anymore—he'd used the notoriety from having cleaned up corruption within police departments and ridden it straight to the governorship, but as some detractors noted, the man couldn't leave well enough alone. So here he was meddling again with the police, and Eve was at the center of it.

While Eve tried to appear confident in most situations, being at the center of a crowd made her nerve-racked and flushed. She was surer of her mission than she was of herself. When one followed a calling, passion was often a driving force greater than self-assuredness.

Whole departments turning to her and lifting glasses made her stomach lurch and waver like the transparent, hovering ghosts glowing about the room who made her work possible. She looked down at the hem of her black dress—simple light wool attire of clean lines and polished buttons she'd designed to look like a police matron's uniform, but in the colors of mourning. When she took on this department, she donned mourning. Not out of sorrow, but in celebration of her coworkers, the dead.

I am a woman of particular purpose…. She thought, an internal rallying cry. Any moment Roosevelt was going to make an announcement about

The Ghost Precinct, the project she'd put everything in her young life on hold to spearhead.

Taking a breath, she steadied her feet, shifting the heel of her black boots on the smooth wooden floor. She glanced in a mirror and tucked an errant thick black lock of hair back into her bun, trying to shift her pallid, nearly sickly looking expression to something that appeared more commanding lest her wide green eyes give away her concerns.

The manner in which the three ghosts at the edges of the room were bobbing insistently in the air meant something. They had something to say and were her most vocal operatives. Vera, Olga, and little Zofia, who was actually wringing her hands. Eve had asked that her operative spirits not come tonight, for fear of distraction, but they had come regardless. She ignored them, though their behavior made her nervous. Something was wrong. But she couldn't ask what. Not now. Not in the spotlight in front of a crowd who didn't trust her.

Roosevelt, dressed in a white suit with a striped waistcoat, his iconic moustache moving with his expressive face as if it were punctuating his dialogue, adjusted his wire-rimmed glasses, lifted a glass, and bid his fellows do the same.

"I give you Miss Evelyn H. Whitby, daughter of Lord and Lady Denbury, and I bid you toast the inception of her Ghost Precinct. Now, because we live in an age of skeptics and charlatans in equal measure, we're not going public about this Precinct beyond our department heads here. We don't need undue fuss; we don't need hysterics. What we know conclusively is that this young woman's talents aided in solving two brutal murders to date. As we near a new century, no one knows what new crimes will come with it, but one thing we can count on is that there will always be the dead, with a perspective none of us have. It's foolish to leave such a resource untapped, especially as this city grows by the thousands every month.

"We await many more resolutions and have directed her to cases that have gone cold. Perhaps, dare I say, she and her colleagues may even garner a few premonitions to stop a crime before it's even begun! To the young lady and her ghosts! Whether you're a believer or not, she has assured me there's nothing to be afraid of!"

There was a polite if less than enthusiastic clap of hands.

*Nothing to be afraid of...*she repeated to herself. *That's exactly your purpose on this earth, to make ghosts a less frightful reality for those who do believe. For those who can see, for those who want to know. You are the voice of the departed, you are their champion. Be proud. Show these people how proud you are to be the advocate for the dead.*

Eve nodded to the politician, squared her shoulders, lifted her flute, and allowed herself to enjoy the distinct, sweet bite of a good champagne, feeling the chill of the dead on the air. If her spirits could not calm her nerves with their presence, at least their drastic temperature wafting toward her warm cheeks made her appear more poised and stoic than nervous in the spotlight.

While she was fairly certain she was the only one present who could fully see and interact with her spirit department, she didn't rule out that some members of the force might be aware that they were being watched from beyond the veil. While the ghosts had disobeyed Eve's orders to stay entirely away tonight, at least they were keeping their distance from the attendees, as some of her friends and family were too affected when more than one was in the room. When she had agreed to be noted in tonight's reception, she'd done everything in her power to avoid a scene.

The intense, inimitable Mister Roosevelt had never tried to convince the New York Metropolitan Police Force that creating a 'Ghost Precinct' was a good idea; he had simply done it. He made it Eve's purview and ensured, thanks to powerful allies, that she had access to departmental services, support, and resources. He had also kept the press out of it lest the Precinct become, as he'd said, "an unnecessary rodeo. I don't want to field calls for you to contact departed loved ones unless they can solve crimes." Roosevelt wasn't a man who much cared what other people thought when he was committed to a cause, and that quality was maybe the only thing she had in common with the bombastic legislator.

When Roosevelt had told her family he wanted to honor Eve and the Precinct, her grandmother Evelyn, whom she was named for, had taken control of the arrangements to ensure the reception was held in the grand downstairs foyer of The Players Club, Edwin Booth's beautiful brownstone complex in Gramercy Park, established in hopes of making the theatre more respectable—a much harder sell after his brother had killed President Lincoln.

While most of the city's grandest clubs were for men only, as was the Players Club's regular membership, Eve fought additional stigma regarding Spiritualists, mediums, psychics and the lot—a hierarchy of respectability that kept a celebration like this relegated only to theatrical spaces. Whether they were believed or exposed as frauds, people passionately loved or hated a woman who spoke with the dead. There was hardly a middle ground. She could not be entirely lauded, and would always be considered suspect. Eve had heard one detractor say that people like her were for 'parlor tricks, not politics.' The man had been a New York congressional representative and had stood in the way of her department when it was first being finalized with the police commissioner. Roosevelt had ignored him and had bid Eve do the same. She was hardly as positioned or as powerful as the Governor, but she tried to follow his lead.

Her parents, Lord and Lady Denbury, were sitting off to the side of the richly appointed foyer. Poised on cushioned benches against the wood-paneled wall, they watched uncomfortably, in elegant but subdued evening dress, matching the tone of mourning dress Eve had taken on out of the kind of respect and engagement she hoped would ensure spirits' ongoing help. The mourning, she felt, was not only a uniform for this work, it was a mission.

To either side were her grandparents, Evelyn looking on in beaming pride in a stunning black gown direct from France, taking the mourning cue from her granddaughter. Her grandfather Gareth looked pleasantly baffled in a plain black suit, choosing to cope with a strange world by way of detached bemusement. This attitude had served him well thus far and kept relations with his clairvoyant wife at their most pleasant.

Eve's parents had come to know the paranormal by violent force. By murder and horror. Her father was a titled English lord who had been targeted by a demonic society, her mother was a middle-class New Yorker. She and Gran had been the only ones who had helped him and it was incredible they had survived at all, having both been targeted by abject evil. They'd survived thanks to cleverness, good friends and Gran's help. They'd fallen in love, married and remained in New York, hoping to have a normal life with their newborn Eve, praying none of what they went through would be passed on to her. They would never fully accept a life lived with ghosts at the fore and Eve could not expect them to.

The gifts Eve manifested placed a distinct strain on the family. Not wishing to bring such loving parents any inconvenience, let alone pain, she had tried to block out her gifts, once.

That effort had nearly killed her at age nine. When she'd tried to stop hearing the dead, migraines had seared her head for weeks, and she couldn't eat or sleep. Only when she opened back up to hear the murmurs of the spirit world could she breathe again, her fever breaking and life returning to her paranormal normal.

The reality of this precinct meant she could never go back on her talents. The dead would never let her. Her parents knew it, as she could tell by their haunted gazes. A new chapter had begun.

Roosevelt was staring at her. So were her ghosts, expectantly. So were all the men.

"Would you like to say a few words, Miss Whitby?" Roosevelt prompted.

"Ah." She wouldn't have liked to, really, as nerves always got the better of her if she was put on the spot in such a manner, but it was necessary.

Taking a deep breath, she thought about what was best to say. The absence of trust in the room felt like an impossible gulf to cross. She wanted to thank her mediums but that seemed odd after not having invited them. She didn't want the patrolmen, detectives and lieutenants to look at a group of four young women of vastly different backgrounds and judge them all as a threat. She wanted that pressure to land solely upon herself, and keep her Sensitives sensitive, not defensive.

She reminded herself that this department was her mission, it was not about her. It was about respect for the great work of mediums and all the good the dead could do for the living. Just like Edwin Booth had sought to lift up the profession of theatre by this grand space. This freed her to speak with a calm, crisp tone.

"In this day and age of charlatans and magicians in the guise of Spiritualism," she said. "I blame no one for their skepticism. In fact, I encourage it. Skepticism offers investigative integrity. A questioning mind solves a case. My specific and unprecedented Precinct hopes to earn continued trust by the thing we can all always agree on: solving crime and easing suffering."

She could see the unsure faces before her, some bemused, some seeming openly hostile. Every woman entering a predominantly male field had encountered these same faces, even without her subject matter being additional fodder for derision. Her nerves crested but she kept talking. She believed, above all, in her mission, and no critic would change that.

"However unorthodox the means," she continued, raising her voice and commanding more of the room, "however unprecedented the methods, our aims are mutual and always will be. Ghosts are far too often misunderstood, and I hope that by working with them in proven, positive ways, we can begin to change the perception of hauntings. Spirits can walk where we cannot, hear what fails our mortal senses, and keep the most vigilant of watches when we must take our rest. I hope you will see them as a help, not a horror." She finished not with a request but a demand: "Thank you for your support."

"Hear, hear!" said Ambassador Bishop, a tall, striking, silver-haired man across the room. Impeccably dressed in a black silk tailcoat and charcoal brocade waistcoat, the diplomat to England and lifelong friend of the family lifted his champagne glass for a second toast. It was Bishop who had gotten Roosevelt involved in the first place, since his present ambassadorship did not carry the same legislative control as when he had been a New York senator. In those days he'd have seen to such a department himself.

Bishop's wife, Clara, a sharp-featured woman many years his junior, with dark golden hair that matched the gold core of her piercing eyes, stood at his elbow in a graceful plum gown. Clara stared at Eve with a fierce pride that held none of her family's hesitance. Eve owed more to Clara than either of them would admit to anyone but each other. Clara nodded at Eve as if she knew she was passing off work she could no longer do herself.

"Hear *indeed*, Ambassador!" Roosevelt exclaimed, grinning at the Bishops. "Now enjoy refreshments and the fine company! I'll be here if any of you men need me and Miss Whitby has been gracious enough to agree to answer some questions from the department present, provided they are posited with all due respect. Respect, and transparency. I didn't clean this filthy force up for nothing. Well, I reckon the Ghost Precinct will be our most *transparent* department yet! Ha!" Roosevelt slapped a hand on a serving table and enjoyed his pun amidst a few groans.

When asked Eve's opinion on Mister Roosevelt, she had once replied that he was a man who wanted to preserve wilderness so he could shoot things within it. That summed him up, she concluded. She found many of his ideas sensible but was often baffled by his road getting there. But no one could deny he was a compelling, larger-than-life character who never failed to surprise.

Gratitude was her most abundant sentiment, if she were asked how she felt in this moment. Thanks to Bishop and Roosevelt's machinations, she'd been given steady employment, without which, like all the many strong working women around her, she'd go mad. The moment she'd signed paperwork on the precinct, the constant, dull ache that rested at the base of her neck even if she wasn't having a migraine had eased. It was as if the whole of the spirit world that clutched at her from behind had released their talons ever so slightly. It was a world that wanted to be seen and acknowledged, and that's why it sought to communicate in such a wide array of methods. Now it was seen in a whole new light and given responsibilities.

At nineteen years old, when most young women of any kind of title and society were very busy with their 'seasons' and hoping for a well-placed marriage, Eve found she had no interest in following the path of her supposed peers in the city. Of course there was the occasional ball she attended due to the pressures of her father's lordship, her gran's high-society dealings, her grandfather's Metropolitan Museum soirees, the Bishops' esteemed gatherings. But theirs were generally philanthropic functions that had great purpose, not dances meant to pair up eligible bachelors with debutantes. The former suited her; the latter bored her.

Her circle attracted a constant parade of ghosts whose chill presence ruined the warmth of a good party. Here at the Players, the fireplaces were roaring as the new electric fixtures were buzzing in a juxtaposition of ancient and modern light and heat, making the room so warm that the ghostly retinue on the margins caused a much-needed draft. But she couldn't keep ignoring them. If she did, they might start throwing things, and now was hardly the best time for a poltergeist.

Roosevelt held up his hand, hailing Eve as if he wished to speak with her, but men in tailcoats blocked his path as he took a step forward. As legislators were forever called upon for favors, the veritable inferno of energy that was Roosevelt was immediately beset by an entourage. Eve took this as a chance to slip away, into another room where the ghosts and she could speak freely.

Glancing around, she moved toward an opening in the crowd, preparing to make her way to whatever empty, dark space she could find in the grand place. But a young detective stepped into her path and she paused with a smile she hoped did not appear strained.

She recognized the dark-haired, clean-shaven, sharp-featured man with rich brown eyes ringed in blue; a distinct gaze that pierced her right to the core. During a recent case, Eve's ghosts had bid her examine a crime scene herself, as they were having trouble describing it. While she had not been welcome at the site, and it was assumed she would both be in the way and taint the evidence, this man had quelled the protesting officers on duty. He had found a place for her to stand within view of the exsanguinated body and take notes. It had been grim but her composure was a test that she'd passed.

"Detective Horowitz, it is good to see you again and I hope you're well. This is a more pleasant scene than when I last saw you."

"Ah, yes." He grimaced. "That ugly bloodletting."

"Have you figured that one out?"

"How a body could be that drained?" he asked. He shook his head with a humorless laugh. "There were suction marks near the puncture wounds—something drew it out of him."

"How odd. I believe in ghosts, but not vampires, detective."

"Well that's reassuring at least." His face transformed from angular to warm for a moment before cooling again.

"Thank you for honoring me this evening," Eve said, bobbing her head.

"I do have a question for you, if you don't mind."

"Go on," she said, glancing at Zofia, a ten-year-old in a simple pinafore, bobbing in the air impatiently, gesturing for her to hurry up with this chat.

"I try, whenever I can, to work in new technologies. Fingerprinting, psychological profiles from alienists, taking exquisite stock of a scene so that not even a hair of evidence is tampered with. In regards to your department... Say one were to believe in poltergeists. To be clear, I don't believe, but if I did, wouldn't a host of spirits be liable to disrupt and thus corrupt a crime scene by moving objects? Couldn't any of the various ways the spirit world has been said to commune with mortals potentially foul a scene?"

She stared at him. It was a valid point.

"My spirits aren't ones for moving things," she began. "They aren't the poltergeist sort, at least not that I've been aware, but it is a cogent point to bring up to them; to be aware of the ways their presences might affect a given environment. To be fair, my ghosts wouldn't leave any additional fingerprints," she offered. The young man twisted his lips as if he wanted to smile but was too focused to allow the indulgence.

"What I have tried, with my contacts, is to cultivate details *beyond* a crime scene," Eve explained. "My ghosts and mediums pick up on expansive aspects, specifics of place, people, setting, weather, clothes, and they're drawn to things the living might find mundane. And they do so in a non-linear manner, so I have to constantly sift for relevance. That's what was so maddening to me at first, why ghosts kept coming and telling me far too many details about seemingly meaningless things. Until I finally saw a pattern in the noise. These patterns led to the arrests and cases solved that Mister Roosevelt so kindly referenced."

"While I am glad of the eventual outcome, how can you be sure all the facts presented to you were real and not just luck?" Horowitz pressed.

Suddenly Roosevelt was behind him like some bold, pouncing apparition. "Because she has spies!" the man cried, waggling his great moustache. "Her ladies, both living and dead, are everywhere and in *everything*," he added delightedly. "And if any man here underestimates a woman's craftiness, or her ability to pick up a litany of detail so intense as to leave you breathlessly disarmed from argument, well then you've never had a single one of them cross with you!"

This broke a distinct layer of ice. The entourage of fine suits swarmed the governor again and Eve edged away, Horowitz following a pace behind.

"When he's right, he's right," Eve said, turning to the detective with a smile. Just as Eve felt that the man was beginning to warm to her, the temperature around her went ice cold. A plummeting of twenty-some degrees wasn't just a draft; it meant only one thing. A ghost wasn't just nearby, but directly behind her, toying with a lock of her hair, threatening to lift it up into thin air. She was familiar with the trick to get her attention. Eve smoothed the lock back down again and gave a sideways glare to the spirit.

"I look forward to your further questions, Detective. But if you'll excuse me for the moment...." she turned away, crossed around the corner of the next threshold and stared into the eyes of the chill directly.

Her best scout, young Zofia, floated before her in full greyscale, dark hair back in a haphazard bun, in a plain work dress blackened just slightly at the hem; the only reminder of her premature death in a garment district fire. Because the ghosts who communed with Eve were full-consciousness spirits, her burned body wasn't what became a shade; this was her silvery soul. The agony of death was long shed—souls were a glowing whole while the body's raw materials returned to dust. Spiritualism's greatest and most comforting gift was this reassurance.

"I'm sorry to disturb you, Eve, I really am, but you have to know..." she said in a thick Polish accent, her ghostly voice never heard above a whisper, no matter how emphatic. "I know you told us to hang back, to not to talk to you, but..."

Eve turned her head away from the crowd, moving into the shadows of the hall beyond so that she couldn't be seen talking to thin air.

"But?" she murmured through clenched teeth.

"Margaret is gone," the spirit replied.

Eve blinked at the spirit. The spirit wavered in the air, blinking back.

"Gone?" Eve prompted, not entirely sure what Zofia meant. The spirit world was full of comings and goings.

"*Gone*, gone," Zofia insisted. "None of us ghosts have any sense of her. Her candle is out. We've tried everything. There is no waking her. There is no summoning her. This world, or the next, we cannot find her. Our Maggie. She's gone."

Eve reeled. What could be worse timing? Just as she was on the cusp of being taken seriously, her best asset was dead. Again.

Printed in the United States
by Baker & Taylor Publisher Services